D1011065

A Christmas Sampler

A

HRISTMAS SAMPLER

Classic Stories of the Season, from Twain to Cheever

Edited by E. A. Crawford
and Teresa Kennedy

FROM THE COLLECTIONS OF THE
NEW YORK PUBLIC LIBRARY

New York

Library of Congress Cataloging-in-Publication Data
A Christmas sampler : classic stories of the season, from Twain to
Cheever / edited by E.A. Crawford and Teresa Kennedy.—1st ed.
p. cm.
ISBN 1-56282-933-5
1. Christmas stories, American. I. Crawford, E. A.
II. Kennedy, Teresa.
PS648.C45C457 1992
813'.010833—dc20 92-15943 CIP

Book design by Richard Oriolo
FIRST EDITION
1 0 9 8 7 6 5 4 3 2 1

Contents

Contents

Introduction

was the night before Christmas, when all through the house / Not a creature was stirring—not even a mouse." Clement Clarke Moore, who wrote those lines in 1823, was not a poet but a Hebrew and Latin scholar. The New York Public Library owns a copy of his *A Compendious Lexicon of the Hebrew Language* and some fifty different versions of *A Visit from St. Nicholas,* which he wrote as a present for his own young children.

But stockings hung from the mantelpiece and visions of sugarplums, to say nothing of eight tiny reindeer, are merely a child's fantasy. They evoke neither the joyful, sacred holiday, nor the obligations, loneliness, and frantic shopping sprees we all know so well. Here is a book to complement whatever mood December finds you in! *A Christmas Sampler* is a collection of some of the best American short stories about Christmas, from the comfortingly traditional to the outrageously contemporary. It is as wide-ranging and diverse as the many voices that represent the vast American landscape. One remembers when the ghost of Hamlet's father vanishes at the crowing of the cock:

> Some say that ever 'gainst that season comes
> Wherein our Savior's birth is celebrated,
> This bird of dawning singeth all night long;
> And then, they say, no spirit dare stir abroad;
> The nights are wholesome; then no planets strike,
> No fairy takes, nor witch hath power to charm,
> So hallow'd and so gracious is that time.

Here is Willa Cather's mythic tale of the Prodigal Son, "The Burglar's Christmas," told from the mother's point of view; Francis P. Church's response to the young but cynical Virginia, "No Santa Claus! Thank God, he lives, and he lives forever . . ."; and Damon Runyan's "The Three Wise Guys," written in quintessential New Yorkese. Mark Twain gives us "Susie's Letter from Santa," and Ntozake Shange, "Christmas for Sassafras, Cypress and Indigo." Christmas brings triumph to Grace Paley's young Jewish immigrant Shirley Abramowitz, as she gets the biggest part in the Christmas Pageant, and Charlie, the East Side doorman, is fired after receiving an excess of misguided generosity in John Cheever's "Christmas Is a Sad Season for the Poor."

Joy, wistfulness, beauty, responsibilities—all may accompany Christmas. But with *A Christmas Sampler,* no one need be lonely.

TIMOTHY S. HEALY
President
The New York Public Library

A Christmas Sampler

Good old-fashioned
Christmas Greetings

CHRISTMAS THOUGHTS

Washington Irving

Washington Irving was born in New York City in 1783 and died in 1859. The youngest of eleven brothers and sisters, Irving was the namesake of then commander-in-chief George Washington. Long considered the "Father of American Literature," Irving was an essayist, historian, and biographer, yet he is primarily remembered for his rendition of the immortal Hudson River legends, Rip Van Winkle *and* The Legend of Sleepy Hollow.

Of all the old festivals, that of Christmas awakens the strongest and most heartfelt associations. There is a tone of solemn and sacred feeling that blends with our conviviality and lifts the spirit to a state of hallowed and elevated enjoyment.

It is a beautiful arrangement, derived from days of yore, that this festival, which commemorates the announcement of the religion of peace and love, has been made the season for gathering together of family connections, and drawing closer again those bands of kindred hearts which the cares, and pleasures, and sorrows of the world are continually operating to cast loose; of calling back the children of a family, who have launched forth in life, once more to assemble about the paternal hearth, there to grow young and loving again among the endearing mementos of childhood.

There is something in the very season of the year that gives a charm to the festivity of Christmas. In the depth of winter, when Nature lies despoiled of her charms, wrapt in her shroud of sheeted snow, we turn for our gratifications to moral sources. Heart calleth unto heart, and we draw our pleasures from the deep wells of living kindness which lie in the quiet recesses of our bosoms.

Amidst the general call to happiness, the bustle of the spirits and stir of the affections, which prevail at this period, what bosom can remain insensible? It is indeed the season of regenerated feeling—the season for kindling not merely the fire of hospitality in the hall, but the genial flame of charity in the heart. He who can turn churlishly away from contemplating the felicity of his fellow-beings and can sit down repining in loneliness, when all around is joyful, wants the genial and social sympathies which constitute the charm of a merry Christmas.

Ruth Welch
I'M WISHING A HAPPY CHRISTMAS
FOR A HAPPY CHILD I KNOW.

How Santa Claus Came to Simpson's Bar

Bret Harte

Bret Harte was born in Albany, New York, in 1836 and died in London in 1902. A transplanted Easterner, Harte came to San Francisco as a young man and went on to earn acclaim with his stories and studies of the region. His firsthand experience of the American West shows up in this marvelous account of Christmas in one of the small mining towns that dotted the California mountains in the days of the gold rush. In fact, it was stories such as this one that made Harte a sensation in literary circles in Boston, where he moved in 1871.

t had been raining in the valley of the Sacramento. The North Fork had overflowed its banks, and Rattlesnake Creek was impassable. The few boulders that had marked the summer ford at Simpson's Crossing were obliterated by a vast sheet of water stretching to the foothills. The upstage was stopped at Granger's; the last mail had been abandoned in the tules, the rider swimming for his life. "An area," remarked the *Sierra Avalanche,* with pensive local pride, "as large as the State of Massachusetts is now under water."

Nor was the weather any better in the foothills. The mud lay deep on the mountain road; wagons that neither physical force nor moral objurgation could move from the evil ways into which they had fallen encumbered the track, and the way to Simpson's Bar was indicated by broken-down teams and hard swearing. And further on, cut off and inaccessible, rained upon and bedraggled, smitten by high winds and threatened by high water, Simpson's Bar, on the eve of Christmas Day, 1862, clung like a swallow's nest to the rocky entablature and splintered capitals of Table Mountain, and shook in the blast.

As night shut down on the settlement, a few lights gleamed through the mist from the windows of cabins on either side of the highway, now crossed and gullied by lawless streams and swept by marauding winds. Happily most of the population were gathered at Thompson's store, clustered around a red-hot stove, at which they silently spat in some accepted sense of social communion that perhaps rendered conversation unnecessary. Indeed, most methods of diversion had long since been exhausted on Simpson's Bar; high water had suspended the regular occupations on gulch and on river, and a consequent lack of money and whiskey had taken the zest from most illegitimate recreation. Even Mr. Hamlin was fain to leave the Bar with fifty dollars in his pocket—the only amount actually realized of the large sums won by him in the successful exercise of his arduous profession. "Ef I was asked," he remarked somewhat later— "ef I was asked to pint out a purty little village where a retired sport as didn't care for money could exercise hisself, frequent and lively, I'd say Simpson's Bar; but for a young man with a large family depending on his exertions, it don't pay." As Mr. Hamlin's family consisted mainly of female adults, this remark is quoted rather to show the breadth of his humor than the exact extent of his responsibilities.

Howbeit, the unconscious objects of this satire sat that evening in the listless apathy begotten of idleness and lack of excitement. Even the sudden splashing of hoofs before the door did not arouse them. Dick Bullen alone paused in the act of scraping out his pipe, and lifted his head, but no other one of the group indicated any interest in, or recognition of, the man who entered.

It was a figure familiar enough to the company, and known in Simpson's Bar as "The Old Man." A man of perhaps fifty years; grizzled and scant of hair, but still fresh and youthful of complexion. A face full of ready but not very powerful sympathy, with a chameleonlike aptitude for taking on the shade and color of contiguous moods and feelings. He had evidently just left some hilarious companions, and did not at first notice the gravity of the group, but clapped the shoulder of the nearest man jocularly, and threw himself into a vacant chair.

"Jest heard the best thing out, boys! Ye know Smiley, over yar—Jim Smiley—funniest man in the Bar? Well, Jim was jest telling the richest yarn about"—

"Smiley's a —— fool," interrupted a gloomy voice.

"A particular —— skunk," added another in sepulchral accents.

A silence followed these positive statements. The Old Man glanced quickly around the group. Then his face slowly changed. "That's so," he said reflectively, after a pause, "certainly a sort of a skunk and suthin' of a fool. In course." He was silent for a moment, as in painful contemplation of the unsavoriness and folly of the unpopular Smiley. "Dismal weather, ain't it?" he added, now fully embarked on the current of prevailing sentiment. "Mighty rough papers on the boys, and no show for money this season. And tomorrow's Christmas."

There was a movement among the men at this announcement, but whether of satisfaction or disgust was not plain. "Yes," continued the Old Man in the lugubrious tone he had within the last few moments unconsciously adopted,— "yes, Christmas, and tonight's Christmas Eve. Ye see, boys, I kinder thought—that is, I sorter had an idee, jest passin' like, you know—that maybe ye'd all like to come over to my house tonight and have a sort of tear round. But I suppose, now, you wouldn't? Don't feel like it, maybe?" he added with anxious sympathy, peering into the faces of his companions.

"Well, I don't know," responded Tom Flynn with some cheerfulness. "P'r'aps we may. But how about your wife, Old Man? What does *she* say to it?"

The Old Man hesitated. His conjugal experience had not been a happy one, and the fact was known to Simpson's Bar. His first wife, a delicate, pretty little woman, had suffered keenly and secretly from the jealous suspicions of her husband, until one day he invited the whole Bar to his house to expose her infidelity. On arriving, the party found the shy, petite creature quietly engaged in her household duties, and retired abashed and discomfited. But the sensitive woman did not easily recover from the shock of this extraordinary outrage. It was with difficulty she regained her equanimity sufficiently to release her lover from the closet in which he was concealed, and escape with him. She left a boy of three years to comfort her bereaved husband. The Old Man's present wife had been his cook. She was large, loyal, and aggressive.

Before he could reply, Joe Dimmick suggested with great directness that it was the "Old Man's house," and that, invoking the Divine Power, if the case were his own, he would invite whom he pleased, even if in so doing he imperiled his salvation. The Powers of Evil, he further remarked, should contend against him vainly. All this delivered with a terseness and vigor lost in this necessary translation.

"In course. Certainly. Thet's it," said the Old Man with a sympathetic frown. "Thar's no trouble about thet. It's my own house, built every stick on it myself. Don't you be afeard o' her, boys. She *may* cut up a trifle rough—ez wimmin do—but she'll come round." Secretly the Old Man trusted to the exaltation of liquor and the power of courageous example to sustain him in such an emergency.

As yet, Dick Bullen, the oracle and leader of Simpson's Bar, had not spoken. He now took his pipe from his lips. "Old Man, how's that yer Johnny gettin' on? Seems to me he didn't look so peart last time I seed him on the bluff heavin' rocks at Chinamen. Didn't seem to take much interest in it. Thar was a gang of 'em by yar yesterday—drownded out up the river—and I kinder thought o' Johnny, and how he'd miss 'em! Maybe now, we'd be in the way ef he wus sick?"

The father, evidently touched not only by this pathetic picture of

Johnny's deprivation, but by the considerate delicacy of the speaker, hastened to assure him that Johnny was better, and that a "little fun might 'liven him up." Whereupon Dick arose, shook himself, and saying, "I'm ready. Lead the way, Old Man: here goes," himself led the way with a leap, a characteristic howl, and darted out into the night. As he passed through the outer room he caught up a blazing brand from the hearth. The action was repeated by the rest of the party, closely following and elbowing each other, and before the astonished proprietor of Thompson's grocery was aware of the intention of his guests, the room was deserted.

The night was pitchy dark. In the first gust of wind their temporary torches were extinguished, and only the red brands dancing and flitting in the gloom like drunken will-o'-the-wisps indicated their whereabouts. Their way led up Pine Tree Canyon, at the head of which a broad, low, bark-thatched cabin burrowed in the mountain-side. It was the home of the Old Man, and the entrance to the tunnel in which he worked when he worked at all. Here the crowd paused for a moment, out of delicate deference to their host, who came up panting in the rear.

"P'r'aps ye'd better hold on a second out yer, whilst I go in and see that things is all right," said the Old Man, with an indifference he was far from feeling. The suggestion was graciously accepted, the door opened and closed on the host, and the crowd, leaning their backs against the wall and cowering under the eaves, waited and listened.

For a few moments there was no sound but the dripping of water from the eaves and the stir and rustle of wrestling boughs above them. Then the men became uneasy, and whispered suggestion and suspicion passed from the one to the other. "Reckon she's caved in his head the first lick!" "Decoyed him inter the tunnel and barred him up, likely." "Got him down and sittin' on him." "Prob'ly biling suthin' to heave on us: stand clear the door, boys!" For just then the latch clicked, the door slowly opened, and a voice said, "Come in out o' the wet."

The voice was neither that of the Old Man nor of his wife. It was the voice of a small boy, its weak treble broken by that preternatural hoarseness which only vagabondage and the habit of premature self-assertion can give. It was the face of a small boy that looked up at theirs—a face that might have been pretty, and even refined, but that it was darkened by evil knowledge from within, and dirt and hard experience from without. He had a blanket around his shoulders, and had evidently just risen from his bed. "Come in," he repeated, "and don't make no noise. The Old Man's in there talking to mar," he continued, pointing to an adjacent room which seemed to be a kitchen, from which the Old Man's voice came in deprecating accents. "Let me be," he added querulously to Dick Bullen, who had caught him up, blanket and all, and was affecting to toss him into the fire, "let go o' me, you d——d old fool, d'ye hear?"

Thus adjured, Dick Bullen lowered Johnny to the ground with a smothered laugh, while the men, entering quietly, ranged themselves around a long table of rough boards which occupied the center of the room. Johnny then gravely proceeded to a cupboard and brought out several articles, which he deposited on the table. "Thar's whiskey. And crackers. And red herons. And cheese." He took a bite of the latter on his way to the table. "And sugar." He scooped up a mouthful en route with a small and very dirty hand. "And terbacker. Thar's dried appils too on the shelf, but I don't admire 'em. Appils is swellin'. Thar," he concluded, "now wade in, and don't be afeard. *I* don't mind the old woman. She don't b'long to *me.* S'long."

He had stepped to the threshold of a small room, scarcely larger than a closet, partitioned off from the main apartment, and holding in its dim recess a small bed. He stood there a moment looking at the company, his bare feet peeping from the blanket, and nodded.

"Hello, Johnny! You ain't goin' to turn in agin, are ye?" said Dick.

"Yes, I are," responded Johnny decidedly.

"Why, wot's up, old fellow?"

"I'm sick."

"How sick?"

"I've got a fevier. And childblains. And roomatiz," returned Johnny, and vanished within. After a moment's pause, he added in the dark, apparently from under the bedclothes—"And biles!"

There was an embarrassing silence. The men looked at each other and at the fire. Even with the appetizing banquet before them, it seemed as if they might again fall into the despondency of Thompson's grocery, when the voice of the Old Man, incautiously lifted, came deprecatingly from the kitchen.

"Certainly! That's so. In course they is. A gang o' lazy, drunken loafers, and that ar Dick Bullen's the ornariest of all. Didn't hev no more *sabe* than to come round yar with sickness in the house and no provision. Thet's what I said: 'Bullen,' sez I, 'it's crazy drunk you are, or a fool,' sez I, 'to think o' such a thing.' 'Staples,' I sez, 'be you a man, Staples, and 'spect to raise H——ll under my roof and invalids lyin' round?' But they would come—they would. Thet's wot you must 'spect o' such trash as lays round the Bar."

A burst of laughter from the men followed this unfortunate exposure. Whether it was overheard in the kitchen, or whether the Old Man's irate companion had just then exhausted all other modes of expressing her contemptuous indignation, I cannot say, but a back door was suddenly slammed with great violence. A moment later and the Old Man reappeared, haply unconscious of the cause of the late hilarious outburst, and smiled blandly.

"The old woman thought she'd jest run over to Mrs. MacFadden's for a sociable call," he explained with jaunty indifference, as he took a seat at the board.

Oddly enough it needed this untoward incident to relieve the embarrassment that was beginning to be felt by the party, and their natural audacity returned with their host. I do not propose to record the convivialities of that evening. The inquisitive reader will accept the statement that the conversation was characterized by the same intellectual exaltation, the same cautious reverence, the same fastidious delicacy, the same rhetorical precision, and the same logical and coherent discourse somewhat later in the evening, which distinguish similar gatherings of the masculine sex in more civilized localities and under more favorable auspices. No glasses were broken in the absence of any; no liquor was uselessly spilt on the floor or table in the scarcity of that article.

It was nearly midnight when the festivities were interrupted. "Hush," said Dick Bullen, holding up his hand. It was the querulous voice of Johnny from his adjacent closet: "O Dad!"

The Old Man arose hurriedly and disappeared in the closet. Presently he reappeared. "His rheumatiz is coming on agin bad," he explained, "and he wants rubbin'." He lifted the demijohn of whiskey from the table and shook it. It was empty. Dick Bullen put down his tin cup with an embarrassed laugh. So did the others. The Old Man examined their contents and said hopefully, "I reckon that's enough; he don't need much. You hold on all o' you for a spell, and I'll be back;" and vanished in the closet with an old flannel shirt and the whiskey. The door closed but imperfectly, and the following dialogue was distinctly audible:

"Now, sonny, whar does she ache worst?"

"Sometimes over yar and sometimes under yer; but it's most powerful from yer to yer. Rub yer, Dad."

A silence seemed to indicate a brisk rubbing. Then Johnny:

"Hevin' a good time out yer, Dad?"

"Yes, sonny."

"Tomorrer's Chrismiss—ain't it?"

"Yes, sonny. How does she feel now?"

"Better. Rub a little furder down. Wot's Chrismiss, anyway? Wot's it all about?"

"Oh, it's a day."

This exhaustive definition was apparently satisfactory, for there was a silent interval of rubbing. Presently Johnny again:

"Mar sez that everywhere else but yer everybody gives things to everybody Chrismiss, and then she jist waded inter you. She sez thar's a man they call Sandy Claws, not a white man, you know, but a kind o' Chinemin, comes down the chimbley night afore Chrismiss and gives things to chillern—boys like me. Puts 'em in their butes! Thet's what she tried to play upon me. Easy now, Pop, whar are you rubbin' to—thet's a mile from the place. She jest made that up, didn't she, jest to aggrewate me and you? Don't rub thar. . . . Why, Dad!"

In the great quiet that seemed to have fallen upon the house the sigh of the near pines and the drip of leaves without was very distinct. Johnny's voice, too, was lowered as he went on, "Don't you take on now, for I'm gettin' all right fast. Wot's the boys doin' out thar?"

The Old Man partly opened the door and peered through. His guests were sitting there sociably enough, and there were a few silver coins and a lean buckskin purse on the table. "Bettin' on suthin'—some little game or 'nother. They're all right," he replied to Johnny, and recommenced his rubbing.

"I'd like to take a hand and win some money," said Johnny reflectively after a pause.

The Old Man glibly repeated what was evidently a familiar formula, that if Johnny would wait until he struck it rich in the tunnel he'd have lots of money, etc., etc.

"Yes," said Johnny, "but you don't. And whether you strike it or I win it, it's about the same. It's all luck. But it's mighty cur'o's about Chrismiss—ain't it? Why do they call it Chrismiss?"

Perhaps from some instinctive deference to the overhearing of his guests, or from some vague sense of incongruity, the Old Man's reply was so low as to be inaudible beyond the room.

"Yes," said Johnny, with some slight abatement of interest, "I've heard o' *him* before. Thar, that'll do, Dad. I don't ache near so bad as I did. Now wrap me tight in this yer blanket. So. Now," he added in a muffled whisper, "sit down yer by me till I go asleep." To assure himself of obedience, he disengaged one hand from the blanket, and grasping his father's sleeve, again composed himself to rest.

For some moments the Old Man waited patiently. Then the unwonted stillness of the house excited his curiosity, and without moving from the bed he cautiously opened the door with his disengaged hand, and looked into the main room. To his infinite surprise it was dark and deserted. But even then a smoldering log on the hearth broke, and by the upspringing blaze he saw the figure of Dick Bullen sitting by the dying embers.

"Hello!"

Dick started, rose, and came somewhat unsteadily toward him.

"Whar's the boys?" said the Old Man.

"Gone up the canyon on a little *pasear.* They're coming back for me in a minit. I'm waitin' round for 'em. What are you starin' at, Old Man?" he added, with a forced laugh; "do you think I'm drunk?"

The Old Man might have been pardoned the supposition, for Dick's eyes were humid and his face flushed. He loitered and lounged back to the chimney, yawned, shook himself, buttoned up his coat, and laughed. "Liquor ain't so plenty as that, Old Man. Now don't you git up," he continued, as the Old Man made a movement to release his sleeve from Johnny's hand. "Don't you mind manners. Sit jest whar you be; I'm goin' in a jiffy. Thar, that's them now."

There was a low tap at the door. Dick Bullen opened it quickly, nodded "good night" to his host, and disappeared. The Old Man would have followed him but for the hand that still unconsciously grasped his sleeve. He could have easily disengaged it: it was small, weak, and emaciated. But perhaps because it *was* small, weak, and emaciated he changed his mind, and drawing his chair closer to the bed, rested his head upon it. In this defenseless attitude the potency of his earlier potations surprised him. The room flickered and faded before his eyes, reappeared, faded again, went out, and left him—asleep.

Meantime Dick Bullen, closing the door, confronted his companions. "Are you ready?" said Staples. "Ready," said Dick; "what's the time?" "Past twelve," was the reply; "can you make it?—it's nigh on fifty miles, the round trip hither and yon." "I reckon," returned Dick shortly. "Whar's the mare?" "Bill and Jack's holdin' her at the crossin'." "Let 'em hold on a minit longer," said Dick.

He turned and re-entered the house softly. By the light of the guttering candle and dying fire he saw that the door of the little room was open. He stepped toward it on tiptoe and looked in. The Old Man had fallen back in his chair, snoring, his helpless feet thrust out in a line with his collapsed shoulders, and his hat pulled over his eyes. Beside him, on a narrow wooden bedstead, lay Johnny, muffled tightly in a blanket that hid all save a strip of forehead and a few curls damp with perspiration. Dick Bullen made a step forward, hesitated, and glanced over his shoulder into the deserted room. Everything was quiet. With a sudden resolution he parted his huge mustaches with both hands and stooped over the sleeping boy. But even as he did so a mischievous blast, lying in wait, swooped down the chimney, rekindled the hearth, and lit up the room with a shameless glow from which Dick fled in bashful terror.

His companions were already waiting for him at the crossing. Two of them were struggling in the darkness with some strange misshapen bulk, which as Dick came nearer took the semblance of a great yellow horse.

It was the mare. She was not a pretty picture. From her Roman nose to her rising haunches, from her arched spine hidden by the stiff *machillas* of a Mexican saddle, to her thick, straight bony legs, there was not a line of equine grace. In her half-blind but wholly vicious white eyes, in her protruding underlip, in her monstrous color, there was nothing but ugliness and vice.

"Now then," said Staples, "stand cl'ar of her heels, boys, and up with you. Don't miss your first holt of her mane, and mind ye get your off stirrup *quick.* Ready!"

There was a leap, a scrambling struggle, a bound, a wild retreat of the crowd, a circle of flying hoofs, two springless leaps that jarred the earth, a rapid play and jingle of spurs, a plunge, and then the voice of Dick somewhere in the darkness. "All right!"

"Don't take the lower road back onless you're hard pushed for time! Don't hold her in downhill! We'll be at the ford at five. G'lang! Hoopa! Mula! GO!"

A splash, a spark struck from the ledge in the road, a clatter in the rocky cut beyond, and Dick was gone.

Sing, O Muse, the ride of Richard Bullen! Sing, O Muse, of chivalrous men! the sacred quest, the doughty deeds, the battery of low churls, the fearsome ride and gruesome perils of the Flower of Simpson's Bar! Alack! she is dainty, this Muse! She will have none of this bucking brute and swaggering, ragged rider, and I must fain follow him in prose, afoot!

It was one o'clock, and yet he had only gained Rattlesnake Hill. For in that time Jovita had rehearsed to him all her imperfections and practiced all her vices. Thrice had she stumbled. Twice had she thrown up her Roman nose in a straight line with the reins, and resisting bit and spur, struck out madly across country. Twice had she reared, and rearing, fallen backward; and twice had the agile Dick, unharmed, regained his seat before she found her vicious legs again. And a mile beyond them, at the foot of a long hill, was Rattlesnake Creek. Dick knew that here was the crucial test of his ability to perform his enterprise, set his teeth grimly, put his knees well into her flanks, and changed his defensive tactics to brisk aggression. Bullied and maddened, Jovita began the descent of the hill. Here the artful Richard pretended to hold her in with ostentatious objurgation and well-feigned cries of alarm. It is unnecessary to add that Jovita instantly ran away. Nor need I state the time made in the descent; it is written in the chronicles of Simpson's Bar. Enough that in another moment, as it seemed to Dick, she was splashing on the overflowed banks of Rattlesnake Creek. As Dick expected, the momentum she had acquired carried her beyond the point of balking, and holding her well together for a mighty leap, they dashed into the middle of the swiftly flowing current. A few moments of kicking, wading, and swimming, and Dick drew a long breath on the opposite bank.

The road from Rattlesnake Creek to Red Mountain was tolerably level. Either the plunge in Rattlesnake Creek had dampened her baleful fire, or the art which led to it had shown her the superior wickedness of her rider, for Jovita no longer wasted her surplus energy in wanton conceits. Once she bucked, but it was from force of habit; once she shied, but it was from a new, freshly painted meetinghouse at the crossing of the county road. Hollows, ditches, gravelly deposits, patches of freshly springing grasses, flew from beneath her rattling hoofs. She began to smell unpleasantly, once or twice she coughed slightly, but there was no abatement of her strength or speed. By two o'clock he had passed Red Mountain and begun the descent to the plain. Ten minutes later the driver of the fast Pioneer coach was overtaken and passed by a "man on a pinto hoss"—an event sufficiently notable for remark. At half past two Dick rose in his stirrups with a great shout. Stars were glittering through the rifted clouds, and beyond him, out of the plain, rose two spires, a flagstaff, and a straggling line of black objects. Dick jingled his spurs and swung his *riata,* Jovita bounded forward, and in another moment they swept into Tuttleville, and drew up before the wooden piazza of "The Hotel of All Nations."

What transpired that night at Tuttleville is not strictly a part of this record. Briefly I may state, however, that after Jovita had been handed over to a sleepy ostler, whom she at once kicked into unpleasant consciousness, Dick sallied out with the barkeeper for a tour of the sleeping town. Lights still gleamed from a few saloons and gambling houses; but avoiding these, they stopped before several closed shops, and by persistent tapping and judicious outcry roused the proprietors from their beds, and made them unbar the doors of their magazines and expose their wares. Sometimes they were met by curses, but oftener by interest and some concern in their needs, and the interview was invariably concluded by a drink. It was three o'clock before this pleasantry was given over, and with a small waterproof bag of India rubber strapped on his shoulders, Dick returned to the hotel. But here he was waylaid by Beauty—Beauty opulent in charms, affluent in dress, persuasive in speech, and Spanish in accent! In vain she repeated the invitation in "Excelsior," happily scorned by all Alpine-climbing youth, and rejected by this child of the Sierras—a rejection softened in this instance by a laugh and his last gold coin. And then he sprang to the saddle and dashed down the lonely street and out into the lonelier plain, where presently the lights, the black line of houses, the spires, and the flagstaff sank into the earth behind him again and were lost in the distance.

The storm had cleared away, the air was brisk and cold, the outlines of adjacent landmarks were distinct, but it was half-past four before Dick reached the meetinghouse and the crossing of the country road. To avoid the rising grade he had taken a longer and more circuitous road, in whose viscid mud Jovita sank fetlock deep at every bound. It was a poor preparation for a steady ascent of five miles more; but Jovita, gathering her legs under her, took it with her usual blind, unreasoning fury, and a half-hour later reached the long level that led to Rattlesnake Creek. Another half-hour would bring him to the creek. He threw the reins lightly upon the neck of the mare, chirruped to her, and began to sing.

Suddenly Jovita shied with a bound that would have unseated a less practiced rider. Hanging to her rein was a figure that had leaped from the bank, and at the same time from the road before her arose a shadowy horse and rider.

"Throw up your hands," commanded the second apparition, with an oath.

Dick felt the mare tremble, quiver, and apparently sink under him. He knew what it meant and was prepared.

"Stand aside, Jack Simpson. I know you, you d——d thief! Let me pass, or—"

He did not finish the sentence. Jovita rose straight in the air with a terrific bound, throwing the figure from her bit with a single shake of her vicious head, and charged with deadly malevolence down on the impediment before her. An oath, a pistol shot, horse and highway man rolled over in the road, and the next moment Jovita was a hundred yards away. But the good right arm of her rider, shattered by a bullet, dropped helplessly at his side.

Without slacking his speed he shifted the reins to his left hand. But a few moments later he was obliged to halt and tighten the saddle girths that had slipped in the onset. This in his crippled condition took some time. He had no fear of pursuit, but looking up he saw that the eastern stars were already paling, and that the distant peaks had lost their ghostly whiteness and now stood out blackly against a lighter sky. Day was upon him. Then completely absorbed in a single idea, he forgot the pain of his wound, and mounting again dashed on toward Rattlesnake Creek. But now Jovita's breath came broken by gasps, Dick reeled in his saddle, and brighter and brighter grew the sky.

Ride, Richard; run, Jovita; linger, O day!

For the last few rods there was a roaring in his ears. Was it exhaustion from loss of blood, or what? He was dazed and giddy as he swept down the hill, and did not recognize his surroundings. Had he taken the wrong road, or was this Rattlesnake Creek?

It was. But the brawling creek he had swam a few hours before had risen, more than doubled its volume, and now rolled a swift and resistless river between him and Rattlesnake Hill. For the first time that night Richard's heart sank within him. The river, the mountain, the quickening east, swam before his eyes. He shut them to recover his self-control. In that brief interval, by some fantastic mental process, the little room at Simpson's Bar and the figures of the sleeping father and son rose upon him. He opened his eyes wildly, cast off his coat, pistol, boots, and saddle, bound his precious pack tightly to his shoulders, grasped the bare flanks of Jovita with his bared knees, and with a shout dashed into the yellow water. A cry rose from the opposite bank as the head of a man and horse struggled for a few moments against the battling current, and then were swept away amidst uprooted trees and whirling driftwood.

The Old Man started and woke. The fire on the hearth was dead, the candle in the outer room flickering in its socket, and somebody was rapping at the door. He opened it, but fell back with a cry before the dripping, half-naked figure that reeled against the doorpost.

"Dick?"

"Hush! Is he awake yet?"

"No; but, Dick—"

"Dry up, you old fool! Get me some whiskey, *quick!*" The Old Man flew and returned with—an empty bottle! Dick would have sworn, but his strength was not equal to the occasion. He staggered, caught at the handle of the door, and motioned to the Old Man.

"Thar's suthin' in my pack yer for Johnny. Take it off. I can't."

The Old Man unstrapped the pack and laid it before the exhausted man.

"Open it, quick."

He did so with trembling fingers. It contained only a few poor toys—cheap and barbaric enough, goodness knows, but bright with paint and tinsel. One of them was broken; another, I fear, was irretrievably ruined by water, and on the third—ah me! there was a cruel spot.

"It don't look like much, that's a fact," said Dick ruefully. . . . "But it's the best we could do. . . . Take 'em, Old Man, and put 'em in his stocking, and tell him—tell him, you know—hold me, Old Man—" The Old Man caught at his sinking figure. "Tell him," said Dick, with a weak little laugh—"tell him Sandy Claus has come."

And even so, bedraggled, ragged, unshaven, and unshorn, with one arm hanging helplessly at his side, Santa Claus came to Simpson's Bar and fell fainting on the first threshold. The Christmas dawn came slowly after, touching the remoter peaks with the rosy warmth of ineffable love. And it looked so tenderly on Simpson's Bar that the whole mountain, as if caught in a generous action, blushed to the skies.

The New Year's
Greetings

CHRISTMAS WITH LEWIS AND CLARK

Meriwether Lewis and William Clark

Meriwether Lewis (1774–1809) and William Clark (1770–1830) undertook their famous expedition in 1804, at the commission of President Thomas Jefferson, to find a route west to the Pacific Ocean. In keeping with American literary tradition, the finest accounts of this grand adventure come from the explorers' own journals, first published by Nicholas Biddle in 1814. The following is an account of their Christmas in this new wilderness called the West.

A Christmas in the wilderness, in 1804, is described by explorers Meriwether Lewis and William Clark.

Tuesday, 25th December 1804. We were awakened before day by a discharge of three platoons from the party. We had told the Indians not to visit us as it was one of our great medicine days, so that the men remained at home and amused themselves various ways, particularly with dancing, in which they take great pleasure. The American flag was hoisted for the first time in the fort; the best provisions we had were brought out, and this, with a little brandy, enabled them to pass the day in great festivity. Wednesday, 25th December 1805. We were awakened at daylight by a discharge of firearms, which was followed by a song from the men, as a compliment to us on the return of Christmas, which we have always been accustomed to observe as a day of rejoicing. After breakfast we divided our remaining stock of tobacco, which amounted to twelve carrots, into two parts; one of which we distributed among such of the party as made use of it; making a present of a handkerchief to the others. The remainder of the day was passed in good spirits, though there was nothing in our situation to excite much gayety.

MRS. PARKINS' CHRISTMAS EVE

Sarah Orne Jewett

Sarah Orne Jewett, a Maine native, was born in 1849 and died in 1909. She was a regular contributor to the Atlantic Monthly, *under the editorship of another of this volume's contributors, William Dean Howells. The author of a number of story collections including* Deephaven *and* The Country of the Pointed Firs, *she is primarily remembered for her work in genre regional studies, being one of the first American authors to give life and voice to her beloved Maine countryside.*

I

ne wintry-looking afternoon the sun was getting low, but still shone with cheerful radiance into Mrs. Lydia Parkins' sitting-room. To point out a likeness between the bareness of the room and the appearance of the outside world on that twenty-first of December might seem ungra-

cious; but there was a certain leaflessness and inhospitality common to both.

The cold, gray wall-paper, and dull, thin furniture; the indescribable poverty and lack of comfort of the room were exactly like the leaflessness and sharpness and coldness of that early winter day—unless the sun shone out with a golden glow as it had done in the latter part of the afternoon; then both the room and the long hillside and frozen road and distant western hills were quite transfigured.

Mrs. Parkins sat upright in one of the six decorous wooden chairs with cane seats; she was trimming a dismal gray-and-black winter bonnet and her work-basket was on the end of the table in front of her, between the windows, with a row of spools on the window-sill at her left. The only luxury she permitted herself was a cricket, a little bench such as one sees in a church pew, with a bit of carpet to cover its top. Mrs. Parkins was so short that she would have been quite off-roundings otherwise in her cane-seated chair; but she had a great horror of persons who put their feet on chair rungs and wore the paint off. She was always on the watch to break the young of this bad habit. She cast a suspicious glance now and then at little Lucy Deems, who sat in another cane-seated chair opposite. The child had called upon Mrs. Parkins before, and was now trying so hard to be good that both her feet had gone to sleep and had come to the prickling stage of that misery. She wondered if her mother were not almost ready to go home.

Mrs. Deems sat in the rocking-chair, full in the sunlight and faced the sun itself, unflinchingly. She was a broad-faced gay-hearted, little woman, and her face was almost as bright as the winter sun itself. One might fancy that they were having a match at trying to outshine one another, but so far it was not Mrs. Deems who blinked and withdrew from the contest. She was just now conscious of little Lucy's depression and anxious looks, and bade her go out to run about a little while and see if there were some of Mrs. Parkins' butternuts left under the big tree.

The door closed, and Mrs. Parkins snapped her thread and said that there was no butternuts out there; perhaps Lucy should have a few in a basket when she was going home.

"Oh, 'taint no matter," said Mrs. Deems, easily. "She was kind of distressed sittin' so quiet; they like to rove about, children does."

"She won't do no mischief?" asked the hostess, timidly.

"Lucy?" laughed the mother. "Why you ought to be better acquainted with Lucy than that, I'm sure. I catch myself wishing she wa'n't quite so still; she takes after her father's folks, all quiet and dutiful, and ain't got the least idea how to enjoy themselves; we was all kind of noisy to our house when I was grown up, and I can't seem to sense the Deems."

"I often wish I had just such a little girl as your Lucy," said Mrs. Parkins, with a sigh. She held her gray-and-black bonnet off with her left hand and looked at it without approval.

"I shall always continue to wear black for Mr. Parkins," she said, "but I had this piece of dark-gray ribbon and I thought I had better use it on my black felt; the felt is sort of rusty, now, and black silk trimmings increase the rusty appearance."

"They do so," frankly acknowledged Mrs. Deems. "Why don't you go an' get you a new one for meetin', Mrs. Parkins? Felts ain't high this season, an' you've got this for second wear."

"I've got one that's plenty good for best," replied Mrs. Parkins, without any change of expression. "It seems best to make this do one more winter." She began to rearrange the gray ribbon, and Mrs. Deems watched her with a twinkle in her eyes; she had something to say, and did not know exactly how to begin, and Mrs. Parkins knew it as well as she did, and was holding her back which made the occasion more and more difficult.

"There!" she exclaimed at last, boldly, "I expect you know what I've come to see you for, an' I can't set here and make talk no longer. May's well ask if you can do anything about the minister's present."

Mrs. Parkins' mouth was full of pins, and she removed them all, slowly, before she spoke. The sun went behind a low snow cloud along the horizon, and Mrs. Deems shone on alone. It was not very warm in the room, and she gathered her woolen shawl closer about her shoulders as if she were getting ready to go home.

"I don't know's I feel to give you anything to-day, Mrs. Deems," said Mrs. Parkins in a resolved tone. "I don't feel much acquainted with the minister's folks. I must say *she* takes a good deal upon herself; I don't like so much of a ma'am."

"She's one of the pleasantest, best women we ever had in town, *I* think," replied Mrs. Deems. "I was tellin' 'em the other day that I always felt as if she brought a pleasant feelin' wherever she came, so sisterly and own-folks-like. They've seen a sight o'trouble and must feel pinched at times, but she finds ways to do plenty o' kindnesses. I never see a mite of behavior in 'em as if we couldn't do enough for 'em because they was ministers. Some minister's folks has such expectin' ways, and the more you do the more you may; but it ain't so with the Lanes. They are always a thinkin' what they can do for other people, an' they do it, too. You never liked 'em, but I can't see why."

"He ain't the ablest preacher that ever was," said Mrs. Parkins.

"I don't care if he ain't; words is words, but a man that lives as Mr. Lane does, is the best o' ministers," answered Mrs. Deems.

"Well, I don't owe 'em nothin' to-day," said the hostess, looking up. "I haven't got it in mind to do for the minister's folks any more than I have; but I may send 'em some apples or somethin', by'n by."

"Jest as you feel," said Mrs. Deems, rising quickly and looking provoked. "I didn't know but what 'twould be a pleasure to you, same's 'tis to the rest of us."

"They ain't been here very long, and I pay my part to the salary, an' 'taint no use to overdo in such cases."

"They've been put to extra expense this fall, and have been very feeling and kind; real interested in all of us, and such a help to the parish as we ain't had for a good while before. Havin' to send their boy to the hospital has made it hard for 'em."

"Well, folks has to have their hard times, and minister's families can't escape. I am sorry about the boy, I'm sure," said Mrs. Parkins, generously. "Don't you go, Mrs. Deems; you ain't been to see me for a good while. I want you to see my bonnet in jest a minute."

"I've got to go way over to the Dilby's, and it's goin' to be dark early. I should be pleased to have you come an' see me. I've got to find Lucy and trudge along."

"I believe I won't rise to see you out o' the door, my lap's so full," said Mrs. Parkins politely, and so they parted. Lucy was hopping up and down by the front fence to keep herself warm and occupied.

"She didn't say anything about the butternuts, did she, mother?" the child asked; and Mrs. Deems laughed and shook her head. Then they walked away down the road together, the big-mittened hand holding fast the little one, and the hooded heads bobbing toward each other now and then, as if they were holding a lively conversation. Mrs. Parkins looked after them two or three times, suspiciously at first, as if she thought they might be talking about her; then a little wistfully. She had come of a saving family and had married a saving man.

"Isn't Mrs. Parkins real poor, mother?" little Lucy inquired in a compassionate voice.

Mrs. Deems smiled, and assured the child that there was nobody so well off in town except Colonel Drummond, so far as money went; but Mrs. Parkins took care neither to enjoy her means herself, nor to let anybody else. Lucy pondered this strange answer for awhile and then began to hop and skip along the rough road, still holding fast her mother's warm hand.

This was the twenty-first of December, and the day of the week was Monday. On Tuesday Mrs. Parkins did her frugal ironing, and on Wednesday she meant to go over to Haybury to put some money into the bank and to do a little shopping. Goods were cheaper in Haybury in some of the large stores, than they were at the corner store at home, and she had the horse and could always get dinner at her cousin's. To be sure, the cousin was always hinting for presents for herself or her children, but Mrs. Parkins could bear that, and always cleared her conscience by asking the boys over in haying-time, though their help cost more than it came to with their growing appetites and the wear and tear of the house. Their mother came for a day's visit now and then, but everything at home depended upon her hard-working hands, as she had been early left a widow with little else to depend upon, until now, when the boys were out of school. One was doing well in the shoe factory and one in a store. Mrs. Parkins was really much attached to her cousin, but she thought if she once began to give, they would always be expecting something.

As has been said, Wednesday was the day set for the visit, but when

Wednesday came it was a hard winter day, cold and windy, with an occasional flurry of snow, and Mrs. Parkins being neuralgic, gave up going until Thursday. She was pleased when she waked Thursday morning to find the weather warmer and the wind stilled. She was weather-wise enough to see snow in the clouds, but it was only eight miles to Haybury and she could start early and come home again as soon as she got her dinner. So the boy who came every morning to take care of her horse and bring in wood was hurried and urged until he nearly lost his breath, and the horse was put into the wagon and, with rare forethought, a piece of salt-pork was wrapped up and put under the wagon-seat; then with a cloud over the re-trimmed bonnet, and a shawl over her Sunday cloak, and mittens over her woolen gloves Mrs. Parkins drove away. All her neighbors knew that she was going to Haybury to put eighty-seven dollars into the bank that the Dilby brothers had paid her for some rye planted and harvested on the halves. Very likely she had a good deal of money beside, that day; she had the best farm in that sterile neighborhood and was a famous manager.

The cousin was a hospitable, kindly soul, very loyal to her relations and always ready with a welcome. Beside, though the ears of Lydia Parkins were deaf to hints of present need and desire, it was more than likely that she would leave her farm and savings to the boys; she was not a person to speak roughly to, or one whom it was possible to disdain. More than this, no truly compassionate heart could fail to pity the thin, anxious, forbidding little woman, who behaved as if she must always be on the defensive against a plundering and begging world.

Cousin Mary Faber, as usual, begged Mrs. Parkins to spend the night; she seemed to take so little pleasure in life that the change might do her good. There would be no expense except for the horse's stabling, Mrs. Faber urged openly, and nobody would be expecting her at home. But Mrs. Parkins, as usual, refused, and feared that the cellar would freeze. It had not been banked up as she liked to have it that autumn, but as for paying the Dilbys a dollar and a quarter for doing it, she didn't mean to please them so much.

"Land sakes! Why don't you feel as rich as you be, an' not mind them little expenses?" said cousin Faber, daringly. "I do declare I don't see how you can make out to grow richer an' poorer at the same time." The good-natured soul could not help laughing as she spoke, and Mrs. Parkins herself really could not help smiling.

"I'm much obliged to you for the pleasure of your company," said cousin Faber, "and it was very considerate of you to bring me that nice piece o' pork." If she had only known what an effort her guest had made to carry it into the house after she had brought it! Twice Mrs. Parkins had pushed it back under the wagon-seat with lingering indecision, and only taken it out at last because she feared that one of those prowling boys might discover it in the wagon and tell his mother. How often she had taken something into her hand to give away and then put it back and taken it again half a dozen times, irresolutely. There were still blind movements of the heart toward generosity, but she had grown more and more skillful at soothing her conscience and finding excuses for not giving.

The Christmas preparations in the busy little town made her uncomfortable, and cheerful cousin Faber's happiness in her own pinched housekeeping was a rebuke. The boys' salaries were very small indeed, this first year or two; but their mother was proud of their steadiness, and still sewed and let rooms to lodgers and did everything she could to earn money. She looked tired and old before her time, and acknowledged to Mrs. Parkins that she should like to have a good, long visit at the farm the next summer and let the boys take their meals with a neighbor. "I never spared myself one step until they were through with their schooling; but now it will be so I can take things a little easier," said the good soul with a wistful tone that was unusual.

Mrs. Parkins felt impatient as she listened; she knew that a small present of money now and then would have been a great help, but she never could make up her mind to begin what promised to be the squandering of her carefully saved fortune. It would be the ruin of the boys, too, if they thought she could be appealed to in every emergency. She would make it up to them in the long run; she could not take her money with her to the next world, and she would make a virtue of necessity.

The afternoon was closing in cold and dark, and the snow came sifting down slowly before Mrs. Parkins was out of the street of Haybury. She had lived too long on a hill not to be weatherwise and for a moment, as the wind buffeted her face and she saw the sky and the horizon line all dulled by the coming storm, she had a great mind to go back to cousin Faber's. If it had been any other time in the year but Christmas eve! The old horse gathered his forces and hurried along as if he had sense enough to be anxious about the weather; but presently the road turned so that the wind was not so chilling and they were quickly out of sight of the town, crossing the level land which lay between Haybury and the hills of Holton. Mrs. Parkins was persuaded that she should get home by dark, and the old horse did his very best. The road was rough and frozen and the wagon rattled and pitched along; it was like a race between Mrs. Parkins and the storm, and for a time it seemed certain that she would be the winner.

The gathering forces of the wind did not assert themselves fully until nearly half the eight miles had been passed, and the snow which had only clung to Mrs. Parkins' blanket-shawl like a white veil at first, and sifted white across the frozen grass of the lowlands, lay at last like a drift on the worn buffalo-robe, and was so deep in the road that it began to clog the wheels. It was a most surprising snow in the thickness of the flakes and the rapidity with which it gathered; it was no use to try to keep the white-knitted cloud over her face, for it became so thick with snow that it blinded and half-stifled her. The darkness began to fall, the snow came thicker and faster, and the horse climbing the drifted hills with the snow-clogged wagon, had to stop again and again. The awful thought suddenly came to Mrs. Parkins' mind that she could not reach home that night, and the next moment she had to acknowledge that she did not know exactly where she was. The thick flakes blinded her; she turned to look behind to see if any one were coming; but she might have been in the middle of an Arctic waste. She felt benumbed and stupid, and again tried to urge the tired horse, and the good creature toiled on desperately. It seemed as if they must have left the lowland far enough behind to be near some houses, but it grew still darker and snowier as they dragged slowly for another mile until it was impossible to get any further, and the horse stopped still and then gave a shake to rid himself of the drift on his back, and turned his head to look inquiringly at his mistress.

Mrs. Parkins began to cry with cold, and fear and misery. She had read accounts of such terrible, sudden storms in the west, and here she was in the night, foodless, and shelterless, and helpless.

"Oh! I'd give a thousand dollars to be safe under cover!" groaned the poor soul. "Oh, how poor I be this minute, and I come right away from that warm house!"

A strange dazzle of light troubled her eyes, and a vision of the brightly lighted Haybury shops, and the merry customers that were hurrying in and out, and the gayety and contagious generosity of Christmas eve mocked at the stingy, little lost woman as she sat there half-bewildered. The heavy flakes of snow caught her eyelashes and chilled her cheeks and melted inside the gray bonnet-strings; they heaped themselves on the top of the bonnet into a high crown that toppled into her lap as she moved. If she tried to brush the snow away, her clogged mitten only gathered more and grew more and more clumsy. It was a horrible, persistent storm; at this rate the horse and driver both would soon be covered and frozen in the road. The gathering flakes were malicious and mysterious; they were so large and flaked so fast down out of the sky.

"My goodness! How numb I be this minute," whispered Mrs. Parkins. And then she remembered that the cashier of the bank had told her that morning when she made her deposit, that everybody else was taking out their money that day; she was the only one who had come to put any in.

"I'd pay every cent of it willin' to anybody that would come along and help me get to shelter," said the poor soul. "Oh, I don't know as I've hoed so's to be worth savin' "; and a miserable sense of shame and defeat beat down whatever hope tried to rise in her heart. What had she tried to do for God and man that gave her a right to think of love and succor now?

Yet it seemed every moment as if help must come and as if this great emergency could not be so serious. Life had been so monotonous to Mrs. Parkins, so destitute of excitement and tragic situations that she could hardly understand, even now, that she was in such great danger. Again she called as loud as she could for help, and the horse whinnied louder still. The only hope was that two men who had passed her some miles back would remember that they had advised her to hurry, and would come back to look for her. The poor, old horse had dragged himself and the wagon to the side of the road under the shelter of some evergreens; Mrs. Parkins slipped down under the buffalo into the bottom of her cold, old wagon, and covered herself as well as she could. There was more than a chance that she might be found frozen under a snow-drift in the morning.

The morning! Christmas morning!

What did the advent of Christmas day hold out for her—buried in the snow-drifts of a December storm!

Anything? Yes, but she knew it not. Little did she dream what this Christmas eve was to bring into her life!

II

Lydia Parkins was a small woman of no great vigor, but as she grew a little warmer under her bed of blankets in the bottom of the old wagon, she came to her senses. She must get out and try to walk on through the snow as far as she could; it was no use to die there in this fearful storm like a rabbit. Yes, and she must unharness the horse and let him find his way; so she climbed boldly down into the knee-deep snow where a drift had blown already. She would not admit the thought that perhaps she might be lost in the snow and frozen to death that very night. It did not seem in character with Mrs. Nathan Parkins, who was the owner of plenty of money in Haybury Bank, and a good farm well divided into tillage and woodland, who had plenty of blankets and comforters at home, and firewood enough, and suitable winter clothes to protect her from the weather. The wind was rising more and more, it made the wet gray-and-black bonnet feel very limp and cold about her head, and her poor head itself felt duller and heavier than ever. She lost one glove and mitten in the snow as she tried to unharness the old horse, and her bare fingers were very clumsy, but she managed to get the good old creature clear, hoping that he would plod on and be known farther along the road and get help for her; but instead of that he only went round and round her and the wagon, floundering and whinnying, and refusing to be driven away. "What kind of a storm is this going to be?" groaned Mrs. Parkins, wading along the road and falling over her dress helplessly. The old horse meekly followed and when she gave a weak, shrill, womanish shout, old Major neighed and shook the snow off his back. Mrs. Parkins knew in her inmost heart, that with such a wind and through such drifts she could not get very far, and at last she lost her breath and sank down at the roadside and the horse went on alone. It was horribly dark and the cold pierced her through and through. In a few minutes she staggered to her feet and went on; she could have cried because the horse was out of sight, but she found it easier following in his tracks.

Suddenly there was a faint twinkle of light on the left, and what a welcome sight it was! The poor wayfarer hastened, but the wind behaved as if it were trying to blow her back. The horse had reached shelter first and somebody had heard him outside and came out and shut the house door with a loud bang that reached Mrs. Parkins' ears. She tried to shout again but she could hardly make a sound. The light still looked a good way off, but presently she could hear voices and see another light moving. She was so tired that she must wait until they came to help her. Who lived in the first house on the left after you passed oak ridge? Why, it couldn't be the Donnells, for they were all away in Haybury, and the house was shut up; this must be the parsonage, and she was off the straight road home. The bewildered horse had taken the left-hand road. "Well," thought Mrs. Parkins, "I'd rather be most anywhere else, but I don't care where 'tis so long as I get under cover. I'm all spent and wore out."

The lantern came bobbing along quickly as if somebody were

hurrying, and wavered from side to side as if it were in a fishing boat on a rough sea. Mrs. Parkins started to meet it, and made herself known to her rescuer.

"I declare, if 'taint the minister," she exclaimed. "I'm Mrs. Parkins, or what's left of her. I've come near bein' froze to death along back here a-piece. I never saw such a storm in all my life."

She sank down in the snow and could not get to her feet again. The minister was a strong man, he stooped and lifted her like a child and carried her along the road with the lantern hung on his arm. She was a little woman and she was not a person given to sentiment, but she had been dreadfully cold and frightened, and now at last she was safe. It was like the good shepherd in the Bible, and Lydia Parkins was past crying; but it seemed as if she could never speak again and as if her heart were going to break. It seemed inevitable that the minister should have come to find her and carry her to the fold; no, to the parsonage; but she felt dizzy and strange again, and the second-best gray-and-black bonnet slipped its knot and tumbled off into the snow without her knowing it.

When Mrs. Parkins opened her eyes a bright light made them shut again directly; then she discovered, a moment afterward, that she was in the parsonage sitting-room and the minister's wife was kneeling beside her with an anxious face; and there was a Christmas tree at the other side of the room, with all its pretty, shining things and gay little candles on the boughs. She was comfortably wrapped in warm blankets, but she felt very tired and weak. The minister's wife smiled with delight: "Now you'll feel all right in a few minutes," she exclaimed. "Think of your being out in this awful storm! Don't try to talk to us yet, dear," she added kindly. "I'm going to bring you a cup of good hot tea. Are you all right? Don't try to tell anything about the storm. Mr. Lane has seen to the horse. Here, I'll put my little red shawl over you, it looks prettier than the blankets, and I'm drying your clothes in the kitchen."

The minister's wife had a sweet face, and she stood for a minute looking down at her unexpected guest; then something in the thin, appealing face on the sofa seemed to touch her heart, and she stooped over and kissed Mrs. Parkins. It happened that nobody had kissed Mrs. Parkins for years, and the tears stole down her cheeks as Mrs. Lane turned away.

As for the minister's wife, she had often thought that Mrs. Parkins had a most disagreeable hard face; she liked her less than any one in the parish, but now as she brightened the kitchen fire, she began to wonder what she could find to put on the Christmas tree for her, and wondered why she never had noticed a frightened, timid look in the poor woman's eyes. "It is so forlorn for her to live all alone on that big farm," said Mrs. Lane to herself, mindful of her own happy home and the children. All three of them came close about their mother at that moment, lame-footed John with his manly pale face, and smiling little Bell and Mary, the girls.

The minister came in from the barn and blew his lantern out and hung it away. The old horse was blanketed as warm as his mistress, and there was a good supper in his crib. It was a very happy household at the parsonage, and Mrs. Parkins could hear their whispers and smothered laughter in the kitchen. It was only eight o'clock after all, and it was evident that the children longed to begin their delayed festivities. The little girls came and stood in the doorway and looked first at the stranger guest and then at their Christmas tree, and after a while their mother came with them to ask whether Mrs. Parkins felt equal to looking on at the pleasuring or whether she would rather go to bed and rest, and sleep away her fatigue.

Mrs. Parkins wished to look on; she was beginning to feel well again, but she dreaded being alone, she could not tell exactly why.

"Come right into the bedroom with me then," said Mrs. Lane, "and put on a nice warm, double gown of mine; 'twill be large enough for you, that's certain, and then if you do wish to move about by-and-by, you will be better able than in the blankets."

Mrs. Parkins felt dazed by this little excitement, yet she was strangely in the mood for it. The reaction of being in this safe and pleasant place, after the recent cold and danger, excited her, and gave her an unwonted power of enjoyment and sympathy. She felt pleased and young, and she wondered what was going to happen. She stood still and let Mrs. Lane brush her gray hair, all tangled with the snow damp, as if she were no older than the little girls themselves; then they went out again to the sitting-room. There was a great fire blazing in the Franklin stove; the minister had cleared a rough bit of the parsonage land the summer before and shown good spirit about it, and these, as Mrs. Parkins saw at once, were some of the pitch-pine roots. She had said when she heard of his hard work, that he had better put the time into his sermons, and she remembered that now with a pang at her heart, and confessed inwardly that she had been mean spirited sometimes toward the Lanes, and it was a good lesson to her to be put at their mercy now. As she sat in her corner by the old sofa in the warm double gown and watched their kindly faces, a new sense of friendliness and hopefulness stole into her heart. "I'm just as warm now as I was cold a while ago," she assured the minister.

The children sat side by side, the lame boy and the two little sisters before the fire, and Mrs. Lane sat on the sofa by Mrs. Parkins, and the minister turned over the leaves of a Bible that lay on the table. It did not seem like a stiff and formal meeting held half from superstition and only half from reverence, but it was as if the good man were telling his household news of some one they all loved and held close to their hearts. He said a few words about the birth of Christ, and of there being no room that night in the inn. Room enough for the Roman soldier and the priest and the tax-gatherer, but no room for Christ; and how we all blame that innkeeper, and then are like him too often in the busy inn of our hearts. "Room for our friends and our pleasures and our gains, and no room for Christ," said the minister sadly, as the children looked soberly into the fire and tried to understand. Then they heard again the story of the shepherds and the star, and it was a more beautiful story than ever, and seemed quite new and wonderful; and then the minister prayed, and gave special thanks for the friend who made one of their household that night, because she had come through such great danger. Afterward the Lanes sang their Christmas hymn, standing about a little old organ which the mother played: "While shepherds watched their flocks by night—"

They sang it all together as if they loved the hymn, and when they stopped and the room was still again, Mrs. Parkins could hear the wind blow outside and the great elm branches sway and creak above the little house, and the snow clicked busily against the windows. There was a curious warmth at her heart; she did not feel frightened or lonely, or cold, or even selfish any more.

They lighted the candles on the Christmas tree, and the young people capered about and were brimming over with secrets and shouted with delight, and the tree shown and glistened brave in its gay trimming of walnuts covered with gold and silver paper, and little bags sewed with bright worsteds, and all sorts of pretty homemade trifles. But when the real presents were discovered, the presents that meant no end of thought and management and secret self-denial, the brightest part of the household love and happiness shone out. One after another they came to bring Mrs. Parkins her share of the little tree's fruit until her lap was full as she sat on the sofa. One little girl brought a bag of candy, though there wasn't much candy on the tree; and the other gave her a bookmark, and the lame boy had a pretty geranium, grown by himself, with a flower on it, and came limping to put it in her hands; and Mrs. Lane brought a pretty hood that her sister had made for her a few weeks before, but her old one was still good and she did not need two. The minister had found a little book of hymns which a friend had given him at the autumn conference, and as Mrs. Parkins opened it, she happened to see these words: "Room to deny ourselves." She didn't know why the tears rushed to her eyes: "I've got to learn to deny myself of being mean," she thought, almost angrily. It was the least she could do, to do something friendly for these kind people; they had taken her in out of the storm with such loving warmth of sympathy; they did not show the least consciousness that she had never spoken a kind word about them since they came to town; that she alone had held aloof when this dear boy, their only son, had fought through an illness which might leave him a cripple for life. She had heard that there was a hope of his being cured if by-and-by his father could carry him to New York to a famous surgeon there. But all the expense of the long journey and many weeks of treatment had seemed impossible. They were so thankful to have him still alive and with them that Christmas night. Mrs. Parkins could see the mother's eyes shine with tears as she looked at him, and the father put out a loving hand to steady him as he limped across the room.

"I wish little Lucy Deems, that lives next neighbor to me, was here to help your girls keep Christmas," said Mrs. Parkins, speaking half-unconsciously. "Her mother has had it very hard; I mean to bring her over some day when the traveling gets good."

"We know Lucy Deems," said the children with satisfaction. Then Mrs. Parkins thought with regret of cousin Faber and her two boys, and was sorry that they were not all at the minister's too. She seemed to have entered upon a new life; she even thought of her dreary home with disapproval, and of its comfortable provisioning in cellar and garret, and of her money in the Haybury bank, with secret shame. Here she was with Mrs. Lane's double gown on, as poor a woman as there was in the world; she had come like a beggar to the Lanes' door that Christmas eve, and they were eagerly giving her house-room and gifts great and small; where were her independence and her riches now? She was a stranger and they had taken her in, and they did it for Christ's sake, and he would bless them, but what was there to say for herself? "Lord, how poor I be!" faltered Lydia Parkins for the second time that night.

There had not been such a storm for years. It was days before people could hear from each other along the blockaded country roads. Men were frozen to death, and cattle; and the telegraph wires were down and the safe and comfortable country side felt as if it had been in the power of some merciless and furious force of nature from which it could never again feel secure. But the sun came out and the blue-jays came back, and the crows, and the white snow melted, and the farmers went to and fro again along the highways. A new peace and good-will showed itself between the neighbors after their separation, but Mrs. Parkins' good-will outshown the rest. She went to Haybury as soon as the roads were well broken, and brought cousin Faber back with her for a visit, and sent her home again with a loaded wagon of supplies. She called in Lucy Deems and gave her a peck basketful of butternuts on New Year's Day, and told her to come for more when these were gone; and, more than all, one Sunday soon afterward, the minister told his people that he should be away for the next two Sundays. The kindness of a friend was going to put a great blessing within his reach, and he added simply, in a faltering voice, that he hoped all his friends would pray for the restoration to health of his dear boy.

Mrs. Parkins sat in her pew; she had not worn so grim an expression since before Christmas. Nobody could tell what secret pangs these gifts and others like them had cost her, yet she knew that only a right way of living would give her peace of mind. She could no longer live in a mean, narrow world of her own making; she must try to take the world as it is, and make the most of her life.

There were those who laughed and said that her stingy ways were frightened out of her on the night of the storm; but sometimes one is taught and led slowly to a higher level of existence unconsciously and irresistibly, and the decisive upward step once taken is seldom retraced. It was not long before Mrs. Deems said to a neighbor cheerfully: "Why, I always knew Mrs. Parkins meant well enough, but she *didn't know how* to do for other folks; she seemed kind of scared to use her own money, as if she didn't have any right to it. Now she is kind of persuaded that she's got the whole responsibility, and just you see how pleased she behaves. She's just a beginnin' to live; she never heard one word o' the first prayer yesterday mornin'; I see her beamin' an' smilin' at the minister's boy from the minute she see him walk up the aisle straight an' well as anybody."

"She goin' to have one of her cousin Faber's sons come over and stop awhile, I hear. He got run down workin' in the shoe factory to Haybury. Perhaps he may take hold and she'll let him take the farm by-an'-by. There, we mustn't expect too much of her," said the other woman compassionately. "I'm sure 'tis a blessed change as far as she's got a'ready. Habits'll live sometimes after they're dead. Folks don't find it so easy to go free of ways they've settled into; life's truly a warfare, ain't it?"

"It is, so," answered Mrs. Deems, soberly. "There comes Mrs.

Parkins this minute, in the old wagon, and my Lucy settin' up 'long side of her as pert as Nathan! Now ain't Mrs. Parkins' countenance got a pleasanter look than it used to wear? Well, the more she does for others, and the poorer she gets, the richer she seems to feel."

"It's a very unusual circumstance for a woman o' her age to turn right about in her tracks. It makes us believe that Heaven takes hold and helps folks," said the neighbor; and they watched the thin, little woman out of sight along the hilly road with a look of pleased wonder on their own faces. It was mid-spring, but Mrs. Parkins still wore her best winter bonnet; as for the old rusty one trimmed with gray, the minister's little girls found it when the snow drifts melted, and carefully hid it away to deck the parsonage scarecrow in the time of corn-planting.

Hearty Christmas Wishes

SUSIE'S LETTER FROM SANTA

Mark Twain

Mark Twain (Samuel Langhorne Clemens) was born in 1835 and died in 1910. During his early childhood, his family relocated to his beloved Hannibal, Missouri, near the Mississippi River that would so profoundly affect his life and career. Young Clemens began his working life on the riverboats, and in fact the pseudonym Mark Twain is a depth call for riverboat pilots. Like many young men of the era, he headed west, working as a journalist, until he met and formed a fast friendship with the man who became his mentor, Bret Harte. Under Harte's tutelage, Twain literally became an overnight success with the publication of his first story, "The Celebrated Jumping Frog of Calaveras County."

Palace of St. Nicholas
In the Moon
Christmas Morning

y dear Susie Clemens:
I have received and read all the letters which you and your little sister have written me by the hand of your mother and your nurses; I have also read

those which you little people have written me with your own hands—for although you did not use any characters that are in grown people's alphabet, you used the characters that all children in all lands on earth and in the twinkling stars use; and as all my subjects in the moon are children and use no characters but that, you will easily understand that I can read your and your baby sister's jagged and fantastic marks without any trouble at all. But I had trouble with those letters which you dictated through your mother and the nurses, for I am a foreigner and cannot read English writing well. You will find that I made no mistakes about the things which you and the baby ordered in your own letters—I went down your chimney at midnight when you were asleep and delivered them all myself—and kissed both of you, too, because you are good children, well trained, nice mannered, and about the most obedient little people I ever saw. But in the letter which you dictated there were some words which I could not make out for certain, and one or two small orders which I could not fill because we ran out of stock. Our last lot of kitchen furniture for dolls has just gone to a very poor little child in the North Star away up in the cold country above the Big Dipper. Your mama can show you that star and you will say: "Little Snow Flake" (for that is the child's name), "I'm glad you got that furniture, for you need it more than I." That is, you must *write* that, with your own hand, and Snow Flake will write you an answer. If you only spoke it she wouldn't hear you. Make your letter light and thin, for the distance is great and the postage very heavy.

There was a word or two in your mama's letter which I couldn't be certain of. I took it to be "a trunk full of doll's clothes." Is that it? I will call at your kitchen door about nine o'clock this morning to inquire. But I must not see anybody and I must not speak to anybody but you. When the kitchen doorbell rings, George must be blindfolded and sent to open the door. Then he must go back to the dining room or the china closet and take the cook with him. You must tell George he must walk on tiptoe and not speak—otherwise he will die someday. Then you must go up to the nursery and stand on a chair or the nurse's bed and put your ear to the speaking tube that leads down to the kitchen and when I whistle through it you must speak in the tube and say, "Welcome, Santa Claus!" Then I will ask whether it was a trunk you ordered or not. If you say it was, I shall ask you what *color* you want the trunk to be. Your mama will help you to name a nice color and then you must tell me every single thing in detail which you want the trunk to contain. Then when I say "Good-bye and a merry Christmas to my little Susie Clemens," you must say "Good-bye, good old Santa Claus, I thank you very much and please tell that little Snow Flake I will look at her star tonight and she must look down here—I will be right in the west bay window; and every fine night I will look at her star and say, 'I know somebody up there and *like* her, too.' " Then you must go down into the library and make George close the doors that open into the main hall and everybody must keep still for a little while. Then while you are waiting I will go to the moon and get those things and in a few minutes I will come down the chimney that belongs to the fireplace that is in the hall—if it is a trunk you want—because I couldn't get such a large thing as a trunk down the nursery chimney, you know.

People may talk if they want, till they hear my footsteps in the hall. Then you tell them to keep quiet a little while until I go up the chimney. Maybe you will not hear my footsteps at all—so you may go now and then and peep through the dining-room doors, and by and by you will see that which you want, right under the piano in the drawing room—for I shall put it there. If I should leave any snow in the hall, you must tell George to sweep it into the fireplace, for I haven't time to do such things. George must not use a broom, but a rag—or he will die someday. You watch George and don't let him run into danger. If my boot should leave a stain on the marble, George must not holystone it away. Leave it there always in memory of my visit; and whenever you look at it or show it to anybody you must let it remind you to be a good little girl. Whenever you are naughty and somebody points to that mark which your good old Santa Claus's boot made on the marble, what will you say, little sweetheart?

Good-bye for a few minutes, till I come down and ring the kitchen doorbell.

Your loving Santa Claus
Whom people sometimes call
"The Man in the Moon"

Best Wishes
for Christmas!

THURLOW'S CHRISTMAS STORY

John Kendrick Bangs

John Kendrick Bangs is little known today, but he is the author of a number of wickedly funny books and stories, including A Houseboat on the Styx. *He was born in Yonkers, New York, in 1862, and died in 1922. Bangs served as the editor for a number of magazines and periodicals during his career, including* Puck, Life, *and* Harper's Weekly. *Bangs was truly a writer's writer, as is evident in the following tale—a Christmas story for anyone who has faced the dread specter of an impending deadline and a bad case of writer's block.*

I

eing the Statement of Henry Thurlow, Author, to George Currier, Editor of the Idler, a Weekly Journal of Human Interest.)

I have always maintained, my dear Currier, that if a man wishes to be considered sane, and has any particular regard for his reputation as a truth-teller, he would better keep silent as to the singular experiences that enter into his life. I have had many such experiences myself; but I have rarely confided them in detail, or otherwise, to those about me, because I know that even the most trustful of my friends would regard them merely as the outcome of an imagination unrestrained by conscience, or of a gradually weakening mind subject to hallucinations. I know them to be true, but until Mr. Edison or some other modern wizard has invented a searchlight strong enough to lay bare the secrets of the mind and conscience of man, I cannot prove to others that they are not pure fabrications, or at least the conjurings of a diseased fancy. For instance, no man would believe me if I were to state to him the plain and indisputable fact that one night last month, on my way up to bed shortly after midnight, having been neither smoking nor drinking, I saw confronting me upon the stairs, with the moonlight streaming through the windows back of me, lighting up its face, a figure in which I recognized my very self in every form and feature. I might describe the chill of terror that struck to the very marrow of my bones, and wellnigh forced me to stagger backward down the stairs, as I noticed in the face of this confronting figure every indication of all the bad qualities which I know myself to possess, of every evil instinct which by no easy effort I have repressed heretofore, and realized that that *thing* was, as far as I knew, entirely independent of my true self, in which I hope at least the moral has made an honest fight against the immoral always. I might describe this chill, I say, as vividly as I felt it at that moment, but it would be of no use to do so, because, however realistic it might prove as a bit of description, no man would believe that the incident really happened; and yet it did happen as truly as I write, and it has happened a dozen times since, and I am certain that it will happen many times again, though I would give all that I possess to be assured that never again should that disquieting creation of mind or matter, whichever it may be, cross my path. The experience has made me afraid almost to be alone, and I have found myself unconsciously and uneasily glancing at my face in mirrors, in the plate-glass of show-windows on the shopping streets of the city, fearful lest I should find some of those evil traits which I have struggled to keep under, and have kept under so far, cropping out there where all the world, all *my* world, can see and wonder at, having known me always as a man of right doing and right feeling. Many a time in the night the thought has come to me with prostrating force, what if that thing were to be seen and recognized by others, myself and yet not my whole self, my unworthy self unrestrained and yet recognizable as Henry Thurlow.

I have also kept silent as to that strange condition of affairs which has tortured me in my sleep for the past year and a half; no one but myself has until this writing known that for that period of time I have had a continuous, logical dream-life; a life so vivid and so dreadfully real to me that I have found myself at times wondering which of the two lives I was living and which I was dreaming; a life in which that other wicked self has dominated, and forced me to a career of shame and horror; a life which, being taken up every time I sleep where it ceased with the awakening from a previous sleep, has made me fear to close my eyes in forgetfulness when others are near at hand, lest, sleeping, I shall let fall some speech that, striking on their ears, shall lead them to believe that in secret there is some wicked mystery connected with my life. It would be of no use for me to tell these things. It would merely serve to make my family and my friends uneasy about me if they were told in their awful detail, and so I have kept silent about them. To you alone, and now for the first time, have I hinted as to the troubles which have oppressed me for many days, and to you they are confided only because of the demand you have made that I explain to you the extraordinary complication in which the Christmas story sent you last week has involved me. You know that I am a man of dignity; that I am not a schoolboy and a lover of childish tricks; and knowing that, your friendship, at least, should have restrained your tongue and pen when, through the former, on Wednesday, you accused me of perpetrating a trifling, and to you excessively embarrassing, practical joke—a charge which, at the moment, I was too overcome to refute; and through the latter, on Thursday, you reiterated the accusation, coupled with a demand for an explanation of my conduct satisfactory to yourself, or my immediate resignation from the staff of the *Idler.* To explain is difficult, for I am certain that you will find the explanation too improbable for credence, but explain I must. The alternative, that of resigning from your staff, affects not only my own welfare, but that of my children, who must be provided for; and if my post with you is taken from me, then are all resources gone. I have not the courage to face dismissal, for I have no sufficient confidence in my powers to please elsewhere to make me easy in my mind, or, if I could please elsewhere, the certainty of finding the immediate employment of my talents which is necessary to me, in view of the at present overcrowded condition of the literary field.

To explain, then, my seeming jest at your expense, hopeless as it appears to be, is my task; and to do so as completely as I can, let me go back to the very beginning.

In August you informed me that you would expect me to provide, as I have heretofore been in the habit of doing, a story for the Christmas issue of the *Idler;* that a certain position in the make-up was reserved for me, and that you had already taken steps to advertise the fact that the story would appear. I undertook the commission, and upon seven different occasions set about putting the narrative into shape. I found great difficulty, however, in doing so. For some reason or other I could not concentrate my mind upon the work. No sooner would I start in on one story than a better one, in my estimation, would suggest itself to me; and all the labor expended on the story already begun would be cast aside, and the new story set in motion. Ideas were plenty enough, but to put them properly upon paper seemed beyond my powers. One story, however, I did finish; but after it had come back to me from my typewriter I read it, and was filled with consternation to discover that it was nothing more nor less than a mass of jumbled sentences, conveying no idea to the mind—a story which had seemed to me in the writing to be coherent had returned to me as a mere bit of incoherence—formless, without ideas—a bit of raving. It was then that I went to you and told you, as you remember, that I was worn out, and needed a month of absolute rest, which you granted. I left my work wholly, and went into the wilderness, where I could be entirely free from everything suggesting labor, and where no summons back to town could reach me. I fished and hunted. I slept; and although, as I have already said, in my sleep I found myself leading a life that was not only not to my taste, but horrible to me in many particulars, I was able at the end of my vacation to come back to town greatly refreshed, and, as far as my feelings went, ready to undertake any amount of work. For two or three days after my return I was busy with other things. On the fourth day after my arrival you came to me, and said that the story must be finished at the very latest by October 15th, and I assured you that you should have it by that time. That night I set about it. I mapped it out, incident by incident, and before starting up to bed had actually written some twelve or fifteen hundred words of the opening chapter—it was to be told in four chapters. When I had gone thus far I experienced a slight return of one of my nervous chills, and, on consulting my watch, discovered that it was after midnight, which was a sufficient explanation of my nervousness: I was merely tired. I arranged my manuscripts on my table so that I might easily take up the work the following morning. I locked up the windows and doors, turned out the lights, and proceeded upstairs to my room.

It was then that I first came face to face with myself—that other self, in which I recognized, developed to the full, every bit of my capacity for an evil life.

Conceive of the situation if you can. Imagine the horror of it, and then ask yourself if it was likely that when next morning came I could by any possibility bring myself to my work-table in fit condition to prepare for you anything at all worthy of publication in the *Idler.* I tried. I implore you to believe that I did not hold lightly the responsibilities of the commission you had intrusted to my hands. You must know that if any of your writers has a full appreciation of the difficulties which are strewn along the path of an editor, I, who have myself had an editorial experience, have it, and so would not, in the nature of things, do anything to add to your troubles. You cannot but believe that I have made an honest effort to fulfil my promise to you.

But it was useless, and for a week after that visitation was it useless for me to attempt the work. At the end of the week I felt better, and again I started in, and the story developed satisfactorily until—*it* came again. That figure which was my own figure, that face which was the evil counterpart of my own countenance, again rose up before me, and once more was I plunged into hopelessness.

Thus matters went on until the 14th day of October, when I received your peremptory message that the story must be forthcoming the following day. Needless to tell you that it was not forthcoming; but what I must tell you, since you do not know it, is that on the evening of the 15th day of October a strange thing happened to me, and in the narration of that incident, which I almost despair of your believing, lies my explanation of the discovery of October 16th, which has placed my position with you in peril.

At half-past seven o'clock on the evening of October 15th I was sitting in my library trying to write. I was alone. My wife and children had gone away on a visit to Massachusetts for a week. I had just finished my cigar, and had taken my pen in hand, when my front-door bell rang. Our maid, who is usually prompt in answering summonses of this nature, apparently did not hear the bell, for she did not respond to its clanging. Again the bell rang, and still did it remain unanswered, until finally, at the third ringing, I went to the door myself. On opening it I saw standing before me a man of, I should say, fifty-odd years of age, tall, slender, pale-faced, and clad in sombre black. He was entirely unknown to me. I had never seen him before, but he had about him such an air of pleasantness and wholesomeness that I instinctively felt glad to see him, without knowing why or whence he had come.

"Does Mr. Thurlow live here?" he asked.

You must excuse me for going into what may seem to you to be petty details, but by a perfectly circumstantial account of all that happened that evening alone can I hope to give a semblance of truth to my story, and that it must be truthful I realize as painfully as you do.

"I am Mr. Thurlow," I replied.

"Henry Thurlow, the author?" he said, with a surprised look upon his face.

"Yes," said I; and then, impelled by the strange appearance of surprise on the man's countenance, I added, "don't I look like an author?"

He laughed and candidly admitted that I was not the kind of looking man he had expected to find from reading my books, and then he entered the house in response to my invitation that he do so. I ushered him into my library, and, after asking him to be seated, inquired as to his business with me.

His answer was gratifying at least. He replied that he had been a reader of my writings for a number of years, and that for some time past he had had a great desire, not to say curiosity, to meet me and tell me how much he had enjoyed certain of my stories.

"I'm a great devourer of books, Mr. Thurlow," he said, "and I have taken the keenest delight in reading your verses and humorous sketches. I may go further, and say to you that you have helped me over many a hard place in my life by your work. At times when I have felt myself worn out with my business, or face to face with some knotty problem in my career, I have found much relief in picking up and reading your books at random. They have helped me to forget my weariness or my knotty problems for the time being; and today, finding myself in this town, I resolved to call upon you this evening and thank you for all that you have done for me."

Thereupon we became involved in a general discussion of literary men and their works, and I found that my visitor certainly did have a pretty thorough knowledge of what has been produced by the writers of today. I was quite won over to him by his simplicity, as well as attracted to him by his kindly opinion of my own efforts, and I did my best to entertain him, showing him a few of my little literary treasures in the way of autograph letters, photographs, and presentation copies of well-known books from the authors themselves. From this we drifted naturally and easily into a talk on the methods of work adopted by literary men. He asked me many questions as to my own methods; and when I had in a measure outlined to him the manner of life which I had adopted, telling him of my days at home, how little detail office-work I had, he seemed much interested with the picture—indeed, I painted the picture of my daily routine in almost too perfect colors, for, when I had finished, he observed quietly that I appeared to him to lead the ideal life, and added that he supposed I knew very little unhappiness.

The remark recalled to me the dreadful reality, that through some perversity of fate I was doomed to visitations of an uncanny order which were practically destroying my usefulness in my profession and my sole financial resource.

"Well," I replied, as my mind reverted to the unpleasant predicament in which I found myself, "I can't say that I know little unhappiness. As a matter of fact, I know a great deal of that undesirable thing. At the present moment I am very much embarrassed through my absolute inability to fulfill a contract into which I have entered, and which should have been filled this morning. I was due today with a Christmas story. The presses are waiting for it, and I am utterly unable to write it."

He appeared deeply concerned at the confession. I had hoped, indeed, that he might be sufficiently concerned to take his departure, that I might make one more effort to write the promised story. His solicitude, however, showed itself in another way. Instead of leaving me, he ventured the hope that he might aid me.

"What kind of a story is it to be?" he asked.

"Oh, the usual ghostly tale," I said, "with a dash of the Christmas flavor thrown in here and there to make it suitable to the season."

"Ah," he observed. "And you find your vein worked out?"

It was a direct and perhaps an impertinent question; but I thought it best to answer it, and to answer it as well without giving him any clew as to the real facts. I could not very well take an entire stranger into my confidence, and describe to him the extraordinary encounters I was having with an uncanny other self. He would not have believed the truth, hence I told him an untruth, and assented to his proposition.

"Yes," I replied, "the vein is worked out. I have written ghost stories for years now, serious and comic, and I am today at the end of my tether—compelled to move forward and yet held back."

"That accounts for it," he said, simply. "When I first saw you tonight at the door I could not believe that the author who had provided me with so much merriment could be so pale and worn and seemingly mirthless. Pardon me, Mr. Thurlow, for my lack of consideration when I told you that you did not appear as I had expected to find you."

I smiled my forgiveness, and he continued:

"It may be," he said, with a show of hesitation—"it may be that I have come not altogether inopportunely. Perhaps I can help you."

I smiled again. "I should be most grateful if you could," I said.

"But you doubt my ability to do so?" he put in. "Oh—well—yes—of course you do; and why shouldn't you? Nevertheless, I have noticed this: at times when I have been baffled in my work a mere hint from another, from one who knew nothing of my work, has carried me on to a solution of my problem. I have read most of your writings, and I have thought over some of them many a time, and I have even had ideas for stories, which, in my own conceit, I have imagined were good enough for you, and I have wished that I possessed your facility with the pen that I might make of them myself what I thought you would make of them had they been ideas of your own."

The old gentleman's pallid face reddened as he said this, and while I was hopeless as to anything of value resulting from his ideas, I could not resist the temptation to hear what he had to say further, his manner was so deliciously simple, and his desire to aid me so manifest. He rattled on with suggestions for a half-hour. Some of them were good, but none were new. Some were irresistibly funny, and did me good because they made me laugh, and I hadn't laughed naturally for a period so long that it made me shudder to think of it, fearing lest I should forget how to be mirthful. Finally I grew tired of his persistence, and, with a very ill-concealed impatience, told him plainly that I could do nothing with his suggestions, thanking him, however, for the spirit of kindliness which had prompted him to offer them. He appeared somewhat hurt, but immediately desisted, and when nine o'clock came he rose up to go. As he walked to the door he seemed to be undergoing some mental struggle, to which, with a sudden resolve, he finally succumbed, for, after having picked up his hat and stick and donned his overcoat, he turned to me and said:

"Mr. Thurlow, I don't want to offend you. On the contrary, it is my dearest wish to assist you. You have helped me, as I have told you. Why may I not help you?"

"I assure you, sir—" I began, when he interrupted me.

"One moment, please," he said, putting his hand into the inside pocket of his black coat and extracting from it an envelope addressed to me. "Let me finish: it is the whim of one who has an affection for you. For ten years I have secretly been at work myself on a story. It is a short one, but it has seemed good to me. I had a double object in seeking you out tonight. I wanted not only to see you, but to read my story to you. No one knows that I have written it; I had intended it as a surprise to my—to my friends. I had hoped to have it published somewhere, and I had come here to seek your advice in the matter. It is a story which I have written and rewritten and rewritten time and time again in my leisure moments during the ten years past, as I have told you. It is not likely that I shall ever write another. I am proud of having done it, but I should be prouder yet if it—if it could in some way help you. I leave it with you, sir, to print or to destroy; and if you print it, to see it in type will be enough for me; to see your name signed to it will be a matter of pride to me. No one will ever be the wiser, for, as I say, no one knows I have written it, and I promise you that no one shall know of it if you decide to do as I not only suggest but ask you to do. No one would believe me after it has appeared as *yours,* even if I should forget my promise and claim it as my own. Take it. It is yours. You are entitled to it as a slight measure of repayment for the debt of gratitude I owe you."

He pressed the manuscript into my hands, and before I could reply had opened the door and disappeared into the darkness of the street. I rushed to the sidewalk and shouted out to him to return, but I might as well have saved my breath and spared the neighborhood, for there was no answer. Holding his story in my hand, I re-entered the house and walked back into my library, where, sitting and reflecting upon the curious interview, I realized for the first time that I was in entire ignorance as to my visitor's name and address.

I opened the envelope hoping to find them, but they were not there. The envelope contained merely a finely written manuscript of thirty-odd pages, unsigned.

And then I read the story. When I began it was with a half-smile upon my lips, and with a feeling that I was wasting my time. The smile soon faded, however; after reading the first paragraph there was no question of wasted time. The story was a masterpiece. It is needless to say to you that I am not a man of enthusiasms. It is difficult to arouse that emotion in my breast, but upon this occasion I yielded to a force too great for me to resist. I have read the tales of Hoffmann and of Poe, the wondrous romances of De La Motte Fouque, the unfortunately little-known tales of the lamented Fitz-James O'Brien, the weird tales of writers of all tongues have been thoroughly sifted by me in the course of my reading, and I say to you now that in the whole of my life I never read one story, one paragraph, one line, that could approach in vivid delineation, in weirdness of conception, in anything, in any quality which goes to make up the truly great story, that story which came into my hands as I have told you. I read it once and was amazed. I read it a second time and was—tempted. It was mine. The writer himself had authorized me to treat it as if it were my own; had voluntarily sacrificed his own claim to its authorship that he might relieve me of my very pressing embarrassment. Not only this; he had almost intimated that in putting my name to his work I should be doing him a favor. Why not do so, then, I asked myself; and immediately my better self rejected the idea as impossible. How could I put out as my own another man's work and retain my self-respect? I resolved on another and better course—to send you the story in lieu of my own with a full statement of the circumstances under which it had come into my possession, when that demon rose up out of the floor at my side, this time more evil of aspect than before, more commanding in its manner. With a groan I shrank back into the cushions of my chair, and by passing my hands over my eyes tried to obliterate forever the offending sight; but it was useless. The uncanny thing approached me, and as truly as I write sat upon the edge of my couch, where for the first time it addressed me.

"Fool!" it said, "how can you hesitate? Here is your position: you have made a contract which must be filled; you are already behind, and in a hopeless mental state. Even granting that between this and tomorrow morning you could put together the necessary number of words to fill the space allotted to you, what kind of a thing do you think that story would make? It would be a mere raving like that other precious effort of August. The public, if by some odd chance it ever reached them, would think your mind was utterly gone; your reputation would go with that verdict. On the other hand, if you do not have the story ready by tomorrow, your hold on the *Idler* will be destroyed. They have their announcements printed, and your name and portrait appear among those of the prominent contributors. Do you suppose the editor and publisher will look leniently upon your failure?"

"Considering my past record, yes," I replied. "I have never yet broken a promise to them."

"Which is precisely the reason why they will be severe with you. You, who have been regarded as one of the few men who can do almost any kind of literary work at will—you, of whom it is said that your 'brains are on tap'—will they be lenient with *you?* Bah! Can't you see that the very fact of your invariable readiness heretofore is going to make your present unreadiness a thing incomprehensible?"

"Then what shall I do?" I asked. "If I can't, I can't, that is all."

"You can. There is the story in your hands. Think what it will do for you. It is one of the immortal stories—"

"You have read it, then?" I asked.

"Haven't you?"

"Yes—but—"

"It is the same," it said, with a leer and a contemptuous shrug. "You and I are inseparable. Aren't you glad?" it added, with a laugh that grated on every fibre of my being. I was too overwhelmed to reply, and it resumed: "It is one of the immortal stories. We agree to that. Published over your name, your name will live. The stuff you write yourself will give you present glory; but when you have been dead ten years people won't remember your name even—unless I get control of you, and in that case there is a very pretty though hardly a literary record in store for you."

Again it laughed harshly, and I buried my face in the pillows of my couch, hoping to find relief there from this dreadful vision.

"Curious," it said. "What you call your decent self doesn't dare look me in the eye! What a mistake people make who say that the man who won't look you in the eye is not to be trusted! As if mere brazenness were a sign of honesty; really, the theory of decency is the most amusing thing in the world. But come, time is growing short. Take that story. The writer gave it to you. Begged you to use it as your own. It is yours. It will make your reputation, and save you with your publishers. How can you hesitate?"

"I shall not use it!" I cried, desperately.

"You must—consider your children. Suppose you lose your connection with these publishers of yours?"

"But it would be a crime."

"Not a bit of it. Whom do you rob? A man who voluntarily came to you, and gave you that of which you rob him. Think of it as it is—and act, only act quickly. It is now midnight."

The tempter rose up and walked to the other end of the room, whence, while he pretended to be looking over a few of my books and pictures, I was aware he was eying me closely, and gradually compelling me by sheer force of will to do a thing which I abhorred. And I—I struggled weakly against the temptation, but gradually, little by little, I yielded, and finally succumbed altogether. Springing to my feet, I rushed to the table, seized my pen, and signed my name to the story.

"There!" I said. "It is done. I have saved my position and made my reputation, and am now a thief!"

"As well as a fool," said the other, calmly. "You don't mean to say you are going to send that manuscript in as it is?"

"Good Lord!" I cried. "What under heaven have you been trying to make me do for the last half hour?"

"Act like a sane being," said the demon. "If you send that manuscript to Currier he'll know in a minute it isn't yours. He knows you haven't an amanuensis, and that handwriting isn't yours. Copy it."

"True!" I answered. "I haven't much of a mind for details tonight. I will do as you say."

I did so. I got out my pad and pen and ink, and for three hours diligently applied myself to the task of copying the story. When it was finished I went over it carefully, made a few minor corrections, signed it, put it in an envelope, addressed it to you, stamped it, and went out to the mail-box on the corner, where I dropped it into the slot, and returned home. When I had returned to my library my visitor was still there.

"Well," it said, "I wish you'd hurry and complete this affair. I am tired, and wish to go."

"You can't go too soon to please me," said I, gathering up the original manuscripts of the story and preparing to put them away in my desk.

"Probably not," it sneered. "I'll be glad to go too, but I can't go until that manuscript is destroyed. As long as it exists there is evidence of your having appropriated the work of another. Why, can't you see that? Burn it!"

"I can't see my way clear in crime!" I retorted. "It is not in my line."

Nevertheless, realizing the value of his advice, I thrust the pages one by one into the blazing log fire, and watched them as they flared and flamed and grew to ashes. As the last page disappeared in the embers the demon vanished. I was alone, and throwing myself down for a moment's reflection upon my couch, was soon lost in sleep.

It was noon when I again opened my eyes, and, ten minutes after I awakened, your telegraphic summons reached me.

"Come down at once," was what you said, and I went; and then came the terrible *dénouement,* and yet a *dénouement* which was pleasing to me since it relieved my conscience. You handed me the envelope containing the story.

"Did you send that?" was your question.

"I did—last night, or rather early this morning. I mailed it about three o'clock," I replied.

"I demand an explanation of your conduct," said you.

"Of what?" I asked.

"Look at your so-called story and see. If this is a practical joke, Thurlow, it's a damned poor one."

I opened the envelope and took from it the sheets I had sent you—twenty-four of them.

They were every one of them as blank as when they left the papermill!

You know the rest. You know that I tried to speak; that my utterance failed me; and that, finding myself unable at the time to control my emotions, I turned and rushed madly from the office, leaving the mystery unexplained. You know that you wrote demanding a satisfactory explanation of the situation or my resignation from your staff.

This, Currier, is my explanation. It is all I have. It is absolute truth. I beg you to believe it, for if you do not, then is my condition a hopeless one. You will ask me perhaps for a *résumé* of the story which I thought I had sent you.

It is my crowning misfortune that upon that point my mind is an absolute blank. I cannot remember it in form or in substance. I have racked my brains for some recollection of some small portion of it to help to make my explanation more credible, but, alas! it will not come back to me. If I were dishonest I might fake up a story to suit the purpose, but I am not dishonest. I came near to doing an unworthy act; I did do an unworthy thing, but by some mysterious provision of fate my conscience is cleared of that.

Be sympathetic, Currier, or, if you cannot, be lenient with me this time. *Believe, believe, believe,* I implore you. Pray let me hear from you at once.

(Signed) HENRY THURLOW.

II

(Being a Note from George Currier, Editor of the Idler, *to Henry Thurlow, Author.)*

Your explanation has come to hand. As an explanation it isn't worth the paper it is written on, but we are all agreed here that it is probably the best bit of fiction you ever wrote. It is accepted for the Christmas issue. Enclosed please find check for one hundred dollars.

Dawson suggests that you take another month up in the Adirondacks. You might put in your time writing up some account of that dream-life you are leading while you are there. It seems to me there are possibilities in the idea. The concern will pay all expenses. What do you say?

(Signed) Yours ever, G. C.

Christmas Greetings

New Relations and Duties
(Excerpt)

Frederick Douglass

Frederick Douglass, renowned abolitionist and journalist, was born a slave in Maryland in 1817 and died in 1895. He took the name Douglass from Sir Walter Scott's Lady of the Lake *when he made his way to freedom in 1838. Douglass became one of the most respected and outspoken abolitionists of the era, one whose life and career was a testament to the strength of the human spirit. His intensely autobiographical journals and memoirs including* The Narrative of the Life of Frederick Douglass, An American Slave; My Bondage and My Freedom; *and* The Life and Times of Frederick Douglass *are very much in keeping with American literary tradition, and his life, so chronicled, serves as a record of championing the rights of others. This account of a Christmas in slavery, excerpted from* My Bondage and My Freedom, *is truly a page from history.*

HANGE OF MASTERS—BENEFITS DERIVED BY THE CHANGE—FAME OF THE FIGHT WITH COVEY—RECKLESS UNCONCERN—AUTHOR'S ABHORRENCE OF SLAVERY—ABILITY TO READ A CAUSE OF PREJUDICE—THE HOLIDAYS—HOW SPENT—SHARP HIT AT SLAV-

ERY—EFFECTS OF HOLIDAYS—A DEVICE OF SLAVERY—DIFFERENCE BETWEEN COVEY AND FREELAND—AN IRRELIGIOUS MASTER PREFERRED TO A RELIGIOUS ONE—CATALOGUE OF FLOGGABLE OFFENSES—HARD LIFE AT COVEY'S USEFUL TO THE AUTHOR—IMPROVED CONDITION NOT FOLLOWED BY CONTENTMENT—CONGENIAL SOCIETY AT FREELAND'S—AUTHOR'S SABBATH SCHOOL INSTITUTED—SECRECY NECESSARY—AFFECTIONATE RELATIONS OF TUTOR AND PUPILS—CONFIDENCE AND FRIENDSHIP AMONG SLAVES—THE AUTHOR DECLINES PUBLISHING PARTICULARS OF CONVERSATIONS WITH HIS FRIENDS—SLAVERY THE INVITER OF VENGEANCE.

My term of actual service to Mr. Edward Covey ended on Christmas day, 1834. I gladly left the snakish Covey, although he was now as gentle as a lamb. My home for the year 1835 was already secured—my next master was already selected. There is always more or less excitement about the matter of changing hands, but I had become somewhat reckless. I cared very little into whose hands I fell—I meant to fight my way. Despite of Covey, too, the report got abroad, that I was hard to whip; that I was guilty of kicking back; that though generally a good tempered negro, I sometimes *"got the devil in me."* These sayings were rife in Talbot County, and they distinguished me among my servile brethren. Slaves, generally, will fight each other, and die at each other's hands; but there are few who are not held in awe by a white man. Trained from the cradle up, to think and feel that their masters are superior, and invested with a sort of sacredness, there are few who can outgrow or rise above the control which that sentiment exercises. I had now got free from it, and the thing was known. One bad sheep will spoil a whole flock. Among the slaves, I was a bad sheep. I hated slavery, slaveholders, and all pertaining to them; and I did not fail to inspire others with the same feeling, wherever and whenever opportunity was presented. This made me a marked lad among the slaves, and a suspected one among the slaveholders. A knowledge of my ability to read and write, got pretty widely spread, which was very much against me.

The days between Christmas day and New Year's are allowed the slaves as holidays. During these days, all regular work was suspended, and there was nothing to do but to keep fires, and look after the stock. This time we regarded as our own, by the grace of our masters, and we, therefore, used it, or abused it, as we pleased. Those who had families at a distance, were now expected to visit them, and to spend with them the entire week. The younger slaves, or the unmarried ones, were expected to see to the cattle, and attend to incidental duties at home. The holidays were variously spent. The sober, thinking and industrious ones of our number, would employ themselves in manufacturing corn brooms, mats, horse collars and baskets, and some of these were very well made. Another class spent their time in hunting opossums, coons, rabbits, and other game. But the majority spent the holidays in sports, ball playing, wrestling, boxing, running foot races, dancing, and drinking whisky; and this latter mode of spending the time was generally most agreeable to their masters. A slave who would work during the holidays was thought, by his master, undeserving of holidays. Such a one had rejected the favor of his master. There was, in this simple act of continued work, an accusation against slaves; and a slave could not help thinking, that if he made three dollars during the holidays, he might make three hundred during the year. Not to be drunk during the holidays was disgraceful; and he was esteemed a lazy and improvident man, who could not afford to drink whisky during Christmas.

The fiddling, dancing and *"jubilee beating,"* was going on in all directions. This latter performance is strickly southern. It supplies the place of a violin, or of other musical instruments, and is played so easily, that almost every farm has its "Juba" beater. The performer improvises as he beats, and sings his merry songs, so ordering the words as to have them fall pat with the movement of his hands. Among a mass of nonsense and wild frolic, once in a while a sharp hit is given to the meanness of slaveholders. Take the following, for an example:

We raise de wheat,
Dey gib us de corn;

We bake de bread,
Dey gib us de cruss;
We sif de meal,
Dey gib us de huss;
We peal de meat,
Dey gib us de skin,
And dat's de way
Dey takes us in.
We skim de pot,
Dey gib us the liquor,
And say dat's good enough for nigger.
Walk over! walk over!
Tom butter and de fat;
Poor nigger you can't get over dat;
Walk over!

This is not a bad summary of the palpable injustice and fraud of slavery, giving—as it does—to the lazy and idle, the comforts which God designed should be given solely to the honest laborer. But to the holiday's.

Judging from my own observation and experience, I believe these holidays to be among the most effective means, in the hands of slaveholders, of keeping down the spirit of insurrection among the slaves.

To enslave men, successfully and safely, it is necessary to have their minds occupied with thoughts and aspirations short of the liberty of which they are deprived. A certain degree of attainable good must be kept before them. These holidays serve the purpose of keeping the minds of the slaves occupied with prospective pleasure, within the limits of slavery. The young man can go wooing; the married man can visit his wife; the father and mother can see their children; the industrious and money loving can make a few dollars; the great wrestler can win laurels; the young people can meet and enjoy each other's society; the drunken man can get plenty of whisky; and the religious man can hold prayer meetings, preach, pray, and exhort during the holidays. Before the holidays, these are pleasures in prospect; after the holidays, they become pleasures of memory, and they serve to keep out thoughts and wishes of a more dangerous character. Were slaveholders at once to abandon the practice of allowing their slaves these liberties, periodically, and to keep them, the year round, closely confined to the narrow circle of their homes, I doubt not that the south would blaze with insurrections. These holidays are conductors or safety valves to carry off the explosive elements inseparable from the human mind, when reduced to the condition of slavery. But for these, the rigors of bondage would become too severe for endurance, and the slave would be forced up to dangerous desperation. Woe to the slaveholder when he undertakes to hinder or to prevent the operation of these electric conductors. A succession of earthquakes would be less destructive, than the insurrectionary fires which would be sure to burst forth in different parts of the south, from such interference.

Thus, the holidays, become part and parcel of the gross fraud, wrongs and inhumanity of slavery. Ostensibly, they are institutions of benevolence, designed to mitigate the rigors of slave life, but, practically, they are a fraud, instituted by human selfishness, the better to secure the ends of injustice and oppression. The slave's happiness is not the end sought, but, rather, the master's safety. It is not from a generous unconcern for the slave's labor that this cessation from labor is allowed, but from a prudent regard to the safety of the slave system. I am strengthened in this opinion, by the fact, that most slaveholders like to have their slaves spend the holidays in such a manner as to be of no real benefit to the slaves. It is plain, that everything like rational enjoyment among the slaves, is frowned upon; and only those wild and low sports, peculiar to semi-civilized people, are encouraged. All the license allowed, appears to have no other object than to disgust the slaves with their temporary freedom, and to make them as glad to return to their work, as they were to leave it. By plunging them into exhausting depths of drunkenness and dissipation, this effect is almost certain to follow. I have known slaveholders resort to cunning tricks, with a view of getting their slaves deplorably drunk. A usual plan is, to make bets on a slave, that he can drink more whisky than any other;

and so to induce a rivalry among them, for the mastery in this degradation. The scenes, brought about in this way, were often scandalous and loathsome in the extreme. Whole multitudes might be found stretched out in brutal drunkenness, at once helpless and disgusting. Thus, when the slave asks for a few hours of virtuous freedom, his cunning master takes advantage of his ignorance, and cheers him with a dose of vicious and revolting dissipation, artfully labeled with the name of LIBERTY. We were induced to drink, I among the rest, and when the holidays were over, we all staggered up from our filth and wallowing, took a long breath, and went away to our various fields of work; feeling, upon the whole, rather glad to go from that which our masters artfully deceived us into the belief was freedom, back again to the arms of slavery. It was not what we had taken it to be, nor what it might have been, had it not been abused by us. It was about as well to be a slave to *master,* as to be a slave to *rum* and *whisky.*

I am the more induced to take this view of the holiday system, adopted by slaveholders, from what I know of their treatment of slaves, in regard to other things. It is the commonest thing for them to try to disgust their slaves with what they do not want them to have, or to enjoy. A slave, for instance, likes molasses; he steals some; to cure him of the taste for it, his master, in many cases, will go away to town, and buy a large quantity of the *poorest* quality, and set it before his slave, and, with whip in hand, compel him to eat it, until the poor fellow is made to sicken at the very thought of molasses. The same course is often adopted to cure slaves of the disagreeable and inconvenient practice of asking for more food, when their allowance has failed them. The same disgusting process works well, too, in other things, but I need not cite them. When a slave is drunk, the slaveholder has no fear that he will plan an insurrection; no fear that he will escape to the north. It is the sober, thinking slave who is dangerous, and needs the vigilance of his master, to keep him a slave.

THE BURGLAR'S CHRISTMAS

Willa Cather

Willa Cather was born in Winchester, Virginia, in 1873 and died in 1947. Moving west to Nebraska with her family when she was a child, Cather went on to grace the American literary tradition with such classics as O Pioneers!, My Antonia, *and* Song of the Lark. *She was described by one critic as "a traditionalist and a conformer . . . a survivor of some distant age." Cather's defense of tradition and the spiritual values is entirely appropriate for a story of Christmas. The following tale is sure to appeal to those among us who want to return, if only for a little while, to a kinder, gentler time.*

wo very shabby-looking young men stood at the corner of Prairie Avenue and Eightieth Street, looking despondently at the carriages that whirled by. It was Christmas Eve, and the streets were full of vehicles: florists' wagons, grocers' carts and carriages. The streets were in that half-

liquid, half-congealed condition peculiar to the streets of Chicago at that season of the year. The swift wheels that spun by sometimes threw the slush of mud and snow over the two young men who were talking on the corner.

"Well," remarked the elder of the two, "I guess we are at our rope's end, sure enough. How do you feel?"

"Pretty shaky. The wind's sharp tonight. If I had had anything to eat I mightn't mind it so much. There is simply no show. I'm sick of the whole business. Looks like there's nothing for it but the lake."

"O, nonsense, I thought you had more grit. Got anything left you can hock?"

"Nothing but my beard, and I am afraid they wouldn't find it worth a pawn ticket," said the younger man ruefully, rubbing the week's growth of stubble on his face.

"Got any folks anywhere? Now's your time to strike 'em if you have."

"Never mind if I have, they're out of the question."

"Well, you'll be out of it before many hours if you don't make a move of some sort. A man's got to eat. See here, I am going down to Longtin's saloon. I used to play the banjo in there with a couple of coons, and I'll bone him for some of his free-lunch stuff. You'd better come along, perhaps they'll fill an order for two."

"How far down is it?"

"Well, it's clear downtown, of course, 'way down on Michigan Avenue."

"Thanks, I guess I'll loaf around here. I don't feel equal to the walk, and the cars—well, the cars are crowded." His features drew themselves into what might have been a smile under happier circumstances.

"No, you never did like street cars, you're too aristocratic. See here, Crawford, I don't like leaving you here. You ain't good company for yourself tonight."

"Crawford? O, yes, that's the last one. There have been so many I forget them."

"Have you got a real name, anyway?"

"O, yes, but it's one of the ones I've forgotten. Don't you worry about me. You go along and get your free lunch. I think I had a row in Longtin's place once. I'd better not show myself there again." As he spoke the young man nodded and turned slowly up the avenue.

He was miserable enough to want to be quite alone. Even the crowd that jostled by him annoyed him. He wanted to think about himself. He had avoided this final reckoning with himself for a year now. He had laughed it off and drunk it off. But now, when all those artificial devices which are employed to turn our thoughts into other channels and shield us from ourselves had failed him, it must come. Hunger is a powerful incentive to introspection.

It is a tragic hour, that hour when we are finally driven to reckon with ourselves, when every avenue of mental distraction has been cut off and our own life and all its ineffaceable failures closes about us like the walls of that old torture chamber of the Inquisition. Tonight, as this man stood stranded in the streets of the city, his hour came. It was not the first time he had been hungry and desperate and alone. But always before there had been some outlook, some chance ahead, some pleasure yet untasted that seemed worth the effort, some face that he fancied was, or would be, dear. But it was not so tonight. The unyielding conviction was upon him that he had failed in everything, had outlived everything. It had been near him for a long time, that Pale Spectre. He had caught its shadow at the bottom of his glass many a time, at the head of his bed when he was sleepless at night, in the twilight shadows when some great sunset broke upon him. It had made life hateful to him when he awoke in the morning before now. But now it settled slowly over him, like night, the endless Northern nights that bid the sun a long farewell. It rose up before him like granite. From this brilliant city with its glad bustle of Yuletide he was shut off as completely as though he were a creature of another species. His days seemed numbered and done, sealed over like the little coral cells at the bottom of the sea. Involuntarily he drew that cold air through his lungs slowly, as though he were tasting it for the last time.

Yet he was but four and twenty, this man—he looked even younger—and he had a father some place down East who had been very proud of him once. Well, he had taken his life into his own hands, and this was what he had made of it. That was all there was to be said. He could remember the hopeful things they used to say about him at college in the old days, before he had cut away and begun to live by his wits, and he found courage to smile at them now. They had read him wrongly. He knew now that he never had the essentials of success, only the superficial agility that is often mistaken for it. He was tow without the tinder, and he had burnt himself out at other people's fires. He had helped other people to make it win, but he himself—he had never touched an enterprise that had not failed eventually. Or, if it survived his connection with it, it left him behind.

His last venture had been with some ten-cent specialty company, a little lower than all the others, that had gone to pieces in Buffalo, and he had worked his way to Chicago by boat. When the boat made up its crew for the outward voyage, he was dispensed with as usual. He was used to that. The reason for it? O, there are so many reasons for failure! His was a very common one.

As he stood there in the wet under the street light he drew up his reckoning with the world and decided that it had treated him as well as he deserved. He had overdrawn his account once too often. There had been a day when he thought otherwise; when he had said he was unjustly handled, that his failure was merely the lack of proper adjustment between himself and other men, that some day he would be recognized and it would all come right. But he knew better than that now, and he was still man enough to bear no grudge against any one—man or woman.

Tonight was his birthday, too. There seemed something particularly amusing in that. He turned up a limp little coat collar to try to keep a little of the wet chill from his throat, and instinctively began to remember all the birthday parties he used to have. He was so cold and empty that his mind seemed unable to grapple with any serious question. He kept thinking about gingerbread and frosted cakes like a child. He could remember the splendid birthday parties his mother used to give him, when all the other little boys in the block came in their Sunday clothes and creaking shoes, with their ears still red from their mother's towel, and the pink and white birthday cake, and the stuffed olives and all the dishes of which he had been particularly fond, and how he would eat and eat and then go to bed and dream of Santa Claus. And in the morning he would awaken and eat again, until by night the family doctor arrived with his castor oil, and poor William used to dolefully say that it was altogether too much to have your birthday and Christmas all at once. He could remember, too, the royal birthday suppers he had given at college, and the stag dinners, and the toasts, and the music, and the good fellows who had wished him happiness and really meant what they said.

And since then there were other birthday suppers that he could not remember so clearly; the memory of them was heavy and flat, like cigarette smoke that has been shut in a room all night, like champagne that has been a day opened, a song that has been too often sung, an acute sensation that has been overstrained. They seemed tawdry and garish, discordant to him now. He rather wished he could forget them altogether.

Whichever way his mind now turned there was one thought that it could not escape, and that was the idea of food. He caught the scent of a cigar suddenly, and felt a sharp pain in the pit of his abdomen and a sudden moisture in his mouth. His cold hands clenched angrily, and for a moment he felt that bitter hatred of wealth, of ease, of everything that is well fed and well housed that is common to starving men. At any rate he had a right to eat! He had demanded great things from the world once: fame and wealth and admiration. Now it was simply bread—and he would have it! He looked about him quickly and felt the blood begin to stir in his veins. In all his straits he had never stolen anything, his tastes were above it. But tonight there would be no tomorrow. He was amused at the way in which the idea excited him. Was it possible there was yet one more experience that would distract him, one thing that had power to excite his jaded interest? Good! He had failed at everything else, now he would see what his chances would be as a common thief. It would be amusing to watch the beautiful consistency of his destiny work itself out even in that role. It would be interesting to add another study to his gallery of futile attempts, and then label them all: "the failure as a journalist," "the failure as a lecturer," "the failure as a business man," "the failure as a thief," and so on, like the titles under the pictures of the Dance of Death. It was time that Childe Roland came to the dark tower.

A girl hastened by him with her arms full of packages. She walked quickly and nervously, keeping well within the shadow, as if she were not accustomed to carrying bundles and did not care to meet any of her friends. As she crossed the muddy street, she made an effort to lift her skirt a little, and as she did so one of the packages slipped unnoticed from beneath her arm. He caught it up and overtook her. "Excuse me, but I think you dropped something."

She started, "O, yes, thank you, I would rather have lost anything than that."

The young man turned angrily upon himself. The package must have contained something of value. Why had he not kept it? Was this the sort of thief he would make? He ground his teeth together. There is nothing more maddening than to have morally consented to crime and then lack the nerve force to carry it out.

A carriage drove up to the house before which he stood. Several richly dressed women alighted and went in. It was a new house, and must have been built since he was in Chicago last. The front door was open and he could see down the hallway and up the staircase. The servant had left the door and gone with the guests. The first floor was brilliantly lighted, but the windows upstairs were dark. It looked very easy, just to slip upstairs to the darkened chambers where the jewels and trinkets of the fashionable occupants were kept.

Still burning with impatience against himself he entered quickly. Instinctively he removed his mud-stained hat as he passed quickly and quietly up the staircase. It struck him as being a rather superfluous courtesy in a burglar, but he had done it before he had thought. His way was clear enough, he met no one on the stairway or in the upper hall. The gas was lit in the upper hall. He passed the first chamber door through sheer cowardice. The second he entered quickly, thinking of something else lest his courage should fail him, and closed the door behind him. The light from the hall shone into the room through the transom. The apartment was furnished richly enough to justify his expectations. He went at once to the dressing case. A number of rings and small trinkets lay in a silver tray. These he put hastily in his pocket. He opened the upper drawer and found, as he expected, several leather cases. In the first he opened was a lady's watch, in the second a pair of old-fashioned bracelets; he seemed to dimly remember having seen bracelets like them before, somewhere. The third case was heavier, the spring was much worn, and it opened easily. It held a cup of some kind. He held it up to the light and then his strained nerves gave way and he uttered a sharp exclamation. It was the silver mug he used to drink from when he was a little boy.

The door opened, and a woman stood in the doorway facing him. She was a tall woman, with white hair, in evening dress. The light from the hall streamed in upon him, but she was not afraid. She stood looking at him a moment, then she threw out her hand and went quickly toward him.

"Willie, Willie! Is it you?"

He struggled to loose her arms from him, to keep her lips from his cheek. "Mother—you must not! You do not understand! O, my God, this is worst of all!" Hunger, weakness, cold, shame, all came back to him, and shook his self-control completely. Physically he was too weak to stand a shock like this. Why could it not have been an ordinary discovery, arrest, the station house and all the rest of it. Anything but this! A hard dry sob broke from him. Again he strove to disengage himself.

"Who is it says I shall not kiss my son? O, my boy, we have waited so long for this! You have been so long in coming, even I almost gave you up."

Her lips upon his cheek burnt him like fire. He put his hand to his throat, and spoke thickly and incoherently: "You do not understand. I did not know you were here. I came here to rob—it is the first time—I swear it—but I am a common thief. My pockets are full of your jewels now. Can't you hear me? I am a common thief!"

"Hush, my boy, those are ugly words. How could you rob your own house? How could you take what is your own? They are all yours, my son, as wholly yours as my great love—and you can't doubt that, Will, do you?"

That soft voice, the warmth and fragrance of her person stole through his chill, empty veins like a gentle stimulant. He felt as though all his strength were leaving him and even consciousness. He held fast to her and bowed his head on her strong shoulder, and groaned aloud.

"O, mother, life is hard, hard!"

She said nothing, but held him closer. And O, the strength of those white arms that held him! O, the assurance of safety in that warm bosom that rose and fell under his cheek! For a moment they stood so, silently. Then they heard a heavy step upon the stair. She led him to a chair and went out and closed the door. At the top of the staircase she met a tall, broad-shouldered man, with iron gray hair, and a face alert and stern. Her eyes were shining and her cheeks on fire, her whole face was one expression of intense determination.

"James, it is William in there, come home. You must keep him at any cost. If he goes this time, I go with him. O, James, be easy with him, he has suffered so." She broke from a command to an entreaty, and laid her hand on his shoulder. He looked questioningly at her a moment, then went in the room and quietly shut the door.

She stood leaning against the wall, clasping her temples with her hands and listening to the low indistinct sound of the voices within. Her own lips moved silently. She waited a long time, scarcely breathing. At last the door opened, and her husband came out. He stopped to say in a shaken voice,

"You go to him now, he will stay. I will go to my room. I will see him again in the morning."

She put her arm about his neck, "O, James, I thank you, I thank you! This is the night he came so long ago, you remember? I gave him to you then, and now you give him back to me!"

"Don't, Helen," he muttered. "He is my son, I have never forgotten that. I failed with him. I don't like to fail, it cuts my pride. Take him and make a man of him." He passed on down the hall.

She flew into the room where the young man sat with his head bowed upon his knee. She dropped upon her knees beside him. Ah, it was so good to him to feel those arms again!

"He is so glad, Willie, so glad! He may not show it, but he is as happy as I. He never was demonstrative with either of us, you know."

"O, my God, he was good enough," groaned the man. "I told him everything, and he was good enough. I don't see how either of you can look at me, speak to me, touch me." He shivered under her clasp again as when she had first touched him, and tried weakly to throw her off.

But she whispered softly,

"This is my right, my son."

Presently, when he was calmer, she rose. "Now, come with me into the library, and I will have your dinner brought there."

As they went downstairs she remarked apologetically, "I will not call Ellen tonight; she has a number of guests to attend to. She is a big girl now, you know, and came out last winter. Besides, I want you all to myself tonight."

When the dinner came, and it came very soon, he fell upon it savagely. As he ate she told him all that had transpired during the years of his absence, and how his father's business had brought them there. "I was glad when we came. I thought you would drift West. I seemed a good deal nearer to you here."

There was a gentle unobtrusive sadness in her tone that was too soft for a reproach.

"Have you everything you want? It is a comfort to see you eat."

He smiled grimly, "It is certainly a comfort to me. I have not indulged in this frivolous habit for some thirty-five hours."

She caught his hand and pressed it sharply, uttering a quick remonstrance.

"Don't say that! I know, but I can't hear you say it—it's too terrible! My boy, food has choked me many a time when I have thought of the possibility of that. Now take the old lounging chair by the fire, and if you are too tired to talk, we will just sit and rest together."

He sank into the depths of the big leather chair with the lions' heads on the arms, where he had sat so often in the days when his feet did not touch the floor and he was half afraid of the grim monsters cut in the polished wood. That chair seemed to speak to him of things long forgotten. It was like the touch of an old familiar friend. He felt a sudden yearning tenderness for the happy little boy who had sat there and dreamed of the big world so long ago. Alas, he had been dead many a summer, that little boy!

He sat looking up at the magnificent woman beside him. He had almost forgotten how handsome she was; how lustrous and sad were the eyes that were set under that serene brow, how impetuous and wayward the mouth even now, how superb the white throat and shoulders! Ah, the wit and grace and fineness of this woman! He remembered how proud he had been of her as a boy when she came to see him at school. Then in the deep red coals of the grate he saw the faces of other women who had come since then into his vexed, disordered life. Laughing faces, with eyes artificially bright, eyes without depth or meaning, features without the stamp of high sensibilities. And he had left this face for such as those!

He sighed restlessly and laid his hand on hers. There seemed refuge and protection in the touch of her, as in the old days when he was afraid of the dark. He had been in the dark so long now, his confidence was so thoroughly shaken, and he was bitterly afraid of the night and of himself.

"Ah, mother, you make other things seem so false. You must feel that I owe you an explanation, but I can't make any, even to myself. Ah, but we make poor exchanges in life. I can't make out the riddle of it all. Yet there are things I ought to tell you before I accept your confidence like this."

"I'd rather you wouldn't, Will. Listen: between you and me there can be no secrets. We are more alike than other people. Dear boy, I know all about it. I am a woman, and circumstances were different with me, but we are of one blood. I have lived all your life before you. You have never had an impulse that I have not known, you have never touched a brink that my feet have not trod. This is your birthday night. Twenty-four years ago I foresaw all this. I was a young woman then and I had hot battles of my own, and I felt your likeness to me.

You were not like other babies. From the hour you were born you were restless and discontented, as I had been before you. You used to brace your strong little limbs against mine and try to throw me off as you did tonight. Tonight you have come back to me, just as you always did after you ran away to swim in the river that was forbidden you, the river you loved because it was forbidden. You are tired and sleepy, just as you used to be then, only a little older and a little paler and a little more foolish. I never asked you where you had been then, nor will I now. You have come back to me, that's all in all to me. I know your every possibility and limitation, as a composer knows his instrument."

He found no answer that was worthy to give to talk like this. He had not found life easy since he had lived by his wits. He had come to know poverty at close quarters. He had known what it was to be gay with an empty pocket, to wear violets in his buttonhole when he had not breakfasted, and all the hateful shams of the poverty of idleness. He had been a reporter on a big metropolitan daily, where men grind out their brains on paper until they have not one idea left—and still grind on. He had worked in a real estate office, where ignorant men were swindled. He had sung in a comic opera chorus and played Harris in an *Uncle Tom's Cabin* company, and edited a socialist weekly. He had been dogged by debt and hunger and grinding poverty, until to sit here by a warm fire without concern as to how it would be paid for seemed unnatural.

He looked up at her questioningly. "I wonder if you know how much you pardon?"

"O, my poor boy, much or little, what does it matter? Have you wandered so far and paid such a bitter price for knowledge and not yet learned that love has nothing to do with pardon or forgiveness, that it only loves, and loves—and loves? They have not taught you well, the women of your world." She leaned over and kissed him, as no woman had kissed him since he left her.

He drew a long sigh of rich content. The old life, with all its bitterness and useless antagonism and flimsy sophistries, its brief delights that were always tinged with fear and distrust and unfaith, that whole miserable, futile, swindled world of Bohemia seemed immeasurably distant and far away, like a dream that is over and done. And as the chimes rang joyfully outside and sleep pressed heavily upon his eyelids, he wondered dimly if the Author of this sad little riddle of ours were not able to solve it after all, and if the Potter would not finally mete out his all comprehensive justice, such as none but he could have, to his Things of Clay, which are made in his own patterns, weak or strong, for his own ends; and if some day we will not awaken and find that all evil is a dream, a mental distortion that will pass when the dawn shall break.

Joyous
Christmas

CHRISTMAS EVERY DAY

William Dean Howells

William Dean Howells was born in Martins Ferry, Ohio, in 1837 and died in 1920. Very much a man of his era, Howells was a self-made and self-educated denizen of the literary circles of the time, serving in various editorial positions on the Atlantic Monthly *from 1866 to 1881. He is recognized as a major influence on the American novel, being one of the first to depart from the earlier oratorical style that so dominated nineteenth-century fiction. His literary voice was at once clear-sighted and warmhearted as is evident in the following story. Christmas comes but once a year and as Howells's fanciful tale implies, there is something to be said for that.*

he little girl came into her papa's study, as she always did Saturday morning before breakfast, and asked for a story. He tried to beg off that morning, for he was very busy, but she would not let him. So he began:

"Well, once there was a little pig—"

She put her hand over his mouth and stopped him at the word. She said she had heard little pig stories till she was perfectly sick of them.

"Well, what kind of story *shall* I tell, then?"

"About Christmas. It's getting to be the season. It's past Thanksgiving already."

"It seems to me," argued her papa, "that I've told as often about Christmas as I have about little pigs."

"No difference! Christmas is more interesting."

"Well!" Her papa roused himself from his writing by a great effort. "Well, then, I'll tell you about the little girl that wanted it Christmas every day in the year. How would you like that?"

"First-rate!" said the little girl; and she nestled into comfortable shape in his lap, ready for listening.

"Very well, then, this little pig—Oh, what are you pounding me for?"

"Because you said little pig instead of little girl."

"I should like to know what's the difference between a little pig and a little girl that wanted it Christmas every day!"

"Papa," said the little girl, warningly, "if you don't go on, I'll *give* it to you!" And at this her papa darted off like lightning, and began to tell the story as fast as he could.

Well, once there was a little girl who liked Christmas so much that she wanted it to be Christmas every day in the year; and as soon as Thanksgiving was over she began to send postal cards to the old Christmas Fairy to ask if she mightn't have it. But the old Fairy never answered any of the postals; and, after a while, the little girl found out that the Fairy was pretty particular, and wouldn't even notice anything but letters, not even correspondence cards in envelopes; but real letters on sheets of paper, and sealed outside with a monogram—or your initial, any way. So, then, she began to send her letters; and in about three weeks—or just the day before Christmas, it was—she got a letter from the Fairy, saying she might have it Christmas every day for a year, and then they would see about having it longer.

The little girl was a good deal excited already, preparing for the old-fashioned, once-a-year Christmas that was coming the next day, and perhaps the Fairy's promise didn't make such an impression on her as it would have made at some other time. She just resolved to keep it to herself, and surprise everybody with it as it kept coming true; and then it slipped out of her mind altogether.

She had a splendid Christmas. She went to bed early, so as to let Santa Claus have a chance at the stockings, and in the morning she was up the first of anybody and went and felt them, and found hers all lumpy with packages of candy, and oranges and grapes, and pocket-books and rubber balls and all kinds of small presents, and her big brother's with nothing but the tongs in them, and her young lady sister's with a new silk umbrella, and her papa's and mamma's with potatoes and pieces of coal wrapped up in tissue paper, just as they always had every Christmas. Then she waited around till the rest of the family were up, and she was the first to burst into the library, when the doors were opened, and look at the large presents laid out on the library-table—books, and portfolios, and boxes of stationery, and breast-pins, and dolls, and little stoves, and dozens of handkerchiefs, and ink-stands, and skates, and snow-shovels, and photograph frames, and little easels, and boxes of watercolors, and Turkish paste, and nougat, and candied cherries, and dolls' houses, and waterproofs—and the big Christmas-tree, lighted and standing in a waste-basket in the middle.

She had a splendid Christmas all day. She ate so much candy that she did not want any breakfast; and the whole forenoon the presents kept pouring in that the expressman had not had time to deliver the night before; and she went 'round giving the presents she had got for other people, and came home and ate turkey and cranberry for dinner, and plum-pudding and nuts and raisins and oranges and more candy, and then went out and coasted and came in with a stomach-ache, crying; and her papa said he would see if his house was turned into that sort of fool's paradise another year; and they had a light supper, and pretty early everybody went to bed cross.

Here the little girl pounded her papa in the back, again.

"Well, what now? Did I say pigs?"

"You made them *act* like pigs."

"Well, didn't they?"

"No matter; you oughtn't to put it into a story."

"Very well, then, I'll take it all out."

Her father went on:

The little girl slept very heavily, and she slept very late, but she was wakened at last by the other children dancing 'round her bed with their stockings full of presents in their hands.

"What is it?" said the little girl, and she rubbed her eyes and tried to rise up in bed.

"Christmas! Christmas! Christmas!" they all shouted, and waved their stockings.

"Nonsense! It was Christmas yesterday."

Her brothers and sisters just laughed. "We don't know about that. It's Christmas to-day, any way. You come into the library and see."

Then all at once it flashed on the little girl that the Fairy was keeping her promise, and her year of Christmases was beginning. She was dreadfully sleepy, but she sprang up like a lark—a lark that had overeaten itself and gone to bed cross—and darted into the library. There it was again! Books, and portfolios, and boxes of stationery, and breast-pins—

"You needn't go over it all, Papa; I guess I can remember just what was there," said the little girl.

Well, and there was the Christmas-tree blazing away, and the family picking out their presents, but looking pretty sleepy, and her father perfectly puzzled, and her mother ready to cry. "I'm sure I don't see how I'm to dispose of all these things," said her mother, and her father said it seemed to him they had had something just like it the day before, but he supposed he must have dreamed it. This struck the little girl as the best kind of joke; and so she ate so much candy she didn't want any breakfast, and went 'round carrying presents, and had turkey and cranberry for dinner, and then went out and coasted, and came in with a—

"Papa!"
"Well, what now?"
"What did you promise, you forgetful thing?"
"Oh! oh, yes!"

Well, the next day, it was just the same thing over again, but everybody getting crosser; and at the end of a week's time so many people had lost their tempers that you could pick up lost tempers everywhere; they perfectly strewed the ground. Even when people tried to recover their tempers they usually got somebody else's, and it made the most dreadful mix.

The little girl began to get frightened, keeping the secret all to herself; she wanted to tell her mother, but she didn't dare to; and she was ashamed to ask the Fairy to take back her gift, it seemed ungrateful and ill-bred, and she thought she would try to stand it, but she hardly knew how she could, for a whole year. So it went on and on, and it was Christmas on St. Valentine's Day, and Washington's Birthday just the same as any day, and it didn't skip even the First of April, though everything was counterfeit that day, and that was some *little* relief.

A MERRY CHRISTMAS

Compliments of the Season

By O. Henry

O. Henry (William Sydney Porter) was born in North Carolina in 1862 and died in 1910. His most famous Christmas story is of course "The Gift of the Magi." Yet in fact he wrote many Christmas stories during his prolific career, each uniquely formed around the most ordinary characters, all of whom somehow manage to transcend their circumstances while under the strange and wonderful influence of the holiday spirit.

There are no more Christmas stories to write. Fiction is exhausted; and newspaper items, the next best, are manufactured by clever young journalists who have married early and have an engagingly pessimistic view of life. Therefore, for seasonable diversion, we are reduced to two very questionable sources—facts and philosophy. We will begin with—whichever you choose to call it.

Children are pestilential little animals with which we have to cope under a bewildering variety of conditions. Especially when childish sorrows overwhelm them are we put to our wits' ends. We exhaust our paltry store of consolation; and then beat them, sobbing, to sleep. Then we grovel in the dust of a million years, and ask God why. Thus we call out of the rat-trap. As for the children, no one understands them except old maids, hunchbacks, and shepherd dogs.

Now come the facts in the case of the Rag-Doll, the Tatterdemalion, and the Twenty-fifth of December.

On the tenth of that month the Child of the Millionaire lost her rag-doll. There were many servants in the Millionaire's palace on the Hudson, and these ransacked the house and grounds, but without finding the lost treasure. The Child was a girl of five, and one of those perverse little beasts that often wound the sensibilities of wealthy parents by fixing their affections upon some vulgar, inexpensive toy instead of upon diamond-studded automobiles and pony phaetons.

The Child grieved sorely and truly, a thing inexplicable to the Millionaire, to whom the rag-doll market was about as interesting as Bay State Gas; and to the Lady, the Child's mother, who was all form—that is, nearly all, as you shall see.

The Child cried inconsolably, and grew hollow-eyed, knock-kneed, spindling, and cory-kilverty in many other respects. The Millionaire smiled and tapped his coffers confidently. The pick of the output of the French and German toymakers was rushed by special delivery to the mansion; but Rachel refused to be comforted. She was weeping for her rag child, and was for a high protective tariff against all foreign foolishness. Then doctors with the finest bedside manners and stop-watches were called in. One by one they chattered futilely about peptomanganate of iron and sea voyages and hypophosphites until their stop-watches showed that Bill Rendered was under the wire for show or place. Then, as men, they advised that the rag-doll be found as soon as possible and restored to its mourning parent. The Child sniffed at therapeutics, chewed a thumb, and wailed for her Betsy. And all this time cablegrams were coming from Santa Claus saying that he would soon be here and enjoining us to show a true Christian spirit and let up on the poolrooms and tontine policies and platoon systems long enough to give him a welcome. Everywhere the spirit of Christmas was diffusing itself. The banks were refusing loans, the pawnbrokers had doubled their gang of helpers, people bumped your shins on the streets with red sleds, Thomas and Jeremiah bubbled before you on the bars while you waited on one foot, holly-wreaths of hospitality were hung in windows of the stores, they who had 'em were getting out their furs. You hardly knew which was the best bet in balls—three, high, moth, or snow. It was no time at which to lose the rag-doll of your heart.

If Doctor Watson's investigating friend had been called in to solve this mysterious disappearance he might have observed on the Millionaire's wall a copy of "The Vampire." That would have quickly suggested, by induction, "A rag and a bone and a hank of hair." "Flip," a Scotch terrier, next to the rag-doll in the Child's heart, frisked through the halls. The hank of hair! Aha! X, the unfound quantity, represented the rag-doll. But, the bone? Well, when dogs find bones they— Done! it was an easy and a fruitful task to examine Flip's forefeet. Look, Watson! Earth—dried earth between the toes. Of course, the dog—but Sherlock was not there. Therefore it devolves. But topography and architecture must intervene.

The Millionaire's palace occupied a lordly space. In front of it was a lawn close-mowed as a South Ireland man's face two days after a shave. At one side of it, and fronting on another street, was a pleasance trimmed to a leaf, and the garage and stables. The Scotch pup had ravished the rag-doll from the nursery, dragged it to a corner of the lawn, dug a hole, and buried it after the manner of careless undertakers. There you have the mystery solved, and no checks to write for the hypodermical wizard or fi'-pun notes to toss to the sergeant. Then let's get down to the heart of the thing, tiresome readers—the Christmas heart of the thing.

Fuzzy was drunk—not riotously or helplessly or loquaciously, as you or I might get, but decently, appropriately, and inoffensively, as becomes a gentleman down on his luck.

Fuzzy was a soldier of misfortune. The road, the haystack, the park bench, the kitchen door, the bitter round of eleemosynary beds-with-shower-bath-attachment, the petty pickings and ignobly garnered largesse of great cities—these formed the chapters of his history.

Fuzzy walked toward the river, down the street that bounded one side of the Millionaire's house and grounds. He saw a leg of Betsy, the lost rag-doll, protruding, like the clue to a Lilliputian murder mystery, from its untimely grave in a corner of the fence. He dragged forth the maltreated infant, tucked it under his arm, and went on his way crooning a road song of his brethren that no doll that has been brought up to the sheltered life should hear. Well for Betsy that she had no ears. And well that she had no eyes save unseeing circles of black; for the faces of Fuzzy and the Scotch terrier were those of brothers, and the heart of no rag-doll could withstand twice to become the prey of such fearsome monsters.

Though you may never knew it Grogan's saloon stands near the river and near the foot of the street down which Fuzzy traveled. In Grogan's, Christmas cheer was already rampant.

Fuzzy entered with his doll. He fancied that as a mummer at the feast of Saturn he might earn a few drops from the wassail cup.

He set Betsy on the bar and addressed her loudly and humorously, seasoning his speech with exaggerated compliments and endearments as one entertaining his lady friend. The loafers and bibbers around caught the farce of it, and roared. The bartender gave Fuzzy a drink. Oh, many of us carry rag-dolls.

"One for the lady?" suggested Fuzzy, impudently, and tucked another contribution to Art beneath his waistcoat.

He began to see possibilities in Betsy. His first-night had been a success. Visions of a vaudeville circuit about town dawned upon him.

In a group near the stove sat "Pigeon" McCarthy, Black Riley, and "One-ear" Mike, well and unfavorably known in the tough shoestring district that blackened the left bank of the river. They passed a newspaper back and forth among themselves. The item that each solid and blunt forefinger pointed out was an advertisement headed "One Hundred Dollars Reward." To earn it one must return the rag-doll lost, strayed, or stolen from the Millionaire's mansion. It seemed that grief still ravaged, unchecked, in the bosom of the too faithful Child. Flip, the terrier, capered and shook his absurd whisker before her, powerless to distract. She wailed for her Betsy in the faces of walking, talking, mamaing, and eye-closing French Mabelles and Violettes. The advertisement was a last resort.

Black Riley came from behind the stove and approached Fuzzy in his one-sided parabolic way.

The Christmas mummer, flushed with success, had tucked Betsy under his arm, and was about to depart to the filling of impromptu dates elsewhere.

"Say, 'Bo," said Black Riley to him, "where did you cop out dat doll?"

"This doll?" asked Fuzzy, touching Betsy with his forefinger to be sure that she was the one referred to. "Why, this doll was presented to me by the Emperor of Beloochistan. I have seven hundred others in my country home in Newport. This doll—"

"Cheese the funny business," said Riley. "You swiped it or picked it up at de house on de hill where—but never mind dat. You want to take fifty cents for de rags, and take it quick. Me brother's kid at home might be wantin' to play wid it. Hey—what?"

He produced the coin.

Fuzzy laughed a gurgling, insolent, alcoholic laugh in his face. Go to the office of Sarah Bernhardt's manager and propose to him that she be released from a night's performance to entertain the Tackytown Lyceum and Literary Coterie. You will hear the duplicate of Fuzzy's laugh.

Black Riley gauged Fuzzy quickly with his blueberry eye as a wrestler does. His hand was itching to play the Roman and wrest the rag Sabine from the extemporaneous merry-andrew who was entertaining an angel unaware. But he refrained. Fuzzy was fat and solid and big. Three inches of well-nourished corporeity, defended from the winter winds by dingy linen, intervened between his vest and trousers. Countless small, circular wrinkles running around his coat-sleeves and knees guaranteed the quality of his bone and muscle. His small, blue eyes, bathed in the moisture of altruism and wooziness, looked upon you kindly, yet without abashment. He was whiskerly, whiskyly, fleshily formidable. So, Black Riley temporized.

"Wot'll you take for it, den?" he asked.

"Money," said Fuzzy, with husky firmness, "cannot buy her."

He was intoxicated with the artist's first sweet cup of attainment. To set a faded-blue, earth-stained rag-doll on a bar, to hold mimic converse with it, and to find his heart leaping with the sense of plaudits earned and his throat scorching with free libations poured in his honor—could base coin buy him from such achievements? You will perceive that Fuzzy had the temperament.

Fuzzy walked out with the gait of a trained sea-lion in search of other cafés to conquer.

Though the dusk of twilight was hardly yet apparent, lights were beginning to spangle the city like pop-corn bursting in a deep skillet. Christmas Eve, impatiently expected, was peeping over the brink of the hour. Millions had prepared for its celebration. Towns would be painted red. You, yourself, have heard the horns and dodged the capers of the Saturnalians.

"Pigeon" McCarthy, Black Riley, and "One-ear" Mike held a hasty converse outside Grogan's. They were narrow-chested, pallid striplings, not fighters in the open, but more dangerous in their ways of warfare than the most terrible of Turks. Fuzzy, in a pitched battle, could have eaten the three of them. In a go-as-you-please encounter he was already doomed.

They overtook him just as he and Betsy were entering Costigan's Casino. They deflected him, and shoved the newspaper under his nose. Fuzzy could read—and more.

"Boys," said he, "you are certainly damn true friends. Give me a week to think it over."

The soul of the real artist is quenched with difficulty.

The boys carefully pointed out to him that advertisements were soulless, and that the deficiencies of the day might not be supplied by the morrow.

"A cool hundred," said Fuzzy, thoughtfully and mushily.

"Boys," said he, "you are true friends. I'll go up and claim the reward. The show business is not what it used to be."

Night was falling more surely. The three tagged at his sides to the foot of the rise on which stood the Millionaire's house. There Fuzzy turned upon them acrimoniously.

"You are a pack of putty-faced beagle-hounds," he roared. "Go away."

They went away—a little way.

In "Pigeon" McCarthy's pocket was a section of one-inch gas-pipe eight inches long. In one end of it and in the middle of it was a lead slug. One-half of it was packed tight with solder. Black Riley carried a slung-shot, being a conventional thug. "One-ear" Mike relied upon a pair of brass knucks—an heirloom in the family.

"Why fetch and carry," said black Riley, "when some one will do it for ye? Let him bring it out to us. Hey—what?"

"We can chuck him in the river," said "Pigeon" McCarthy, "with a stone tied to his feet."

"Youse guys make me tired," said "One-ear" Mike sadly. "Ain't progress ever appealed to none of yez? Sprinkle a little gasoline on 'im, and drop 'im on the Drive—well?"

Fuzzy entered the Millionaire's gate and zigzagged toward the softly glowing entrance of the mansion. The three goblins came up to the gate and lingered—one on each side of it, one beyond the roadway. They fingered their cold metal and leather, confident.

Fuzzy rang the door-bell, smiling foolishly and dreamily. An atavistic instinct prompted him to reach for the button of his right glove. But he wore no gloves; so his left hand dropped, embarrassed.

The particular menial whose duty it was to open doors to silks and laces shied at first sight of Fuzzy. But a second glance took in his passport, his card of admission, his surety of welcome—the lost rag-doll of the daughter of the house dangling under his arm.

Fuzzy was admitted into a great hall, dim with the glow from unseen lights. The hireling went away and returned with a maid and the Child. The doll was restored to the mourning one. She clasped her lost darling to her breast; and then with the inordinate selfishness and candor of childhood, stamped her foot and whined hatred and fear of the odious being who had rescued her from the depths of sorrow and despair. Fuzzy wriggled himself into an ingratiatory attitude and essayed the idiotic smile and blattering small talk that is supposed to charm the budding intellect of the young. The Child bawled, and was dragged away, hugging her Betsy close.

There came the Secretary, pale, poised, polished, gliding in pumps, and worshipping pomp and ceremony. He counted out into Fuzzy's hand ten ten-dollar bills; then dropped his eye upon the door, transferred it to James, its custodian, indicated the obnoxious earner of the reward with the other, and allowed his pumps to waft him away to secretarial regions.

James gathered Fuzzy with his own commanding optic and swept him as far as the front door.

When the money touched Fuzzy's dingy palm his first instinct was to take to his heels; but a second thought restrained him from that blunder of etiquette. It was his; it had been given him. It—and, oh, what an elysium it opened to the gaze of his mind's eye! He had tumbled to the foot of the ladder; he was hungry, homeless, friendless, ragged, cold, drifting; and he held in his hand the key to a paradise of the mud-honey that he craved. The fairy doll had waved a wand with her rag-stuffed hand; and now wherever he might go the enchanted palaces with shining foot-rests and magic red fluids in gleaming glassware would be open to him.

He followed James to the door.

He paused there as the flunky drew open the great mahogany portal for him to pass into the vestibule.

Beyond the wrought-iron gates in the dark highway Black Riley and his two pals casually strolled, fingering under their coats the inevitably fatal weapons that were to make the reward of the rag-doll theirs.

Fuzzy stopped at the Millionaire's door and bethought himself. Like little sprigs of mistletoe on a dead tree, certain living green thoughts and memories began to decorate his confused mind. He was quite drunk, mind you, and the present was beginning to fade. Those wreaths and festoons of holly with their scarlet berries making the great hall gay—where had he seen such things before? Somewhere he had known polished floors and odors of fresh flowers in winter, and—some one was singing a song in the house that he thought he had heard before. Some one singing and playing a harp. Of course, it was Christmas—Fuzzy thought he must have been pretty drunk to have overlooked that.

And then he went out of the present, and there came back to him out of some impossible, vanished, and irrevocable past a little, pure-white, transient, forgotten ghost—the spirit of *noblesse oblige.* Upon a gentleman certain things devolve.

James opened the outer door. A stream of light went down the graveled walk to the iron gate. Black Riley, McCarthy, and "One-ear" Mike saw, and carelessly drew their sinister cordon closer about the gate.

With a more imperious gesture than James' master had ever used or could ever use, Fuzzy compelled the menial to close the door. Upon a gentleman certain things devolve. Especially at the Christmas season.

"It is cust—customary," he said to James, the flustered, "when a gentleman calls on Christmas Eve to pass the compliments of the season with the lady of the house. You und'stand? I shall not move step till I pass compl'ments season with lady the house. Und'stand?"

There was an argument. James lost. Fuzzy raised his voice and sent it through the house unpleasantly. I did not say he was a gentleman. He was simply a tramp being visited by a ghost.

A sterling silver bell rang. James went back to answer it, leaving Fuzzy in the hall. James explained somewhere to some one.

Then he came and conducted Fuzzy to the library.

The Lady entered a moment later. She was more beautiful and holy than any picture that Fuzzy had seen. She smiled, and said something about a doll. Fuzzy didn't understand that; he remembered nothing about a doll.

A footman brought in two small glasses of sparkling wine on a stamped sterling-silver waiter. The Lady took one. The other was handed to Fuzzy.

As his fingers closed on the slender glass stem his disabilities dropped from him for one brief moment. He straightened himself; and Time, so disobliging to most of us, turned backward to accommodate Fuzzy.

Forgotten Christmas ghosts whiter than the false beards of the most opulent Kris Kringle were raising in the fumes of Grogan's whisky. What had the Millionaire's mansion to do with a long wainscoted Virginia hall, where the riders were grouped around a silver punch-bowl drinking the ancient toast of the House? And why should the patter of the cab horses' hoofs on the frozen street be in any wise related to the sound of the saddled hunters stamping under the shelter of the west veranda? And what had Fuzzy to do with any of it?

The Lady, looking at him over her glass, let her condescending smile fade away like a false dawn. Her eyes turned serious. She saw something beneath the rags and Scotch terrier whiskers that she did not understand. But it did not matter.

Fuzzy lifted his glass and smiled vacantly.

"P-pardon, lady," he said, "but couldn't leave without exchangin' comp'ments sheason with lady th' house. 'Gainst princ'ples gen'leman do sho."

And then he began the ancient salutation that was a tradition in the House when men wore lace ruffles and powder.

"The blessings of another year—"

Fuzzy's memory failed him. The Lady prompted:

"—Be upon this hearth."

"—The guest—" stammered Fuzzy.

"—And upon her who—" continued the Lady, with a leading smile.

"Oh, cut it out," said Fuzzy, ill-manneredly. "I can't remember. Drink hearty."

Fuzzy had shot his arrow. They drank. The Lady smiled again the smile of her caste. James enveloped Fuzzy and re-conducted him toward the front door. The harp music still softly drifted through the house.

Outside, Black Riley breathed on his cold hands and hugged the gate.

"I wonder," said the Lady to herself, musing, "who—but there were so many who came. I wonder whether memory is a curse or a blessing to them after they have fallen so low."

Fuzzy and his escort were nearly at the door. The Lady called: "James!"

James stalked back obsequiously, leaving Fuzzy waiting unsteadily, with his brief spark of the divine fire gone.

Outside, Black Riley stamped his cold feet and got a firmer grip on his section of gas-pipe.

"You will conduct this gentleman," said the Lady, "downstairs. Then tell Louis to get out the Mercedes and take him to whatever place he wishes to go."

A MERRY CHRISTMAS
To wish you all the
joys and toys that
Santa Claus can carry.

Yes Virginia, There Is a Santa Claus

By Francis P. Church

Francis P. Church was an editorial writer for the New York Sun *when he responded to a letter from Virginia O'Hanlon, a little girl with a big question on her mind. Dated September 21, 1897, Virginia's letter read:*

Dear Editor:

I am 8 years old. Some of my little friends say there is no Santa Claus. Papa says "If you see it in The Sun, *it's so." Please tell me the truth, is there a Santa Claus?*

Virginia O'Hanlon
115 West 95th Street
New York City

Unaware that his reply to Virginia would survive nearly a century of Christmases to come, the name Francis Church has become synonymous with the true spirit of the American Christmas.

Yes, Virginia, there is a Santa Claus. He exists as certainly as love and generosity and devotion exist, and you know that they abound and give to your life its highest beauty and joy. Alas! how dreary would be the world if there were no Santa Claus! It would be as dreary as if there were no Virginias.

There would be no childlike faith then, no poetry, no romance to make tolerable this existence. We should have no enjoyment, except in sense and sight. The eternal light with which childhood fills the world would be extinguished. Not believe in Sant Claus! You might as well not believe in fairies! You might get your papa to hire men to watch in all the chimneys on Christmas Eve to catch Santa Claus, but even if they did not see Santa Claus coming down, what would that prove? Nobody sees Santa Claus, but that is no sign that there is no Santa Claus. The most real things in the world are those that no children or men can see. Did you ever see fairies dancing on the lawn? Of course not, but that's no proof that they are not there. Nobody can conceive or imagine all the wonders there are unseen or unseeable in the world. . . . No Santa Claus! Thank God he lives, and he lives forever. A thousand years from now, Virginia, nay, ten times ten thousand years from now, he will continue to make glad the heart of childhood.

FORESTIER

THE TWELFTH GUEST

Mary Wilkins Freeman

Mary E. Wilkins Freeman was born in Randolph, Massachusetts, in 1852 and died in 1930. Among her works are more than twenty-five Christmas stories that appeared in newspapers and magazines of the day. She is considered one of the finest writers of her era, and her work has long been admired by critics and scholars alike. The following eerie tale of "The Twelfth Guest" first appeared in an 1889 issue of Harper's New England Monthly Magazine.

I don't see how it happened, for my part," Mrs. Childs said. "Paulina, you set the table."

"You counted up yesterday how many there'd be, and you said twelve; don't you know you did, mother? So I didn't count to-day. I just put on the plates," said Paulina, smilingly defensive.

Paulina had something of a helpless and gentle look when she smiled. Her mouth was rather large, and the upper jaw full, so the smile seemed hardly under her control. She was quite pretty; her complexion was so delicate and her eyes so pleasant.

"Well, I don't see how I made such a blunder," her mother remarked further, as she went on pouring the tea.

On the opposite side of the table were a plate, a knife and fork, and a little dish of cranberry sauce, with an empty chair before them. There was no guest to fill it.

"It's a sign somebody's comin' that's hungry," Mrs. Childs' brother's wife said, with soft effusiveness which was out of proportion to the words.

The brother was carving the turkey. Caleb Childs, the host, was an old man, and his hands trembled. Moreover, no one, he himself least of all, ever had any confidence in his ability in such directions. Whenever he helped himself to gravy, his wife watched anxiously lest he should spill it, and he always did. He spilled some to-day. There was a great spot on the beautiful clean table-cloth. Caleb set his cup and saucer over it quickly, with a little clatter because of his unsteady hand. Then he looked at his wife. He hoped she had not seen, but she had.

"You'd better have let John give you the gravy," she said, in a stern aside.

John, rigidly solicitous, bent over the turkey. He carved slowly and laboriously, but everybody had faith in him. The shoulders to which a burden is shifted have the credit of being strong. His wife, in her best black dress, sat smilingly, with her head canted a little to one side. It was a way she had when visiting. Ordinarily she did not assume it at her sister-in-law's house, but this was an extra occasion. Her fine manners spread their wings involuntarily. When she spoke about the sign, the young woman next her sniffed.

"I don't take any stock in signs," said she, with a bluntness which seemed to crash through the other's airiness with such force as to almost hurt itself. She was a distant cousin of Mr. Childs. Her husband and three children were with her.

Mrs. Childs' unmarried sister, Maria Stone, made up the eleven at the table. Maria's gaunt face was unhealthily red about the pointed nose and the high cheek-bones; her eyes looked with a steady sharpness through her spectacles.

"Well, it will be time enough to believe the sign when the twelfth one comes," said she, with a summary air. She had a judicial way of speaking. She had taught school ever since she was sixteen, and now she was sixty. She had just given up teaching. It was to celebrate that, and her final home-coming, that her sister was giving a Christmas dinner instead of a Thanksgiving one this year. The school had been in session during Thanksgiving week.

Maria Stone had scarcely spoken when there was a knock on the outer door, which led directly into the room. They all started. They were a plain, unimaginative company, but for some reason a thrill of superstitious and fantastic expectation ran through them. No one arose. They were all silent for a moment, listening and looking at the empty chair in their midst. Then the knock came again.

"Go to the door, Paulina," said her mother.

The young girl looked at her half fearfully, but she rose at once, and went and opened the door. Everybody stretched around to see. A girl stood on the stone step looking into the room. There she stood, and never said a word. Paulina looked around at her mother, with her innocent, half-involuntary smile.

"Ask her what she wants," said Mrs. Childs.

"What do you want?" repeated Paulina, like a sweet echo.

Still the girl said nothing. A gust of north wind swept into the room. John's wife shivered, then looked around to see if any one had noticed it.

"You must speak up quick an' tell what you want, so we can shut the door; it's cold," said Mrs. Childs.

The girl's small sharp face was sheathed in an old worsted hood; her eyes glared out of it like a frightened cat's. Suddenly she turned to go. She was evidently abashed by the company.

"Don't you want somethin' to eat?" Mrs. Childs asked, speaking up louder.

"It ain't—no matter." She just mumbled it.

"What?"

She would not repeat it. She was quite off the step by this time.

"You make her come in, Paulina," said Maria Stone, suddenly. "She wants something to eat, but she's half scared to death. You talk to her."

"Hadn't you better come in, and have something to eat?" said Paulina, shyly persuasive.

"Tell her she can sit right down here by the stove, where it's warm, and have a good plate of dinner," said Maria.

Paulina fluttered softly down to the stone step. The chilly snow-wind came right in her sweet, rosy face. "You can have a chair by the stove, where it's warm, and a good plate of dinner," said she.

The girl looked at her.

"Won't you come in?" said Paulina, of her own accord, and always smiling.

The stranger made a little hesitating movement forward.

"Bring her in, quick! and shut the door," Maria called out then. And Paulina entered with the girl stealing timidly in her wake.

"Take off your hood an' shawl," Mrs. Childs said, "an' sit down here by the stove, an' I'll give you some dinner." She spoke kindly. She was a warm-hearted woman, but she was rigidly built, and did not relax too quickly into action.

But the cousin, who had been observing, with head alertly raised, interrupted. She cast a mischievous glance at John's wife—the empty chair was between them. "For pity's sake!" cried she; "you ain't goin' to shove her off in the corner? Why, here's this chair. She's the twelfth one. Here's where she ought to sit." There was a mixture of heartiness and sport in the young woman's manner. She pulled the chair back from the table. "Come right over here," said she.

There was a slight flutter of consternation among the guests. They were all narrow-lived country people. Their customs had made deeper grooves in their roads; they were more fastidious and jealous of their social rights than many in higher positions. They eyed this forlorn girl, in her faded and dingy woollens which fluttered airily and showed their pitiful thinness.

Mrs. Childs stood staring at the cousin. She did not think she could be in earnest.

But she was. "Come," said she; "put some turkey in this plate, John."

"Why, it's jest as the rest of you say," Mrs. Childs said, finally, with hesitation. She looked embarrassed and doubtful.

"Say! Why, they say just as I do," the cousin went on. "Why shouldn't they? Come right around here." She tapped the chair impatiently.

The girl looked at Mrs. Childs. "You can go an' sit down there where she says," she said, slowly, in a constrained tone.

"Come," called the cousin again. And the girl took the empty chair, with the guests all smiling stiffly.

Mrs. Childs began filling a plate for the new-comer.

Now that her hood was removed, one could see her face more plainly. It was thin, and of that pale brown tint which exposure gives to some blond skins. Still there was a tangible beauty which showed through all that. Her fair hair stood up softly, with a kind of airy roughness which caught the light. She was apparently about sixteen.

"What's your name?" inquired the school-mistress sister, suddenly.

The girl started. "Christine," she said, after a second.

"What?"

"Christine."

A little thrill ran around the table. The company looked at each other. They were none of them conversant with the Christmas legends, but at that moment the universal sentiment of them seemed to seize upon their fancies. The day, the mysterious appearance of the girl, the name, which was strange to their ears—all startled them, and gave them a vague sense of the supernatural. They, however, struggled against it with their matter-of-fact pride, and threw it off directly.

"Christine what?" Maria asked further.

The girl kept her scared eyes on Maria's face, but she made no reply.

"What's your other name? Why don't you speak?"

Suddenly she rose.

"What are you goin' to do?"

"I'd—rather—go, I guess."

"What are you goin' for? You ain't had your dinner."

"I—can't tell it," whispered the girl.

"Can't tell your name?"

She shook her head.

"Sit down, and eat your dinner," said Maria.

There was a strong sentiment of disapprobation among the company. But when Christine's food was actually before her, and she seemed to settle down upon it, like a bird, they viewed her with more toleration. She was evidently half starved. Their discovery of that fact gave them at once a fellow-feeling toward her on this feast-day, and a complacent sense of their own benevolence.

As the dinner progressed the spirits of the party appeared to rise, and a certain jollity which was almost hilarity prevailed. Beyond providing the strange guest plentifully with food, they seemed to ignore her entirely. Still nothing was more certain than the fact that they did not. Every outburst of merriment was yielded to with the most thorough sense of her presence, which appeared in some subtle way to excite it. It was as if this forlorn twelfth guest were the foreign element needed to produce a state of nervous effervescence in those staid, decorous people who surrounded her. This taste of mystery and unusualness, once fairly admitted, although reluctantly, to their unaccustomed palates, served them as wine with their Christmas dinner.

It was late in the afternoon when they arose from the table. Christine went directly for her hood and shawl, and put them on. The others, talking among themselves, were stealthily observant of her. Christine began opening the door.

"Are you goin' home now?" asked Mrs. Childs.

"No, marm."

"Why not?"

"I ain't got any."

"Where did you come from?"

The girl looked at her. Then she unlatched the door.

"Stop!" Mrs. Childs cried, sharply. "What are you goin' for? Why don't you answer?"

She stood still, but did not speak.

"Well, shut the door up, an' wait a minute," said Mrs. Childs.

She stood close to a window, and she stared out scrutinizingly. There was no house in sight. First came a great yard, then wide stretches of fields; a desolate gray road curved around them on the left. The sky was covered with still, low clouds; the sun had not shone out that day. The ground was all bare and rigid. Out in the yard some gray hens were huddled together in little groups for warmth; their red combs showed out. Two crows flew up, away over on the edge of the field.

"It's goin' to snow," said Mrs. Childs.

"I'm afeard it is," said Caleb, looking at the girl. He gave a sort of silent sob, and brushed some tears out of his old eyes with the back of his hands.

"See here a minute, Maria," said Mrs. Childs.

The two women whispered together; then Maria stepped in front of the girl, and stood, tall and stiff and impressive.

"Now, see here," said she; "we want you to speak up and tell us your other name, and where you came from, and not keep us waiting any longer."

"I—*can't.*" They guessed what she said from the motion of her head. She opened the door entirely then and stepped out.

Suddenly Maria made one stride forward and seized her by her shoulders, which felt like knife-blades through the thin clothes. "Well," said she, "we've been fussing long enough; we've got all these dishes to clear away. It's bitter cold, and it's going to snow, and you ain't going out of this house one step to-night, no matter what you are. You'd ought to tell us who you are, and it ain't many folks that would keep you if you wouldn't; but we ain't goin' to have you found dead in the road, for our own credit. It ain't on your account. Now you just take those things off again, and go and sit down in that chair."

Christine sat in the chair. Her pointed chin dipped down on her neck, whose poor little muscles showed above her dress, which sagged away from it. She never looked up. The women cleared off the table, and cast curious glances at her.

After the dishes were washed and put away, the company were all assembled in the sitting-room for an hour or so; then they went home. The cousin, passing through the kitchen to join her husband, who was waiting with his team at the door, ran hastily up to Christine.

"You stop at my house when you go to-morrow morning," said she. "Mrs. Childs will tell you where 'tis—half a mile below here."

When the company were all gone, Mrs. Childs called Christine into the sitting-room. "You'd better come in here and sit now," said she. "I'm goin' to let the kitchen fire go down; I ain't goin' to get another regular meal; I'm jest goin' to make a cup of tea on the sittin'-room stove by-an'-by."

The sitting-room was warm, and restrainedly comfortable with its ordinary village furnishings—its ingrain carpet, its little peaked clock on a corner of the high black shelf, its red-covered card-table, which had stood in the same spot for forty years. There was a little newspaper-covered stand, with some plants on it, before a window. There was one red geranium in blossom.

Paulina was going out that evening. Soon after the company went she commenced to get ready; and her mother and aunt seemed to be helping her. Christine was alone in the sitting-room for the greater part of an hour.

Finally the three women came in, and Paulina stood before the sitting-room glass for a last look at herself. She had on her best red cashmere, with some white lace around her throat. She had a red geranium flower with some leaves in her hair. Paulina's brown hair, which was rather thin, was very silky. It was apt to part into little soft strands on her forehead. She wore it brushed smoothly back. Her mother would not allow her to curl it.

The two older women stood looking at her. "Don't you think she looks nice, Christine?" Mrs. Childs asked, in a sudden overflow of love and pride, which led her to ask sympathy from even this forlorn source.

"Yes, marm." Christine regarded Paulina, in her red cashmere and geranium flower, with sharp, solemn eyes. When she really looked at any one, her gaze was as unflinching as that of a child.

There was a sudden roll of wheels in the yard.

"Willard's come!" said Mrs. Childs. "Run to the door an' tell him you'll be right out, Paulina, an' I'll get your things ready."

After Paulina had been helped into her coat and hood, and the wheels had bowled out of the yard with a quick dash, the mother turned to Christine.

"My daughter's gone to a Christmas tree over to the church," said she. "That was Willard Morris that came for her. He's a real nice young man that lives about a mile from here."

Mrs. Childs' tone was at once gently patronizing and elated.

When Christine was shown to a little back bedroom that night, nobody dreamed how many times she was to occupy it. Maria and Mrs. Childs, who after the door was closed set a table against it softly and erected a tiltish pyramid of milk pans, to serve as an alarm signal in case the strange guest should try to leave her room with evil intentions, were fully convinced that she would depart early on the following morning.

"I dun know but I've run an awful risk keeping her," Mrs. Childs said. "I don't like her not tellin' where she come from. Nobody knows but she belongs to a gang of burglars, an' they've kind of sent her on ahead to spy out things an' unlock the doors for 'em."

"I know it," said Maria. "I wouldn't have had her stay for a thousand dollars if it hadn't looked so much like snow. Well, I'll get up an' start her off early in the morning."

But Maria Stone could not carry out this resolution. The next morning she was ill with a sudden and severe attack of erysipelas. Moreover, there was a hard snow-storm, the worst of the season; it would have been barbarous to have turned the girl out-of-doors on such a morning. Moreover, she developed an unexpected capacity for usefulness. She assisted Paulina about the housework with timid alacrity, and Mrs. Childs could devote all her time to her sister.

"She takes right hold as if she was used to it," she told Maria. "I'd rather keep her a while than not, if I only knew a little more about her."

"I don't believe but what I could get it out of her after a while if

I tried," said Maria, with her magisterial air, which illness could not subdue.

However, even Maria, with all her well-fostered imperiousness, had no effect on the girl's resolution; she continued as much of a mystery as ever. Still the days went on, then the weeks and months, and she remained in the Childs family.

None of them could tell exactly how it had been brought about. The most definite course seemed to be that her arrival had apparently been the signal for a general decline of health in the family. Maria had hardly recovered when Caleb Childs was laid up with the rheumatism; then Mrs. Childs had a long spell of exhaustion from overwork in nursing. Christine proved exceedingly useful in these emergencies. Their need of her appeared to be the dominant, and only outwardly evident, reason for her stay; still there was a deeper one which they themselves only faintly realized—this poor young girl, who was rendered almost repulsive to these honest downright folk by her persistent cloak of mystery, had somehow, in a very short time, melted herself, as it were, into their own lives. Christine asleep of a night in her little back bedroom, Christine of a day stepping about the house in one of Paulina's old gowns, became a part of their existence, and a part which was not far from the nature of a sweetness to their senses.

She still retained her mild shyness of manner, and rarely spoke unless spoken to. Now that she was warmly sheltered and well fed, her beauty became evident. She grew prettier every day. Her cheeks became softly dimpled; her hair turned golden. Her language was rude and illiterate, but its very uncouthness had about it something of a soft grace.

She was really prettier than Paulina.

The two girls were much together, but could hardly be said to be intimate. There were few confidences between them, and confidences are essential for the intimacy of young girls.

Willard Morris came regularly twice a week to see Paulina, and everybody spoke of them as engaged to each other.

Along in August Mrs. Childs drove over to town one afternoon and bought a piece of cotton cloth and a little embroidery and lace.

Then some fine sewing went on, but with no comment in the household. Mrs. Childs had simply said, "I guess we may as well get a few things made up for you, Paulina, you're getting rather short." And Paulina had sewed all day long, with a gentle industry, when the work was ready.

There was a report that the marriage was to take place on Thanksgiving Day. But about the first of October Willard Morris stopped going to the Childs house. There was no explanation. He simply did not come as usual on Sunday night, nor the following Wednesday, nor the next Sunday. Paulina kindled her little parlor fire, whose sticks she had laid with maiden preciseness; she arrayed herself in her best gown and ribbons. When at nine o'clock Willard had not come, she blew out the parlor lamp, shut up the parlor stove, and went to bed. Nothing was said before her, but there was much talk and surmise between Mrs. Childs and Maria, and a good deal of it went on before Christine.

It was a little while after the affair of Cyrus Morris's note, and they wondered if it could have anything to do with that. Cyrus Morris was Willard's uncle, and the note affair had occasioned much distress in the Childs family for a month back. The note was for twenty-five hundred dollars, and Cyrus Morris had given it to Caleb Childs. The time, which was two years, had expired on the first of September, and then Caleb could not find the note.

He had kept it in his old-fashioned desk, which stood in one corner of the kitchen. He searched there a day and half a night, pulling all the soiled, creasy old papers out of the drawers and pigeon-holes before he would answer his wife's inquiries as to what he had lost.

Finally he broke down and told. "I've lost that note of Morris'," said he. "I dun know what I'm goin' to do."

He stood looking gloomily at the desk with its piles of papers. His rough old chin dropped down on his breast.

The women were all in the kitchen, and they stopped and stared.

"Why, father," said his wife, "where have you put it?"

"I put it here in this top drawer, and it ain't there."

"Let *me* look," said Maria, in a confident tone. But even Maria's energetic and self-assured researches failed. "Well, it ain't here," said she. "I don't know what you've done with it."

"I don't believe you put it in that drawer, father," said his wife.

"It was in there two weeks ago. I see it."

"Then you took it out afterwards."

"I ain't laid hands on't."

"You must have; it couldn't have gone off without hands. You know you're kind of forgetful, father."

"I guess I know when I've took a paper out of a drawer. I know a leetle somethin' yit."

"Well, I don't suppose there'll be any trouble about it, will there?" said Mrs. Childs. "Of course he knows he give the note, an' had the money."

"I dun know as there'll be any trouble, but I'd ruther give a hundred dollar than had it happen."

After dinner Caleb shaved, put on his other coat and hat, and trudged soberly up the road to Cyrus Morris's. Cyrus Morris was an elderly man, who had quite a local reputation for wealth and business shrewdness. Caleb, who was lowly natured and easily impressed by another's importance, always made a call upon him quite a formal affair, and shaved and dressed up.

He was absent about an hour to-day. When he returned he went into the sitting-room, where the women sat with their sewing. He dropped into a chair, and looked straight ahead, with his forehead knitted.

The women dropped their work and looked at him, and then at each other.

"What did he say, father?" Mrs. Childs asked at length.

"Say! He's a rascal, that's what he is, an' I'll tell him so, too."

"Ain't he going' to pay it?"

"No, he ain't."

"Why, father, I don't believe it! You didn't get hold of it straight," said his wife.

"You'll see."

"Why, what did he say?"

"He didn't say anything."

"Doesn't he remember he had the money and gave the note, and has been paying interest on it?" queried Maria.

"He jest laughed, an' said 'twa'n't accordin' to law to pay unless I showed the note an' give it up to him. He said he couldn't be sure but I'd want him to pay it over ag'in. *I know where that note is!*"

Caleb's voice had deep meaning in it. The women stared at him.

"Where?"

"It's in Cyrus Morris' desk—that's where it is."

"Why, father, you're crazy!"

"No, I ain't crazy, nuther. I know what I'm talkin' about. I—"

"It's just where you put it," interrupted Maria, taking up her sewing with a switch; "and I wouldn't lay the blame onto anybody else."

"You'd ought to ha' looked out for a paper like that," said his wife. "I guess I should if it had been me. If you've gone an' lost all that money through your carelessness, you've done it, that's all I've got to say. I don't see what we're goin' to do."

Caleb bent forward and fixed his eyes upon the women. He held up his shaking hand impressively. *"If* you'll stop talkin' just a minute," said he, "I'll tell you what I was goin' to. Now I'd like to know just one thing: *Wa'n't Cyrus Morris alone in that kitchen as* much as fifteen minutes a week ago to-day? Didn't you leave him there while you went to look arter me? Wa'n't the key in the desk? Answer me *that!*"

His wife looked at him with cold surprise and severity. "I wouldn't talk in any such way as that if I was you, father," said she. "It don't show a Christian spirit. It's jest layin' the blame of your own carelessness onto somebody else. You're all the one that's to blame. An' when it comes to it, you'd never ought to let Cyrus Morris have the money anyhow. I could have told you better. I knew what kind of a man he was."

"He's a rascal," said Caleb, catching eagerly at the first note of foreign condemnation in his wife's words. "He'd ought to be put in state's-prison. I don't think much of his relations nuther. I don't want nothin' to do with 'em, an' I don't want none of my folks to."

Paulina's soft cheeks flushed. Then she suddenly spoke out as she had never spoken in her life.

"It doesn't make it out because he's a bad man that his relations are," said she. "You haven't any right to speak so, father. And I guess you won't stop me having anything to do with them, if you want to."

She was all pink and trembling. Suddenly she burst out crying, and ran out of the room.

"You'd ought to be ashamed of yourself, father," exclaimed Mrs. Childs.

"I didn't think of her takin' on it so," muttered Caleb, humbly. "I didn't mean nothin'."

Caleb did not seem like himself through the following days. His simple old face took on an expression of strained thought, which made it look strange. He was tottering on a height of mental effort and worry which was almost above the breathing capacity of his innocent and placid nature. Many a night he rose, lighted a candle, and tremulously fumbled over his desk until morning, in the vain hope of finding the missing note.

One night, while he was so searching, some one touched him softly on the arm.

He jumped and turned. It was Christine. She had stolen in silently.

"Oh, it's you!" said he.

"Ain't you found it?"

"Found it? No; an' I sha'n't, nuther." He turned away from her and pulled out another drawer. The girl stood watching him wistfully. "It was a big yellow paper," the old man went on—"a big yellow paper, an' I'd wrote on the back on't, 'Cyrus Morris's note.' An' the interest he'd paid was set down on the back on't, too."

"It's too bad you can't find it," said she.

"It ain't no use lookin'; it ain't here, an' that's the hull on't. It's in *his* desk. I ain't got no more doubt on't than nothin' at all."

"Where—does he keep his desk?"

"In his kitchen; it's jest like this one."

"Would this key open it?"

"I dun know but 'twould. But it ain't no use. I s'pose I'll have to lose it." Caleb sobbed silently and wiped his eyes.

A few days later he came, all breathless, into the sitting-room. He could hardly speak; but he held out a folded yellow paper, which fluttered and blew in his unsteady hand like a yellow maple leaf in an autumn gale.

"Look-a-here!" he gasped—"look-a-here!"

"Why, for goodness' sake, what's the matter?" cried Maria. She and Mrs. Childs and Paulina were there, sewing peacefully.

"Jest look-a-*here!*"

"Why, for mercy's sake, what is it, father? Are you crazy?"

"It's—the *note!*"

"What note? Don't get so excited, father."

"Cyrus Morris' note. That's what note 'tis. Look-a-here!"

The women all arose and pressed around him, to look at it.

"Where *did* you find it, father?" asked his wife, who was quite pale.

"I suppose it was just where you put it," broke in Maria, with sarcastic emphasis.

"No, it wa'n't. No, it wa'n't, nuther. Don't you go to crowin' too quick, Maria. That paper was just where I told you 'twas. What do you think of that, hey?"

"Oh, father, you didn't!"

"It was layin' right there in his desk. That's where 'twas. Jest where I knew—"

"Father, you didn't go over there an' take it!"

The three women stared at him with dilated eyes.

"No, I didn't."

"Who did?"

The old man jerked his head toward the kitchen door. "She."

"Who?"

"Christiny."

"How did she get it?" asked Maria, in her magisterial manner, which no astonishment could agitate.

"She saw Cyrus and Mis' Morris ride past, an' then she run over there, an' she got in through the window an' got it; that's how." Caleb braced himself like a stubborn child, in case any exception were taken to it all.

"It beats everything I ever heard," said Mrs. Childs, faintly.

"Next time you'll believe what I tell you!" said Caleb.

The whole family were in a state of delight over the recovery of the note; still Christine got rather hesitating gratitude. She was sharply questioned, and rather reproved than otherwise.

This theft, which could hardly be called a theft, aroused the old distrust of her.

"It served him just right, and it wasn't stealing, because it didn't belong to him; and I don't know what you would have done if she hadn't taken it," said Maria; "but, for all that, it went all over me."

"So it did over me," said her sister. "I felt just as you did, an' I felt as if it was real ungrateful too, when the poor child did it just for us."

But there were no such misgivings for poor Caleb, with his money, and his triumph over iniquitous Cyrus Morris. He was wholly and unquestioningly grateful.

"It was a blessed day when we took that little girl in," he told his wife.

"I hope it'll prove so," said she.

Paulina took her lover's desertion quietly. She had just as many soft smiles for every one; there was no alteration in her gentle, obliging ways. Still her mother used to listen at her door, and she knew that she cried instead of sleeping many a night. She was not able to eat much, either, although she tried to with pleasant willingness when her mother urged her.

After a while she was plainly grown thin, and her pretty color had faded. Her mother could not keep her eyes from her.

"Sometimes I think I'll go an' ask Willard myself what this kind of work means," she broke out with an abashed abruptness one afternoon. She and Paulina happened to be alone in the sitting-room.

"You'll kill me if you do, mother," said Paulina. Then she began to cry.

"Well, I won't do anything you don't want me to, of course," said her mother. She pretended not to see that Paulina was crying.

Willard had stopped coming about the first of October; the time wore on until it was the first of December, and he had not once been to the house, and Paulina had not exchanged a word with him in the meantime.

One night she had a fainting-spell. She fell heavily while crossing the sitting-room floor. They got her on to the lounge, and she soon revived; but her mother had lost all control of herself. She came out into the kitchen and paced the floor.

"Oh, my darlin'!" she wailed. "She's goin' to die. What shall I do? All the child I've got in the world. An' he's killed her! That *scamp!* I wish I could get my hands on him. Oh, Paulina, Paulina, to think it should come to this!"

Christine was in the room, and she listened with eyes dilated and lips parted. She was afraid that shrill wail would reach Paulina in the next room.

"She'll hear you," she said, finally.

Mrs. Childs grew quieter at that, and presently Maria called her into the sitting-room.

Christine stood thinking for a moment. Then she got her hood and shawl, put on her rubbers, and went out. She shut the door softly, so nobody should hear. When she stepped forth she plunged knee-deep into snow. It was snowing hard, as it had been all day. It was a cold storm, too; the wind was bitter. Christine waded out of the yard and down the street. She was so small and light that she staggered when she tried to step firmly in some tracks ahead of her. There was a full moon behind the clouds, and there was a soft white light in spite of the storm. Christine kept on down the street, in the direction of Willard Morris's house. It was a mile distant. Once in a while she stopped and turned herself about, that the terrible wind might smite her back instead of her face. When she reached the house she waded painfully through the yard to the side-door and knocked. Pretty soon it opened, and Willard stood there in the entry, with a lamp in his hand.

"Good-evening," said he, doubtfully, peering out.

"Good-evenin'." The light shone on Christine's face. The snow clung to her soft hair, so it was quite white. Her cheeks had a deep, soft color, like roses; her blue eyes blinked a little in the lamp-light, but seemed rather to flicker like jewels or stars. She panted softly through her parted lips. She stood there, with the snow-flakes driving in light past her, and "She looks like an angel," came swiftly into Willard Morris's head before he spoke.

"Oh, it's you," said he.

Christine nodded.

Then they stood waiting. "Why, won't you come in?" said Willard, finally, with an awkward blush. "I declare I never thought. I ain't very polite."

She shook her head. "No, thank you," said she.

"Did—you want to see mother?"

"No."

The young man stared at her in increasing perplexity. His own fair, handsome young face got more and more flushed. His forehead wrinkled. "Was there anything you wanted?"

"No, I guess not," Christine replied, with a slow softness.

Willard shifted the lamp into his other hand and sighed. "It's a pretty hard storm," he remarked, with an air of forced patience.

"Yes."

"Didn't you find it terrible hard walking?"

"Some."

Willard was silent again. "See here, they're all well down at your house, ain't they?" said he, finally. A look of anxious interest had sprung into his eyes. He had begun to take alarm.

"I guess so."

Suddenly he spoke out impetuously. "Say, Christine, I don't know what you came here for; you can tell me afterwards. I don't know what you'll think of me, but—Well, I want to know something. Say—well, I haven't been 'round for quite a while. You don't—suppose—they've cared much, any of them?"

"I don't know."

"Well, I don't suppose you do, but—you might have noticed. Say, Christine, you don't think she—you know whom I mean—cared anything about my coming, do you?"

"I don't know," she said again, softly, with her eyes fixed warily on his face.

"Well, I guess she didn't; she wouldn't have said what she did if she had."

Christine's eyes gave a sudden gleam. "What did she say?"

"Said she wouldn't have anything more to do with me," said the young man, bitterly. "She was afraid I would be up to just such tricks as my uncle was, trying to cheat her father. That was too much for me. I wasn't going to stand that from any girl." He shook his head angrily.

"She didn't say it."

"Yes, she did; her own father told my uncle so. Mother was in the next room and heard it."

"No, she didn't say it," the girl repeated.

"How do you know?"

"I heard her say something different." Christine told him.

"I'm going right up there," cried he, when he heard that. "Wait a minute, and I'll go along with you."

"I dun know as you'd better—to-night," Christine said, looking out towards the road, evasively. "She—ain't been very well tonight."

"Who? Paulina? What's the matter?"

"She had a faintin'-spell jest before I came out," answered Christine, with stiff gravity.

"Oh! Is she real sick?"

"She was some better."

"Don't you suppose I could see her just a few minutes? I wouldn't stay to tire her," said the young man, eagerly.

"I dun know."

"I must, anyhow."

Christine fixed her eyes on his with a solemn sharpness. "What makes you want to?"

"What makes me want to? Why, I'd give ten years to see her five minutes."

"Well, mebbe you could come over a few minutes."

"Wait a minute," cried Willard. "I'll get my hat."

"I'd better go first, I guess. The parlor fire'll be to light."

"Then had I better wait?"

"I guess so."

"Then I'll be along in about an hour. Say, you haven't said what you wanted."

Christine was off the step. "It ain't any matter," murmured she.

"Say—she didn't send you?"

"No, she didn't."

"I didn't mean that. I didn't suppose she did," said Willard, with an abashed air. "What did you want, Christine?"

"There's somethin' I want you to promise," said she, suddenly.

"What's that?"

"Don't you say anything about Mr. Childs."

"Why, how can I help it?"

"He's an old man, an' he was so worked up he didn't know what he was sayin'. They'll all scold him. Don't say anything."

"Well, I won't say anything. I don't know what I'm going to tell her, though."

Christine turned to go.

"You didn't say what 'twas you wanted," called Willard again.

But she made no reply. She was pushing through the deep snow out of the yard.

It was quite early yet, only a few minutes after seven. It was eight when she reached home. She entered the house without any one seeing her. She pulled off her snowy things, and went into the sitting-room.

Paulina was alone there. She was lying on the lounge. She was very pale, but she looked up and smiled when Christine entered.

Christine brought the fresh out-door air with her. Paulina noticed it. "Where have you been?" whispered she.

Then Christine bent over her, and talked fast in a low tone.

Presently Paulina raised herself and sat up. "To-night?" cried she, in an eager whisper. Her cheeks grew red.

"Yes; I'll go make the parlor fire."

"It's all ready to light." Suddenly Paulina threw her arms around Christine and kissed her. Both girls blushed.

"I don't think I said one thing to him that you wouldn't have wanted me to," said Christine.

"You didn't—ask him to come?"

"No, I didn't, honest."

When Mrs. Childs entered, a few minutes later, she found her daughter standing before the glass.

"Why, Paulina!" cried she.

"I feel a good deal better, mother," said Paulina.

"Ain't you goin' to bed?"

"I guess I won't quite yet."

"I've got it all ready for you. I thought you wouldn't feel like sittin' up."

"I guess I will; a little while."

Soon the door-bell rang with a sharp peal. Everybody jumped—Paulina rose and went to the door.

Mrs. Childs and Maria, listening, heard Willard's familiar voice, then the opening of the parlor door.

"It's *him!*" gasped Mrs. Childs. She and Maria looked at each other.

It was about two hours before the soft murmur of voices in the parlor ceased, the outer door closed with a thud, and Paulina came into the room. She was blushing and smiling, but she could not look in any one's face at first.

"Well," said her mother, "who was it?"

"Willard. It's all right."

It was not long before the fine sewing was brought out again, and presently two silk dresses were bought for Paulina. It was known about that she was to be married on Christmas Day. Christine assisted in the preparation. All the family called to mind afterwards the obedience so ready as to be loving which she yielded to their biddings during those few hurried weeks. She sewed, she made cake, she ran of errands, she wearied herself joyfully for the happiness of this other young girl.

About a week before the wedding, Christine, saying good-night when about to retire one evening, behaved strangely. They remembered it afterwards. She went up to Paulina and kissed her when saying good-night. It was something which she had never before done. Then she stood in the door, looking at them all. There was a sad, almost a solemn, expression on her fair girlish face.

"Why, what's the matter?" said Maria.

"Nothin'," said Christine. "Good-night."

That was the last time they ever saw her. The next morning Mrs. Childs, going to call her, found her room vacant. There was a great alarm. When they did not find her in the house nor the neighborhood, people were aroused, and there was a search instigated. It was prosecuted eagerly, but to no purpose. Paulina's wedding evening came, and Christine was still missing.

Paulina had been married, and was standing beside her husband, in the midst of the chattering guests, when Caleb stole out of the room. He opened the north door, and stood looking out over the dusky fields. "Christiny!" he called, "Christiny!"

Presently he looked up at the deep sky, full of stars, and called again—"Christiny! Christiny!" But there was no answer save in light. When Christine stood in the sitting-room door and said good-night, her friends had their last sight and sound of her. Their Twelfth Guest had departed from their hospitality forever.

CAROL CLUB
SANTACLAUS STARTS FOR EARTH AT 11.P.M.
Louis Wain.

How Claus Made the First Toy

L. Frank Baum

L. Frank Baum, a native of New York State, was born on May 15, 1856, and died in Hollywood in 1919. Famous for the children's classic The Wizard of Oz, *Baum was the author of more than sixty books for children including thirteen additional books in the Oz series and* Father Goose. *The following excerpt is taken from* The Life and Adventures of Santa Claus, *first published in 1902 and dedicated to the author's son, Harry Neal Baum.*

Truly our Claus had wisdom, for his good fortune but strengthened his resolve to befriend the little ones of his own race. He knew his plan was approved by the immortals, else they would not have favored him so greatly.

So he began at once to make acquaintance

with mankind. He walked through the Valley to the plain beyond, and crossed the plain in many directions to reach the abodes of men. These stood singly or in groups of dwellings called villages, and in nearly all the houses, whether big or little, Claus found children.

The youngsters soon came to know his merry, laughing face and the kind glance of his bright eyes; and the parents, while they regarded the young man with some scorn for loving children more than their elders, were content that the girls and boys had found a playfellow who seemed willing to amuse them.

So the children romped and played games with Claus, and the boys rode upon his shoulders, and the girls nestled in his strong arms and the babies clung fondly to his knees. Wherever the young man chanced to be, the sound of childish laughter followed him; and to understand this better you must know that children were much neglected in those days and received little attention from their parents, so that it became to them a marvel that so goodly a man as Claus devoted his time to making them happy. And those who knew him were, you may be sure, very happy indeed. The sad faces of the poor and abused grew bright for once; the cripple smiled despite his misfortune; the ailing ones hushed their moans and the grieved ones their cries when their merry friend came nigh to comfort them.

Only at the beautiful palace of the Lord of Lerd and at the frowning castle of the Baron Braun was Claus refused admittance. There were children at both places; but the servants at the palace shut the door in the young stranger's face, and the fierce Baron threatened to hang him from an iron hook on the castle walls. Whereupon Claus sighed and went back to the poorer dwellings where he was welcome.

After a time the winter drew near.

The flowers lived out their lives and faded and disappeared; the beetles burrowed far into the warm earth; the butterflies deserted the meadows; and the voice of the brook grew hoarse, as if it had taken cold.

One day snowflakes filled all the air in the Laughing Valley, dancing boisterously toward the earth and clothing in pure white raiment the roof of Claus's dwelling.

At night Jack Frost rapped at the door.

"Come in!" cried Claus.

"Come out!" answered Jack, "for you have a fire inside."

So Claus came out. He had known Jack Frost in the Forest, and liked the jolly rogue, even while he mistrusted him.

"There will be rare sport for me to-night, Claus!" shouted the sprite. "Isn't this glorious weather? I shall nip scores of noses and ears and toes before daybreak."

"If you love me, Jack, spare the children," begged Claus.

"And why?" asked the other, in surprise.

"They are tender and helpless," answered Claus.

"But I love to nip the tender ones!" declared Jack. "The older ones are tough, and tire my fingers."

"The young ones are weak, and can not fight you," said Claus.

"True," agreed Jack, thoughtfully. "Well, I will not pinch a child this night—if I can resist the temptation," he promised. "Good-night, Claus!"

"Good-night."

The young man went in and closed the door, and Jack Frost ran on to the nearest village.

Claus threw a log on the fire, which burned up brightly. Beside the hearth sat Blinkie, a big cat given him by Peter the Knook. Her fur was soft and glossy, and she purred never-ending songs of contentment.

"I shall not see the children again soon," said Claus to the cat, who kindly paused in her song to listen. "The winter is upon us, the snow will be deep for many days, and I shall be unable to play with my little friends."

The cat raised a paw and stroked her nose thoughtfully, but made no reply. So long as the fire burned and Claus sat in his easy chair by the hearth she did not mind the weather.

So passed many days and many long evenings. The cupboard was always full, but Claus became weary with having nothing to do more than to feed the fire from the big wood-pile the Knooks had brought him.

One evening he picked up a stick of wood and began to cut it with his sharp knife. He had no thought, at first, except to occupy his time, and he whistled and sang to the cat as he carved away portions of the stick. Puss sat up on her haunches and watched him, listening at the same time to her master's merry whistle, which she loved to hear even more than her own purring songs.

Claus glanced at puss and then at the stick he was whittling, until presently the wood began to have a shape, and the shape was like the head of a cat, with two ears sticking upward.

Claus stopped whistling to laugh, and then both he and the cat looked at the wooden image in some surprise. Then he carved out the eyes and the nose, and rounded the lower part of the head so that it rested upon a neck.

Puss hardly knew what to make of it now, and sat up stiffly, as if watching with some suspicion what would come next.

Claus knew. The head gave him an idea. He plied his knife carefully and with skill, forming slowly the body of the cat, which he made to sit upon its haunches as the real cat did, with her tail wound around her two front legs.

The work cost him much time, but the evening was long and he had nothing better to do. Finally he gave a loud and delighted laugh at the result of his labors and placed the wooden cat, now completed, upon the hearth opposite the real one.

Puss thereupon glared at her image, raised her hair in anger, and uttered a defiant mew. The wooden cat paid no attention, and Claus, much amused, laughed again.

Then Blinkie advanced toward the wooden image to eye it closely and smell of it intelligently: eyes and nose told her the creature was wood, in spite of its natural appearance; so puss resumed her seat and her purring, but as she neatly washed her face with her padded paw she cast more than one admiring glance at her clever master. Perhaps she felt the same satisfaction we feel when we look upon good photographs of ourselves.

The cat's master was himself pleased with his handiwork, without knowing exactly why. Indeed, he had great cause to congratulate himself that night, and all the children throughout the world should have joined him in rejoicing. For Claus had made his first toy.

GREETINGS

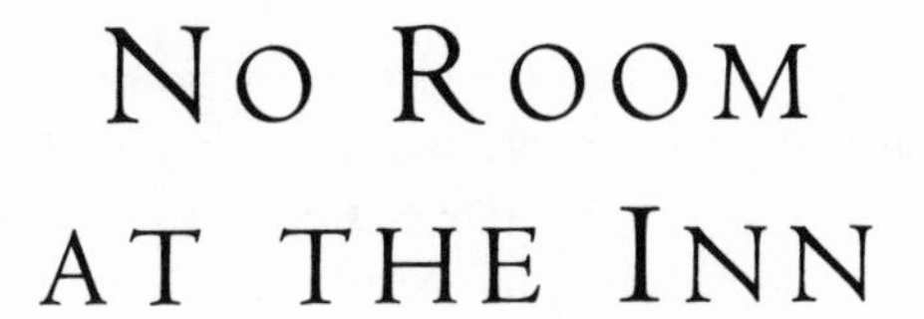

No Room at the Inn

Edna Ferber

Edna Ferber was born in 1887 in Kalamazoo, Michigan, and died in New York in 1968. One of the premiere women of American letters, she was a champion of ordinary people, and her work enjoyed huge commercial success during her lifetime. Two of her classics, Showboat *and* Giant, *were brought to an even wider audience through the movie adaptations. Her Christmas story "No Room at the Inn" is a retelling of a biblical tale, set against the backdrop of World War II.*

"NOBODY" IS BORN IN NO MAN'S LAND

PRAGUE, OCT. 25 (UP)—*A baby born in the no man's land south of Brno, where 200 Jewish refugees have been living in a ditch between Germany and Czechoslovakia for two weeks, was named Niemand (Nobody) today.*

She had made every stitch herself. Literally, every stitch, and the sewing was so fairylike that the eye scarcely could see it. Everything was new, too. She had been almost unreasonable about that, considering Joe's meager and uncertain wage and the frightening time that had come upon the world. Cousin Elisabeth had offered to give her some of the clothing that her baby had outgrown, but Mary had refused, politely, to accept these.

"That is dear and good of you, 'Lisbeth," Mary had said. "I know it seems ungrateful, maybe, and even silly not to take them. It's hard to tell you how I feel. I want everything of his to be new. I want to make everything myself. Every little bit myself."

Cousin Elisabeth was more than twice as old as Mary. She understood everything. It was a great comfort to have Elisabeth so near, with her wisdom and her warm sympathy. "No, I don't think it's silly at all. I know just how you feel. I felt the same way when my John was coming." She laughed then, teasingly: "How does it happen you're so sure it's going to be a boy? You keep saying 'he' all the time."

Mary had gone calmly on with her sewing, one infinitesimal stitch after the other, her face serene. "I know. I know." She glanced up at her older cousin, fondly. "I only hope he'll be half as smart and good as your little John."

Elisabeth's eyes went to the crib where the infant lay asleep. "Well, if I say so myself, John certainly is smart for his age. But then"—hastily, for fear that she should seem too proud—"but, then, Zach and I are both kind of middle-aged. And they say the first child of middle-aged parents is likely to be unusually smart."

The eighteen-year-old Mary beamed at this. "Joe's middle-aged!" she boasted happily. Then she blushed the deep, flaming crimson of youth and innocence; for Joe's astonishment at the first news of the child's coming had been as great as her own. It was like a miracle wrought by some outside force.

Cousin Elisabeth had really made the match between the young girl and the man well on in years. People had thought it strange; but this Mary, for all her youth, had a wisdom and sedateness beyond her years, and an unexpected humor, too, quiet and strangely dry, such as one usually finds associated with long observation and experience. Joe was husband, father, brother to the girl. It was wonderful. They were well mated. And now, when life in this strange world had become so frightening, so brutal, so terrible, it was more than ever wonderful to have his strength and goodness and judgment as a shield and staff. She knew of younger men, hotheaded, who had been taken away in the night and never again heard from. Joe went quietly about his business. But each morning as he left her he said, "Stay at home until I come back this evening. Or, if you must do your marketing, take Elisabeth with you. I'll stop by and tell her to call for you. Don't go into the streets alone."

"I'll be all right," she said. "Nobody would hurt me." For here pregnant women were given special attention. The government wanted children for future armies.

"Not our children," Joe said bitterly.

So they lived quietly, quietly they obeyed the laws; they went nowhere. Two lower-middle-class people. Dreadful, unspeakable things were happening; but such things did not happen to her and to her husband and to her unborn child. Everything would right itself. It must.

Her days were full. There were the two rooms to keep clean, the marketing, the cooking, the sewing. The marketing was a tiring task, for one had to run from shop to shop to get a bit of butter, an egg for Joe, a piece of meat however coarse and tough. Sometimes when she came back to the little flat in the narrow street and climbed the three flights of stairs, the beads of sweat stood on her lip and forehead and her breath came painfully, for all her youth. Still, it was glorious to be able at night to show Joe a pan of coffeecake, or a meat ball, or even a pat of pretty good butter. On Friday she always tried her hardest to get a fowl, however skinny, or a bit of lamb because Friday was the eve of the Sabbath. She rarely could manage it; but that made all the sweeter her triumph when she did come home, panting up the stairs, with her scrap of booty.

Mary kept her sewing in a wicker basket neatly covered over with a clean white cloth. The little pile grew and grew. Joe did not know that she had regularly gone without a midday meal in order to save even that penny or two for the boy's furnishings. Sometimes Joe would take the sewing from her busy hands and hold it up, an absurd fragment of cloth, a miniature garment that looked the smaller in contrast with his great, work-worn hand. He would laugh as he held it, dangling. It seemed so improbable that anything alive and sentient should be small enough to fit into this scrap of cloth. Then, in the midst of his laugh, he would grow serious. He would stare at her and she at him and they would listen, hushed, as for a dreaded and expected sound on the stairs.

Floors to scrub, pots and pans to scour, clothes to wash, food to cook, garments to sew. It was her life, it was for Joe, it was enough and brimming over. Hers was an enormous pride in keeping things in order, the pride of possession inherited from peasant ancestors. Self-respect.

The men swarmed up the stairway so swiftly that Mary and Joe had scarcely heard their heavy boots on the first landing before they were kicking at the door and banging it with their fists. Joe sprang to his feet and she stood up, one hand at her breast and in that hand a pink knitted hood, no bigger than a fist, that she was knitting. Then they were in the room; they filled the little clean room with their clamor and their oaths and their great brown-clad bodies. They hardly looked at Joe and Mary, they ransacked the cupboards, they pulled out the linen and the dishes, they trampled these. One of the men snatched the pink cap from her hand and held it up and then put in on his own big, round head, capering with a finger in his mouth.

"Stop that!" said the one in charge. "We've no time for such foolishness." And snatched off the pink hood, and blew his nose into it, and threw it in a corner.

In the cupboard they came upon the little cakes. She had saved drippings, she had skimmed such bits of rare fat as came their way, she had used these to fashion shortening for four little cakes, each with a dab of dried plum on top. Joe had eaten two for his supper and there had been two left for his breakfast. She had said she did not want any. Cakes made her too fat. It was bad for the boy.

"Look!" yelled the man who had found these. "Cakes! These swine have cakes to eat, so many that they can leave them uneaten in the cakebox." He broke one between his fingers, sniffed it like a dog, then bolted it greedily.

"Enough of this!" yelled the man in authority. "Stop fooling and come on! You want to stay in this pigsty all night! There's a hundred more. Come on. Out!"

Then they saw Mary, big as she was, and they made a joke of this, and one of them poked her a little with his finger, and still Joe did nothing; he was like a man standing asleep with his eyes wide open. Then they shoved them both from the room. As they went, Mary made a gesture toward the basket in the corner—the basket that had been covered so neatly with the clean white cloth. Her hand was outstretched; her eyes were terrible. The little stitches so small that even she had scarcely been able to see them, once she had pricked them into the cloth.

The man who had stuffed the cakes into his mouth was now hurriedly wiping his soiled boots with a bit of soft white, kneeling by the overturned basket as he did so. He was very industrious and concentrated about it, as they were taught to be thorough about everything. His tongue was out a little way between his strong yellow teeth and he rubbed away industriously. Then, at an impatient oath from the leader, he threw the piece of cloth into a corner with the rest of the muddied, trampled garments and hurried after so that he was there to help load them into the truck with the others huddled close.

Out of the truck and on the train they bumped along for hours—or it may have been days. Mary had no sense of time. Joe pillowed her head on his breast and she even slept a little, like a drugged thing, her long lashes meeting the black smudges under her eyes. There was no proper space for them all; they huddled on the floor and in the passages. Soon the scene was one of indescribable filth. Children cried, sometimes women screamed hysterically, oftenest they sat, men and women, staring into space. The train puffed briskly along with the businesslike efficiency characteristic of the country.

It was intereting to see these decent middle-class people reduced to dreadful squalor, to a sordidness unthought of in their lives. From time to time the women tried to straighten their clothing, to wash their bodies, but the cup of water here and there was needed for refreshment. Amidst these stenches and sounds, amidst the horror and degradation, Joe and Mary sat, part of the scene, yet apart from it. She had wakened curiously refreshed. It was as though a dream she had dreamed again and again, only to awake in horror, had really come to pass, and so, seeing it come true, she was better able to bear it, knowing the worst of it. Awake, she now laid his head in its turn on her breast and through exhaustion he slept, his eyes closed flutteringly but his face and hands clenched even in sleep. Joe had aged before her eyes, overnight. A strong and robust man, of sturdy frame, he had withered; there were queer hollows in his temples and blue veins throbbed there in welts she had never before seen.

Big though she was with her burden, she tried to help women younger and older than she. She was, in fact, strangely full of strength and energy, as often is the case with pregnant women.

The train stopped, and they looked out, and there was nothing. It started again, and they came to the border of the next country. Men in uniform swarmed amongst them, stepping over them and even on them as if they were vermin. Then they talked together and alighted from the train, and the train backed until it came again to the open fields where there was nothing. Barren land, and no sign of habitation. It was nowhere. It was nothing. It was neither their country nor the adjoining country. It was no man's land.

They could not enter here, they could not turn back there. Out they went, shoved and pushed, between heaven and hell, into purgatory. Lost souls.

They stumbled out into the twilight. It was October, it was today. Nonsense, such things do not happen, this is a civilized world, they told themselves. Not like this, to wander until they dropped and died.

They walked forward together, the two hundred of them, dazedly but with absurd purposefulness, too, as if they were going somewhere. The children stumbled and cried and stumbled again. Shed, barn, shelter there was none. There was nothing.

And then that which Mary had expected began to take place. Her pains began, wave on wave. Her eyes grew enormous and her face grew very little and thin and old. Presently she could no longer walk with the rest. They came upon a little flock of sheep grazing in a spot left still green in the autumn, and near by were two shepherds and a tiny donkey hardly bigger than a dog.

Joe went to the shepherds, desperate. "My wife is ill. She is terribly ill. Let me take your donkey. There must be some place near by—an inn. Some place."

One of the shepherds, less oafish than the other, and older, said, "There's an inn, but they won't take her."

"Here," said Joe, and held out a few poor coins that had been in his pocket. "Let her ride just a little way."

The fellow took the coins. "All right. A little way. I'm going home. It's suppertime. She can ride a little way."

So they hoisted her to the donkey's back and she crouched there, but presently it was her time, and she slipped off and they helped her to the ditch by the side of the road.

She was a little silly by now, what with agony and horror. "Get all the nice clean things, Joe. The linen things, they're in the box in the cupboard. And call Elisabeth. Put the kettle on to boil. No, not my best nightgown, that comes later, when everything is over and I am tidy again. Men don't know."

Her earth rocked and roared and faces were blurred and distorted and she was rent and tortured and she heard someone making strange noises like an animal in pain, and then there came merciful blackness.

When she awoke there were women bending over her, and they had built a fire from bits of wood and dried grass, and in some miraculous way there was warm water and strips of cloth and she felt and then saw the child by her side in the ditch and he was swaddled in decent wrappings. She was beyond the effort of questioning, but at the look in her eyes the woman bending over her said, "It's a boy. A fine boy." And she held him up. He waved his tiny arms and his hair was bright in the reflection of the fire behind him. But they crowded too close around her, and Joseph waved them away with one arm and slipped his other under her head and she looked up at him and even managed to smile.

As the crowd parted there was the sound of an automobile that came to a grinding halt. They were officials, you could see that easily enough, with their uniforms and their boots and their proud way of walking.

"Hr-r-rmph!" they said. "Here, all of you. Now then, what's all this! We had a hell of a time finding you, we never would have got here if we hadn't seen the light in the sky from your fire. Now, then, answer to roll call; we've got the names of all of you, so speak up or you'll wish you had."

They called the roll of the two hundred and each answered, some timidly, some scornfully, some weeping, some cringing, some courageously.

"Mary!" they called. "Mary."

She opened her eyes. "Mary," she said, in little more than a whisper.

"That must be the one," they said amongst themselves, the three. "That's the one had the kid just born." They came forward then and saw the woman Mary and the newborn babe in the ditch. "Yep, that's it. Born in a ditch to one of these damned Jews."

"Well, let's put it on the roll call. Might as well get it in now, before it grows up and tries to sneak out. What d'you call it? Heh, Mary?" He prodded her a little, not too roughly, with the toe of his boot.

She opened her eyes again and smiled a little as she looked up at him and then at the boy in her arms. She smiled while her eyes were clouded with agony.

"Niemand," she whispered.

"What's that? Speak up. Can't hear you."

She concentrated all her energies, she formed her lips to make sound again, and licked them because they were quite dry, and said once more, "Niemand . . . Nobody."

One man wrote it down, but the first man stared as though he resented being joked with, a man of his position. But at the look in her eyes he decided that she had not been joking. He stared and stared at the boy, the firelight shining on his tiny face, making a sort of halo of his hair.

"Niemand, eh? That the best you can do for him! . . . Jesus! . . . Well, cheer up, he's a fine-looking boy. He might grow up to be quite a kid, at that."

Season's Greetings

One Christmas Eve

Langston Hughes

Poet and author Langston Hughes was born in Joplin, Missouri, in 1902, and died in New York City in 1967. One critic has described his work as "a spontaneous art . . . his stories, like his poems, are for readers who will judge them with their hearts as well as their heads." The following story is taken from The Ways of White Folks, *published in 1934.*

tanding over the hot stove cooking supper, the colored maid, Arcie, was very tired. Between meals today, she had cleaned the whole house for the white family she worked for, getting ready for Christmas tomorrow. Now her back ached and her head felt faint from sheer fatigue. Well, she would be off in a little while, if only the

Missus and her children would come on home to dinner. They were out shopping for more things for the tree which stood all ready, tinsel-hung and lovely in the living-room, waiting for its candles to be lighted.

Arcie wished she could afford a tree for Joe. He'd never had one yet, and it's nice to have such things when you're little. Joe was five, going on six. Arcie, looking at the roast in the white folks' oven, wondered how much she could afford to spend tonight on toys. She only got seven dollars a week, and four of that went for her room and the landlady's daily looking after Joe while Arcie was at work.

"Lord, it's more'n a notion raisin' a child," she thought.

She looked at the clock on the kitchen table. After seven. What made white folks so darned inconsiderate? Why didn't they come on home here to supper? They knew she wanted to get off before all the stores closed. She wouldn't have time to buy Joe nothin' if they didn't hurry. And her landlady probably wanting to go out and shop, too, and not be bothered with little Joe.

"Dog gone it!" Arcie said to herself. "If I just had my money, I might leave the supper on the stove for 'em. I just got to get to the stores fo' they close." But she hadn't been paid for the week yet. The Missus had promised to pay her Christmas Eve, a day or so ahead of time.

Arcie heard a door slam and talking and laughter in the front of the house. She went in and saw the Missus and her kids shaking snow off their coats.

"Ummm-mm! It's swell for Christmas Eve," one of the kids said to Arcie. "It's snowin' like the deuce, and mother came near driving through a stop light. Can't hardly see for the snow. It's swell!"

"Supper's ready," Arcie said. She was thinking how her shoes weren't very good for walking in snow.

It seemed like the white folks took as long as they could to eat that evening. While Arcie was washing dishes, the Missus came out with her money.

"Arcie," the Missus said, "I'm so sorry, but would you mind if I just gave you five dollars tonight? The children have made me run short of change, buying presents and all."

"I'd like to have seven," Arcie said. "I needs it."

"Well, I just haven't got seven," the Missus said. "I didn't know you'd want all your money before the end of the week, anyhow. I just haven't got it to spare."

Arcie took five. Coming out of the hot kitchen, she wrapped up as well as she could and hurried by the house where she roomed to get little Joe. At least he could look at the Christmas trees in the windows downtown.

The landlady, a big light yellow woman, was in a bad humor. She said to Arcie, "I thought you was comin' home early and get this child. I guess you know I want to go out, too, once in awhile."

Arcie didn't say anything for, if she had, she knew the landlady would probably throw it up to her that she wasn't getting paid to look after a child both night and day.

"Come on, Joe," Arcie said to her son, "let's us go in the street."

"I hears they got a Santa Claus downtown," Joe said, wriggling into his worn little coat. "I wants to see him."

"Don't know 'bout that," his mother said, "but hurry up and get your rubbers on. Stores'll all be closed directly."

It was six or eight blocks downtown. They trudged along through the falling snow, both of them a little cold. But the snow was pretty!

The main street was hung with bright red and blue lights. In front of the City Hall there was a Christmas tree—but it didn't have no presents on it, only lights. In the store windows there were lots of toys—for sale.

Joe kept on saying, "Mama, I want . . ."

But mama kept walking ahead. It was nearly ten, when the stores were due to close, and Arcie wanted to get Joe some cheap gloves and something to keep him warm, as well as a toy or two. She thought she might come across a rummage sale where they had children's clothes. And in the ten-cent store, she could get some toys.

"O-oo! Lookee . . .," little Joe kept saying, and pointing at things in the windows. How warm and pretty the lights were, and the shops, and the electric signs through the snow.

It took Arcie more than a dollar to get Joe's mittens and things he needed. In the A & P Arcie bought a big box of hard candies for 49¢.

And then she guided Joe through the crowd on the street until they came to the dime store. Near the ten-cent store they passed a moving picture theatre. Joe said he wanted to go in and see the movies.

Arcie said, "Ump-un! No, child! This ain't Baltimore where they have shows for colored, too. In these here small towns, they don't let colored folks in. We can't go in there."

"Oh," said little Joe.

In the ten-cent store, there was an awful crowd. Arcie told Joe to stand outside and wait for her. Keeping hold of him in the crowded store would be a job. Besides she didn't want him to see what toys she was buying. They were to be a surprise from Santa Claus tomorrow.

Little Joe stood outside the ten-cent store in the light, and the snow, and people passing. Gee, Christmas was pretty. All tinsel and stars and cotton. And Santa Claus a-coming from somewhere, dropping things in stockings. And all the people in the streets were carrying things, and the kids looked happy.

But Joe soon got tired of just standing and thinking and waiting in front of the ten-cent store. There were so many things to look at in the other windows. He moved along up the block a little, and then a little more, walking and looking. In fact, he moved until he came to the white folks' picture show.

In the lobby of the moving picture show, behind the plate-glass doors, it was all warm and glowing and awful pretty. Joe stood looking in, and as he looked his eyes began to make out, in there blazing beneath holly and colored streamers and the electric stars of the lobby, a marvellous Christmas tree. A group of children and grown-ups, white, of course, were standing around a big jovial man in red beside the tree. Or was it a man? Little Joe's eyes opened wide. No, it was not a man at all. It was Santa Claus!

Little Joe pushed open one of the glass doors and ran into the lobby of the white moving picture show. Little Joe went right through the crowd and up to where he could get a good look at Santa Claus. And Santa Claus was giving away gifts, little presents for children, little boxes of animal crackers and stick-candy canes. And behind him on the tree was a big sign (which little Joe didn't know how to read).

It said, to those who understood, MERRY XMAS FROM SANTA CLAUS TO OUR YOUNG PATRONS.

Around the lobby, other signs said, WHEN YOU COME OUT OF THE SHOW STOP WITH YOUR CHILDREN AND SEE OUR SANTA CLAUS. And another announced, GEM THEATRE MAKES ITS CUSTOMERS HAPPY—SEE OUR SANTA.

And there was Santa Claus in a red suit and a white beard all sprinkled with tinsel snow. Around him were rattles and drums and rocking horses which he was not giving away. But the signs on them said (could little Joe have read) that they would be presented from the stage on Christmas Day to the holders of the lucky numbers. Tonight, Santa Claus was only giving away candy, and stick-candy canes, and animal crackers to the kids.

Joe would have liked terribly to have a stick-candy cane. He came a little closer to Santa Claus, until he was right in the front of the crowd. And then Santa Claus saw Joe.

Why is it that lots of white people always grin when they see a Negro child? Santa Claus grinned. Everybody else grinned, too, looking at little black Joe—who had no business in the lobby of a white theatre. Then Santa Claus stooped down and slyly picked up one of his lucky number rattles, a great big loud tin-pan rattle such as they use in cabarets. And he shook it fiercely right at Joe. That was funny. The white people laughed, kids and all. But little Joe didn't laugh. He was scared. To the shaking of the big rattle, he turned and fled out of the warm lobby of the theatre, out into the street where the snow was and the people. Frightened by laughter, he had begun to cry. He went looking for his mama. In his heart he never thought Santa Claus shook great rattles at children like that—and then laughed.

In the crowd on the street he went the wrong way. He couldn't find the ten-cent store or his mother. There were too many people, all white people, moving like white shadows in the snow, a world of white people.

It seemed to Joe an awfully long time till he suddenly saw Arcie, dark and worried-looking, cut across the side-walk through the passing crowd and grab him. Although her arms were full of packages, she still managed with one free hand to shake him until his teeth rattled.

"Why didn't you stand where I left you?" Arcie demanded loudly. "Tired as I am, I got to run all over the streets in the night lookin' for you. I'm a great mind to wear you out."

When little Joe got his breath back, on the way home, he told his mama he had been in the moving picture show.

"But Santa Claus didn't give me nothin'," Joe said tearfully. "He made a big noise at me and I runned out."

"Serves you right," said Arcie, trudging through the snow. "You had no business in there. I told you to stay where I left you."

"But I seed Santa Claus in there," little Joe said, "so I went in."

"Huh! That wasn't no Santa Claus," Arcie explained. "If it was, he wouldn't a-treated you like that. That's a theatre for white folks—I told you once—and he's just a old white man."

"Oh . . .," said little Joe.

CHRISTMAS CHEER

May your Christmas be cheerful
And merry and glad;
The very best Christmas
That ever you've had;
May the Day bring glad greetings,
Good neighbors to call,
And so many presents
You can't count them all!

THE WORST CHRISTMAS STORY

Christopher Morley

Christopher Morley was born in Haverford, Pennsylvania, in 1890 and died in 1957. He had a long and varied career including that of essayist, poet, and radio personality, and was among the regular staff of contributors to The Saturday Review. *More a household name in his twenties and early thirties, Morley called himself "overpraised in his youth, and underpraised in his maturity." Yet the lively wit and sophisticated humor that made him famous are readily apparent in the following story, with its less-than-respectful echoes of O. Henry's Christmas tale "The Gift of the Magi."*

We had been down to an East Side settlement house on Christmas afternoon. I had watched my friend Dove Dulcet, in moth-riddled scarlet

and cotton wool trimmings, play Santa Claus for several hundred adoring urchins and their parents. He had done this for many years, but I had never before seen him insist on the amiable eccentricity of returning uptown still wearing the regalia of the genial saint. But Dove is always unusual, and I thought—as did the others who saw him, in the subway and elsewhere—it was a rather kindly and innocent concession to the hilarity of the day.

When we had got back to his snug apartment he beamed at me through his snowy fringes of false whisker, and began rummaging in the tall leather boots of his costume. From each one he drew a bottle of chianti.

"From a grateful parent on Mulberry Street," he said. "My favorite bootlegger lives down that way, and I've been playing Santa to his innumerable children for a number of years. The garb attributed—quite inaccurately, I expect—to Saint Nicholas of Bari, has its uses. Even the keenest revenue agent would hardly think of holding up poor old Santa."

He threw off his trappings, piled some logs on the fire, and we sat down for our annual celebration. Dove and I have got into the habit of spending Christmas together. We are both old bachelors, with no close family ties, and we greatly enjoy the occasion. It isn't wholly selfish, either, for we usually manage to spice our fun with a little unexpected charity in some of the less fortunate quarters of the town.

As my friend uncorked the wicker-bound bottles I noticed a great pile of Christmas mail on his table.

"Dove, you odd fish," I said. "Why don't you open your letters? I should have thought that part of the fun of Christmas is hurrying to look through the greetings from friends. Or do you leave them to the last, to give them greater savor?"

He glanced at the heap, with a curious expression on his face.

"The Christmas cards?" he said. "I postpone them as long as I possibly can. It's part of my penance."

"What on earth do you mean?"

He filled two glasses, passed one to me, and sat down beside the cheerful blaze.

"Here's luck, old man!" he said. "Merry Christmas."

I drank with him, but something evasive in his manner impelled me to repeat my question.

"What a ferret you are, Ben!" he said. "Yes, I put off looking at the Christmas cards as long as I dare. I suppose I'll have to tell you. It's one of the few skeletons in my anatomy of melancholy that you haven't exhumed. It's a queer kind of Christmas story."

He reached over to the table, took up a number of the envelopes, and studied their handwritings. He tore them open one after another, and read the enclosed cards.

"As I expected," he said. "Look here, it's no use your trying to make copy out of this yarn. No editor would look at it. It runs counter to all the good old Christmas tradition."

"My dear Dove," I said, "if you've got a Christmas story that's 'different,' you've got something that editors will pay double for."

"Judge for yourself," he said. From the cards in his lap he chose four and gave them to me. "Begin by reading those."

Completely mystified, I did so.

The first showed a blue bird perched on a spray of holly. The verse read:

Our greeting is "Merry Christmas!"
None better could we find,
And tho' you are now out of sight,
You're ever in our mind.

The second card said, below a snow scene of mid-Victorian characters alighting from a stage coach at the hospitable door of a country mansion:

Should you or your folk ever call at our door
You'll be welcome, we promise you—nobody more;
We wish you the best of the Joy and Cheer
That can come with Christmas and last through the year!

The third, with a bright picture of three stout old gentlemen in scarlet waistcoats, tippling before an open fire:

Jolly old Yule, Oh the jolly old Yule
Blesses rich man and poor man and wise man and fool—
Be merry, old friend, in this bright winter weather,
And you'll Yule and I'll Yule, we'll all Yule together!

The fourth—an extremely ornate vellum leaflet, gilded with Oriental designs and magi on camels—ran thus:

I pray the prayer the Easterners do;
May the Peace of Allah abide with you—
Through days of labor and nights of rest
May the love of Allah make you blest.

"Well," I said, "of course I wouldn't call them great poetry, but the sentiments are generous enough. Surely it's the spirit in which they're sent that counts. It doesn't seem like you to make fun—"

Dulcet leaned forward. "Make fun?" he said. "Heavens, I'm not making fun of them. The ghastly thing is, I wrote those myself."

There was nothing to say, so I held my peace.

"You didn't know, I trust, that at one time I was regarded as the snappiest writer of greeting sentiments (so the trade calls them) in the business? That was long ago, but the sentiments themselves, and innumerable imitations of them, go merrily on. You see, out of the first ten cards that I picked up, four are my own composition. Can you imagine the horror of receiving, every Christmas, every New Year, every Easter, every birthday, every Halloween, every Thanksgiving, cards most of which were written by yourself? And when I think of the honest affection with which those cards were chosen for me by my unsuspecting friends, and contrast their loving simplicity with—"

He broke off, and refilled the glasses.

"I told you," he said, "that this was the worst Christmas story in the world! But I must try to tell it a little better, at any rate. Well, it has some of the traditional ingredients.

"You remember the winter of the Great Panic—1906, wasn't it? I had a job in an office downtown, and was laid off. I applied everywhere for work—nothing doing. I had been writing a little on the side, verses and skits for the newspapers, but I couldn't make enough that way to live on. I had an attic in an old lodging house on Gay Street. (The Village was still genuine then, no hokum about it.) I used to reflect on the irony of that name, Gay Street, when I was walking about trying not to see the restaurants, they made me feel so hungry. I still get a queer feeling in the pit of my stomach when I pass by Gonfarone's—there was a fine thick savor of spaghetti and lentil soup that used to float out from the basement as I went along Eighth Street.

"There was a girl in it too, of course. You'll smile when I tell you who she was. Peggy Cassell, who does the magazine covers. Yes, she's prosperous enough now—so are we all. But those were the days!

"It's the old bachelors who are the real sentimentalists, hey? But by Jove, how I adored that girl! She was fresh from upstate somewhere, studying at the League, and doing small illustrating jobs to make ends approach. I was as green and tender as she. I was only twenty-five, you know. To go up to what Peggy called her studio—which was only a bleak bedroom she shared with another girl—and smoke cigarettes and see her wearing a smock and watch her daub away at a thing she intended to be a 'portrait' of me, was my idea of high tide on the seacoast of Bohemia. Peggy would brew cocoa in a chafing dish and then the other girl would tactfully think of some errand, and we'd sit, timidly and uncomfortably, with our arms around each other, and talk about getting married some day, and prove by Cupid's grand old logarithms that two can live cheaper than one. I used to recite to her that ripping old song 'My Peggy is a young thing. And I'm not very auld,' and it would knock us both cold.

"The worst of it was, poor Peggy was almost as hard up as I was. In fact, we were both so hard up that I'm amazed we didn't get married, which is what people usually do when they have absolutely no prospects. But with all her sweet sentiment Peggy had a streak of sound caution. And as a matter of fact, I think she was better off than I was, because she did get a small allowance from home. Anyway, I was nearly desperate, tearing my heart out over the thought of this brave little creature facing the world for the sake of her art, and so on. She complained of the cold, and I remember taking her my steamer rug off my own bed, telling her I was too warm. After that I used to shingle myself over with newspapers when I went to bed. It was bitter on Gay Street that winter.

"But I said this was a Christmas Story. So it is. It began like this. About Hallowe'en I had a little poem in *Life*—nothing of any account, but a great event to me, my first appearance in Big Time journalism. Well, one day I got a letter from a publisher in Chicago asking permission to reprint it on a card. He said also that my verses had just the right touch which was needed in such things, and that I could probably do some 'holiday greetings' for him. He would be glad to see some Christmas 'sentiments,' he said, and would pay one dollar each for any he could use.

"You can imagine that it didn't take me long to begin tearing off sentiments though I stipulated, as a last concession to my honor, that my name should not be used. There was no time to lose: it was now along in November, and these things—to be sold to the public for Christmas a year later—must be submitted as soon as possible so that they could be illustrated and ready for the salesmen to take on the road in January.

"Picture, then, the young author of genial greeting cards, sitting ironically in the chilliest attic on Gay Street—a dim and draughty little elbow of the city—and attempting to ignite his wits with praise of the glowing hearth and the brandied pudding. The room was heated only by a small gas stove, one burner of which had been scientifically sealed by the landlady; an apparatus, moreover, in which asphyxia was the partner of warmth. When that sickly sweetish gust became too overpotent, see the author throw up the window and retire to bed, meditating under a mountain of newsprint further applause of wintry joy and fellowship. I remember one sentiment—very likely it is among the pile on the table here: it is a great favorite—which went:

May blazing log and steaming bowl
And wreaths of mistletoe and holly
Remind you of a kindred soul
Whose love for you is warm and jolly!

"My, how cold it was the night I wrote that."

Dove paused, prodded the logs to a brighter flame, and leaned closer to the chimney as though feeling a reminiscent chill.

"Well, as Christmas itself drew nearer, I became more and more agitated. I had sent in dozens of these compositions; each batch was duly acknowledged, and highly praised. The publisher was pleased to say that I had a remarkable aptitude for 'greetings'; my Christmas line, particularly, he applauded as being full of the robust and hearty spirit of the old-fashioned Yule. My Easter touch, he felt, was a little thin and tepid by comparison. So I redoubled my metrical cheer. I piled the logs higher and higher upon my imaginary hearth; I bore in cups of steaming wassail; blizzards drummed at my baronial window panes; stage coaches were halted by drifts axle-deep; but within the circle of my mid-Victorian halloo, all was mirth: beauty crowded beneath the pale mistletoe; candles threw a tawny shine; the goose was carved and the port wine sparkled. And all the while, if you please, it was December of the panic winter; no check had yet arrived from the delighted publisher; I had laid aside other projects to pursue this golden phantom; I ate once a day, and sometimes kept warm by writing my mellow outbursts of gladness in the steam-heated lobbies of hotels.

"I had said nothing to Peggy about this professional assumption of Christmas heartiness. For one thing, I had talked to her so much, and with such youthful ardor, of my literary ambitions and ideals, that I feared her ridicule; for another, my most eager hope was to surprise her with an opulent Christmas present. She, poor dear, was growing a trifle threadbare, too; she had spoken, now and then, of some sort of fur neckpiece she had seen in shop windows; this, no less, was my secret ambition. And so, as the streets grew brighter with the approach of the day, and still the publisher delayed his remittance, I wrote him a masterly letter. It was couched in the form of a Christmas greeting from me to him; it acknowledged the validity of his contention that he had postponed a settlement because I was still submitting more and more masterpieces and he planned to settle en bloc; but it pointed out the supreme and tragic irony of my having to pass a Christmas in starvation and misery because I had spent so much time dispersing altruistic and factitious good will.

"As I waited anxiously for a reply, I was further disquieted by distressing behavior on Peggy's part. She had been rather strange with me for some time, which I attributed partly to my own shabby appearance and wretched preoccupation with my gruesome task. She had rallied me—some time before—on my mysterious mien, and I may have been clumsy in my retorts. Who can always know just the right accent with which to chaff a woman? At any rate, she had—with some suddenly assumed excuse of propriety—forbidden me the hospitality of her bedroom studio; even my portrait (which we had so blithely imagined as a national triumph in future years when we both stood at the crest of our arts) had been discontinued. We wandered the streets together, quarrelsome and unhappy; we could agree about nothing. In spite of this, I nourished my hopeful secret, still believing that when my check came, and enabled me to mark the Day of Days with the coveted fur, all would be happier than ever.

"It was two days before Christmas, and you may elaborate the picture with all the traditional tints of Dickens pathos. It was cold and snowy and I was hungry, worried, and forlorn. I was walking along Eighth Street wondering whether I could borrow enough money to telegraph to Chicago. Just by the Brevoort I met Peggy, and to my chagrin and despair she was wearing a beautiful new fur neckpiece—a tippet, I think they used to call them in those days. She looked a different girl: her face was pink, her small chin nestled adorably into the fur collar, her eyes were bright and merry. Well, I was only human, and I guess I must have shown my wretched disappointment. Of course she hadn't known that I hoped to surprise her in just that way, and when I blurted out something to that effect, she spoke tartly.

" 'You!' she cried. 'How could you buy me anything like that? I suppose you'd like me to tramp around in the snow all winter and catch my death of cold!'

"In spite of all the Christmas homilies I had written about good will and charity and what not, I lost my temper.

" 'Ah,' I said bitterly, 'I see it all now! I wasn't prosperous enough, so you've found someone else who can afford to buy furs for you. That's why you've kept me away from the studio, eh? You've got some other chap on the string.'

"I can still see her little flushed face, rosy with wind and snow, looking ridiculously stricken as she stood on that wintry corner. She began to say something, but I was hot with the absurd rage of youth. All my weeks of degradation on Gay Street suddenly boiled up in my mind. I was grotesquely melodramatic and absurd.

" 'A rich lover!' I sneered. 'Go ahead and take him! I'll stick to poverty and my ideals. You can have the furs and fleshpots!'

"Well, you never know how a woman will take things. To my utter amazement, instead of flaming up with anger, she burst into tears. But I was too proud and troubled to comfort her.

" 'Yes, you're right,' she sobbed. 'I had such fine dreams, but I couldn't stick it out. I'm not worthy of your ideals. I guess I've sold myself.' She turned and ran away down the slippery street, leaving me flabbergasted.

"I walked around and around Washington Square, not knowing what to do. She had as good as admitted that she had thrown me over for some richer man. And yet I didn't feel like giving her up without a struggle. Perhaps it all sounds silly now, but it was terribly real then.

"At last I went back to Gay Street. On the hall table was a letter from the publisher, with a check for fifty dollars. He had accepted fifty of the hundred or so pieces I had sent, and said if I would consider going to Chicago he would give me a position on his staff as Assistant Greeting Editor. 'Get into a good sound business,' he wrote. 'There will never be a panic in the Greeting line.'

"When I read that letter I was too elated to worry about anything. I would be able to fix things with Peggy somehow. I would say to her, in a melting voice. 'My Peggy is a young thing,' and she would tumble. She must love me still, or she wouldn't have cried. I rushed round to her lodging house, and went right upstairs without giving her a chance to deny me. I knocked, and when she came to the door she looked frightened and ill. She tried to stop me, but I burst in and waved the letter in front of her.

" 'Look at this, Peggy darling!' I shouted. 'We're going to be rich and infamous. I didn't tell you what I was doing, because I was afraid you'd be ashamed of me, after all my talk about high ideals. But anything is better than starving and freezing on Gay Street, or doing without the furs that pretty girls need.'

"She read the letter, and looked up at me with the queerest face.

" 'Now no more nonsense about the other man,' I said. 'I'll buy you a fur for Christmas that'll put his among camphor balls. Who is he, anyway?'

"She surprised me again, for this time she began to laugh.

" 'It's the same one,' she said. 'I mean, the same publisher—your friend in Chicago. Oh Dove, I've been doing drawings for Christmas cards, and I think they must be yours.'

"It was true. Her poor little cold studio was littered with sketches for Christmas drawings—blazing fires and ruddy Georgian squires with tankards of hissing ale and girls in sprigged muslin being coy under the mistletoe. And when she showed me the typewritten verses the publisher had sent her to illustrate, they were mine, sure enough. She had had her check a day sooner than I, and had rushed off to buy herself the fur her heart yearned for.

" 'I was so ashamed of doing the work,' she said—with her head on my waistcoat—'that I didn't dare tell you.' "

Dove sighed, and leaned back in his chair. A drizzle of rain and sleet tinkled on the window pane, but the fire was a core of rosy light.

"Not much of a Christmas story, eh?" he said. "Do you wonder, now, that I hesitate to look back at the cards I wrote and Peggy illustrated?"

"But what happened?" I asked. "It seems a nice enough story as far as you've gone."

"Peggy was a naughty little hypocrite," he said. "I found out that she wasn't really ashamed of illustrating my Greetings at all. She thought they were lovely. She honestly did. And presently she told me she simply couldn't marry a man who would capitalize Christmas. She said it was too sacred."

Merry Christmas

The Snow Too Deep

Oliver La Farge

Oliver La Farge was born in New York in 1901 and died in 1963. A novelist, anthropologist, and scholar noted for his work and studies among Native Americans of the Southwest, he served as president of the American Association of Indian Affairs. He won the Pulitzer Prize in 1929 for his much acclaimed novel Laughing Boy.

hen Consuelo was a little girl Christmas loomed up brilliant long in advance. What she had been told by her older brother and older sisters—especially Carmen, just two years her senior and still free of disillusionment—what she herself remembered, and what she invented in telling her little sister, Pepita, about the delightful sights and experiences of the feast of Christmas all combined as simple fact. The short reach of her memory seemed long, as long as the meaning of "always." It had always happened like this; it always would. And the pleasure of anticipation grew stronger each year. One began thinking of Christmas with the first frosts, along about the time one began thinking of snow and sleds. Another Christmas was on its way, as certain as the seasons themselves. If anyone had suggested that the seasons were uncertain or that Christmas itself might fail, probably she would not have understood, and if she had, more than likely she would have rejected the thought as foolish, or the kind of tasteless humor some grown-ups indulge in.

How it happened that the Bacas developed the magnificent Christmas celebration they did puzzles me. Don José came of a family of purely Spanish descent that was powerful in the region about Las Vegas, New Mexico, on the southern slopes of the Sangre de Cristo Mountains. He must have been reared in a strongly Spanish tradition, and he had something of his ancestors' cultural orientation toward Spain, through Mexico City as the point of linkage and distribution—much as many educated Western Anglo-Americans retain an orientation toward Britain through New York. He procured his bride's wedding chest from the Southern capital and took her there on her honeymoon, and it was there, too, that he later found a governess for his younger daughters. As I have told, although Doña Marguerite grew up at Rociada, she was reared in a strongly French tradition.

One would expect, then, that Don José and Doña Marguerite would delight their children with the songs and processions of the *posadas,* the breaking of *piñatas*—fanciful pottery birds filled with small gifts—or the setting of shoes by the fireplace to receive *étrennes* on New Year's Eve. Actually, apart from Mass on Christmas Day, with its singing of the ancient *alabados*—hymns of praise—the only exotic touch to their celebration was serving tamales in the course of the morning, a pleasant custom to which all New Mexico, Anglo- or Spanish-American, subscribes. For the rest, they observed the Anglo-

Dutch practices centering around Santa Claus and the tree—but without the business of stockings—in a manner to make almost anyone retrospectively envious.

The day before Christmas there would be no sign of tree or gifts; if you did not know for sure, you might wonder if there would be any. The preparations for the huge dinner on Christmas afternoon, however, began days in advance and could not be concealed. Doña Marguerite is a petite, brisk woman with a neat, fast step; the recurrent clicking of her heels when she is at work on a feast is unmistakable. Even in a big house, one would catch the sound, along with her instructions—in Spanish to the maids, in English with occasional spurts of French to her two older daughters—her exclamations of despair over the whole project when something went wrong, occasionally her annoyance, and her helpers answering her in kind and with equal feeling. During these preparations Carmen, Consuelo, and Pepita were in the kitchen as much as they were allowed to be, dainty, black-haired, oval-faced, large-eyed, voracious little creatures savoring a delicious torment.

The indications of great eating to come were titillating in themselves but even more exciting because they were the sign of the greater wonder that would precede the feast. Christmas Eve was quiet; the little girls were full of expectation and on their best behavior. They had supper early, as always, and afterward they passed the evening until bedtime as nearly as possible as on other evenings. At the usual hour they were sent to bed, but on this one night the three of them slept together in a big four-poster, and, moreover, on this night alone Count, the bloodhound, was allowed in the room with them and took his place at the foot of the bed. They thought they would not be able to sleep; they hoped to stay awake. For a time they whispered, but in the end sleep always captured them.

In the dead of night, as it seemed to them—somewhere between ten and eleven o'clock—they were wakened by the loud ringing of sleigh bells, not at a distance on the road but close at hand and overhead. They knew, of course, that the sound came from on top of the roof. They were into slippers and dressing gowns by the time their mother came for them, but just as the traitor drowsiness always overcame them, so they were never quick enough to get downstairs in time to catch a glimpse of Santa Claus.

Behind him, he left the miracle of the Christmas tree, fully expected and yet breath-stopping, so that you had to stand for a moment in the doorway and absorb it before you went in. It was always a fragrant, fresh-cut fir, tall enough almost to touch the ceiling of that high-ceilinged room, decorated, candle-lit, with the presents massed at its foot. And part of the special quality of the occasion came from the fact that it all took place so late at night after that glorious awakening. Soon after Santa Claus had passed by, visitors from the village would begin to drop in for a glass of wine and a bit of fruitcake. These arrivals, usually one man at a time, occasionally a man and wife, out of the snow and cold—the slight stamping inside the door and the removal of outer garments, the gesture of brushing rime off a heavy mustache, the people formal, rustic, and yet socially graceful, Don José's and Doña Marguerite's welcoming Spanish, the faint smell of wine to spice the smells of the tree, the candles, and the fire—were an essential part of Consuelo's impression of the real beginning of Christmas.

That was the way it was, with the day of prayer and fine eating to come after. That was how it had always been and always would be—until the year of the big snow. In the autumn of that year, an exceptionally early snowfall, in the latter part of September, turned the three little girls' thoughts toward Christmas. The snow was gone within twenty-four hours, but then it was unseasonably cold, not only at night but also in the daytime, which was most unusual before December. Don José studied weather reports and the almanacs, talked to Las Vegas on the hand-cranked telephone, and consulted with Señor Juan. When it snowed again before the month was out, and the white covering, thin though it was, lay for over a week in the shade and was slow to melt even on the sunny slopes, he sent a number of teams to the city to bring back a supply of cottonseed cakes.

The Bacas' Wineglass-2 ranch operation was conducted in good part on the land that Doña Marguerite's father had originally owned, grazed under National Forest permits, or leased. It lay within the mountains, which meant that Don José wintered several thousand head of his sheep, his beef herd, and most of his horses on what was properly summer range. The animals were held within fairly easy reach of Rociada, on pastures where trees and cliffs gave shelter and south slopes caught the sun's full strength, and they were carried through that part of the winter during which they could not rustle for themselves by the rich store of hay harvested from the Rociada meadows. As far back as anyone could remember, that had sufficed, but this year the signs were not good.

It started snowing in earnest the second week of October. Sleds and sleighs appeared early. In that favored land it is unusual for snow to last more than a week or so anywhere that the sun strikes, until one passes above the eight-thousand-foot level, but this year the cold held through the brightest days even in the valleys. The nights were bitter. What at first had seemed to the children an early, extra bonus of winter fun became too much of a good thing.

November carried on from where October left off. Several times Amadeo Lobato was a day late with the mail, having been unable to get through with his buggy. Automobiles were little used; they remained in their shelters, their radiators drained. Week by week, the snow grew deeper. Don José was constantly out on horseback, plowing his way to this camp or that, or to the horse pasture, to make sure that the men did not relax their efforts under the conditions they faced. Getting the feed to the various pastures was a constant battle of seizing upon the spells of clear weather to break open the roads—no more than cross-country cart tracks, at best—and then stockpiling as rapidly as possible.

Along in December, Don José began feeding the cottonseed cakes to the animals, to supplement the hay, which otherwise would not last through the long feeding period he foresaw. The animals were not ranging at all; they bunched together in narrow trampled areas where the shelter was best. The mail came through erratically. Other traffic with Las Vegas and the railroad was almost completely stopped. A few men from Rociada village, who still believed that the game laws were nothing but an unwarranted attempt to restrict their traditional rights, and who were hardy enough to fight their way through the drifts, built up their family stocks with snowbound deer and elk.

Consuelo heard her father say that the herders were feeding cakes to the sheep; the idea pleased her. It was nice for the poor sheep out in the frozen distances to be given a little cake. One day when she had made her way to the barn, she examined the stuff. It looked like cake. She asked Juan Grande, who was there, and he said yes, those were *queques.* She took one, turned it over in her hands, examined it. It looked like spicecake and had a promising heaviness. She tried it. It was foul, oily, revolting; she could not spit the stuff out fast enough. It was days before she forgave Juan for laughing at her.

In all other years, on a bright day in mid-December the younger children and Doña Marguerite would take a wagon, or go on foot, driving a burro, to gather what they miscall kinnikinnick. This is a ground vine, known as *toje* in the local Spanish. It has close-massed, shiny dark green leaves and red berries, and makes an excellent substitute for holly. Properly speaking, kinnikinnick is a mixture of the dried leaves and bark of certain plants, used by the Indians (the word is of Algonquian origin) as a substitute for tobacco, or to mix with it. As far as I know, no one smokes the ground vine. The trips for kinnikinnick were picnics, the last of the year—gay occasions, bright with small adventures, charged with the imminence of Christmas. They were the first preparation for the great event. There was no question of any such expedition this year, which was not going like any other. The unchangeable had been changed.

When Doña Marguerite recalls the winter of the big snow, she is likely to speak of what happened to Mr. Goldfarb—"such a nice man, poor thing." Goldfarb's story, in its main outlines, was a classic one of the western frontier—the merchant who came out to the new country with a stock-in-trade he could carry on his back or pack on a single mule and, by intense thrift and drive, built that stake up into a solid business. It differed in that this man came West comparatively late; nonetheless, after twenty industrious years he was within reaching distance of at least modest wealth.

That fall, the prices of sheep and wool were at a record low, as a result of the slump following the First World War, but there were signs that times were improving and that sheep and wool, like other commodities, were due to rise sharply before spring. Goldfarb saw his opportunity. Putting up his store in Las Vegas as security, he raised all the money his credit would stand and invested it in a flock of slightly over three thousand ewes and the corresponding complement of rams, the latter mostly registered stock. To winter them, he leased several miles of good grass on an open, level, almost treeless mesa top south of Las Vegas. Ideally, he should have leased lower country, but in ordinary years sheep wintered well on that range.

The region of Las Vegas is notoriously a place of driving winter winds. That year, the snow-laden winds prowled like a siege of wolves. The coyotes came out of the mountains early, to skulk about the edges of the city and awaken the dogs to frenzy, until the nights were maniacal with barking and the answering, challenging, mocking howls. Out on the open mesas, the snow drove and piled, and there, too, the predators quested.

Goldfarb's herders were simply hired hands. There were no old friendships and family loyalties between him and them to induce them to maintain punishing vigilance despite the whip of the winter. He himself, with his business to run, could not be constantly visiting the camps. Snow, sleet, wind, and cold made the men keep close to their huts and their fires. The sheep drifted, looking for shelter that did not exist, until they fetched up against the fences. By December the covering of ice and snow was too deep for them to scrape through it to grass, and they could not fight through its cold mass to find and browse on those bushes and shrubs that still reached the surface. The snow piled on the animals as they huddled. When God sent a bright, still noon, the snow melted; at sundown it froze into little cloud-colored balls of ice on their wool.

The sheep had to be fed. Goldfarb went to buy hay, as many others were doing. The going price that fall had been fifteen dollars a ton, baled and delivered; suddenly it was sixty dollars and haul it yourself, and he had no more credit. As his sheep hungered and grew weak, the coyotes moved in on them, but the wild beasts could not kill as fast as cold and starvation. Before the month was out, there was nothing left of his twenty years of effort but the frozen carcasses on the mesa.

If the snow was white and cold and deep below Las Vegas, in the mountain valleys it was just as gleamingly white, and colder and deeper. Day after day, Don José and Señor Juan put on their sheepskin-lined jackets, pulled their chaps over their heaviest trousers, muffled the lower part of their faces, and rode out to the camps, to return weary, cold, hungry, with icicles on the mufflers across their mouths. Day after day, the men went up on the roof of the big roadhouse to shovel off snow, and sometimes in the night Consuelo wakened to the sound of the shovels scraping overhead. There was no longer such a thing as a mail day; Amadeo was using a sleigh with a team, and even so he rarely got through to the ranch.

When their parents suggested to the girls that Santa Claus might not be able to make it that year, they did not at first believe it possible that this could happen. It took time for them to accustom themselves to the idea that there could be winters too severe for even a saint who lived at the North Pole to travel through, and to accept the uncertainty of what they had supposed the most certain thing in life. It was an acceptance that did not come easily.

The paths between the big house and the bunkhouse, the commissary, and the barns had become trenches with walls nearly as high as a man's head. The children played in them, exploring a novelty. These, they decided, were what was meant by the word "tunnel." When the sun was out, it made a bright zone along the upper part of one wall; it edged the opposite crest with jewels. Below, the shade was luminous. On a day of overcast, Consuelo, on some errand of her own, stopped midway in a tunnel. With her mittened hand, she scraped at one wall. She decided to make a *nicho,* in which she might set a saint modeled of snow. She scraped away until, her hand getting chilled through the red wool, she stopped to warm it under her armpit. This was the snow that was too deep for Santa Claus. She looked up, considering its depth. Above, the sky was leaden; it made her feel the dead weight of winter and the promise of yet more flakes shortly. It was not the thickness of the cold white blanket that would stop Santa, she decided; it was the whole nature of the season. Without having words for it, she felt the smothering quality of *too much.* The tunnel became desolate. She would not put a saint there, a snow saint, a cold saint. She hurried back to the house.

Ordinarily, the three girls liked to lie in front of the fire evenings and watch the gold sparks that winked and ran through the soot at the back. They called the sparks Indians, and made a game of counting them. Now, without anything being said, they dropped this game. Everything to do with the fireplace was a reminder of Christmas, and the erratic, ascending course of the spark Indians had too often carried their thoughts on, up, and out to the North Pole.

Pino came home from college. He reached Rociada, thanks to a favorable break in the weather. Don José was able to reach Sápello in the sleigh, and Pino got that far from Las Vegas in a car driven by a cousin. Hardly was he in the house before he had on his boots, his chaps, and the rest of his gear to take over some of the burden of patroling the camps. It was time, too, to throw the rams in with the ewes, and under the circumstances the big creatures had to be carted to the flocks.

So far, the stock was wintering well; their shelter was good, and there was adequate feed for them. The principal trouble was with the coyotes raiding the sheep. The coyotes had grown bold, and in the freezing nights the dogs were not always able to keep them off. To the eastward there was a special breed of beasts of prey, descendants of coyotes and a variety of hound that a rancher had imported to hunt them but that had fraternized instead. Pino once described them as the "most marvelous animals" he had ever known.

Don José and Pino decided that Pino could probably get through to Las Vegas by car, so three days before Christmas he set out on a last-minute sortie for green vegetables, celery, fruit, and Christmas gifts for the youngsters. He did get to the city and accomplish his shopping, but on the way back, late in the day, his motor failed on Nine Mile Hill, some forty miles from home, and he had to stay there until a man in a wagon gave him a lift back to Las Vegas, well after sundown. One of his ears was frozen. He got home by relays, on Christmas Eve, virtually empty-handed, with his ear swollen and black. Amadeo had managed another mail delivery that morning.

Carmen, Consuelo, and Pepita by then were in full mourning over the defeat of Santa Claus. They cheered up somewhat when their parents told them that the whole family would have supper together and at the grown-ups' hour. They would eat in the kitchen, Doña Marguerite said, instead of in the dining room, to save fuel. They all sat down—Don José, Doña Marguerite, Pino, and the three little girls. The two older girls, one at college, one at boarding school, had not come home for this holiday. Christmas Eve being a day of fast, the meal was meatless and simple, but good—*chicos, tortitas de huevos, chile colorado* made without meat, and other such fast-day dishes, which are delicacies in themselves. The parents led the conversation around to the variety of Christmas customs among different peoples, and especially to the custom of hanging stockings to be filled by Santa Claus. The girls were interested; the subject, although painful, was fascinating. They discussed the pros and cons of Christmas stockings, and considered the very odd idea, proffered by their mother, that one might have these but no Christmas tree.

When the meal had ended, the family still remained at the table, talking. Suddenly Don José stiffened, listening. Everyone fell silent. "What was that I heard?" he said.

Carmen said immediately, "Sleigh bells!"

They all listened intently. Definitely there was a sound of bells, but was it outside or in the living room? The three girls were out of their chairs instantly. Carmen managed to whisper "Santa" in a way that had the quality of a shout; then they were on the run, through the dining room to the living room, their elders following more sedately. Consuelo was in the lead, because her chair had been nearest the door.

As they broke into the living room, they slowed down, not knowing quite what to expect. There was no tree, but the mantelpiece was rich with boughs and ornaments, and under these hung three of their stockings—the sturdy, long, woolen ones—bulging with gifts. The three little girls went to them almost timidly.

Naturally, they did not notice that all their presents were of the kind usually purchased from the mail-order houses; even had they known enough for that, they would never have thought to scrutinize a miracle. Santa Claus had made it, after all—with a light pack, to be sure, for obvious reasons, but he had made it. When their parents and Pino had had time to express their astonishment, they handed the stockings down to the children. The two maids and Juan Chico, who had not been in the kitchen during supper, came in from the hall and added their exclamations. The children settled down before the fire, blissful with their presents. It was already past their bedtime, but Doña Marguerite said nothing. Shortly, Amadeo and Tomás Lobato knocked at the door, stamping and brushing off snow, and Doña Marguerite sent one of the maids for the fruitcake while Don José brought the decanter of sherry from the dining room. Everything was in order, and Christmas was a certainty after all.

Consuelo went to bed hugging a new fluffy rabbit. Tucked in, she lay feeling the cold that seeped in through the narrow opening at the bottom of the window. She heard the faint thud and squeak of horses plodding in over cold snow, the icy jingle of a spur, and a man's voice speaking wearily. That would be Señor Juan and one of the hands coming in late from a mission to one of the farther camps. She was glad that they would soon be in the warmth. She snuggled farther down in the bed with the rabbit, mentally telling it her secret, a secret more wonderful even than Christmas stockings or gifts. She had been first into the living room, and she had seen—with her own eyes she, and she only, had seen—Santa Claus's red-clad legs and his boots just disappearing up the chimney.

Merry Christmas, Marge!

Alice Childress

Alice Childress was born in Charleston, South Carolina, in 1920. She has had a long and varied career including that of playwright, essayist, novelist, and screenwriter. She joined the American Negro Theater in Harlem in 1940 and has said that no matter what form her writing may take, she is always influenced by the drama. The following entry is one of many conversations between Mildred and her friend Marge. The collected stories were most recently reprinted in 1986 in Like One of the Family: Conversations from a Domestic's Life.

erry Christmas, Marge! Girl, I just want to sit down and catch my breath for a minute. . . . I had a half a day off and went Christmas shopping. Them department stores is just like a madhouse. They had a record playin' real loud all over Crumbleys. . . . "Peace on Earth." Well sir!

I looked 'round at all them scuffling' folks and I begun to wonder. . . . What is peace?

You know Marge, I hear so much talk about peace. I see it written on walls and I hear about it on the radio, and at Christmas time you can't cut 'round the corner without hearin' it blarin' out of every store front. . . . Peace . . . Peace . . . Peace.

Marge, what is peace? . . . Well, you're partly right, it do mean not havin' any wars . . . but I been doin' some deep thinkin' since I left Crumbleys and I been askin' myself. . . . How would things have to be in order for *me* to be at peace with the world? . . . Why thank you, dear. . . . I will take an eggnog. Nobody can make it like you do. . . . That's some good. I tell you.

And it begun to come to my mind. . . . If I had no cause to hate "white folks" that would be good and if I could like most of 'em . . . *that* would be peace. . . . Don't laugh, Marge, 'cause I'm talkin' some deep stuff now!

If I could stand in the street and walk in any direction that my toes was pointin' and go in one of them pretty apartment houses and say, "Give me an apartment please?" and the man would turn and say, "Why, it would be a pleasure, mam. We'll notify you 'bout the first vacancy." . . . That would be peace.

Do you hear me? If I could stride up to any employment agency without havin' the folk at the desk stutterin' and stammerin'. . . . *That,* my friend, would be peace also. If I could ride a subway or a bus and not see any signs pleadin' with folks to be "tolerant" . . . "regardless" of what I am . . . I know that would be peace 'cause then there would be no need for them signs.

If you and me could have a cool glass of lemonade or a hot cup of coffee anywhere . . . and I mean *anywhere* . . . wouldn't that be peace? If all these little children 'round here had their mamas takin' care of them instead of other folks' children . . . that would be peace, too. . . . Hold on, Marge! Go easy on that eggnog . . . it goes to my head so fast. . . .

Oh yes, if nobody wanted to kill nobody else and I could pick up a newspaper and not read 'bout my folks gettin' the short end of every stick . . . that would mean more peace.

If all mamas and daddies was sittin' back safe and secure in the knowledge that they'd have toys and goodies for their children . . . that would bring on a little more peace. If eggs and butter would stop flirtin' 'round the dollar line, I would also consider that a peaceful sign. . . . Oh, darlin' let's don't talk 'bout the meat!

Yes girl! You are perfectly right. . . . If our menfolk would *make* over us a little more, THAT would be peaceful, too.

When all them things are fixed up the way I want 'em I'm gonna spend one peaceful Christmas . . . and do you know what I'd do? . . . Look Marge . . . I told you now, don't give me too much of that eggnog. . . . My dear, I'd catch me a plane for Alageorgia somewhere and visit all my old friends and we'd go 'round from door to door hollerin' "Christmas Gift!" Then we'd go down to Main Street and ride front, middle, and rear on the street-car and the "whitefolk" would wave and cry out, "Merry Christmas, neighbors!" . . . Oh hush now! . . . They would do this because they'd understand *peace.*

And we'd all go in the same church and afterwards we'd all go in the same movie and see Lena Horne actin' and singin' all the way through a picture. . . . I'd have to visit a school so that I could see a black teacher teachin' white kids . . . an' when I see this . . . I'll sing out . . . Peace, it's *truly* wonderful!

Then I'd go and watch the black Governor and the white Mayor unveiling a bronze statue of Frederick Douglass and John Brown shakin' hands. . . .

When I was ready to leave, I'd catch me a pullman back to New York. . . . Now that's what you'd call "sleepin' in heavenly peace." When I got home the bells and the horns would be ringin' and tootin' "Happy New Year!" . . . and there wouldn't be no mothers mournin' for their soldier sons. . . . Children would be prancin' 'round and ridin' Christmas sleds through the sparklin' snow . . . and the words "lynch," "murder," and "kill" would be crossed out of every dictionary . . . and nobody would write peace on no walls . . . 'cause it would *be* peace . . . and our hearts would be free!

What? . . . No, I ain't crazy, either! All that is gonna happen

. . . just as sure as God made little apples! I promise you that! . . . and do you know who's gonna be here to see it? *Me* girl . . . yes, your friend Mildred! Let's you and me have another eggnog on that. . . . Here's to it. MERRY XMAS Marge! PEACE!

SOMETHING GOOD SHOULD COME FROM THIS!
CHRISTMAS GREETINGS

The Three Wise Guys

Damon Runyon

Damon Runyon was born in 1884 and died in 1946. Famous for his contributions to the American literary scene as both journalist and short story author, Runyon's work served to lay the foundation for much of what we consider "modern" fiction. As seen in the following story, with its realistic, first-person narrative, use of the present tense, and brilliant humor, Runyon survives as a modern voice in a modern age.

An exciting Christmas story which will greatly surprise those citizens who have been wondering what became of Miss Clarabelle Cobb, who was once the town's most beautiful doll

One cold winter afternoon I am standing at the bar in Good Time Charley's little drum in West 49th Street, partaking of a mixture of rock candy and rye whisky, and this is a most surprising thing for me to be doing, as I am by no means a rumpot, and very seldom indulge in alcoholic beverages in any way, shape, manner, or form.

But when I step into Good Time Charley's on the afternoon in question, I am feeling as if maybe I have a touch of grippe coming on, and Good Time Charley tells me that there is nothing in this world as good for a touch of grippe as rock candy and rye whisky, as it assassinates the germs at once.

It seems that Good Time Charley always keeps a stock of rock candy and rye whisky on hand for touches of the grippe, and he gives me a few doses immediately, and in fact Charley takes a few doses with me, as he says there is no telling but what I am scattering germs of my touch of the grippe all around the joint, and he must safeguard his health. We are both commencing to feel much better when the door opens, and who comes in but a guy by the name of Blondy Swanson.

This Blondy Swanson is a big, six-foot-two guy, with straw-colored hair, and pink cheeks, and he is originally out of Harlem, and it is well known to one and all that in his day he is the largest puller on the Atlantic seaboard. In fact, for upwards of ten years, Blondy is bringing wet goods into New York from Canada, and one place and another, and in all this time he never gets a fall, which is considered a phenomenal record for an operator as extensive as Blondy.

Well, Blondy steps up alongside me at the bar, and I ask him if he cares to have a few doses of rock candy and rye whisky with me and Good Time Charley, and Blondy says he will consider it a privilege and a pleasure, because, he says, he always has something of a sweet tooth. So we have these few doses, and I say to Blondy Swanson that I hope and trust that business is thriving with him.

"I have no business," Blondy Swanson says, "I retire from business."

Well, if J. Pierpont Morgan, or John D. Rockefeller, or Henry Ford step up and tell me they retire from business, I will not be more astonished than I am by this statement from Blondy Swanson, and in fact not as much. I consider Blondy's statement the most important commercial announcement I hear in many years, and naturally I ask him why he makes such a decision, and what is to become of thousands of citizens who are dependent on him for merchandise.

"Well," Blondy says, "I retire from business because I am one hundred per cent American citizen. In fact," he says, "I am a patriot. I serve my country in the late war. I am cited at Château-Thierry. I always vote the straight Democratic ticket, except," he says, "when we figure it better to elect some Republican. I always stand up when the band plays 'The Star-Spangled Banner.' One year I even pay an income tax," Blondy says.

And of course I know that many of these things are true, although I remember hearing rumors that if the draft officer is along half an hour later than he is, he will not see Blondy for heel dust, and that what Blondy is cited for at Château-Thierry is for not robbing the dead.

But of course I do not speak of these matters to Blondy Swanson, because Blondy is not such a guy as will care to listen to rumors, and may become indignant, and when Blondy is indignant he is very difficult to get along with.

"Now," Blondy says, "I am a bootie for a long time, and supply very fine merchandise to my trade, as everybody knows, and it is a respectable business, because one and all in this country are in favor of it, except the prohibitionists. But," he says, "I can see into the future, and I can see that one of these days they are going to repeal the prohibition law, and then it will be most unpatriotic to be bringing in wet goods from foreign parts in competition with home industry. So I retire," Blondy says.

"Well, Blondy," I say, "your sentiments certainly do you credit, and if we have more citizens as high minded as you are, this will be a better country."

"Furthermore," Blondy says, "there is no money in booting any more. All the booties in this country are broke. I am broke myself," he says. "I just lose the last piece of property I own in the world, which is the twenty-five-G home I build in Atlantic City, figuring to spend the rest of my days there with Miss Clarabelle Cobb, before she takes a runout powder on me. Well," Blondy says, "if I only listen to Miss Clarabelle Cobb, I will now be an honest clerk in a gents' furnishings store, with maybe a cute little apartment up around 110th

Street, and children running all around and about."

And with this, Blondy sighs heavily, and I sigh with him, because the romance of Blondy Swanson and Miss Clarabelle Cobb is well known to one and all on Broadway.

It goes back a matter of anyway six years when Blondy Swanson is making money so fast he can scarcely stop to count it, and at this time Miss Clarabelle Cobb is the most beautiful doll in this town, and many citizens almost lose their minds just gazing at her when she is a member of Mr. Georgie White's Scandals, including Blondy Swanson.

In fact, after Blondy Swanson sees Miss Clarabelle Cobb in just one performance of Mr. Georgie White's Scandals, he is never quite the same guy again. He goes to a lot of bother meeting up with Miss Clarabelle Cobb, and then he takes to hanging out around Mr. Georgie White's stage door, and sending Miss Clarabelle Cobb ten-pound boxes of candy, and floral horseshoes, and wreaths, and also packages of trinkets, including such articles as diamond bracelets, and brooches, and vanity cases, for there is no denying that Blondy is a fast guy with a dollar.

But it seems that Miss Clarabelle Cobb will not accept any of these offerings, except the candy and the flowers, and she goes so far as to return a sable coat that Blondy sends her one very cold day, and she is openly criticized for this action by some of the other dolls in Mr. Georgie White's Scandals, for they say that after all there is a limit even to eccentricity.

But Miss Clarabelle Cobb states that she is not accepting valuable offerings from any guy, and especially a guy who is engaged in trafficking in the demon rum, because she says that his money is nothing but blood money that comes from breaking the law of the land, although, as a matter of fact, this is a dead wrong rap against Blondy Swanson, as he never handles a drop of rum in his life, but only Scotch, and furthermore he keeps himself pretty well straightened out with the law.

The idea is, Miss Clarabelle Cobb comes of very religious people back in Akron, Ohio, and she is taught from childhood that rum is a terrible thing, and personally I think it is myself, except in cocktails, and furthermore, the last thing her mamma tells her when she leaves for New York is to beware of any guys who come around offering her diamond bracelets and fur coats, because her mamma says such guys are undoubtedly snakes in the grass, and probably on the make.

But while she will not accept his offerings, Miss Clarabelle Cobb does not object to going out with Blondy Swanson now and then, and putting on the chicken Mexicaine, and the lobster Newburg, and other items of this nature, and any time you put a good-looking young guy and a beautiful doll together over the chicken Mexicaine and the lobster Newburg often enough, you are apt to have a case of love on your hands.

And this is what happens to Blondy Swanson and Miss Clarabelle Cobb, and in fact they become in love more than somewhat, and Blondy Swanson is wishing to marry Miss Clarabelle Cobb, but one night over a batch of lobster Newburg, she says to him like this:

"Blondy," she says, "I love you, and," she says, "I will marry you in a minute if you get out of trafficking in rum. I will marry you if you are out of the rum business, and do not have a dime, but I will never marry you as long as you are dealing in rum, no matter if you have a hundred million."

Well, Blondy says he will get out of the racket at once, and he keeps saying this every now and then for a year or so, and the chances are that several times he means it, but when a guy is in this business in those days as strong as Blondy Swanson it is not so easy for him to get out, even if he wishes to do so. And then one day Miss Clarabelle Cobb has a talk with Blondy, and says to him as follows:

"Blondy," she says, "I still love you, but you care more for your business than you do for me. So I am going back to Ohio," she says. "I am sick and tired of Broadway, anyhow. Some day when you are really through with the terrible traffic you are now engaged in, come to me."

And with this, Miss Clarabelle Cobb takes plenty of outdoors on Blondy Swanson, and is seen no more in these parts. At first Blondy thinks she is only trying to put a little pressure on him, and will be back, but as the weeks become months, and the months finally count up into years, Blondy can see that she is by no means clowning with him. Furthermore, he never hears from her, and all he knows is she is back in Akron, Ohio.

Well, Blondy is always promising himself that he will soon pack in on hauling wet goods, and go look up Miss Clarabelle Cobb and marry her, but he keeps putting it off, and putting it off, until finally one day he hears that Miss Clarabelle Cobb marries some legitimate guy in Akron, and this is a terrible blow to Blondy, indeed, and from this day he never looks at another doll again, or anyway not much.

Naturally, I express my deep sympathy to Blondy about being broke, and I also mention that my heart bleeds for him in his loss of Miss Clarabelle Cobb, and we have a few doses of rock candy and rye whisky on both propositions, and by this time Good Time Charley runs out of rock candy, and anyway it is a lot of bother for him to be mixing it up with the rye whisky, so we have the rye whisky without the rock candy, and personally I do not notice much difference.

Well, while we are standing there at the bar having our rye whisky without the rock candy, who comes in but an old guy by the name of The Dutchman, who is known to one and all as a most illegal character in every respect. In fact, The Dutchman has no standing whatever in the community, and I am somewhat surprised to see him appear in Good Time Charley's, because The Dutchman is generally a lammie from some place, and the gendarmes everywhere are always anxious to have a chat with him. The last I hear of The Dutchman he is in college somewhere out West for highway robbery, although afterwards he tells me it is a case of mistaken identity. It seems he mistakes a copper in plain clothes for a groceryman.

The Dutchman is an old-fashioned looking guy of maybe fifty-odd, and he has gray hair, and a stubby gray beard, and he is short, and thickset, and always good-natured, even when there is no call for it, and to look at him you will think there is no more harm in him than there is in a preacher, and maybe not as much.

As The Dutchman comes in, he takes a peek all around and about as if he is looking for somebody in particular, and when he sees

Blondy Swanson he moves up alongside Blondy and begins whispering to Blondy until Blondy pulls away and tells him to speak freely.

Now The Dutchman has a very interesting story, and it goes like this: it seems that about eight or nine months back The Dutchman is mobbed up with a party of three very classy heavy guys who make quite a good thing of going around knocking off safes in small-town jugs, and post offices, and stores in small towns, and taking the money, or whatever else is valuable in these safes. This is once quite a popular custom in this country, although it dies out to some extent of late years because they improve the brand of safes so much it is a lot of bother knocking them off, but it comes back during the depression when there is no other way of making money, until it is a very prosperous business again. And of course this is very nice for old-time heavy guys, such as The Dutchman, because it gives them something to do in their old age.

Anyway, it seems that this party The Dutchman is with goes over into Pennsylvania one night on a tip from a friend and knocks off a safe in a factory office, and gets a pay roll amounting to maybe fifty G's. But it seems that while they are making their getaway in an automobile, the gendarmes take out after them, and there is a chase, during which there is considerable blasting back and forth.

Well, finally in this blasting, the three guys with The Dutchman get cooled off, and The Dutchman also gets shot up quite some, and he abandons the automobile out on an open road, taking the money, which is in a gripsack, with him, and he somehow manages to escape the gendarmes by going across country, and hiding here and there.

But The Dutchman gets pretty well petered out, what with his wounds, and trying to lug the gripsack, and one night he comes to an old deserted barn, and he decides to stash the gripsack in this barn, because there is no chance he can keep lugging it around much longer. So he takes up a few boards in the floor of the barn, and digs a nice hole in the ground underneath and plants the gripsack there, figuring to come back some day and pick it up.

Well, The Dutchman gets over into New Jersey one way and another, and lays up in a town by the name of New Brunswick until his wounds are healed, which requires considerable time as The Dutchman cannot take it nowadays as good as he can when he is younger.

Furthermore, even after The Dutchman recovers and gets to thinking of going after the stashed gripsack, he finds he is about half out of confidence, which is what happens to all guys when they commence getting old, and he figures that it may be a good idea to declare somebody else in to help him, and the first guy he thinks of is Blondy Swanson, because he knows Blondy Swanson is a very able citizen in every respect.

"Now, Blondy," The Dutchman says, "if you like my proposition, I am willing to cut you in for fifty per cent, and fifty per cent of fifty G's is by no means pretzels in these times."

"Well, Dutchman," Blondy says, "I will gladly assist you in this enterprise on the terms you state. It appeals to me as a legitimate proposition, because there is no doubt this dough is coming to you, and from now on I am strictly legit. But in the meantime, let us have some more rock candy and rye whisky, without the rock candy, while we discuss the matter further."

But it seems that The Dutchman does not care for rock candy and rye whisky, even without the rock candy, so Blondy Swanson and me and Good Time Charley continue taking our doses, and Blondy keeps getting more enthusiastic about The Dutchman's proposition until finally I become enthusiastic myself, and I say I think I will go along as it is an opportunity to see new sections of the country, while Good Time Charley states that it will always be the great regret of his life that his business keeps him from going, but that he will provide us with an ample store of rock candy and rye whisky, without the rock candy, in case we run into any touches of the grippe.

Well, anyway, this is how I come to be riding around in an old can belonging to The Dutchman on a very cold Christmas Eve with The Dutchman and Blondy Swanson, although none of us happen to think of it being Christmas Eve until we notice that there seems to be holly wreaths in windows here and there as we go bouncing along the roads, and finally we pass a little church that is all lit up, and somebody opens the door as we are passing, and we see a big Christmas tree inside the church, and it is a very pleasant sight, indeed, and in fact it makes me a little homesick, although of course the chances are I will not be seeing any Christmas trees even if I am home.

We leave Good Time Charley's along mid-afternoon, with The Dutchman driving this old can of his, and all I seem to remember about the trip is going through a lot of little towns so fast they seem strung together, because most of the time I am dozing in the back seat.

Blondy Swanson is riding in the front seat with The Dutchman and Blondy also cops a little snooze now and then as we are going along, but whenever he happens to wake up he pokes me awake, too, so we can take a dose of rock candy and rye whisky, without the rock candy. So in many respects it is quite an enjoyable journey.

I recollect the little church because we pass it right after we go busting through a pretty fair-sized town, and I hear The Dutchman say the old barn is now only a short distance away, and by this time it is dark, and colder than a deputy sheriff's heart, and there is snow on the ground, although it is clear overhead, and I am wishing I am back in Mindy's restaurant wrapping myself around a nice T-bone steak, when I hear Blondy Swanson ask The Dutchman if he is sure he knows where he is going, as this seems to be an untraveled road, and The Dutchman states as follows:

"Why," he says, "I know I am on the right road. I am following the big star you see up ahead of us, because I remember seeing this star always in front of me when I am going along this road before."

So we keep following the star, but it turns out that it is not a star at all, but a light shining from the window of a ramshackle old frame building pretty well off to one side of the road and on a rise of ground, and when The Dutchman sees this light, he is greatly nonplussed, indeed, and speaks as follows:

"Well," he says, "this looks very much like my barn, but my barn does not call for a light in it. Let us investigate this matter before we go any farther."

So The Dutchman gets out of the old can, and slips up to one side of the building and peeks through the window, and then he comes back and motions for Blondy and me to also take a peek through this window, which is nothing but a square hole cut in the side of the building with wooden bars across it, but no window panes, and what we behold inside by the dim light of a lantern hung on a nail on a post is really most surprising.

There is no doubt whatever that we are looking at the inside of a very old barn, for there are several stalls for horses, or maybe cows, here and there, but somebody seems to be living in the barn, as we can see a table, and a couple of chairs, and a tin stove, in which there is a little fire, and on the floor in one corner is what seems to be a sort of a bed.

Furthermore, there seems to be somebody lying on the bed and making quite a fuss in the way of groaning and crying and carrying on generally in a loud tone of voice, and there is no doubt that it is the voice of a doll, and anybody can tell that this doll is in some distress.

Well, here is a situation, indeed, and we move away from the barn to talk it over.

The Dutchman is greatly discouraged, because he gets to thinking that if this doll is living in the barn for any length of time, his plant may be discovered. He is willing to go away and wait awhile, but Blondy Swanson seems to be doing quite some thinking, and finally Blondy says like this:

"Why," Blondy says, "the doll in this barn seems to be sick, and only a bounder and a cad will walk away from a sick doll, especially," Blondy says, "a sick doll who is a total stranger to him. In fact, it will take a very large heel to do such a thing. The idea is for us to go inside and see if we can do anything for this sick doll," Blondy says.

Well, I say to Blondy Swanson that the chances are the doll's ever-loving husband, or somebody, is in town, or maybe over to the nearest neighbors digging up assistance, and will be back in a jiffy, and that this is no place for us to be found.

"No," Blondy says, "it cannot be as you state. The snow on the ground is anyway a day old. There are no tracks around the door of this old joint, going or coming, and it is a cinch if anybody knows there is a sick doll here, they will have plenty of time to get help before this. I am going inside and look things over," Blondy says.

Naturally, The Dutchman and I go, too, because we do not wish to be left alone outside, and it is no trouble whatever to get into the barn, as the door is unlocked, and all we have to do is walk in. And when we walk in with Blondy Swanson leading the way, the doll on the bed on the floor half raises up to look at us, and although the light of the lantern is none too good, anybody can see that this doll is nobody but Miss Clarabelle Cobb, although personally I see some change in her since she is in Mr. Georgie White's Scandals.

She stays half raised up on the bed looking at Blondy Swanson for as long as you can count ten, if you count fast, then she falls back and starts crying and carrying on again, and at this The Dutchman kneels down on the floor beside her to find out what is eating her.

All of a sudden The Dutchman jumps up and speaks to us as follows:

"Why," he says, "this is quite a delicate situation, to be sure. In fact," he says, "I must request you guys to step outside. What we really need for this case is a doctor, but it is too late to send for one. However, I will endeavor to do the best I can under the circumstances."

Then The Dutchman starts taking off his overcoat, and Blondy Swanson stands looking at him with such a strange expression on his kisser that The Dutchman laughs out loud, and says like this:

"Do not worry about anything, Blondy," The Dutchman says. "I am maybe a little out of practice since my old lady put her checks back in the rack, but she leaves eight kids alive and kicking, and I bring them all in except one, because we are seldom able to afford a croaker."

So Blondy Swanson and I step out of the barn and after a while The Dutchman calls us and we go back into the barn to find he has a big fire going in the stove, and the place nice and warm.

Miss Clarabelle Cobb is now all quieted down, and is covered with The Dutchman's overcoat, and as we come in The Dutchman tiptoes over to her and pulls back the coat and what do we see but a baby with a noggin no bigger than a crab apple and a face as wrinkled as some old pappy guy's, and The Dutchman states that it is a boy, and a very healthy one, at that.

"Furthermore," The Dutchman says, "the mamma is doing as well as can be expected. She is as strong a doll as ever I see," he says, "and all we have to do now is send out a croaker when we go through town just to make sure there are no complications. But," The Dutchman says, "I guarantee the croaker will not have much to do."

Well, the old Dutchman is as proud of this baby as if it is his own, and I do not wish to hurt his feelings, so I say the baby is a darberoo, and a great credit to him in every respect, and also to Miss Clarabelle Cobb, while Blondy Swanson just stands there looking at it as if he never sees a baby before in his life, and is greatly astonished.

It seems that Miss Clarabelle Cobb is a very strong doll, just as The Dutchman states, and in about an hour she shows signs of being wide awake, and Blondy Swanson sits down on the floor beside her, and she talks to him quite a while in a low voice, and while they are talking The Dutchman pulls up the floor in another corner of the barn, and digs around underneath a few minutes, and finally comes up with a gripsack covered with dirt, and he opens this gripsack and shows me it is filled with lovely, large coarse banknotes.

Later Blondy Swanson tells The Dutchman and me the story of Miss Clarabelle Cobb, and parts of this story are rather sad. It seems that after Miss Clarabelle Cobb goes back to her old house in Akron, Ohio, she winds up marrying a young guy by the name of Joseph Hatcher, who is a bookkeeper by trade, and has a pretty good job in Akron, so Miss Clarabelle Cobb and this Joseph Hatcher are as happy as anything together for quite a spell.

Then about a year before the night I am telling about, Joseph Hatcher is sent by his firm to these parts where we find Miss Clarabelle Cobb, to do the bookkeeping in a factory there, and one night a few months afterwards, when Joseph Hatcher is staying after hours in the factory office working on his books, a mob of wrong gees breaks into the joint, and sticks him up, and blows open the safe, taking away a large sum of money and leaving Joseph Hatcher tied up like a turkey.

When Joseph Hatcher is discovered in this predicament the next morning, what happens but the gendarmes put the sleeve on him, and place him in the pokey, saying the chances are Joseph Hatcher is in and in with the safe blowers, and that he tips them off the dough is in the safe, and it seems that the guy who is especially fond of this idea is a guy by the name of Ambersham, who is manager of the factory, and a very hard-hearted guy, at that.

And now, although this is eight or nine months back, there is Joseph Hatcher still in the pokey awaiting trial, and it is 7 to 5 anywhere in town that the judge throws the book at him when he finally goes to bat, because it seems from what Miss Clarabelle Cobb tells Blondy Swanson that nearly everybody figures Joseph Hatcher is guilty.

But of course Miss Clarabelle Cobb does not put in with popular opinion about her ever-loving Joe, and she spends the next few months trying to spring him from the pokey, but she has no potatoes, and no way of getting any potatoes, so things go from bad to worse with Miss Clarabelle Cobb.

Finally, she finds herself with no place to live in town, and she happens to run into this old barn, which is on an abandoned property owned by a doctor in town by the name of Kelton, and it seems that he is a kind-hearted guy, and he gives her permission to use it any way she wishes. So Miss Clarabelle moves into the barn, and the chances are there is many a time when she wishes she is back in Mr. Georgie White's Scandals.

Now The Dutchman listens to this story with great interest, especially the part about Joseph Hatcher being left tied up in the factory office, and finally The Dutchman states as follows:

"Why, my goodness," The Dutchman says, "there is no doubt but what this is the very same young guy we are compelled to truss up the night we get this gripsack. As I recollect it, he wishes to battle for his employer's dough, and I personally tap him over the coco with a blackjack.

"But," he says, "he is by no means the guy who tips us off about the dough being there. As I remember it now, it is nobody but the guy whose name you mention in Miss Clarabelle Cobb's story. It is this guy Ambersham, the manager of the joint, and come to think of it, he is supposed to get his bit of this dough for his trouble, and it is only fair that I carry out this agreement as the executor of the estate of my late comrades, although," The Dutchman says, "I do not approve of his conduct toward this Joseph Hatcher. But," he says, "the first thing for us to do is to get a doctor out here to Miss Clarabelle Cobb, and I judge the doctor for us to get is this Doc Kelton she speaks of."

So The Dutchman takes the gripsack and we get into the old can and head back the way we come, although before we go I see Blondy Swanson bend down over Miss Clarabelle Cobb, and while I do not wish this to go any farther, I will take a paralyzed oath I see him plant a small kiss on the baby's noggin, and I hear Miss Clarabelle Cobb speak as follows:

"I will name him for you, Blondy," she says. "By the way, Blondy, what is your right name?"

"Olaf," Blondy says.

It is now along in the early morning and not many citizens are stirring as we go through town again, with Blondy in the front seat again holding the gripsack on his lap so The Dutchman can drive, but finally we find a guy in an all-night lunch counter who knows where Doc Kelton lives, and this guy stands on the running board of the old can and guides us to a house in a side street, and after pounding on the door quite a spell, we roust the Doc out and Blondy goes inside to talk with him.

He is in there quite a spell, but when he comes out he says everything is okay, and that Doc Kelton will go at once to look after Miss Clarabelle Cobb, and take her to a hospital, and Blondy states that he leaves a couple of C's with the Doc to make sure Miss Clarabelle Cobb gets the best of care.

"Well," The Dutchman says, "we can afford a couple of C's out of what we have in this gripsack, but," he says, "I am still wondering if it is not my duty to look up this Ambersham, and give him his bit."

"Dutchman," Blondy says, "I fear I have some bad news for you.

The gripsack is gone. This Doc Kelton strikes me as a right guy in every respect, especially," Blondy says, "as he states to me that he always half suspects there is a wrong rap in on Miss Clarabelle Cobb's ever-loving Joe, and that if it is not for this guy Ambersham agitating all the time other citizens may suspect the same thing, and it will not be so tough for Joe.

"So," Blondy says, "I tell Doc Kelton the whole story, about Ambersham and all, and I take the liberty of leaving the gripsack with him to be returned to the rightful owners, and Doc Kelton says if he does not have Miss Clarabelle Cobb's Joe out of the sneezer, and this Ambersham on the run out of town in twenty-four hours, I can call him a liar. But," Blondy says, "let us now proceed on our way, because I only have Doc Kelton's word that he will give us twelve hours' leeway before he does anything except attend to Miss Clarabelle Cobb, as I figure you need this much time to get out of sight, Dutchman."

Well, The Dutchman does not say anything about all this news for a while, and seems to be thinking the situation over, and while he is thinking he is giving his old can a little more gas than he intends, and she is fairly popping along what seems to be the main drag of the town when a gendarme on a motorcycle comes up alongside us, and motions The Dutchman to pull over to the curb.

He is a nice-looking young gendarme, but he seems somewhat hostile as he gets off his motorcycle, and walks up to us very slow, and asks us where the fire is.

Naturally, we do not say anything in reply, which is the only thing to say to a gendarme under these circumstances, so he speaks as follows:

"What are you guys carrying in this old skillet, anyway?" he says. "Stand up, and let me look you guys over."

And then as we stand up, he peeks into the front and back of the car, and under our feet, and all he finds is a bottle which once holds some of Good Time Charley's rock candy and rye whisky without the rock candy, but which is now very empty, and he holds this bottle up, and sniffs at the nozzle, and asks what is formerly in this bottle, and

I tell him the truth when I tell him it is once full of medicine, and The Dutchman and Blondy Swanson nod their heads in support of my statement. But the gendarme takes another sniff, and then he says like this:

"Oh," he says, very sarcastic, "wise guys, eh? Three wise guys, eh? Trying to kid somebody, eh? Medicine, eh?" he says. "Well, if it is not Christmas Day I will take you in and hold you just on suspicion. But I will be Santa Claus to you, and let you go ahead, wise guys."

And then after we get a few blocks away, The Dutchman speaks as follows:

"Yes," he says, "that is what we are, to be sure. We are wise guys. If we are not wise guys, we will still have the gripsack in this car for the copper to find. And if the copper finds the gripsack, he will wish to take us to the jail house for investigation, and if he wishes to take us there I fear he will not be alive at this time, and we will be in plenty of heat around and about, and personally," The Dutchman says, "I am sick and tired of heat."

And with this The Dutchman puts a large Betsy back in a holster under his left arm, and turns on the gas, and as the old can begins leaving the lights of the town behind, I ask Blondy if he happens to notice the name of this town.

"Yes," Blondy says, "I notice it on a signboard we just pass. It is Bethlehem, Pa."

Greetings

STRANGE STORY OF A TRAVELER TO BETHLEHEM

John Evans

John Evans was the religious editor of the Chicago Tribune *when he wrote "Strange Story of a Traveler to Bethlehem." First published in that paper on Christmas Day, 1943, the dateline read: "Bethlehem, Judea, December 25—In the 36th Year of the Reign of Herod—Special." It was later included in Dr. Evans' book* I Saw His Glory, *published in 1943.*

ur caravan was rerouted at Gaza as it proceeded northward to accommodate my employer, Eleazar, a rich Jewish glass merchant of Alexandria, who had to deliver some luxury merchandise to customers in the new Zion district of Jerusalem in time for a winter festival.

But here we are, stalled in this miserable village of Bethlehem. Eleazar thinks the crowds which held us up will slacken so that we can proceed tomorrow. Seldom do caravans travel northward along this route. Usually they travel the coastal plain, but despite nasty weather here in this rock pile of a country there is fascination in this historic land, even for a Roman.

Ostensibly, the crowds stalling us here are en route to a Roman census taking; but Eleazar, with a wink, spoke of today's anniversary of the country's liberation a century and a half ago from the tyranny of Syrian-Greek despotism. Even my tolerant country does not like any of its mandated peoples to remember their past victories too well.

Since we left the coastal route our troubles mostly were this incessant drizzle, chill winds, fog. The cold penetrates to the marrow, but last night's strange incident, together with Eleazar's stories about his peculiar people, has made up for some of the discomfort.

Eleazar, now on what he calls his last pilgrimage to the city of his fathers, warned against expectation of hospitality by his people here in Judea. They will be distant and aloof, he said, but he told me of their traditions in a way which made one feel a kindly sympathy for those who remained here in this desolate and unproductive land in order to conserve a rich cultural and religious tradition reaching back more than a thousand years.

Here, off all main trade routes, and by holding firm against all outside influences, the garden of tradition blooms where nothing else will grow. Eleazar said the temple at Jerusalem really supports the whole of Judea. In addition to being a religious center it is virtually a bank with its own coinage, a very rich institution that conquerors would like to plunder. Part of its wealth comes from exchange fees, for sacrificial animals must be purchased in temple coins.

But Eleazar explained with a shrug that our caravan would be as comfortable in the open as in these leaky, mud-roofed houses. He added that Jerusalem will hang out no welcome sign to me, a Roman on unofficial business. You see, he said, the sphere of influence of Rome is constantly widening just as that of Macedonian Greece did a couple of centuries ago. A bitter war and incredible feats of heroism by a few followers of a man they called "The Hammerer" were necessary to the freedom of this tiny religious commonwealth.

Now another conflict looms as the people on today's festival recall "The Hammerer's" exploits and look to the dynasty he established. Even though the Roman senate set up Herod's present throne in part to end that dynasty, the wily Herod married into "The Hammerer's" line. Herod is a sort of naturalized Jew, but is really a descendant of the hated Edomites.

How Judea hates this "Edomite slave" who rules over it! But he has kept the land peaceful and reasonably prosperous. Did he not keep Judea out of the hands of Cleopatra, and did he not quell the rebellion in Galilee with an iron hand? And did he not rebuild the temple and fortify Jerusalem impregnably against any possible attack?

Yes, but did he not rebuild Samaria into a hated Greek city, and help build pagan temples elsewhere? But his wickedness and pagan spirit are now catching up with him. He spends more and more time each year at Callirrhoe Hot Springs and is sick most of the time. His jealousies are becoming furious.

Recently he became suspicious of the ambitions of his sons, who, through their mother, are members of "The Hammerer's" dynasty and he is not. He summarily recalled them from Rome and executed his own sons, as he put their mother to death twenty-two years ago. Herod strikes instantly and ruthlessly when he thinks his power is threatened.

A few days ago he was unbelievably cruel. He sentenced some tiny infants to death because he had heard mere rumors from eastern travelers that the foretold time had come for a son to be born in the great David's dynasty. Tradition said this king would be God's anointed and would set up universal reign, even over Rome!

But with all his violent tempers and cruelty, the people are worried about what will happen when he dies. From accounts of his sickness, that time is not far off. Will the country then suffer partition and resulting civil violence leading to further intervention by Rome? A large section of the people, particularly in Galilee, want to attack now, just as "The Hammerer" did. But that means war, and the loss of temple revenue from pilgrims. Ruination would ensue.

Here in Bethlehem the main business is sheep raising. The sheep are certified by the priests for temple sacrifices and economic conditions are good. What they want more than anything else is peace, so they tolerate Herod but worry about the state of his health.

These worries were accentuated last night by a strange incident. Drivers heard a commotion in stables where our caravan animals are kept. We did not want to run into further trouble and delay so Eleazar and I went out, despite the late night chill, to see if something else would stall us longer.

To our amazement, the sky was clear, and a brilliant star not known to these people seemed to shine directly into one of the stables. On approaching we learned that a young woman from Galilee had become a mother in the stable, where the young woman and her husband had been forced to go because the village was crowded. Eleazar explained that a new and brilliant star would be one of the sure signs of the birth of David's divinely anointed descendant.

Then frightened shepherds began arriving in the village. They told of hearing heavenly songs in the sky telling of peace to men of good will. While still terror-struck, they saw an angel who bade them be unafraid; that good news was breaking on the world. . . .

> *"For unto you is born this day in the city of David a Saviour, which is the anointed of the Lord. And this shall be a sign unto you; ye shall find the babe wrapped in swaddling clothes, lying in a manger," the angel said.*

In an awe-stricken voice, Eleazar whispered to me that Bethlehem is David's city; that here the great king would be born. He turned back to the stable, and I, following him, entered. The loveliness of the scene was unforgettable; the light of the star on two beautiful faces, mother and babe, with the glow forming a crown around the baby's head. The husband knelt before the manger as in adoration.

Before parting with Eleazar for the short remainder of the night, I asked him if there should be anything to these strange things. His moist eye glistened in the star's light.

"I think there is," he said. "I am sure of it."

THE SEASON'S GREETINGS

A CHRISTMAS CARILLON

By Hortense Calisher

Hortense Calisher was born in 1911 in New York City and has been called one of the most literate practitioners of modern American fiction. The winner of four O. Henry awards for short stories and two Guggenheim Fellowships, Calisher has been called the most acclaimed short story writer of the last half of the century. Her gifts come to the fore in beautifully crafted, highly controlled works such as this—a rare Christmas tale from a rare and talented author.

About four weeks before Christmas, Grorley, in combined shame and panic, began to angle for an invitation to somewhere, anywhere, for Christmas Day. By this time, after six months of living alone in the little Waverly Place flat to which he had gone as soon as he and his wife had decided to separate, he had become all too well reacquainted with his own peculiar mechanism in regard to solitude. It was a mechanism that had its roots in the jumbled lack of privacy of an adolescence spent in the dark, four-room apartment to which his parents had removed themselves and three children after his father's bankruptcy in '29. Prior to that, Grorley's childhood had been what was now commonly referred to as Edwardian—in a house where servants and food smells kept their distance until needed, and there were no neurotic social concerns about the abundance of either—a house where there was always plush under the buttocks, a multiplicity of tureens and napery at table, lace on the pillow, and above all that general expectancy of creature comfort and spiritual order which novelists now relegated to the days before 1914.

That it had lasted considerably later, Grorley knew, since this had been the year of his own birth, but although he had been fifteen when they had moved, it was the substantial years before that had faded to fantasy. Even now, when he read or said the word "reality," his mind reverted to Sunday middays in the apartment house living room, where the smudgy daylight was always diluted by lamps, the cheaply stippled walls menaced the oversized furniture, and he, his father and brother and sister, each a claustrophobe island of irritation, were a constant menace to one another. Only his mother, struggling alone in the kitchen with the conventions of roast chicken and gravy, had perhaps achieved something of the solitude they all had craved. To Grorley even now, the smell of roasting fowl was the smell of a special kind of Sunday death.

Only once before now had he lived alone, and then, too, it had been in the Village, not far from where he presently was. After his graduation from City College he had worked a year, to save up for a master's in journalism, and then, salving his conscience with the thought that he had at least paid board at home for that period, he had left his family forever. The following year, dividing his time between small-time newspaper job and classes, living in his $27 per month place off Morton Street, he had savored all the wonders of the single doorkey opening on the quiet room, of the mulled book and the purring clock, of the smug decision not to answer the phone or to let even the most delightful invader in. Now that he looked back on it, of course, he recalled that the room had rung pretty steadily with the voices of many such who had been admitted, but half the pleasure had been because it had been at his own behest. That had been a happy time, when he had been a gourmet of loneliness, prowling bachelor-style on the edge of society, dipping inward when he chose. Of all the habitations he had had since, that had been the one whose conformations he remembered best, down to the last, worn dimple of brick. When he had house hunted, last June, he had returned instinctively to the neighborhood of that time. Only a practicality born of superstition had kept him from hunting up the very street, the very house.

He had had over two years of that earlier freedom, although the last third of it had been rather obscured by his courtship of Eunice. Among the girl students of the Village there had been quite a few who, although they dressed like ballerinas and prattled of art like painters' mistresses, drew both their incomes and their morality from good, solid middle-class families back home. Eunice had been the prettiest and most sought after of these, and part of her attraction for some, and certainly for Grorley, had been that she seemed to be, quite honestly, one of those rare girls who were not particularly eager to marry and settle down. Grorley had been so entranced at finding like feelings in a girl—and in such a beautiful one—that he had quite forgotten that in coaxing her out of her "freedom" he was persuading himself out of his own.

He hadn't realized this with any force until the children came, two within the first four years of the marriage. Before that, in the first fusion of love, it had seemed to Grorley that two could indeed live more delightfully alone than one, and added to this had been that wonderful release from jealousy which requited love brings—half the great comfort of the loved one's presence being that, *ipso facto,* she is with no one else. During this period of happy, though enlarged privacy, Grorley confided to Eunice some, though not all, of his feelings about family life and solitude. He was, he told her, the kind of person who needed to be alone a great deal—although this of course excepted her. But they must never spend their Sundays and holidays frowsting in the house like the rest of the world, sitting there stuffed and droning, with murder in their hearts. They must always have plans laid well in advance, plans which would keep the two of them emotionally limber, so to speak, and *en plein air.* Since these plans were always pleasant—tickets to the Philharmonic, with after-theater suppers, hikes along the Palisades, fishing expeditions to little-known ponds back of the Westchester parkways, whose intricacies Grorley, out of a history of Sunday afternoons, knew as well as certain guides knew Boca Raton—Eunice was quite willing to accede. In time she grew very tactful, almost smug, over Grorley's little idiosyncrasy, and he sometimes heard her on the phone, fending people off. "Not Sunday. Gordon and I have a thing about holidays, you know." By this time, too, they had both decided that, although Grorley would keep his now very respectable desk job at the paper, his real destiny was to "write"; and to Eunice, who respected "imagination" as only the unimaginative can, Grorley's foible was the very proper defect of a noble intelligence.

But with the coming of the children, it was brought home to Grorley that he was face-to-face with one of those major rearrangements of existence for which mere tact would not suffice. Eunice, during her first pregnancy, was as natural and unassuming about it as a man could wish; she went on their Sunday sorties to the very last, and maintained their gallant privacy right up to the door of the delivery room. But the child of so natural a mother was bound to be natural, too. It contracted odd fevers whenever it wished and frequently on Sundays, became passionately endeared to their most expensive sitter or would have none at all, and in general permeated their lives as only the most powerfully frail of responsibilities can. And when the second one arrived, it did so, it seemed to Grorley, only to egg the other one on.

There came a morning, the Christmas morning of the fourth year, when Grorley, sitting in the odor of baked meat, first admitted that his hydra-headed privacy was no longer a privacy at all. He had created, he saw, his own monster; sex and the devil had had their sport with him, and he was, in a sense that no mere woman would understand, all too heavily "in the family way." Looking at Eunice, still neat, still very pretty, but with her lovely mouth pursed with maternity, her gaze sharp enough for *Kinder* and *Küche,* but abstract apparently for him, he saw that she had gone over to the enemy and was no longer his. Eunice had become "the family," too.

It was as a direct consequence of this that Grorley wrote the book which was his making. Right after that fatal morning, he had engaged a room in a cheap downtown hotel (he and Eunice were living out in Astoria at the time), with the intention, as he explained to Eunice, of writing there after he left the paper, and coming home weekends. He had also warned her that, because of the abrasive effects of family life, it would probably be quite some time before "the springs of reverie"—a phrase he had lifted from Ellen Glasgow—would start churning. His real intention was, of course, to prowl, and for some weeks thereafter he joined the company of those men who could be found, night after night, in places where they could enjoy the freedom of not having gone home where they belonged.

To his surprise, he found, all too quickly, that though his intentions were of the worst, he had somehow lost the moral force to pursue them. He had never been much for continuous strong drink, and that crude *savoir-faire* which was needed for the preliminaries to lechery seemed to have grown creaky with the years. He took to spending odd hours in the newspaper morgue, correlating, in a half-hearted way, certain current affairs that interested him. After some months, he suddenly realized that he had enough material for a book. It found a publisher almost immediately. Since he was much more a child of his period than he knew, he had hit upon exactly that note between disaffection and hope which met response in the breasts of those who regarded themselves as permanent political independents. His book was an instant success with those who thought of themselves as thinking for themselves (if they had only had time for it). Quick to capitalize upon this, Grorley's paper gave him a biweekly column, and he developed a considerable talent for telling men of good will, over Wednesday breakfast, the very thing they had been saying to one another at Tuesday night dinner.

Grorley spent the war years doing this, always careful to keep his column, like his readers, one step behind events. With certain minor changes, he kept, too, that scheme of life which had started him writing, changing only, with affluence, to a more comfortable hotel. In time, also, that *savoir-faire* whose loss he had mourned returned to him, and his success at his profession erased any guilts he might otherwise have had—a wider experience, he told himself, being not only necessary to a man of his trade, but almost unavoidable in the practice of it. He often congratulated himself at having achieved, in a country which had almost completely domesticated the male, the perfect pattern for a man of temperament, and at times he became almost insufferable to some of his married men friends, when he dilated on the contrast between his "continental" way of life and their own. For by then, Grorley had reversed himself—it was his weekends and holidays that were now spent cozily *en famille.* It was pleasant, coming back to the house in Tarrytown on Friday evenings, coming back from the crusades to find Eunice and the whole household decked out, literally and psychologically, for his return. One grew sentimentally fond of children whom one saw only under such conditions—Grorley's Saturdays were now spent, as he himself boasted, "on all fours," in the rejuvenating air of the skating rinks, the museums, the woods, and the zoos. Sundays and holidays he and Eunice often entertained their relatives, and if, as the turkey browned, he had a momentary twinge of his old *mal de famille,* he had but to remember that his hat was, after all, only hung in the hall.

It was only some years after the war that Eunice began to give trouble. Before that, their double ménage had not been particularly unusual—almost all the households of couples their age had been upset in one way or another, and theirs had been more stable than many. During the war years Eunice had had plenty of company for her midweek evenings; all over America women had been managing bravely behind the scenes. But now that families had long since paired off again, Eunice showed a disquieting tendency to want to be out in front.

"No, you'll have to come home for good," she said to Grorley, at the end of their now frequent battles. "I'm tired of being a short-order wife."

"The trouble with you," said Grorley, "is that you've never adjusted to postwar conditions."

"That was your nineteen forty-six column," said Eunice. "If you must quote yourself, pick one a little more up-to-date." Removing a jewel-encrusted slipper-toe from the fender, she made a feverish circle of the room, the velvet panniers of her housegown swinging dramatically behind her. She was one of those women who used their charge accounts for retaliation. With each crisis in their deteriorating relationship, Grorley noted gloomily, Eunice's wardrobe had improved.

"Now that the children are getting on," he said, "you ought to have another interest. A hobby."

Eunice made a hissing sound. "Nineteen forty-seven!" she said.

In the weeks after, she made her position clear. Men, she told him, might have provided the interest he suggested, but when a woman had made a vocation of one, it wasn't easy to start making a hobby of several. It was hardly much use swishing out in clouds of Tabu at seven, if one had to be back to feel Georgie's forehead at eleven. Besides, at their age, the only odd men out were likely to be hypochondriacs, or bachelors still dreaming of mother, or very odd men indeed.

"All the others," she said nastily, "are already on somebody else's hearth rug. Or out making the rounds with you." Worst of all, she seemed to have lost her former reverence for Grorley's work. If he'd been a novelist or a poet, she said (she even made use of the sticky word "creative"), there'd have been more excuse for his need to go off into the silence. As it was, she saw no reason for his having to be so broody over analyzing the day's proceedings at the U.N. If he wanted an office, that should take care of things very adequately. But if he did not wish to live *with* her, then he could not go on *living* with her.

"Mentally," she said, "you're still in the Village. Maybe you better go back there."

Things were at this pass when Grorley's paper sent him to London on an assignment that kept him there for several months. He was put up for membership in one or two exclusively masculine clubs, and in their leonine atmosphere his outraged vanity—("creative" indeed!)—swelled anew. Finally, regrettably near the end of his stay, he met up with a redheaded young woman named Vida who worked for a junior magazine by day, wrote poetry by night, and had once been in America for three weeks. She and Grorley held hands over the mutual hazards of the "creative" life, and on her lips the word was like a caress. For a woman, too, she was remarkably perceptive about the possessiveness of other women. "Yes, quite," she had said. "Yes, quite."

When she and Grorley made their final adieu in her Chelsea flat, she held him, for just a minute, at arm's length. "I shall be thinking of you over there, in one of those ghastly, what do you call them, *living rooms,* of yours. Everybody matted together, and the floor all over children—like beetles. Poor dear. I should think those living rooms must be the curse of the American family. Poor, poor dear."

On his return home in June, Grorley and Eunice agreed on a six-month trial separation prior to a divorce. Eunice showed a rather unfeeling calm in the lawyer's office, immediately afterward popped the children in camp, and went off to the Gaspé with friends. Grorley took a sublet on the apartment in Waverly Place. It was furnished in a monastic modern admirably suited to the novel he intended to write, that he had promised Vida to write.

He had always liked summers in town, when the real *aficionados* of the city took over, and now this summer seemed to him intoxicating, flowing with the peppery currents of his youth. In the daytime his freedom slouched unshaven; in the evenings the streets echoed and banged with life, and the moon made a hot harlequinade of every alley. He revisited the San Remo, Julius's, Chumley's, Jack Delaney's, and all the little Italian bars with backyard restaurants, his full heart and wallet carrying him quickly into the camaraderie of each. Occasionally he invited home some of the remarkables he met on his rounds—a young Italian bookie, a huge St. Bernard of a woman who drove a taxi and had once lived on a barge on the East River, an attenuated young couple from Chapel Hill who were honeymooning at the New School. Now and then a few of his men friends from uptown joined him in a night out. A few of these, in turn, invited him home for the weekend, but although he kept sensibly silent on the subject of their fraternal jaunts, he detected some animus in the hospitality of their wives.

By October, Grorley was having a certain difficulty with his weekends. His list of bids to the country was momentarily exhausted, and his own ideas had begun to flag. The children, home from camp, had aged suddenly into the gang phase; they tore out to movies and jamborees of their own, were weanable from these only by what Grorley could scrape up in the way of rodeos and football games, and assumed, once the afternoon's treat was over, a faraway look of sufferance. Once or twice, when he took them home, he caught himself hoping that Eunice would ask him in for a drink, a chat that might conceivably lead to dinner, but she was always out, and Mrs. Lederer, the housekeeper, always pulled the children in as if they were packages whose delivery had been delayed, gave him a nasty nod, and shut the door.

For a few weekends he held himself to his desk, trying to work up a sense of dedication over the novel, but there was no doubt that it was going badly. Its best juice had been unwisely expended in long, analytic letters to Vida, and now, in her airmail replies, which bounced steadily and enthusiastically over the Atlantic, it began to seem more her novel than his. The Sunday before Thanksgiving, he made himself embark on a ski-train to Pittsfield, working up a comforting sense of urgency over the early rising and the impedimenta to be checked. The crowd on the train was divided between a band of Swiss and German perfectionists who had no conversation, and a horde of young couples, rolling on the slopes like puppies, who had too much. Between them, Grorley's privacy was respected to the point of insult. When he returned that night, he tossed his gear into a corner, where it wilted damply on his landlord's blond rug, made himself a hot toddy—with a spasm of self-pity over his ability to do for himself—and sat down to face his fright. For years, his regular intervals at home had been like the chewed coffee bean that renewed the wine-taster's palate. He had lost the background from which to rebel.

Thanksgiving Day was the worst. The day dawned oyster-pale and stayed that way. Grorley slept as late as he could, then went out for a walk. The streets were slack, without the twitch of crowds, and the houses had a tight look of inner concentration. He turned toward the streets which held only shops, and walked uptown as far as Rockefeller Center. The rink was open, with its usual cast of characters—ricocheting children, a satiny, professional twirler from the Ice Show, and several solemn old men who skated upright in some Euclidian absorption of their own. Except for a few couples strolling along in the twin featurelessness of love, the crowd around the rink was type-cast, too. Here, it told itself, it participated in life; here in this flying spectacle of flag and stone it could not possibly be alone. With set, shy smiles, it glanced sideways at its neighbors, rounded its shoulders to the wind, turned up its collar, and leaned closer to the musical bonfire of the square. Grorley straightened up, turned on his heel, smoothed down his collar, and walked rapidly toward Sixth Avenue. He filled himself full of ham and eggs in one of the quick-order places that had no season, taxied home, downed a drink, swallowed two Seconal tablets, and went to bed.

The next morning, seated at his desk, he took a relieved look at the street. People were hard at their normal grind again; for a while the vacuum was past. But Christmas was not going to catch him alone. He picked up the phone. At the end of the day he was quite heartened. Although he had not yet turned up an invitation for Christmas Day, he had netted himself a cocktail party (which might easily go on to dinner) for two days before, a bid to an eggnog party on New Year's Day, and one weekend toward the middle of December. A lot of people did things impromptu. A phone call now and then would fix him up somehow.

But by Christmas week he was haggard. He had visualized himself as bidden to share, in a pleasantly avuncular capacity, some close friend's family gathering; he had seen himself as indolently and safely centered, but not anchored, in the bright poinsettia of their day. Apparently their vision of him was cast in a harsher mold; they returned his innuendoes with little more than a pointed sympathy. Only two propositions had turned up, one from a group of men, alone like himself for one reason or another, who were forming a party at an inn in the Poconos, and one from a waif-like spinster—"Last Christmas was my last one with dear Mother"—who offered to cook dinner for him in her apartment. Shuddering, he turned down both of these. The last thing he wanted to do on that day was to ally himself with *waifs* of any description; on that day he very definitely wanted to be safely inside some cozy family cocoon, looking out at *them*.

Finally, the day before Christmas, he thought of the Meechers. Ted was that blue-ribbon bore, the successful account-executive who believed his own slogans, and his wife, a former social worker, matched him in her own field. Out of Ted's sense of what was due his position in the agency and Sybil's sense of duty to the world, they had created a model home in Chappaqua, equipped with four children, two Bedlingtons, a games room, and a part-time pony. Despite this, they were often hard up for company, since most people could seldom be compelled twice to their table, where a guest was the focus of a constant stream of self-congratulation from either end. Moreover, Ted had wormed his way into more than one stag party at Grorley's, and could hardly refuse a touch. And their Christmas, whatever its other drawbacks, would be a four-color job, on the best stock.

But Ted's voice, plum-smooth when he took the phone from his secretary, turned reedy and doubtful when he heard Grorley's inquiry. "Uh-oh! 'Fraid that puts me on the spot, fella. Yeah. Kind of got it in the neck from Sybil, last time I came home from your place. Yeah. Had a real old-fashioned hassle. Guess I better not risk reminding her just yet. But, say! How about coming up here right now, for the office party?"

Grorley declined, and hung up. Off-campus boy this time of year, that's what I am, he thought. He looked at his mantelpiece crowded with its reminders—greetings from Grace and Bill, Jane and Tom, Peg and Jack, Etcetera and Mrs. Etcetera. On top of the pile was another airmail from Vida, received that morning, picture enclosed. Sans the red in the hair, without the thrush tones of the assenting voice, she looked a little long in the teeth. Her hands and feet, he remembered, were always cold. Somehow or other, looking at the picture, he didn't think that central heating would improve them. "The living room is the curse," she'd said. That's it, he thought; that's it. And this, Vida, is the season of the living room.

He looked down into the street. The Village was all right for the summer, he thought. But now the periphery of the season had changed. In summer, the year spins on a youth-charged axis, and a man's muscles have a spurious oil. But this is the end toward which it spins. Only three hundred days to Christmas. Only a month—a week. And then, every year, the damned day itself, catching him with its holly claws, sounding its platitudes like carillons.

Down at the corner, carols bugled steamily from a mission soup-kitchen. There's no escape from it, he thought. Turn on the radio, and its alleluia licks you with tremolo tongue. In every store window flameth housegown, nuzzleth slipper. In all the streets the heavenly shops proclaim. The season has shifted inward, Grorley, and you're on the outside, looking in.

He moved toward the phone, grabbed it, and dialed the number before he remembered that you had to dial the code for Tarrytown. He replaced the receiver. Whatever he had to say, and he wasn't quite sure what, or how, it wasn't for the ears of the kids or the Lederer woman. He jammed on his hat. Better get there first, get inside the door.

Going up to Grand Central in the cab, he pressed his face against the glass. Everything had been taken care of weeks ago—the kids had been sent their two-wheelers, and he had mailed Eunice an extra-large check—one he hadn't sent through the lawyer. But at five o'clock, Fifth Avenue still shone like an enormous blue sugarplum revolving in a tutti-frutti rain of light. Here was the season in all its questionable glory—the hallmarked joy of giving, the good will *diamanté.* But in the cosmetic air, people raised tinted faces, walked with levitated step.

In the train, he avoided the smoker, and chose an uncrowded car up front. At his station, he waited until all the gleaming car muzzles pointed at the train had picked up their loads and gone, then walked through the main street which led to his part of town. All was lit up here, too, with a more intimate, household shine. He passed the pink damp of a butcher's, the bright fuzz of Woolworth's. "Sold out!" said a woman, emerging. "'s try the A & P." He walked on, invisible, his face pressed to the shop window of the world.

At Schlumbohn's Credit Jewelry Corner he paused, feeling for the wallet filled with cash yesterday for the still not impossible yes over the phone. This was the sort of store that he and Eunice, people like them, never thought of entering. It sold watches pinned to cards, zircons, musical powder-boxes, bracelets clasped with fat ten-carat hearts, Rajah pearl necklaces and Truelove blue-white diamonds. Something for Everybody, it said. He opened the door.

Inside, a magnetic salesgirl nipped him toward her like a pin. He had barely stuttered his wants before he acquired an Add-a-Pearl necklace for Sally, two Genuine Pinseal handbags for his mother-in-law and Mrs. Lederer, and a Stag-horn knife with three blades, a nailfile, and a corkscrew, for young George. He had left Eunice until last, but with each purchase, a shabby, telephoning day had dropped from him. Dizzy with participation, he surveyed the mottoed store.

"Something . . . something for the wife," he said.

"Our lovely Lifetime Watch, perhaps? Or Something in Silver, for the House?" The clerk tapped her teeth, gauging him.

He leaned closer, understanding suddenly why housewives, encysted in lonely houses, burbled confidences to the grocer, made an audience of the milkman. "We've had a—Little Tiff."

"Aw-w," said the clerk, adjusting her face. "Now . . . let me see. . . ." She kindled suddenly, raised a sibylline finger, beckoned him farther down the counter, and drew out a tray of gold charms. Rummaging among them with a long, opalescent nail, she passed over minute cocktail shakers, bird cages, tennis rackets, a tiny scroll bearing the words. "If you can see this, you're too darn close," and seized a trinket she held up for view. A large gold shamrock, hung on a chain by a swivel through its middle, it bore the letter I. on its upper leaf, on its nether one the letter U. She reversed it. L.O.V.E. was engraved across the diameter of the other side. The clerk spun it with her accomplished nail. "See?" she said. "Spin it! Spin it and it says I. L.O.V.E. U!"

"Hmmm . . ." said Grorley, clearing his throat. "Well . . . guess you can't fob some women off with just a diamond bracelet." She tittered dutifully. But, as she handed it to him with his other packages, and closed the glass door behind him, he saw her shrug something, laughing, to another clerk. She had seen that he was not Schlumbohn's usual, after all.

As he walked up his own street he felt that he was after all hardly anybody's usual, tonight. It was a pretty street, of no particular architectural striving. Not a competitive street, except sometimes in summer, on the subject of gardens. And, of course, now. In every house the tree was up and lit, in the window nearest the passer-by. Here was his own, with the same blue lights that had lasted, with some tinkering on his part, year after year. Eunice must have had a man in to fix them.

He stopped on the path. A man in. She was pretty, scorned, and—he had cavalierly assumed—miserable. He had taken for granted that his family, in his absence, would have remained reasonably static. They always had. He'd been thinking of himself. Silently, he peeled off another layer of self-knowledge. He still was.

He walked up the steps wondering what kind of man might rise to be introduced, perhaps from his own armchair. One of her faded, footballish resurrections from Ohio State U., perhaps: Gordon, this is Jim Jerk, from home. Or would she hand it to him at once? Would it be: *Dear,* this is Gordon.

The door was unlocked. He closed it softly behind him, and stood listening. This was the unmistakable quiet of an empty house—as if the secret respiration of all objects in it had just stopped at his entrance. The only light downstairs was the glowing tree. He went up the stairs.

In the bedroom, the curtains were drawn, the night light on. The bed was piled with an abandoned muddle of silver wrappings, tissue paper, ribbons. He dropped the presents on the bed, tossed his hat after them, let his coat slip down on the familiar chair, and parted the curtains. It had a good view of the river, his house. He stood there, savoring it.

He was still there when a car door slammed and the family came up the path. The Christmas Eve pantomime, of course, held every year at the village hall. Georgie had on one of those white burnooses they always draped the boys in, and Sally, in long dress and coned hat, seemed to be a medieval lady. He saw that this year she had the waist for it. Eunice and Mrs. Lederer walked behind them. He tapped on the glass.

They raised their faces in tableau. The children waved, catcalled, and disappeared through the downstairs door. Mrs. Lederer followed them. Below, Eunice stared upward, in the shine from the tree-window. Behind him, he heard that sound made only by children—the noise of bodies falling up a staircase. As they swarmed in on him, she disappeared.

"You shoulda been to the hall," said Georgie, seizing him. "Christmas at King Arthur's court. I was a knight."

"Was it corny!" said Sally, from a distance. She caught sight of herself in a pier glass. "I was Guinevere."

"Had to do some last-minute shopping," said Grorley.

"I saw my bike!" said Georgie. "It's in the cellar."

"Oh . . . Georgie!" said Sally.

"Well, I couldn't help seeing it."

"Over there are some Christmas Eve presents," said Grorley.

"Open now?" they said. He nodded. They fell upon them.

"Gee," said Georgie, looking down at the knife. "Is that neat!" From his tone it was clear that he, at least, was Schlumbohn's usual.

"Oh, Dad!" Sally had the necklace around her neck. She raised her arms artistically above her head, in the fifth position, minced forward, and placed their slender wreath around Grorley's neck. As she hung on him, sacklike, he felt that she saw them both, a tender picture, in some lurking pier glass of her mind.

The door opened, and Eunice came in. She shut it behind her with a "not before the servants" air, and stood looking at him. Her face was blurred at the edges; she hadn't decked herself out for anybody. She looked the way a tired, pretty woman, of a certain age and responsibilities, might look at the hour before dinner, at the moment when age and prettiness tussle for her face, and age momentarily has won.

"Look what I got!" Georgie brandished the knife.

"And mine!" Sally undulated herself. "Mums! Doesn't it just *go!*" She stopped, looking from father to mother, her face hesitant, but shrewd.

"Open yours, Mums. Go on."

"Later," said Eunice. "Right now I think Mrs. Lederer wants you both to help with the chestnuts."

"No fair, no fair," said Georgie. "You saw ours."

"Do what your mother says," said Grorley. The paternal phrase, how it steadied him, was almost a hearthstone under his feet.

"Oh, well," said Eunice, wilting toward the children, as she invariably did when he was stern with them. Opening the package he indicated, she drew out the bauble. Georgie rushed to look at it, awarded it a quick, classifying disinterest, and returned to his knife.

"Oo—I know how to work those! Margie's sister has one," said Sally. She worked it. "If that isn't corny!" she gurgled. Eunice's head was bent over the gift. Sally straightened up, gave her and Grorley a swift, amending glance. "But cute!" she said. She flushed. Then, with one of the lightning changes that were the bane of her thirteen years, she began to cry. "Honestly, it's sweet!" she said.

Grorley looped an arm around her, gave her a squeeze and a kiss. "Now, shoo," he said. "Both of you."

When he turned back to the room, Eunice was looking out the window, chin up, her face not quite averted. Recognizing the posture, he quailed. It was the stance of the possessor of the stellar role—of the nightingale with her heart against the thorn. It was the stance of the woman who demands her scene.

He sighed, rat-tatted his fingers on a table top. "Well," he said. "Guess this is the season the corn grows tall."

A small movement of her shoulder. The back of her head to him. Now protocol demanded that he talk, into her silence, dredging his self-abasement until he hit upon some remark which made it possible for her to turn, to rend it, to show it up for the heartless, illogical, tawdry remark that it was. He could repeat a list of the game birds of North America, or a passage from the Congressional Record. The effect would be the same.

"Go on," he said, "get it over with. I deserve it. I just want you to know . . . mentally, I'm out of the Village."

She turned, head up, nostrils dilated. Her mouth opened. "Get it ov—!" Breath failed her. But not for long.

Much later, they linked arms in front of the same window. Supper had been eaten, the turkey had been trussed, the children at last persuaded into their beds. That was the consolatory side of family life, Grorley thought—the long, Olympian codas of the emotions were cut short by the niggling detail. Women thought otherwise, of course. In the past, he had himself.

Eunice began clearing off the bed. "What's in those two? Father's and Mother's?"

"Oh Lord. I forgot Father."

"Never mind. I'll look in the white-elephant box." The household phrase—how comfortably it rang. She looked up. "What's in these then?"

"For Mother and Mrs. Lederer. Those leather satchel-things. Pin-seal."

"Both the same, I'll bet."

He nodded.

Eunice began to laugh. "Oh, Lord. How they'll hate it." She continued to laugh, fondly, until Grorley smirked response. This, too, was familiar. Masculine gifts: the inappropriateness thereof.

But Eunice continued to laugh, steadily, hysterically, clutching her stomach, collapsing into a chair. "It's that hat," she said. "It's that s-specimen of a hat!"

Grorley's hat lay on the bed, where he had flung it. Brazenly dirty, limp denizen of bars, it reared sideways on a crest of tissue paper, one curling red whorl of ribbon around its crown. "L-like something out of Hogarth," she said. "The R-rounder's Return."

Grorley forced a smile. "You can buy me another."

"Mmmm . . . for Christmas." She stopped laughing. "You know . . . I think that's what convinced me—your coming back tonight. Knowing you—that complex of yours. Suppose I felt if you meant to stand us through the holidays, you meant to stand us for good."

Grorley coughed, bent to stuff some paper into the wastebasket. In fancy, he was stuffing in a picture, too, portrait of Vida, woman of imagination, outdistanced forever by the value of a woman who had none.

Eunice yawned. "Oh . . . I forgot to turn out the tree."

"I'll go down."

"Here, take this along." She piled his arms with crushed paper. In grinning afterthought, she clapped the hat on his head.

He went to the kitchen and emptied his arms in the bin. The kitchen was in chaos, the cookery methods of *alt Wien* demanding that each meal rise like a phoenix from a flaming muddle belowstairs. Tomorrow, as Mrs. Lederer mellowed with wine, they would hear once again of her grandfather's house, where the coffee was not even *roasted* until the guests' carriages appeared in the driveway.

In the dining room, the table was set in state, from damask to silver nut dishes. Father would sit there. He was teetotal, but anecdotalism signs no pledge. His jousts as purchasing agent for the city of his birth now left both narrator and listener with the impression that he had built it as well. They would hear from Mother, too. It was unfortunate that her bit of glory—her grandfather had once attended Grover Cleveland—should have crystallized itself in that one sentence so shifty for false teeth—"Yes, my father was a physician, you know."

Grorley sighed, and walked into the living room. He looked out, across the flowing blackness of the river. There to the south, somewhere in that jittering corona of yellow lights, was the apartment. He shuddered pleasurably, thinking of all the waifs in the world tonight. His own safety was too new for altruism; it was only by a paring of luck as thin as this pane of glass that he was safely here—on the inside, looking out.

Behind him, the tree shone—that *trompe l'oeil* triumphant—yearly symbol of how eternally people had to use the spurious to catch at the real. If there was an angel at the top, then here was the devil at its base—that, at this season, anybody who opened his eyes and ears too wide caught the poor fools, caught himself, hard at it. Home is where the heart . . . the best things in life are . . . spin it and it says I. L.O.V.E. U.

Grorley reached up absently and took off his hat. This is middle age, he thought. Stand still and hear the sound of it, bonging like carillons, the gathering sound of all the platitudes, sternly coming true.

He looked down at the hat in his hand. It was an able hat; not every hat could cock a snook like that one. From now on, he'd need every ally he could muster. Holding it, he bent down and switched off the tree. He was out of the living room and halfway up the stairs, still holding it, before he turned back. Now the house was entirely dark, but he needed no light other than the last red sputter of rebellion in his heart. He crept down, felt along the wall, clasped a remembered hook. Firmly, he hung his hat in the hall. Then he turned, and went back up the stairs.

The Loudest Voice

Grace Paley

Grace Paley was born in New York City in 1922. Confining herself to short stories, her work has met with acclaim from critics, feminists, and lovers of literature everywhere. This selection—"The Loudest Voice"—is full of life and humor. It gives us a rare glimpse of Christmas from a singular point of view.

There is a certain place where dumb-waiters boom, doors slam, dishes crash; every window is a mother's mouth bidding the street shut up, go skate somewhere else, come home. My voice is the loudest.

There, my own mother is still as full of

breathing as me and the grocer stands up to speak to her. "Mrs. Abramowitz," he says, "people should not be afraid of their children."

"Ah, Mr. Bialik," my mother replies, "if you say to her or her father 'Ssh,' they say, 'In the grave it will be quiet.' "

"From Coney Island to the cemetery," says my papa. "It's the same subway; it's the same fare."

I am right next to the pickle barrel. My pinky is making tiny whirlpools in the brine. I stop a moment to announce: "Campbell's Tomato Soup. Campbell's Vegetable Beef Soup. Cambell's S-c-otch Broth . . ."

"Be quiet," the grocer says, "the labels are coming off."

"Please, Shirley, be a little quiet," my mother begs me.

In that place the whole street groans: Be quiet! Be quiet! but steals from the happy chorus of my inside self not a tittle or a jot.

There, too, but just around the corner, is a red-brick building that has been old for many years. Every morning the children stand before it in double lines which must be straight. They are not insulted. They are waiting anyway.

I am usually among them. I am, in fact, the first, since I begin with "A."

One cold morning the monitor tapped me on the shoulder. "Go to Room 409, Shirley Abramowitz," he said. I did as I was told. I went in a hurry up a down staircase to Room 409, which contained sixth-graders. I had to wait at the desk without wiggling until Mr. Hilton, their teacher, had time to speak.

After five minutes he said, "Shirley?"

"What?" I whispered.

He said, "My! My! Shirley Abramowitz! They told me you had a particularly loud, clear voice and read with lots of expression. Could that be true?"

"Oh yes," I whispered.

"In that case, don't be silly; I might very well be your teacher someday. Speak up, speak up."

"Yes," I shouted.

"More like it," he said. "Now, Shirley, can you put a ribbon in your hair or a bobby pin? It's too messy."

"Yes!" I bawled.

"Now, now, calm down." He turned to the class. "Children, not a sound. Open at page 39. Read till 52. When you finish, start again." He looked me over once more. "Now, Shirley, you know, I suppose, that Christmas is coming. We are preparing a beautiful play. Most of the parts have been given out. But I still need a child with a strong voice, lots of stamina. Do you know what stamina is? You do? Smart kid. You know, I heard you read 'The Lord is my shepherd' in Assembly yesterday. I was very impressed. Wonderful delivery. Mrs. Jordan, your teacher, speaks highly of you. Now listen to me, Shirley Abramowitz, if you want to take the part and be in the play, repeat after me, 'I swear to work harder than I ever did before.' "

I looked to heaven and said at once, "Oh, I swear." I kissed my pinky and looked at God.

"That is an actor's life, my dear," he explained. "Like a soldier's, never tardy or disobedient to his general, the director. Everything," he said, "absolutely everything will depend on you."

That afternoon, all over the building, children scraped and scrubbed the turkeys and the sheaves of corn off the schoolroom windows. Goodbye Thanksgiving. The next morning a monitor brought red paper and green paper from the office. We made new shapes and hung them on the walls and glued them to the doors.

The teachers became happier and happier. Their heads were ringing like the bells of childhood. My best friend Evie was prone to evil, but she did not get a single demerit for whispering. We learned "Holy Night" without an error. "How wonderful!" said Miss Glacé, the student teacher. "To think that some of you don't even speak the language!" We learned "Deck the Halls" and "Hark! The Herald Angels" . . . They weren't ashamed and we weren't embarrassed.

Oh, but when my mother heard about it all, she said to my father: "Misha, you don't know what's going on there. Cramer is the head of the Tickets Committee."

"Who?" asked my father. "Cramer? Oh yes, an active woman."

"Active? Active has to have a reason. Listen," she said sadly, "I'm surprised to see my neighbors making tra-la-la for Christmas."

My father couldn't think of what to say to that. Then he decided:

"You're in America! Clara, you wanted to come here. In Palestine the Arabs would be eating you alive. Europe you had pogroms. Argentina is full of Indians. Here you got Christmas. . . . Some joke, ha?"

"Very funny, Misha. What is becoming of you? If we came to a new country a long time ago to run away from tyrants, and instead we fall into a creeping pogrom, that our children learn a lot of lies, so what's the joke? Ach, Misha, your idealism is going away."

"So is your sense of humor."

"That I never had, but idealism you had a lot of."

"I'm the same Misha Abramovitch, I didn't change an iota. Ask anyone."

"Only ask me," says my mama, may she rest in peace. "I got the answer."

Meanwhile the neighbors had to think of what to say, too.

Marty's father said: "You know, he has a very important part, my boy."

"Mine also," said Mr. Sauerfeld.

"Not my boy!" said Mrs. Kleig. "I said to him no. The answer is no. When I say no! I mean no!"

The rabbi's wife said, "It's disgusting!" But no one listened to her. Under the narrow sky of God's great wisdom she wore a strawberry-blond wig.

Every day was noisy and full of experience. I was Right-hand Man. Mr. Hilton said: "How could I get along without you, Shirley?"

He said: "Your mother and father ought to get down on their knees every night and thank God for giving them a child like you."

He also said: "You're absolutely a pleasure to work with, my dear, dear child."

Sometimes he said: "For God's sakes, what did I do with the script? Shirley! Shirley! Find it."

Then I answered quietly: "Here it is, Mr. Hilton."

Once in a while, when he was very tired, he would cry out: "Shirley, I'm just tired of screaming at those kids. Will you tell Ira Pushkov not to come in till Lester points to that star the second time?"

Then I roared: "Ira Pushkov, what's the matter with you? Dope!

Mr. Hilton told you five times already, don't come in till Lester points to that star the second time."

"Ach, Clara," my father asked, "What does she do there till six o'clock she can't even put the plates on the table?"

"Christmas," said my mother coldly.

"Ho! Ho!" my father said. "Christmas. What's the harm? After all, history teaches everyone. We learn from reading this is a holiday from pagan times also, candles, lights, even Chanukah. So we learn it's not altogether Christian. So if they think it's a private holiday, they're only ignorant, not patriotic. What belongs to history, belongs to all men. You want to go back to the Middle Ages? Is it better to shave your head with a secondhand razor? Does it hurt Shirley to learn to speak up? It does not. So maybe someday she won't live between the kitchen and the shop. She's not a fool."

I thank you, Papa, for your kindness. It is true about me to this day. I am foolish but I am not a fool.

That night my father kissed me and said with great interest in my career, "Shirley, tomorrow's your big day. Congrats."

"Save it," my mother said. Then she shut all the windows in order to prevent tonsillitis.

In the morning it snowed. On the street corner a tree had been decorated for us by a kind city administration. In order to miss its chilly shadow our neighbors walked three blocks east to buy a loaf of bread. The butcher pulled down black window shades to keep the colored lights from shining on his chickens. Oh, not me. On the way to school, with both my hands I tossed it a kiss of tolerance. Poor thing, it was a stranger in Egypt.

I walked straight into the auditorium past the staring children. "Go ahead, Shirley!" said the monitors. Four boys, big for their age, had already started work as propmen and stagehands.

Mr. Hilton was very nervous. He was not even happy. Whatever he started to say ended in a sideward look of sadness. He sat slumped in the middle of the first row and asked me to help Miss Glacé. I did this, although she thought my voice too resonant and said, "Show-off!"

Parents began to arrive long before we were ready. They wanted to make a good impression. From among the yards of drapes I peeked out at the audience. I saw my embarrassed mother.

Ira, Lester, and Meyer were pasted to their beards by Miss Glacé. She almost forgot to thread the star on its wire, but I reminded her. I coughed a few times to clear my throat. Miss Glacé looked around and saw that everyone was in costume and on line waiting to play his part. She whispered, "All right . . ." Then:

Jackie Sauerfeld, the prettiest boy in first grade, parted the curtains with his skinny elbow and in a high voice sang out:

Parents dear
We are here
To make a Christmas play in time.
It we give
In narrative
And illustrate with pantomime.

He disappeared.

My voice burst immediately from the wings to the great shock of Ira, Lester, and Meyer, who were waiting for it but were surprised all the same.

"I remember, I remember, the house where I was born . . ."

Miss Glacé yanked the curtain open and there it was, the house—an old hayloft, where Celia Kornbluh lay in the straw with Cindy Lou, her favorite doll. Ira, Lester, and Meyer moved slowly from the wings toward her, sometimes pointing to a moving star and sometimes ahead to Cindy Lou.

It was a long story and it was a sad story. I carefully pronounced all the words about my lonesome childhood, while little Eddie Braunstein wandered upstage and down with his shepherd's stick, looking for sheep. I brought up lonesomeness again, and not being understood at all except by some women everybody hated. Eddie was too small for that and Marty Groff took his place, wearing his father's prayer shawl. I announced twelve friends, and half the boys in the fourth grade gathered round Marty, who stood on an orange crate while my voice harangued. Sorrowful and loud, I declaimed about love and God and Man, but because of the terrible deceit of Abie Stock we came suddenly to a famous moment. Marty, whose remembering tongue I was, waited at the foot of the cross. He stared desperately at the audience. I groaned, "My God, my God, why hast thou forsaken me?" The soldiers who were sheiks grabbed poor Marty to pin him up to die, but he wrenched free, turned again to the audience, and spread his arms aloft to show despair and the end. I murmured at the top of my voice, "The rest is silence, but as everyone in this room, in this city—in this world—now knows, I shall have life eternal."

That night Mrs. Kornbluh visited our kitchen for a glass of tea.

"How's the virgin?" asked my father with a look of concern.

"For a man with a daughter, you got a fresh mouth, Abramovitch."

"Here," said my father kindly, "have some lemon, it'll sweeten your disposition."

They debated a little in Yiddish, then fell in a puddle of Russian and Polish. What I understood next was my father, who said, "Still and all, it was certainly a beautiful affair, you have to admit, introducing us to the beliefs of a different culture."

"Well, yes," said Mrs. Kornbluh. "The only thing . . . you know Charlie Turner—that cute boy in Celia's class—a couple others? They got very small parts or no part at all. In very bad taste, it seemed to me. After all, it's their religion."

"Ach," explained my mother, "what could Mr. Hilton do? They got very small voices; after all, why should they holler? The English language they know from the beginning by heart. They're blond like angels. You think it's so important they should get in the play? Christmas . . . the whole piece of goods . . . they own it."

I listened and listened until I couldn't listen any more. Too sleepy, I climbed out of bed and kneeled. I made a little church of my hands and said, "Hear, O Israel . . ." Then I called out in Yiddish, "Please, good night, good night. Ssh." My father said, "Ssh yourself," and slammed the kitchen door.

I was happy. I fell asleep at once. I had prayed for everybody: my talking family, cousins far away, passersby, and all the lonesome Christians. I expected to be heard. My voice was certainly the loudest.

Oh, Joseph, I'm So Tired

By Richard Yates

Richard Yates was born in Yonkers, New York, in 1926, and is the author of the novels Revolutionary Road, Disturbing the Peace, *and* A Good School. *His work has met with consistent critical acclaim, yet has not met with the large popular audience it surely deserves. A memoir of childhood that takes place through the holiday season, "Oh, Joseph, I'm So Tired" weaves together a hard-eyed glimpse of childhood, history, and the darker sides of innocence.*

hen Franklin D. Roosevelt was President-elect there must have been sculptors all over America who wanted a chance to model his head from life, but my mother had connections. One of her closest friends and neighbors, in the Greenwich Village courtyard where we lived, was an amiable man named Howard Whitman who had recently lost his job as a reporter on the *New York Post.* And one of Howard's former colleagues from the *Post* was now employed in the press office of Roosevelt's New York headquarters. That would make it easy for her to get in—or, as she said, to get an entrée—and she was confident she could take it from there. She was confident about everything she did in those days, but it never quite disguised a terrible need for support and approval on every side.

She wasn't a very good sculptor. She had been working at it for only three years, since breaking up her marriage to my father, and there was still something stiff and amateurish about her pieces. Before the Roosevelt project her specialty had been "garden figures"—a life-size little boy whose legs turned into the legs of a goat at the knees and another who knelt among ferns to play the pipes of Pan; little girls who trailed chains of daisies from their upraised arms or walked beside a spread-winged goose. These fanciful children, in plaster painted green to simulate weathered bronze, were arranged on home-made wooden pedestals to loom around her studio and to leave a cleared space in the middle for the modeling stand that held whatever she was working on in clay.

Her idea was that any number of rich people, all of them gracious and aristocratic, would soon discover her: they would want her sculpture to decorate their landscaped gardens, and they would want to make her their friend for life. In the meantime, a little nationwide publicity as the first woman sculptor to "do" the President-elect certainly wouldn't hurt her career.

And, if nothing else, she had a good studio. It was, in fact, the best of all the studios she would have in the rest of her life. There were six or eight old houses facing our side of the courtyard, with their backs to Bedford Street, and ours was probably the showplace of the row because the front room on its ground floor was two stories high. You went down a broad set of brick steps to the tall front windows and the front door; then you were in the high, wide, light-flooded studio. It was big enough to serve as a living room, too, and so along with the green garden children it contained all the living-room furniture from the house we'd lived in with my father in the suburban town of Hastings-on-Hudson, where I was born. A second-floor balcony ran along the far end of the studio, with two small bedrooms and a tiny bathroom tucked away upstairs; beneath that, where the ground floor continued through to the Bedford Street side, lay the only part of the apartment that might let you know we didn't have much money. The ceiling was very low and it was always dark in there; the small windows looked out underneath an iron sidewalk grating, and the bottom of that street cavity was thick with strewn garbage. Our roach-infested kitchen was barely big enough for a stove and sink that were never clean, and for a brown wooden icebox with its dark, ever-melting block of ice; the rest of that area was our dining room, and not even the amplitude of the old Hastings dining-room table could brighten it. But our Majestic radio was in there, too, and that made it a cozy place for my sister Edith and me: we liked the children's programs that came on in the late afternoons.

We had just turned off the radio one day when we went out into the studio and found our mother discussing the Roosevelt project with Howard Whitman. It was the first we'd heard of it, and we must have interrupted her with too many questions because she said "Edith? Billy? That's enough, now. I'll tell you all about this later. Run out in the garden and play."

She always called the courtyard "the garden," though nothing grew there except a few stunted city trees and a patch of grass that never had a chance to spread. Mostly it was bald earth, interrupted here and there by brick paving, lightly powdered with soot and scattered with the droppings of dogs and cats. It may have been six or eight houses long, but it was only two houses wide, which gave it a hemmed-in, cheerless look; its only point of interest was a dilapidated marble fountain, not much bigger than a birdbath, which stood near our house. The original idea of the fountain was that water would drip evenly from around the rim of its upper tier and tinkle into its lower basin, but age had unsettled it; the water spilled in a single ropy stream from the only inch of the upper tier's rim that stayed clean. The lower basin was deep enough to soak your feet in on a hot day, but there wasn't much pleasure in that because the underwater part of the marble was coated with brown scum.

My sister and I found things to do in the courtyard every day, for all of the two years we lived there, but that was only because Edith was an imaginative child. She was eleven at the time of the Roosevelt project, and I was seven.

"Daddy?" she asked in our father's office uptown one afternoon. "Have you heard Mommy's doing a head of President Roosevelt?"

"Oh?" He was rummaging in his desk, looking for something he'd said we might like.

"She's going to take his measurements and stuff here in New York," Edith said, "and then after the Inauguration, when the sculpture's done, she's going to take it to Washington and present it to him in the White House." Edith often told one of our parents about the other's more virtuous activities; it was part of her long, hopeless effort to bring them back together. Many years later she told me she thought she had never recovered, and never would, from the shock of their breakup: she said Hastings-on-Hudson remained the happiest time of her life, and that made me envious because I could scarcely remember it at all.

"Well," my father said. "That's really something, isn't it." Then he found what he'd been looking for in the desk and said, "Here we go; what do you think of these?" They were two fragile perforated sheets of what looked like postage stamps, each stamp bearing the insignia of an electric light bulb in vivid white against a yellow background, and the words "More light."

My father's office was one of many small cubicles on the twenty-third floor of the General Electric building. He was an assistant regional sales manager in what was then called the Mazda Lamp Division—a modest job, but good enough to have allowed him to rent into a town like Hastings-on-Hudson in better times—and these "More light" stamps were souvenirs of a recent sales convention. We told him the stamps were neat—and they were—but expressed some doubt as to what we might do with them.

"Oh, they're just for decoration," he said. "I thought you could paste them into your schoolbooks, or—you know—whatever you want. Ready to go?" And he carefully folded the sheets of stamps and put them in his inside pocket for safekeeping on the way home.

Between the subway exit and the courtyard, somewhere in the West Village, we always walked past a vacant lot where men stood huddled around weak fires built of broken fruit crates and trash, some of them warming tin cans of food held by coat-hanger wire over the flames. "Don't stare," my father had said the first time. "All those men are out of work, and they're hungry."

"Daddy?" Edith inquired. "Do you think Roosevelt's good?"

"Sure I do."

"Do you think all the Democrats are good?"

"Well, most of 'em, sure."

Much later I would learn that my father had participated in local Democratic Party politics for years. He had served some of his political friends—men my mother described as dreadful little Irish people from Tammany Hall—by helping them to establish Mazda Lamp distributorships in various parts of the city. And he loved their social gatherings, at which he was always asked to sing.

"Well, of course, you're too young to remember Daddy's singing," Edith said to me once after his death in 1942.

"No, I'm not; I remember."

"But I mean really remember," she said. "He had the most beautiful tenor voice I've ever heard. Remember 'Danny Boy'?"

"Sure."

"Ah, God, that was something," she said, closing her eyes. "That was really—that was really something."

When we got back to the courtyard that afternoon, and back into the studio, Edith and I watched our parents say hello to each other. We always watched that closely, hoping they might drift into conversation and sit down together and find things to laugh about, but they never did. And it was even less likely than usual that day because my mother had a guest—a woman named Sloane Cabot who was her best friend in the courtyard, and who greeted my father with a little rush of false, flirtatious enthusiasm.

"How've you been, Sloane?" he said. Then he turned back to his former wife and said "Helen? I hear you're planning to make a bust of Roosevelt."

"Well, not a bust," she said. "A head. I think it'll be more effective if I cut it off at the neck."

"Well, good. That's fine. Good luck with it. Okay, then." He gave his whole attention to Edith and me. "Okay. See you soon. How about a hug?"

And those hugs of his, the climax of his visitation rights, were unforgettable. One at a time we would be swept up and pressed hard into the smells of linen and whiskey and tobacco; the warm rasp of his jaw would graze one cheek and there would be a quick moist kiss near the ear; then he'd let us go.

He was almost all the way out of the courtyard, almost out in the street, when Edith and I went racing after him.

"Daddy! Daddy! You forgot the stamps!"

He stopped and turned around, and that was when we saw he was crying. He tried to hide it—he put his face nearly into his armpit as if that might help him search his inside pocket—but there is no way to disguise the awful bloat and pucker of a face in tears.

"Here," he said. "Here you go." And he gave us the least convincing smile I had ever seen. It would be good to report that we stayed and talked to him—that we hugged him again—but we were too embarrassed for that. We took the stamps and ran home without looking back.

"Oh, aren't you excited, Helen?" Sloane Cabot was saying. "To be meeting him, and talking to him and everything, in front of all those reporters?"

"Well, of course," my mother said, "but the important thing is to get the measurements right. I hope there won't be a lot of photographers and silly interruptions."

Sloane Cabot was some years younger than my mother, and strikingly pretty in a style often portrayed in what I think are called Art Deco illustrations of that period: straight dark bangs, big eyes, and a big mouth. She too was a divorced mother, though her former husband had vanished long ago and was referred to only as "that bastard" or "that cowardly son of a bitch." Her only child was a boy of Edith's age named John, whom Edith and I liked enormously.

The two women had met within days of our moving into the courtyard, and their friendship was sealed when my mother solved the problem of John's schooling. She knew a Hastings-on-Hudson family who would appreciate the money earned from taking in a boarder, so John went up there to live and go to school, and came home only on weekends. The arrangement cost more than Sloane could comfortably afford, but she managed to make ends meet and was forever grateful.

Sloane worked in the Wall Street district as a private secretary. She talked a lot about how she hated her job and her boss, but the good part was that her boss was often out of town for extended periods: that gave her time to use the office typewriter in pursuit of her life's ambition, which was to write scripts for the radio.

She once confided to my mother that she'd made up both of her names: "Sloane" because it sounded masculine, the kind of name a woman alone might need for making her way in the world, and "Cabot" because—well, because it had a touch of class. Was there anything wrong with that?

"Oh, Helen," she said. "This is going to be wonderful for you. If you get the publicity—if the papers pick it up, and the newsreels—you'll be one of the most interesting personalities in America."

Five or six people were gathered in the studio on the day my mother came home from her first visit with the President-elect.

"Will somebody get me a drink?" she asked, looking around in mock helplessness. "Then I'll tell you all about it."

And with the drink in her hand, with her eyes as wide as a child's, she told us how a door had opened and two big men had brought him in.

"Big men," she insisted. "Young, strong men, holding him up under the arms, and you could see how they were straining. Then you saw this *foot* come out, with these awful metal braces on the shoe, and then the *other* foot. And he was sweating, and he was panting for breath, and his face was—I don't know—all bright and tense and horrible." She shuddered.

"Well," Howard Whitman said, looking uneasy, "he can't help being crippled, Helen."

"Howard," she said impatiently, "I'm only trying to tell you how *ugly* it was." And that seemed to carry a certain weight. If she was an authority on beauty—on how a little boy might kneel among ferns to play the pipes of Pan, for example—then surely she had earned her credentials as an authority on ugliness.

"*Any*way," she went on, "they got him into a chair, and he wiped most of the sweat off his face with a handkerchief—he was still out of breath—and after a while he started talking to some of the other men there; I couldn't follow that part of it. Then finally he turned to me with this smile of his. Honestly, I don't know if I can describe that smile. It isn't something you can see in the newsreels; you have to be there. His eyes don't change at all, but the corners of his mouth go up as if they're being pulled by puppet strings. It's a frightening smile. It makes you think: this could be a dangerous man. This could be an evil man. Well anyway, we started talking, and I spoke right up to him. I said 'I didn't vote for you, Mr. President.' I said 'I'm a good Republican and I voted for President Hoover.' He said 'Why are you here, then?' or something like that, and I said 'Because you have a very interesting head.' So he gave me the smile again and he said 'What's interesting about it?' And I said 'I like the bumps on it.' "

By then she must have assumed that every reporter in the room was writing in his notebook, while the photographers got their flashbulbs ready; tomorrow's papers might easily read:

GAL SCULPTOR TWITS FDR
ABOUT "BUMPS" ON HEAD

At the end of her preliminary chat with him she got down to business, which was to measure different parts of his head with her calipers. I knew how that felt: the cold, trembling points of those clay-encrusted calipers had tickled and poked me all over during the times I'd served as model for her fey little woodland boys.

But not a single flashbulb went off while she took and then recorded the measurements, and nobody asked her any questions; after a few nervous words of thanks and good-bye she was out in the corridor again among all the hopeless, craning people who couldn't get in. It must have been a bad disappointment, and I imagine she tried to make up for it by planning the triumphant way she'd tell us about it when she got home.

"Helen?" Howard Whitman inquired, after most of the other visitors had gone. "Why'd you tell him you didn't vote for him?"

"Well, because it's true. I *am* a good Republican; you know that."

She was a storekeeper's daughter from a small town in Ohio; she had probably grown up hearing the phrase "good Republican" as an index of respectability and clean clothes. And maybe she had come to relax her standards of respectability, maybe she didn't even care much about clean clothes anymore, but "good Republican" was worth clinging to. It would be helpful when she met the customers for her garden figures, the people whose low, courteous voices would welcome her into their lives and who would almost certainly turn out to be Republicans, too.

"I believe in the aristocracy!" she often cried, trying to make herself heard above the rumble of voices when her guests were discussing communism, and they seldom paid her any attention. They liked her well enough: she gave parties with plenty of liquor, and she was an agreeable hostess if only because of her touching eagerness to please; but in any talk of politics she was like a shrill, exasperating child. She believed in the aristocracy.

She believed in God, too, or at least in the ceremony of St. Luke's Episcopal Church, which she attended once or twice a year. And she believed in Eric Nicholson, the handsome middle-aged Englishman who was her lover. He had something to do with the American end of a British chain of foundries: his company cast ornamental objects into bronze and lead. The cupolas of college and high-school buildings all over the East, the lead-casement windows for Tudor-style homes in places like Scarsdale and Bronxville—these were some of the things Eric Nicholson's firm had accomplished. He was always self-deprecating about his business, but ruddy and glowing with its success.

My mother had met him the year before, when she'd sought help in having one of her garden figures cast into bronze, to be "placed on consignment" with some garden-sculpture gallery from which it would never be sold. Eric Nicholson had persuaded her that lead would be almost as nice as bronze and much cheaper; then he'd asked her out to dinner, and that evening changed our lives.

Mr. Nicholson rarely spoke to my sister or me, and I think we were both frightened of him, but he overwhelmed us with gifts. At first they were mostly books—a volume of cartoons from *Punch,* a partial set of Dickens, a book called *England in Tudor Times* containing tissue-covered color plates that Edith liked. But in the summer of 1933, when our father arranged for us to spend two weeks with our mother at a small lake in New Jersey, Mr. Nicholson's gifts became a cornucopia of sporting goods. He gave Edith a steel fishing rod with a reel so intricate that none of us could have figured it out even if we'd known how to fish, a wicker creel for carrying the fish she would never catch, and a sheathed hunting knife to be worn at her waist. He gave me a short axe whose head was encased in a leather holster and strapped to my belt—I guess this was for cutting firewood to cook the fish—and a cumbersome net with a handle that hung from an elastic shoulder strap, in case I should be called upon to wade in and help Edith land a tricky one. There was nothing to do in that New Jersey village except take walks, or what my mother called good hikes; and every day, as we plodded out through the insect-humming weeds in the sun, we wore our full regalia of useless equipment.

That same summer Mr. Nicholson gave me a three-year subscription to *Field and Stream,* and I think that impenetrable magazine was the least appropriate of all his gifts because it kept coming in the mail for such a long, long time after everything else had changed for us: after we'd moved out of New York to Scarsdale, where Mr. Nicholson had found a house with a low rent, and after he had abandoned my mother in that house—with no warning—to return to England and to the wife from whom he'd never really been divorced.

But all that came later; I want to go back to the time between Franklin D. Roosevelt's election and his Inauguration, when his head was slowly taking shape on my mother's modeling stand.

Her original plan had been to make it life-size, or larger than life-size, but Mr. Nicholson urged her to scale it down for economy in the casting, and so she made it only six or seven inches high. He persuaded her, too, for the second time since he'd known her, that lead would be almost as nice as bronze.

She had always said she didn't mind at all if Edith and I watched her work, but we had never much wanted to; now it was a little more interesting because we could watch her sift through many photographs of Roosevelt cut from newspapers until she found one that would help her execute a subtle plane of cheek or brow.

But most of our day was taken up with school. John Cabot might go to school in Hastings-on-Hudson, for which Edith would always yearn, but we had what even Edith admitted was the next best thing: we went to school in our bedroom.

During the previous year my mother had enrolled us in the public school down the street, but she'd begun to regret it when we came home with lice in our hair. Then one day Edith came home accused of having stolen a boy's coat, and that was too much. She withdrew us both, in defiance of the city truant officer, and pleaded with my father to help her meet the cost of a private school. He refused. The rent she paid and the bills she ran up were already taxing him far beyond the terms of the divorce agreement; he was in debt; surely she must realize he was lucky even to have a job. Would she ever learn to be reasonable?

It was Howard Whitman who broke the deadlock. He knew of an inexpensive, fully accredited mail-order service called The Calvert School, intended mainly for the homes of children who were invalids. The Calvert School furnished weekly supplies of books and materials and study plans; all she would need was someone in the house to administer the program and to serve as a tutor. And someone like Bart Kampen would be ideal for the job.

"The skinny fellow?" she asked. "The Jewish boy from Holland or wherever it is?"

"He's very well educated, Helen," Howard told her. "And he speaks fluent English, and he'd be very conscientious. And he could certainly use the money."

We were delighted to learn that Bart Kampen would be our tutor. With the exception of Howard himself, Bart was probably our favorite among the adults around the courtyard. He was twenty-eight or so, young enough so that his ears could still turn red when he was teased by children; we had found that out in teasing him once or twice about such matters as that his socks didn't match. He was tall and very thin and seemed always to look startled except when he was comforted enough to smile. He was a violinist, a Dutch Jew who had emigrated the year before in the hope of joining a symphony orchestra and eventually of launching a concert career. But the symphonies weren't hiring then, nor were lesser orchestras, so Bart had gone without work for a long time. He lived alone in a room on Seventh Avenue, not far from the courtyard, and people who liked him used to worry that he might not have enough to eat. He owned two suits, both cut in a way that must have been stylish in the Netherlands at the time: stiff, heavily padded shoulders and a nipped-in waist; they would probably have looked better on someone with a little more meat on his bones. In shirtsleeves, with the cuffs rolled back, his hairy wrists and forearms looked even more fragile than you might have expected, but his long hands were shapely and strong enough to suggest authority on the violin.

"I'll leave it entirely up to you, Bart," my mother said when he asked if she had any instructions for our tutoring. "I know you'll do wonders with them."

A small table was moved into our bedroom, under the window, and three chairs placed around it. Bart sat in the middle so that he could divide his time equally between Edith and me. Big, clean, heavy brown envelopes arrived in the mail from The Calvert School once a week, and when Bart slid their fascinating contents onto the table it was like settling down to begin a game.

Edith was in the fifth grade that year—her part of the table was given over to incomprehensible talk about English and History and Social Studies—and I was in the first. I spent my mornings asking Bart to help me puzzle out the very opening moves of an education.

"Take your time, Billy," he would say. "Don't get impatient with this. Once you have it you'll see how easy it is, and then you'll be ready for the next thing."

At eleven each morning we would take a break. We'd go downstairs and out to the part of the courtyard that had a little grass. Bart would carefully lay his folded coat on the sidelines, turn back his shirt cuffs, and present himself as ready to give what he called airplane rides. Taking us one at a time, he would grasp one wrist and one ankle; then he'd whirl us off our feet and around and around, with himself as the pivot, until the courtyard and the buildings and the city and the world were lost in the dizzying blur of our flight.

After the airplane rides we would hurry down the steps into the studio, where we'd usually find that my mother had set out a tray bearing three tall glasses of cold Ovaltine, sometimes with cookies on the side and sometimes not. I once overheard her telling Sloane Cabot she thought the Ovaltine must be Bart's first nourishment of the day—and I think she was probably right, if only because of the way his hand would tremble in reaching for his glass. Sometimes she'd forget to prepare the tray and we'd crowd into the kitchen and fix it ourselves; I can never see a jar of Ovaltine on a grocery shelf without remembering those times. Then it was back upstairs to school again. And during that year, by coaxing and prodding and telling me not to get impatient, Bart Kampen taught me to read.

It was an excellent opportunity for showing off. I would pull books down from my mother's shelves—mostly books that were the gifts of Mr. Nicholson—and try to impress her by reading mangled sentences aloud.

"That's wonderful, dear," she would say. "You've really learned to read, haven't you."

Soon a white and yellow "More light" stamp was affixed to every page of my Calvert First Grade Reader, proving I had mastered it, and others were accumulating at a slower rate in my arithmetic workbook. Still other stamps were fastened to the wall beside my place at the school table, arranged in a proud little white and yellow thumb-smudged column that rose as high as I could reach.

"You shouldn't have put your stamps on the wall," Edith said.

"Why?"

"Well, because they'll be hard to take off."

"Who's going to take them off?"

That small room of ours, with its double function of sleep and learning, stands more clearly in my memory than any other part of our home. Someone should probably have told my mother that a girl and boy of our ages ought to have separate rooms, but that never occurred to me until much later. Our cots were set foot-to-foot against the wall, leaving just enough space to pass alongside them to the school table, and we had some good conversations as we lay waiting for sleep at night. The one I remember best was the time Edith told me about the sound of the city.

"I don't mean just the loud noises," she said, "like the siren going by just now, or those car doors slamming, or all the laughing and shouting down the street; that's just close-up stuff. I'm talking about something else. Because you see there are millions and millions of people in New York—more people than you can possibly imagine, ever—and most of them are doing something that makes a sound. Maybe talking, or playing the radio, maybe closing doors, maybe putting their forks down on their plates if they're having dinner, or dropping their shoes if they're going to bed—and because there are so many of them, all those little sounds add up and come together in a kind of hum. But it's so faint—so very, very faint—that you can't hear it unless you listen very carefully for a long time."

"Can you hear it?" I asked her.

"Sometimes. I listen every night, but I can only hear it sometimes. Other times I fall asleep. Let's be quiet now, and just listen. See if you can hear it, Billy."

And I tried hard, closing my eyes as if that would help, opening my mouth to minimize the sound of my breathing, but in the end I had to tell her I'd failed. "How about you?" I asked.

"Oh, I heard it," she said. "Just for a few seconds, but I heard it. You'll hear it too, if you keep trying. And it's worth waiting for. When you hear it, you're hearing the whole city of New York."

The high point of our week was Friday afternoon, when John Cabot came home from Hastings. He exuded health and normality; he brought fresh suburban air into our bohemian lives. He even transformed his mother's small apartment, while he was there, into an enviable place of rest between vigorous encounters with the world. He subscribed to both *Boy's Life* and *Open Road for Boys,* and these seemed to me to be wonderful things to have in your house, if only for the illustrations. John dressed in the same heroic way as the boys shown in those magazines, corduroy knickers with ribbed stockings pulled taut over his muscular calves. He talked a lot about the Hastings high-school football team, for which he planned to try out as soon as he was old enough, and about Hastings friends whose names and personalities grew almost as familiar to us as if they were friends of our own. He taught us invigorating new ways to speak, like saying "What's the diff?" instead of "What's the difference?" And he was better even than Edith at finding new things to do in the courtyard.

You could buy goldfish for ten or fifteen cents apiece in Woolworth's then, and one day we brought home three of them to keep in the fountain. We sprinkled the water with more Woolworth's granulated fish food than they could possibly need, and we named them after ourselves: "John," "Edith," and "Billy." For a week or two Edith and I would run to the fountain every morning, before Bart came for school, to make sure they were still alive and to see if they had enough food, and to watch them.

"Have you noticed how much bigger Billy's getting?" Edith asked me. "He's huge. He's almost as big as John and Edith now. He'll probably be bigger than both of them."

Then one weekend when John was home he called our attention to how quickly the fish could turn and move. "They have better reflexes than humans," he explained. "When they see a shadow in the water, or anything that looks like danger, they get away faster than you can blink. Watch." And he sank one hand into the water to make a grab for the fish named Edith, but she evaded him and fled. "See that?" he asked. "How's that for speed. Know something? I bet you could shoot an arrow in there, and they'd get away in time. Wait." To prove his point he ran to his mother's apartment and came back with the handsome bow and arrow he had made at summer camp (going to camp every summer was another admirable thing about John); then he knelt at the rim of the fountain like the picture of an archer, his bow steady in one strong hand and the feathered end of the arrow tight against the bowstring in the other. He was taking aim at the fish named Billy. "Now, the velocity of this arrow," he said in a voice weakened by his effort, "is probably more than a car going eighty miles an hour. It's probably more like an airplane, or maybe even more than that. Okay; watch."

The fish named Billy was suddenly floating dead on the surface, on his side, impaled a quarter of the way up the arrow with parts of his pink guts dribbled along the shaft.

I was too old to cry, but something had to be done about the shock and rage and grief that filled me as I ran from the fountain, heading blindly for home, and half-way there I came upon my mother. She stood looking very clean, wearing a new coat and dress I'd never seen before and fastened to the arm of Mr. Nicholson. They were either just going out or just coming in—I didn't care which—and Mr. Nicholson frowned at me (he had told me more than once that boys of my age went to boarding school in England), but I didn't care about that either. I bent my head into her waist and didn't stop crying until long after I'd felt her hands stroking my back, until after she had assured me that goldfish didn't cost much and I'd have another one soon, and that John was sorry for the thoughtless thing he'd done. I had discovered, or rediscovered, that crying is a pleasure—that it can be a pleasure beyond all reckoning if your head is pressed in your mother's waist and her hands are on your back, and if she happens to be wearing clean clothes.

There were other pleasures. We had a good Christmas Eve in our house that year, or at least it was good at first. My father was there, which obliged Mr. Nicholson to stay away, and it was nice to see how relaxed he was among my mother's friends. He was shy, but they seemed to like him. He got along especially well with Bart Kampen.

Howard Whitman's daughter Molly, a sweet-natured girl of about my age, had come in from Tarrytown to spend the holidays with him, and there were several other children whom we knew but rarely saw. John looked very mature that night in a dark coat and tie, plainly aware of his social responsibilities as the oldest boy.

After a while, with no plan, the party drifted back into the dining-room area and staged an impromptu vaudeville. Howard started it: he brought the tall stool from my mother's modeling stand and sat his daughter on it, facing the audience. He folded back the opening of a brown paper bag two or three times and fitted it onto her head; then he took off his suit coat and draped it around her backwards, up to the chin; he went behind her, crouched out of sight, and worked his hands through the coatsleeves so that when they emerged they appeared to be hers. And the sight of a smiling little girl in a paper-bag hat, waving and gesturing with huge, expressive hands, was enough to make everyone laugh. The big hands wiped her eyes and stroked her chin and pushed her hair behind her ears; then they elaborately thumbed her nose at us.

Next came Sloane Cabot. She sat very straight on the stool with her heels hooked over the rungs in such a way as to show her good legs to their best advantage, but her first act didn't go over.

"Well," she began, "I was at work today—you know my office is on the fortieth floor—when I happened to glance up from my typewriter and saw this big old man sort of crouched on the ledge outside the window, with a white beard and a funny red suit. So I ran to the window and opened it and said 'Are you all right?' Well, it was Santa Claus, and he said 'Of course I'm all right; I'm used to high places. But listen, miss: can you direct me to number seventy-five Bedford Street?' "

There was more, but our embarrassed looks must have told her we knew we were being condescended to; as soon as she'd found a way to finish it she did so quickly. Then, after a thoughtful pause, she tried something else that turned out to be much better.

"Have you children ever heard the story of the first Christmas?" she asked. "When Jesus was born?" And she began to tell it in the kind of hushed, dramatic voice she must have hoped might be used by the narrators of her more serious radio plays.

". . . And there were still many miles to go before they reached Bethlehem," she said, "and it was a cold night. Now, Mary knew she would very soon have a baby. She even knew, because an angel had told her, that her baby might one day be the saviour of all mankind. But she was only a young girl"—here Sloane's eyes glistened, as if they might be filling with tears—"and the traveling had exhausted her. She was bruised by the jolting gait of the donkey and she ached all over, and she thought they'd never, ever get there, and all she could say was 'Oh, Joseph, I'm so tired.' "

The story went on through the rejection at the inn, and the birth in the stable, and the manger, and the animals, and the arrival of the three kings; when it was over we clapped a long time because Sloane had told it so well.

"Daddy?" Edith asked. "Will you sing for us?"

"Oh, well, thanks, honey," he said, "but no; I really need a piano for that. Thanks anyway."

The final performer of the evening was Bart Kampen, persuaded by popular demand to go home and get his violin. There was no surprise in discovering that he played like a professional, like something you might easily hear on the radio; the enjoyment came from watching how his thin face frowned over the chin rest, empty of all emotion except concern that the sound be right. We were proud of him.

Some time after my father left a good many other adults began to arrive, most of them strangers to me, looking as though they'd already been to several other parties that night. It was very late, or rather very early Christmas morning, when I looked into the kitchen and saw Sloane standing close to a bald man I didn't know. He held a trembling drink in one hand and slowly massaged her shoulder with the other; she seemed to be shrinking back against the old wooden icebox. Sloane had a way of smiling that allowed little wisps of cigarette smoke to escape from between her almost-closed lips while she looked you up and down, and she was doing that. Then the man put his drink on top of the icebox and took her in his arms, and I couldn't see her face anymore.

Another man, in a rumpled brown suit, lay unconscious on the dining-room floor. I walked around him and went into the studio, where a good-looking young woman stood weeping wretchedly and three men kept getting in each other's way as they tried to comfort her. Then I saw that one of the men was Bart, and I watched while he outlasted the other two and turned the girl away toward the door. He put his arm around her and she nestled her head in his shoulder; that was how they left the house.

Edith looked jaded in her wrinkled party dress. She was reclining in our old Hastings-on-Hudson easy chair with her head tipped back and her legs flung out over both the chair's arms, and John sat cross-legged on the floor near one of her dangling feet. They seemed to have been talking about something that didn't interest either of them much, and the talk petered out altogether when I sat on the floor to join them.

"Billy," she said, "do you realize what time it is?"

"What's the diff?" I said.

"You should've been in bed hours ago. Come on. Let's go up."

"I don't feel like it."

"Well," she said, "I'm going up, anyway," and she got laboriously out of the chair and walked away into the crowd.

John turned to me and narrowed his eyes unpleasantly. "Know something?" he said. "When she was in the chair that way I could see everything."

"Huh?"

"I could see everything. I could see the crack, and the hair. She's beginning to get hair."

I had observed these features of my sister many times—in the bathtub, or when she was changing her clothes—and hadn't found them especially remarkable; even so, I understood at once how remarkable they must have been for him. If only he had smiled in a bashful way we might have laughed together like a couple of regular fellows out of *Open Road for Boys,* but his face was still set in that disdainful look.

"I kept looking and looking," he said, "and I had to keep her talking so she wouldn't catch on, but I was doing fine until you had to come over and ruin it."

Was I supposed to apologize? That didn't seem right, but nothing else seemed right either. All I did was look at the floor.

When I finally got to bed there was scarcely time for trying to hear the elusive sound of the city—I had found that a good way to keep from thinking of anything else—when my mother came blundering in. She'd had too much to drink and wanted to lie down, but instead of going to her own room she got into bed with me. "Oh," she said. "Oh, my boy. Oh, my boy." It was a narrow cot and there was no way to make room for her; then suddenly she retched, bolted to her feet, and ran for the bathroom, where I heard her vomiting. And when I moved over into the part of the bed she had occupied my face recoiled quickly, but not quite in time, from the slick mouthful of puke she had left on her side of the pillow.

For a month or so that winter we didn't see much of Sloane because she said she was "working on something big. Something really big." When it was finished she brought it to the studio, looking tired but prettier than ever, and shyly asked if she could read it aloud.

"Wonderful," my mother said. "What's it about?"

"That's the best part. It's about us. All of us. Listen."

Bart had gone for the day and Edith was out in the courtyard by herself—she often played by herself—so there was nobody for an audience but my mother and me. We sat on the sofa and Sloane arranged herself on the tall stool, just as she'd done for telling the Bethlehem story.

"There is an enchanted courtyard in Greenwich Village," she read. "It's only a narrow patch of brick and green among the irregular shapes of very old houses, but what makes it enchanted is that the people who live in it, or near it, have come to form an enchanted circle of friends.

"None of them have enough money and some are quite poor, but they believe in the future; they believe in each other, and in themselves.

"There is Howard, once a top reporter on a metropolitan daily newspaper. Everyone knows Howard will soon scale the journalistic heights again, and in the meantime he serves as the wise and humorous sage of the courtyard.

"There is Bart, a young violinist clearly destined for virtuosity on the concert stage, who just for the present must graciously accept all lunch and dinner invitations in order to survive.

"And there is Helen, a sculptor whose charming works will someday grace the finest gardens in America, and whose studio is the favorite gathering place for members of the circle."

There was more like that, introducing other characters, and toward the end she got around to the children. She described my sister as "a lanky, dreamy tomboy," which was odd—I had never thought of Edith that way—and she called me "a sad-eyed, seven-year-old philosopher," which was wholly baffling. When the introduction was over she paused a few seconds for dramatic effect and then went into the opening episode of the series, or what I suppose would be called the "pilot."

I couldn't follow the story very well—it seemed to be mostly an excuse for bringing each character up to the microphone for a few lines apiece—and before long I was listening only to see if there would be any lines for the character based on me. And there were, in a way. She announced my name—"Billy"—but then instead of speaking she put her mouth through a terrible series of contortions, accompanied by funny little bursts of sound, and by the time the words came out I didn't care what they were. It was true that I stuttered badly—I wouldn't get over it for five or six more years—but I hadn't expected anyone to put it on the radio.

"Oh, Sloane, that's marvelous," my mother said when the reading was over. "That's really exciting."

And Sloane was carefully stacking her typed pages in the way she'd probably been taught to do in secretarial school, blushing and smiling with pride. "Well," she said, "it probably needs work, but I do think it's got a lot of potential."

"It's perfect," my mother said. "Just the way it is."

Sloane mailed the script to a radio producer and he mailed it back with a letter typed by some radio secretary, explaining that her material had too limited an appeal to be commercial. The radio public was not yet ready, he said, for a story of Greenwich Village life.

Then it was March. The new President promised that the only thing we had to fear was fear itself, and soon after that his head came packed in wood and excelsior from Mr. Nicholson's foundry.

It was a fairly good likeness. She had caught the famous lift of the chin—it might not have looked like him at all if she hadn't—and everyone told her it was fine. What nobody said was that her original plan had been right, and Mr. Nicholson shouldn't have interfered: it was too small. It didn't look heroic. If you could have hollowed it out and put a slot in the top, it might have made a serviceable bank for loose change.

The foundry had burnished the lead until it shone almost silver in the highlights, and they'd mounted it on a sturdy little base of heavy black plastic. They had sent back three copies: one for the White House presentation, one to keep for exhibition purposes, and an extra one. But the extra one soon toppled to the floor and was badly damaged—the nose mashed almost into the chin—and my mother might have burst into tears if Howard Whitman hadn't made everyone laugh by saying it was now a good portrait of Vice President Garner.

Charlie Hines, Howard's old friend from the *Post* who was now a minor member of the White House staff, made an appointment for my mother with the President late on a weekday morning. She arranged for Sloane to spend the night with Edith and me; then she took an evening train down to Washington, carrying the sculpture in a cardboard box, and stayed at one of the less expensive Washington hotels. In the morning she met Charlie Hines in some crowded White House anteroom, where I guess they disposed of the cardboard box, and he took her to the waiting room outside the Oval Office. He sat with her as she held the naked head in her lap, and when their turn came he escorted her in to the President's desk for the presentation. It didn't take long. There were no reporters and no photographers.

Afterwards Charlie Hines took her out to lunch, probably because he'd promised Howard Whitman to do so. I imagine it wasn't a first-class restaurant, more likely some bustling, no-nonsense place favored by the working press, and I imagine they had trouble making conversation until they settled on Howard, and on what a shame it was that he was still out of work.

"No, but do you know Howard's friend Bart Kampen?" Charlie asked. "The young Dutchman? The violinist?"

"Yes, certainly," she said. "I know Bart."

"Well, Jesus, there's *one* story with a happy ending, right? Have you heard about that? Last time I saw Bart he said 'Charlie, the Depression's over for me,' and he told me he'd found some rich, dumb, crazy woman who's paying him to tutor her kids."

I can picture how she looked riding the long, slow train back to New York that afternoon. She must have sat staring straight ahead or out the dirty window, seeing nothing, her eyes round and her face held in a soft shape of hurt. Her adventure with Franklin D. Roosevelt had come to nothing. There would be no photographs or interviews or feature articles, no thrilling moments of newsreel coverage; strangers would never know of how she'd come from a small Ohio town, or of how she'd nurtured her talent through the brave, difficult, one-woman journey that had brought her to the attention of the world. It wasn't fair.

All she had to look forward to now was her romance with Eric Nicholson, and I think she may have known even then that it was faltering—his final desertion came the next fall.

She was forty-one, an age when even romantics must admit that youth is gone, and she had nothing to show for the years but a studio crowded with green plaster statues that nobody would buy. She believed in the aristocracy, but there was no reason to suppose the aristocracy would ever believe in her.

And every time she thought of what Charlie Hines had said about Bart Kampen—oh, how hateful; oh, how hateful—the humiliation came back in wave on wave, in merciless rhythm to the clatter of the train.

She made a brave show of her homecoming, though nobody was there to greet her but Sloane and Edith and me. Sloane had fed us, and she said "There's a plate for you in the oven, Helen," but my mother said she'd rather just have a drink instead. She was then at the onset of a long battle with alcohol that she would ultimately lose; it must have seemed bracing that night to decide on a drink instead of dinner. Then she told us "all about" her trip to Washington, managing to make it sound like a success. She talked of how thrilling it was to be actually inside the White House; she repeated whatever small, courteous thing it was that President Roosevelt had said to her on receiving the head. And she had brought back souvenirs: a handful of note-size White House stationery for Edith, and a well-used briar pipe for me. She explained that she'd seen a very distinguished-looking man smoking the pipe in the waiting room outside the Oval

Office; when his name was called he had knocked it out quickly into an ashtray and left it there as he hurried inside. She had waited until she was sure no one was looking; then she'd taken the pipe from the ashtray and put it in her purse. "Because I knew he must have been somebody important," she said. "He could easily have been a member of the Cabinet, or something like that. Anyway, I thought you'd have a lot of fun with it." But I didn't. It was too heavy to hold in my teeth and it tasted terrible when I sucked on it; besides, I kept wondering what the man must have thought when he came out of the President's office and found it gone.

Sloane went home after a while, and my mother sat drinking alone at the dining-room table. I think she hoped Howard Whitman or some of her other friends might drop in, but nobody did. It was almost our bedtime when she looked up and said "Edith? Run out in the garden and see if you can find Bart."

He had recently bought a pair of bright tan shoes with crepe soles. I saw those shoes trip rapidly down the dark brick steps beyond the windows—he seemed scarcely to touch each step in his buoyance—and then I saw him come smiling into the studio, with Edith closing the door behind him. "Helen!" he said. "You're back!"

She acknowledged that she was back. Then she got up from the table and slowly advanced on him, and Edith and I began to realize we were in for something bad.

"Bart," she said, "I had lunch with Charlie Hines in Washington today."

"Oh?"

"And we had a very interesting talk. He seems to know you very well."

"Oh, not really; we've met a few times at Howard's, but we're not really—"

"And he said you'd told him the Depression was over for you because you'd found some rich, dumb, crazy woman who was paying you to tutor her kids. Don't interrupt me."

But Bart clearly had no intention of interrupting her. He was backing away from her in his soundless shoes, retreating past one stiff green garden child after another. His face looked startled and pink.

"I'm not a rich woman, Bart," she said, bearing down on him. "And I'm not dumb. And I'm not crazy. And I can recognize ingratitude and disloyalty and sheer, rotten viciousness and *lies* when they're thrown in my face."

My sister and I were halfway up the stairs jostling each other in our need to hide before the worst part came. The worst part of these things always came at the end, after she'd lost all control and gone on shouting anyway.

"I want you to get out of my house, Bart," she said. "And I don't ever want to see you again. And I want to tell you something. All my life I've hated people who say 'Some of my best friends are Jews.' Because *none* of my friends are Jews, or ever will be. Do you understand me? *None* of my friends are Jews, or ever will be."

The studio was quiet after that. Without speaking, avoiding each other's eyes, Edith and I got into our pajamas and into bed. But it wasn't more than a few minutes before the house began to ring with our mother's raging voice all over again, as if Bart had somehow been brought back and made to take his punishment twice.

". . . And I said '*None* of my friends are Jews, or ever will be . . .' "

She was on the telephone, giving Sloane Cabot the highlights of the scene, and it was clear that Sloane would take her side and comfort her. Sloane might know how the Virgin Mary felt on the way to Bethlehem, but she also knew how to play my stutter for laughs. In a case like this she would quickly see where her allegiance lay, and it wouldn't cost her much to drop Bart Kampen from her enchanted circle.

When the telephone call came to an end at last there was silence downstairs until we heard her working with the ice pick in the icebox: she was making herself another drink.

There would be no more school in our room. We would probably never see Bart again—or if we ever did, he would probably not want to see us. But our mother was ours; we were hers; and we lived with that knowledge as we lay listening for the faint, faint sound of millions.

SEASONS GREETINGS

Christmas for Sassafras, Cypress and Indigo

Ntozake Shange

Ntozake Shange was born in Trenton, New Jersey, in 1948 and is the author of the highly successful choreopoem For Colored Girls Who Have Considered Suicide/When the Rainbow Is Enuf. *The following story was first published in the December issue of* Essence *magazine in 1982. Unique in its own right, the story nevertheless offers an interesting echo of Louisa May Alcott and the March family of* Little Women.

ilda Effania couldn't wait till Christmas. The Christ Child was born. Hallelujah. Hallelujah. The girls were home. The house was humming. Hilda Effania just a singing, cooking up a storm. Up before dawn. Santa's elves barely up the chimney. She chuckled. This was gonna be some mornin'. Yes, indeed. There was nothing too good for her girls. Matter of fact, what folks never dreamt of would only just about do. That's right, all her babies home for Christmas Day. Hilda Effania cooking up a storm. Little Jesus Child lyin' in his Manger. Praise the Lord for all these gifts. Hilda Effania justa singin':

Poor little Jesus Child, Born in a Manger
Sweet little Jesus Child
& they didn't know who you were.

Breakfast with Hilda Effania & Her Girls on Christmas Morning

Hilda's Turkey Hash

1 pound diced cooked turkey meat (white & dark)
2 medium onions, diced
1 red sweet pepper, diced
1 full boiled potato, diced
1 tablespoon cornstarch
3 tablespoons butter
Salt to taste, pepper too
(A dash of corn liquor, optional)

In a heavy skillet, put your butter. Sauté your onions & red pepper. Add your turkey, once your onions are transparent. When the turkey's sizzling, add your potato. Stir. If consistency is not to your liking, add the cornstarch to thicken, the corn liquor to thin. Test to see how much salt & pepper you want, & don't forget your cayenne.

Catfish / The Way Albert Liked It

½ cup flour
½ cup cornmeal
Salt
Pepper
½ cup buttermilk
3 beaten eggs
Oil for cooking
Lemons
6 fresh catfish

Sift flour and cornmeal. Season with your salt & pepper. Mix the beaten eggs well with the buttermilk. Dip your fish in the egg & milk. Then roll your fish in the cornmeal-flour mix. Get your oil spitting hot in a heavy skillet. Fry your fish, not too long, on both sides. Your lemon wedges are for your table.

Trio Marmalade

1 tangerine	Sugar
1 papaya	Cold Water
1 lemon	

Delicately grate rinds of fruits. Make sure you have slender pieces of rind. Chop up your pulp, leaving the middle section of each fruit. Put the middles of the fruits and the seeds somewhere else in a cotton wrap. Add three times the amount of pulp & rind. That's the measure for your water. Keep this sitting overnight. Get up the next day & boil this for a half hour. Drop your wrapped seed bag in there. Boil that, too. & mix in an exact equal of your seed bag with your sugar (white or brown). Leave it be for several hours. Come back. Get it boiling again. Don't stop stirring. You can test it & test it, but you'll know when it jells. Put on your table or in jars you seal while it's hot.

Now you have these with your hominy grits. (I know you know how to make hominy grits.) Fried eggs, sunny-side up. Ham-sliced bacon, butter rolls & Aunt Haydee's Red Pimiento Jam. I'd tell you that receipt, but Aunt Haydee never told nobody how it is you make that. I keep a jar in the pantry for special occasions. I get one come harvest.

Mama's breakfast simmering way downstairs drew the girls out of their sleep. Indigo ran to the kitchen. Sassafrass turned back over on her stomach to sleep a while longer, there was no House Mother ringing a cowbell. Heaven. Cypress brushed her hair, began her daily *pliés* & leg stretches. Hilda Effania sat at her kitchen table, drinking strong coffee with Magnolia Milk, wondering what the girls would think of her tree.

"Merry Christmas, Mama." Indigo gleamed. "May I please have some coffee with you? Nobody else is up yet. Then we can go see the tree, can't we, when they're all up. Should I go get 'em?" Indigo was making herself this coffee as quickly as she could, before Hilda Effania said "no." But Hilda was so happy Indigo could probably have had a shot of bourbon with her coffee.

"Only half a cup, Indigo. Just today." Hilda watched Indigo moving more like Cypress. Head erect, back stretched tall, with some of Sassafrass' easy coyness.

"So you had a wonderful time last night at your first party?"

"Oh, yes, Mama." Indigo paused. "But you know what?" Indigo sat down by her mother with her milk tinged with coffee. She stirred her morning treat, serious as possible. She looked her mother in the eyes. "Mama, I don't think boys are as much fun as everybody says."

"What do you mean, darling?"

"Well, they dance. & I guess eventually you marry 'em. But I like my fiddle so much more. I even like my dolls better than boys. They're fun, but they can't talk about important things."

Hilda Effania giggled. Indigo was making her own path at her own pace. There'd be not one more boy-crazy, obsessed-with-romance child in her house. This last one made more sense out of the world than either of the other two. Alfred would have liked that. He liked independence.

"Good morning, Mama. Merry Christmas." Sassafrass was still tying her bathrobe as she kissed her mother.

"Merry Christmas, Indigo. I see Santa left you a cup of coffee."

"This is not my first cup of coffee. I had some on my birthday, too."

"Oh, pardon me. I didn't realize you were so grown. I've been away, you know?" Sassafrass was never very pleasant in the morning. Christmas was no exception. Indigo & her mother exchanged funny faces. Sassafrass wasn't goin' to spoil this day.

"Good morning. Good morning. Good morning, everyone." Cypress flew through the kitchen: *coupé jeté en tournant.*

"Merry Christmas, Cypress," the family shouted in unison.

"Oh, Mama, you musta been up half the night cooking what all I'm smelling." Cypress started lifting pot tops, pulling the oven door open.

"Cypress, you know I can't stand for nobody to be looking in my food till I serve it. Now, come on away from my stove."

Cypress turned to her mama, smiling. "Mama, let's go look at the tree."

"I haven't finished my coffee," Sassafrass yawned.

"You can bring it with you. That's what I'm gonna do," Indigo said with sweet authority.

The tree glistened by the front window of the parlor. Hilda Effania had covered it, of course, with cloth & straw. Satin ribbons of scarlet, lime, fuchsia, bright yellow, danced on the fat limbs of the pine. Tiny straw angels of dried palm swung from the upper branches. Apples shining, next to candy canes & gingerbread men, brought shouts of joy & memory from the girls, who recognized their own handiwork. The black satin stars with appliqués of the Christ Child Cypress had made when she was ten. Sassafrass fingered the lyres she fashioned for the children singing praises of the little Jesus: little burlap children with lyres she'd been making since she could thread a needle, among the miniatures of Indigo's dolls. Hilda Effania had done something else special for this Christmas, though. In silk frames of varied pastels were the baby pictures of her girls & one of her wedding day: Hilda Effania & Alfred, November 30, 1946.

Commotion. Rustling papers. Glee & Surprise. Indigo got a very tiny laced brassiere from Cypress. Sassafrass had given her a tiny pair of earrings, dangling golden violins. Indigo had made for both her sisters dolls in their very own likenesses. Both five feet tall, with hips & bras. Indigo had dressed the dolls in the old clothes Cypress & Sassafrass had left at home.

"Look in their panties," Indigo blurted. Cypress felt down in her doll's panties. Sassafrass pulled her doll's drawers. They both found velvet sanitary napkins with their names embroidered cross the heart of silk.

"Oh, Indigo. You're kidding. You're not menstruating, are you?"

"Indigo, you got your period?"

"Yes, she did." Hilda Effania joined, trying to change the subject. She'd known Indigo was making dolls, but not that the dolls had their period.

"Well, what else did you all get?" Hilda asked provocatively.

Cypress pulled out an oddly shaped package wrapped entirely in gold sequins. "Mama, this is for you." The next box was embroidered continuously with Sassafrass' name. "Here, guess whose?" Cypress held Indigo's shoulders. Indigo had on her new bra over her nightgown. Waiting for her mother & sister to open their gifts, Cypress did *tendues.* "Hold still, Indigo. If you move, my alignment goes off."

"Oh, Cypress, this is just lovely." Hilda Effania didn't know what else to say. Cypress had given her a black silk negligee with a very revealing bed jacket. "I certainly have to think when I could wear this & you all won't be home to see it."

"Aw, Mama. Try it on," Cypress pleaded.

"Yeah, Mama. Put that on. It looks so nasty." Indigo squinched up her face, giggled.

"Oh, Cypress, these are so beautiful. I can hardly believe it." Sassafras held the embroidered box open. In the box lined with beige raw silk were seven cherry-wood hand-carved crochet needles of different gauges.

"Bet not one white girl up to the Callahan School has ever in her white life laid eyes on needles like that!" Cypress hugged her sister, flexed her foot. "Indigo, you got to put that bra on under your clothes, not on top of 'em! Mama, would you look at this little girl?"

Hilda Effania had disappeared. "I'm trying on this scandalous thing, Cypress. You all look for your notes at the foot of the tree." She shouted from her bedroom, thinking she looked pretty good for a widow with three most grown girls.

Hilda Effania always left notes for the girls explaining where their Christmas from Santa was. This practice began the first year Sassafrass had doubted that a fat white man came down her chimney to bring her anything. Hilda solved that problem by leaving notes from Santa Claus for all the children. That way they had to go search the house, high & low, for their gifts. Santa surely had to have been there. Once school chums & reality interfered with this myth, Hilda continued the practice of leaving her presents hidden away. She liked the idea that each child experienced her gift in privacy. The special relationship she nurtured with each was protected from rivalries, jokes & Christmas confusions. Hilda Effania loved thinking that she'd managed to give her daughters a moment of their own.

My Oldest Darling, Sassafrass,
In the back of the pantry is something from Santa. In a red box by the attic window is something your father would want you to have. Out by the shed in a bucket covered with straw is a gift from your Mama.
Love to you,
Mama

Darling Cypress,
Underneath my hat boxes in the 2nd floor closet is your present from Santa. Look behind the tomatoes I canned last year for what I got you in your Papa's name. My own choice for you is under your bed.
XOXOX,
Mama

Sweet Little Indigo,
This is going to be very simple. Santa left you something outside your violin. I left you a gift by the outdoor stove on the right hand side. Put your coat on before you go out there. And the special something I got you from your Daddy is way up in the china cabinet. Please, be careful.
I love you so much,
Mama

In the back of the pantry between the flour & rice, Sassafrass found a necklace of porcelain roses. Up in the attic across from Indigo's mound of resting dolls, there was a red box all right, with a woven blanket of mohair, turquoise & silver. Yes, her father would have wanted her to have a warm place to sleep. Running out to the shed, Sassafrass knocked over the bucket filled with straw. There on the ground lay eight skeins of her mother's finest spun cotton, dyed so many colors. Sassafrass sat out in the air feeling her yarns.

Cypress wanted her mother's present first. Underneath her bed, she felt tarlatan. A tutu. Leave it to Mama. Once she gathered the whole thing out where she could see it, Cypress started to cry. A tutu *juponnage,* reaching to her ankles, rose & lavender. The waist was a wide sash with the most delicate needlework she'd ever seen. Tiny toe shoes in white & pink graced brown ankles tied with ribbons. Unbelievable. Cypress stayed in her room dancing in her tutu till lunchtime. Then she found *The Souls of Black Folks* by DuBois near the tomatoes from her Papa's spirit. She was the only one who'd insisted on calling him Papa, instead of Daddy or Father. He didn't mind. So she guessed he wouldn't mind now. "Thank you so much, Mama & Papa." Cypress slowly went to the 2nd floor closet where she found Santa'd left her a pair of opal earrings. To thank her mother Cypress did a complete *port de bras,* in the Cecchetti manner, by her mother's vanity. The mirrors inspired her.

Indigo had been very concerned that anything was near her fiddle that she hadn't put there. Looking at her violin, she knew immediately what her gift from Santa was. A brand-new case. No second-hand battered thing from Uncle John. Indigo approached her instrument slowly. The case was out of crocodile skin, lined with white velvet. Plus, Hilda Effania had bought new rosin, new strings. Even cushioned the fiddle with cleaned raw wool. Indigo carried her new case with her fiddle outside to the stove where she found a music stand holding *A Practical Method for Violin* by Nicolas Laoureux. "Oh, my. She's right about that. Mama would be real mad if I never learned to read music." Indigo looked through the pages, understanding nothing. Whenever she was dealing with something she didn't understand, she made it her business to learn. With great difficulty, she carried her fiddle, music stand & music book into the house. Up behind the wine glasses that Hilda Effania rarely used, but dusted regularly, was a garnet bracelet from the memory of her father. Indigo figured the bracelet weighed so little, she would definitely be able to wear it every time she played her fiddle. Actually, she could wear it while conversing with the Moon.

Hilda Effania decided to chance fate & spend the rest of the morning in her fancy garb from Cypress. The girls were silent when she entered the parlor in black lace. She looked like she did in those hazy photos from before they were born. Indigo rushed over to the easy chair & straightened the pillows.

"Mama, I have my present for you." Hilda Effania swallowed hard. There was no telling what Indigo might bring her.

"Well, Sweetheart. I'm eager for it. I'm excited, too."

Indigo opened her new violin case, took out her violin, made motions of tuning it (which she'd already done). In a terribly still moment, she began "My Buddy," Hilda Effania's mother's favorite song. At the end, she bowed to her mother. Her sisters applauded.

Sassafrass gave her mother two things: a woven hanging of twined ikat using jute and raffia, called "You Know Where We Came From, Mama"; & six amethysts with holes drilled through, for her mother's creative weaving.

"Mama, you've gotta promise me you won't have a bracelet or a ring or something made from them. Those are for your very own pieces." Sassafrass wanted her mother to experience weaving as an expression of herself, not as something the family did for Miz Fitzhugh. Hilda Effania was still trying to figure out where in the devil she could put this "hanging," as Sassafrass had called it.

"Oh, no, dear. I wouldn't dream of doing anything with these stones but what you intended."

When the doorbell rang, Hilda Effania didn't know what to do with herself. Should she run upstairs? Sit calmly? Run get her house robe? She had no time to do any of that. Indigo opened the door.

"Merry Christmas, Miz Fitzhugh. Won't you come in?" Hilda sank back in the easy chair. Cypress casually threw her mother an afghan to cover herself. Miz Fitzhugh in red wool suit, tailored green satin shirt, red tam, all of Hilda's design, and those plain brown pumps white women like, wished everyone a "Merry Christmas." She said

Mathew, her butler, would bring some sweetbreads & venison over later, more toward the dinner hour. Miz Fitzhugh liked Sassafrass the best of the girls. That's why she'd sponsored her at the Callahan School. The other two, the one with the gall to want to be a ballerina & the headstrong one with the fiddle, were much too much for Miz Fitzhugh. They didn't even wanta be weavers. What was becoming of the Negro, refusing to ply an honorable trade.

Nevertheless, Miz Fitzhugh hugged each one with her frail blue-veined arms, gave them their yearly checks for their savings accounts she'd established when each was born. There be no talk that her Negroes were destitute. What she didn't know was that Hilda Effania let the girls use that money as they pleased. Hilda believed every family needed only one mother. She was the mother to her girls. That white lady was mighty generous, but she wasn't her daughters' mama or manna from Heaven. If somebody needed taking care of, Hilda Effania determined that was her responsibility, knowing in her heart that white folks were just peculiar.

"Why, Miz Fitzhugh, that's right kindly of you," Hilda honeyed.

"Why, Hilda, you know I feel like the girls were my very own," Miz Fitzhugh confided. Cypress began a series of violent *ronds de jambe.* Sassafrass picked up all the wrapping papers as if it were the most important thing in the world. Indigo felt some huge anger coming over her. Next thing she knew, Miz Fitzhugh couldn't keep her hat on. There was a wind justa pushing, blowing Miz Fitzhugh out the door. Because she had blue blood or blue veins, whichever, Indigo knew Miz Fitzhugh would never act like anything strange was going on. She'd let herself be blown right out the door with her white kid gloves, red tailored suit & all. Waving good-bye, shouting, "Merry Christmas," Miz Fitzhugh vanished as demurely as her station demanded.

Sucha raucous laughing & carrying on rarely came out of Hilda Effania's house like it did after Miz Fitzhugh'd been blown away. Hilda Effania did an imitation of her, hugging the girls.

"But Miz Fitzhugh, do the other white folks know you touch your Negroes?" Hilda responded, "Oh, I don't tell anyone!"

Eventually, they all went to their rooms, to their private fantasies & preoccupations. Hilda was in the kitchen working the fat off her goose, fiddling with the chestnut stuffing, wondering how she would handle the house when it was really empty again. It would be empty; not even Indigo would be home come January.

"Yes, Alfred. I think I'm doing right by 'em. Sassafrass is in that fine school with rich white children. Cypress is studying classical ballet with Effie in New York City. Imagine that? I'm sending Indigo out to Difuskie with Aunt Haydee. Miz Fitzhugh's promised me a tutor for her. She doesn't want the child involved in all the violence 'bout the white & the colored going to school together, the integration. I know you know what I mean, 'less up there's segregated too.

"No, Alfred, I'm not blaspheming. I just can't imagine another world. I'm trying to, though. I want the girls to live the good life. Like what we planned. Nice husbands. Big houses. Children. Trips to Paris & London. Going to the opera. Knowing nice people for friends. Remember we used to say we were the nicest, most interesting folks we'd ever met? Well, I don't want it to be that way for our girls. You know, I'm sort of scared of being here by myself. I can always talk to you, though. Can't I?

"I'ma tell Miz Fitzhugh that if she wants Indigo in Difuskie, that tutor will have to be a violin teacher. Oh, Alfred, you wouldn't believe what she can do on that fiddle. If you could only see how Cypress dances. Sassafrass' weavings. I wish you were here sometimes, so we could tell the world to look at what all we, Hilda Effania & Alfred, brought to this world."

Once her Christmas supper was organized in the oven, the frigerator, the sideboard, Hilda Effania slept in her new negligee, Alfred's WWII portrait close to her bosom.

I send these
Jolly minstrels
To sing their
sweetest song
To make your
Christmas merry
And happy
all day long

Christmas Is a Sad Season for the Poor

John Cheever

John Cheever is an undisputed master of the American short story. He was born in Massachusetts in 1912 and died in 1982. His wry look at the "underprivileged" in this Christmas tale is a departure from his usual suburban settings; nonetheless, the story is sure to warm the heart and pique the intelligence of even the most cynical urban veterans.

hristmas is a sad season. The phrase came to Charlie an instant after the alarm clock had waked him, and named for him an amorphous depression that had troubled him all the previous evening. The sky outside his window was black. He sat up in bed and pulled the light chain that hung in front of his nose. Christmas is a very sad day of the year, he thought. Of all the millions of people in New York, I am practically the only one who has to get up in the cold black of 6 A.M. on Christmas Day in the morning; I am practically the only one.

He dressed, and when he went downstairs from the top floor of the rooming house in which he lived, the only sounds he heard were the coarse sounds of sleep; the only lights burning were lights that had been forgotten. Charlie ate some breakfast in an all-night lunchwagon and took an Elevated train uptown. From Third Avenue, he walked over to Sutton Place. The neighborhood was dark. House after house put into the shine of the street lights a wall of black windows. Millions and millions were sleeping, and this general loss of consciousness generated an impression of abandonment, as if this were the fall of the city, the end of time. He opened the iron-and-glass doors of the apartment building where he had been working for six months as an elevator operator, and went through the elegant lobby to a locker room at the back. He put on a striped vest with brass buttons, a false ascot, a pair of pants with a light-blue stripe on the seam, and a coat. The night elevator man was dozing on the little bench in the car. Charlie woke him. The night elevator man told him thickly that the day doorman had been taken sick and wouldn't be in that day. With the doorman sick, Charlie wouldn't have any relief for lunch, and a lot of people would expect him to whistle for cabs.

Charlie had been on duty a few minutes when 14 rang—a Mrs. Hewing, who, he happened to know, was kind of immoral. Mrs. Hewing hadn't been to bed yet, and she got into the elevator wearing a long dress under her fur coat. She was followed by her two funny-looking dogs. He took her down and watched her go out into the dark and take her dogs to the curb. She was outside for only a few minutes. Then she came in and he took her up to 14 again. When she got off the elevator, she said, "Merry Christmas, Charlie."

"Well, it isn't much of a holiday for me, Mrs. Hewing," he said. "I think Christmas is a very sad season of the year. It isn't that people around here ain't generous—I mean, I got plenty of tips—but, you see, I live alone in a furnished room and I don't have any family or anything, and Christmas isn't much of a holiday for me."

"I'm sorry, Charlie," Mrs. Hewing said. "I don't have any family myself. It is kind of sad when you're alone, isn't it?" She called her dogs and followed them into her apartment. He went down.

It was quiet then, and Charlie lighted a cigarette. The heating plant in the basement encompassed the building at that hour in a regular and profound vibration, and the sullen noises of arriving steam heat began to resound, first in the lobby and then to reverberate up through all the sixteen stories, but this was a mechanical awakening, and it didn't lighten his loneliness or his petulance. The black air outside the glass doors had begun to turn blue, but the blue light seemed to have no source; it appeared in the middle of the air. It was a tearful light, and as it picked out the empty street he wanted to cry. Then a cab drove up, and the Walsers got out, drunk and dressed in evening clothes, and he took them up to their penthouse. The Walsers got him to brooding about the difference between his life in a furnished room and the lives of the people overhead. It was terrible.

Then the early churchgoers began to ring, but there were only three of these that morning. A few more went off to church at eight o'clock, but the majority of the building remained unconscious, although the smell of bacon and coffee had begun to drift into the elevator shaft.

At a little after nine, a nursemaid came down with a child. Both the nursemaid and the child had a deep tan and had just returned, he knew, from Bermuda. He had never been to Bermuda. He, Charlie, was a prisoner, confined eight hours a day to a six-by-eight elevator cage, which was confined, in turn, to a sixteen-story shaft. In one building or another, he had made his living as an elevator operator for ten years. He estimated the average trip at about an eighth of a mile, and when he thought of the thousands of miles he had traveled, when he thought that he might have driven the car through the mists above the Caribbean and set it down on some coral beach in Bermuda, he held the narrowness of his travels against his passengers, as if it were not the nature of the elevator but the pressure of their lives that confined him, as if they had clipped his wings.

He was thinking about this when the DePauls, on 9, rang. They wished him a merry Christmas.

"Well, it's nice of you to think of me," he said as they descended, "but it isn't much of a holiday for me. Christmas is a sad season when you're poor. I live alone in a furnished room. I don't have any family."

"Who do you have dinner with, Charlie?" Mrs. DePaul asked.

"I don't have any Christmas dinner," Charlie said. "I just get a sandwich."

"Oh, Charlie!" Mrs. DePaul was a stout woman with an impulsive heart, and Charlie's plaint struck at her holiday mood as if she had been caught in a cloudburst. "I do wish we could share our Christmas dinner with you, you know," she said. "I come from Vermont, you know, and when I was a child, you know, we always used to have a great many people at our table. The mailman, you know, and the schoolteacher, and just anybody who didn't have any family of their own, you know, and I wish we could share our dinner with you the way we used to, you know, and I don't see any reason why we can't. We can't have you at the table, you know, because you couldn't leave the elevator—could you?—but just as soon as Mr. DePaul has carved the goose, I'll give you a ring, and I'll arrange a tray for you, you know, and I want you to come up and at least share our Christmas dinner."

Charlie thanked them, and their generosity surprised him, but he wondered if, with the arrival of friends and relatives, they wouldn't forget their offer.

Then old Mrs. Gadshill rang, and when she wished him a merry Christmas, he hung his head.

"It isn't much of a holiday for me, Mrs. Gadshill," he said. "Christmas is a sad season if you're poor. You see, I don't have any family. I live alone in a furnished room."

"I don't have any family either, Charlie," Mrs. Gadshill said. She spoke with a pointed lack of petulance, but her grace was forced. "That is, I don't have any children with me today. I have three children and seven grandchildren, but none of them can see their way to coming East for Christmas with me. Of course, I understand their problems. I know that it's difficult to travel with children during the holidays, although I always seemed to manage it when I was their age, but people feel differently, and we mustn't condemn them for the things we can't understand. But I know how you feel, Charlie. I haven't any family either. I'm just as lonely as you."

Mrs. Gadshill's speech didn't move him. Maybe she was lonely, but she had a ten-room apartment and three servants and bucks and bucks and diamonds and diamonds, and there were plenty of poor kids in the slums who would be happy at a chance at the food her cook threw away. Then he thought about poor kids. He sat down on a chair in the lobby and thought about them.

They got the worst of it. Beginning in the fall, there was all this excitement about Christmas and how it was a day for them. After Thanksgiving, they couldn't miss it. It was fixed so they couldn't miss it. The wreaths and decorations everywhere, and bells ringing, and trees in the park, and Santa Clauses on every corner, and pictures in the magazines and newspapers and on every wall and window in the city told them that if they were good, they would get what they wanted. Even if they couldn't read, they couldn't miss it. They couldn't miss it even if they were blind. It got into the air the poor kids inhaled. Every time they took a walk, they'd see all the expensive toys in the store windows, and they'd write letters to Santa Claus, and their mothers and fathers would promise to mail them, and after the kids had gone to sleep, they'd burn the letters in the stove. And when it came Christmas morning, how could you explain it, how could you tell them that Santa Claus only visited the rich, that he didn't know about the good? How could you face them when all you had to give them was a balloon or a lollipop?

On the way home from work a few nights earlier, Charlie had seen a woman and a little girl going down Fifty-ninth Street. The little girl was crying. He guessed she was crying, he knew she was crying, because she'd seen all the things in the toy-store windows and couldn't understand why none of them were for her. Her mother did housework, he guessed, or maybe was a waitress, and he saw them going back to a room like his, with green walls and no heat, on Christmas Eve, to eat a can of soup. And he saw the little girl hang up her ragged stocking and fall asleep, and he saw the mother looking through her purse for something to put into the stocking— This reverie was interrupted by a bell on 11. He went up, and Mr. and Mrs. Fuller were waiting. When they wished him a merry Christmas, he said, "Well, it isn't much of a holiday for me, Mrs. Fuller. Christmas is a sad season when you're poor."

"Do you have any children, Charlie?" Mrs. Fuller asked.

"Four living," he said. "Two in the grave." The majesty of his lie overwhelmed him. "Mrs. Leary's a cripple," he added.

"How sad, Charlie," Mrs. Fuller said. She started out of the elevator when it reached the lobby, and then she turned. "I want to give your children some presents, Charlie," she said. "Mr. Fuller and I are going to pay a call now, but when we come back, I want to give you some things for your children."

He thanked her. Then the bell rang on 4, and he went up to get the Westons.

"It isn't much of a holiday for me," he told them when they wished him a merry Christmas. "Christmas is a sad season when you're poor. You see, I live alone in a furnished room."

"Poor Charlie," Mrs. Weston said. "I know just how you feel. During the war, when Mr. Weston was away, I was all alone at Christmas. I didn't have any Christmas dinner or a tree or anything. I just scrambled myself some eggs and sat there and cried." Mr. Weston, who had gone into the lobby, called impatiently to his wife. "I know just how you feel, Charlie," Mrs. Weston said.

By noon, the climate in the elevator shaft had changed from bacon and coffee to poultry and game, and the house, like an enormous and complex homestead, was absorbed in the preparations for a domestic feast. The children and their nursemaids had all returned from the park. Grandmothers and aunts were arriving in limousines. Most of the people who came through the lobby were carrying packages wrapped in colored paper, and were wearing their best furs and new clothes. Charlie continued to complain to most of the tenants when they wished him a merry Christmas, changing his story from the lonely bachelor to the poor father, and back again, as his mood changed, but this outpouring of melancholy, and the sympathy it aroused, didn't make him feel any better.

At half past one, 9 rang, and when he went up, Mr. DePaul was standing in the door of their apartment holding a cocktail shaker and a glass. "Here's a little Christmas cheer, Charlie," he said, and he poured Charlie a drink. Then a maid appeared with a tray of covered dishes, and Mrs. DePaul came out of the living room. "Merry Christmas, Charlie," she said. "I had Mr. DePaul carve the goose early, so that you could have some, you know. I didn't want to put the dessert on the tray, because I was afraid it would melt, you know, so when we have our dessert, we'll call you."

"And what is Christmas without presents?" Mr. DePaul said, and he brought a large, flat box from the hall and laid it on top of the covered dishes.

"You people make it seem like a real Christmas to me," Charlie said. Tears started into his eyes. "Thank you, thank you."

"Merry Christmas! Merry Christmas!" they called, and they watched him carry his dinner and his present into the elevator. He took the tray and the box into the locker room when he got down. On the tray, there was a soup, some kind of creamed fish, and a serving of goose. The bell rang again, but before he answered it, he tore open the DePauls' box and saw that it held a dressing gown. Their generosity and their cocktail had begun to work on his brain, and he went jubilantly up to 12. Mrs. Gadshill's maid was standing in the door with a tray, and Mrs. Gadshill stood behind her. "Merry Christmas, Charlie!" she said. He thanked her, and tears came into his eyes again. On the way down, he drank off the glass of sherry on Mrs. Gadshill's tray. Mrs. Gadshill's contribution was a mixed grill. He ate the lamb chop with his fingers. The bell was ringing again, and he wiped his face with a paper towel and went up to 11. "Merry Christmas, Charlie," Mrs. Fuller said, and she was standing in the door with her arms full of packages wrapped in silver paper, just like a picture in an advertisement, and Mr. Fuller was beside her with an arm around her, and they both looked as if they were going to cry. "Here are some things I want you to take home to your children," Mrs. Fuller said. "And here's something for Mrs. Leary and here's something for you. And if you want to take these things out to the elevator, we'll have your dinner ready for you in a minute." He carried the things into the elevator and came back for the tray. "Merry Christmas, Charlie!" both of the Fullers called after him as he closed the door. He took their dinner and their presents into the locker room and tore open the box that was marked for him. There was an alligator wallet in it, with Mr. Fuller's initials in the corner. Their dinner was also goose, and he ate a piece of the meat with his fingers and was washing it down with a cocktail when the bell rang. He went up again. This time it was the Westons. "Merry Christmas, Charlie!" they said, and they gave him a cup of eggnog, a turkey dinner, and a present. Their gift was also a dressing gown. Then 7 rang, and when he went up, there was another dinner and some more toys. Then 14 rang, and when he went up, Mrs. Hewing was standing in the hall, in a kind of negligee, holding a pair of riding boots in one hand and some neckties in the other. She had been crying and drinking. "Merry Christmas, Charlie," she said tenderly. "I wanted to give you something, and I've been thinking about you all morning, and I've been all over the apartment, and these are the only things I could find that a man might want. These are the only things that Mr. Brewer left. I don't suppose you'd have any use for the riding boots, but wouldn't you like the neckties?" Charlie took the neckties and thanked her and hurried back to the car, for the elevator bell had rung three times.

By three o'clock, Charlie had fourteen dinners spread on the table and the floor of the locker room, and the bell kept ringing. Just as he started to eat one, he would have to go up and get another, and he was in the middle of the Parsons' roast beef when he had to go up and get the DePauls' dessert. He kept the door of the locker room closed, for he sensed that the quality of charity is exclusive and that his friends would have been disappointed to find that they were not the only ones to try to lessen his loneliness. There were goose, turkey, chicken, pheasant, grouse, and pigeon. There were trout and salmon, creamed scallops and oysters, lobster, crab meat, whitebait, and clams. There were plum puddings, mince pies, mousses, puddles of melted ice cream, layer cakes, *Torten*, éclairs, and two slices of Bavarian cream. He had dressing gowns, neckties, cuff links, socks, and handkerchiefs, and one of the tenants had asked for his neck size and then given him three green shirts. There were a glass teapot filled, the label said, with jasmine honey, four bottles of after-shave lotion, some alabaster bookends, and a dozen steak knives. The avalanche of charity he had precipitated filled the locker room and made him hesitant, now and then, as if he had touched some wellspring in the female heart that would bury him alive in food and dressing gowns. He had made almost no headway on the food, for all the servings were preternaturally large, as if loneliness had been counted on to generate in him a brutish appetite. Nor had he opened any of the presents that had been given to him for his imaginary children, but he had drunk everything they sent down, and around him were the dregs of Martinis, Manhattans, Old-Fashioneds, champagne-and-raspberry-shrub cocktails, eggnogs, Bronxes, and Side Cars.

His face was blazing. He loved the world, and the world loved him. When he thought back over his life, it appeared to him in a rich and wonderful light, full of astonishing experiences and unusual friends. He thought that his job as an elevator operator—cruising up and down through hundreds of feet of perilous space—demanded the nerve and the intellect of a birdman. All the constraints of his life—the green walls of his room and the months of unemployment—dissolved. No one was ringing, but he got into the elevator and shot it at full speed up to the penthouse and down again, up and down, to test his wonderful mastery of space.

A bell rang on 12 while he was cruising, and he stopped in his flight long enough to pick up Mrs. Gadshill. As the car started to fall, he took his hands off the controls in a paroxysm of joy and shouted, "Strap on your safety belt, Mrs. Gadshill! We're going to make a loop-the-loop!" Mrs. Gadshill shrieked. Then, for some reason, she sat down on the floor of the elevator. Why was her face so pale, he wondered; why was she sitting on the floor? She shrieked again. He grounded the car gently, and cleverly, he thought, and opened the door. "I'm sorry if I scared you, Mrs. Gadshill," he said meekly. "I was only fooling." She shrieked again. Then she ran out into the lobby, screaming for the superintendent.

The superintendent fired Charlie and took over the elevator himself. The news that he was out of work stung Charlie for a minute. It was his first contact with human meanness that day. He sat down in the locker room and gnawed on a drumstick. His drinks were beginning to let him down, and while it had not reached him yet, he felt a miserable soberness in the offing. The excess of food and presents around him began to make him feel guilty and unworthy. He regretted bitterly the lie he had told about his children. He was a single man with simple needs. He had abused the goodness of the people upstairs. He was unworthy.

Then up through this drunken train of thought surged the sharp figure of his landlady and her three skinny children. He thought of them sitting in their basement room. The cheer of Christmas had passed them by. This image got him to his feet. The realization that he was in a position to give, that he could bring happiness easily to someone else, sobered him. He took a big burlap sack, which was used for collecting waste, and began to stuff it, first with his presents and then with the presents for his imaginary children. He worked with the haste of a man whose train is approaching the station, for he could hardly wait to see those long faces light up when he came in the door. He changed his clothes, and, fired by a wonderful and unfamiliar sense of power, he slung his bag over his shoulder like a regular Santa Claus, went out the back way, and took a taxi to the Lower East Side.

The landlady and her children had just finished off a turkey, which had been sent to them by the local Democratic Club, and they were stuffed and uncomfortable when Charlie began pounding on the door, shouting "Merry Christmas!" He dragged the bag in after him and dumped the presents for the children onto the floor. There were dolls and musical toys, blocks, sewing kits, an Indian suit, and a loom, and it appeared to him that, as he had hoped, his arrival in the basement dispelled its gloom. When half the presents had been opened, he gave the landlady a bathrobe and went upstairs to look over the things he had been given for himself.

Now, the landlady's children had already received so many presents by the time Charlie arrived that they were confused with receiving, and it was only the landlady's intuitive grasp of the nature of charity that made her allow the children to open some of the presents while Charlie was still in the room, but as soon as he had gone, she stood between the children and the presents that were still unopened. "Now, you kids have had enough already," she said. "You kids have got your share. Just look at the things you got there. Why, you ain't even played with the half of them. Mary Anne, you ain't even looked at that doll the Fire Department give you. Now, a nice thing to do would be to take all this stuff that's left over to those poor people on Hudson Street—them Deckkers. They ain't got nothing." A beatific light came into her face when she realized that she could give, that she could bring cheer, that she could put a healing finger on a case needier than hers, and—like Mrs. DePaul and Mrs. Weston, like Charlie himself and like Mrs. Deckker, when Mrs. Deckker was to think, subsequently, of the poor Shannons—first love, then charity, and then a sense of power drove her. "Now, you kids help me get all this stuff together. Hurry, hurry, hurry," she said, for it was dark then, and she knew that we are bound, one to another, in licentious benevolence for only a single day, and that day was nearly over. She was tired, but she couldn't rest, she couldn't rest.

DRAWING NAMES

Bobbie Ann Mason

Bobbie Ann Mason was born May 1, 1940, in Mayfield, Kentucky, and has written several books, including In Country. *Her first story collection,* Shiloh and Other Stories, *published in 1982, made a sensational debut and earned her the coveted P.E.N. Hemingway Award for First Fiction. "Drawing Names" is from that collection. It is a story that clearly illustrates, in Mason's understated style, not only the reality of family relationships at holiday time, but the spirit underlying it all.*

On Christmas Day, Carolyn Sisson went early to her parents' house to help her mother with the dinner. Carolyn had been divorced two years before, and last Christmas, coming alone, she felt uncomfortable. This year she had invited her lover, Kent Ballard, to join the family gathering.

She had even brought him a present to put under the tree, so he wouldn't feel left out. Kent was planning to drive over from Kentucky Lake by noon. He had gone there to inspect his boat because of an ice storm earlier in the week. He felt compelled to visit his boat on the holiday, Carolyn thought, as if it were a sad old relative in a retirement home.

"We're having baked ham instead of turkey," Mom said. "Your daddy never did like ham baked, but whoever heard of fried ham on Christmas? We have that all year round and I'm burnt out on it."

"I love baked ham," said Carolyn.

"Does Kent like it baked?"

"I'm sure he does." Carolyn placed her gifts under the tree. The number of packages seemed unusually small.

"It don't seem like Christmas with drawed names," said Mom.

"Your star's about to fall off." Carolyn straightened the silver ornament at the tip of the tree.

"I didn't decorate as much as I wanted to. I'm slowing down. Getting old, I guess." Mom had not combed her hair and she was wearing a workshirt and tennis shoes.

"You always try to do too much on Christmas, Mom."

Carolyn knew the agreement to draw names had bothered her mother. But the four daughters were grown, and two had children. Sixteen people were expected today. Carolyn herself could not afford to buy fifteen presents on her salary as a clerk at J. C. Penney's, and her parents' small farm had not been profitable in years.

Carolyn's father appeared in the kitchen and he hugged her so tightly she squealed in protest.

"That's all I can afford this year," he said, laughing.

As he took a piece of candy from a dish on the counter, Carolyn teased him. "You'd better watch your calories today."

"Oh, not on Christmas!"

It made Carolyn sad to see her handsome father getting older. He was a shy man, awkward with his daughters, and Carolyn knew he had been deeply disappointed over her failed marriage, although he had never said so. Now he asked, "Who bought these 'toes'?"

He would no longer say "nigger toes," the old name for the chocolate-covered creams.

"Hattie Smoot brought those over," said Mom. "I made a pants suit for her last week," she said to Carolyn. "The one that had stomach bypass?"

"When Pee Wee McClain had that, it didn't work and they had to fix him back like he was," said Dad. He offered Carolyn a piece of candy, but she shook her head no.

Mom said, "I made Hattie a dress back last spring for her boy's graduation, and she couldn't even find a pattern big enough. I had to 'low a foot. But after that bypass, she's down to a size twenty."

"I think we'll all need a stomach bypass after we eat this feast you're fixing," said Carolyn.

"Where's Kent?" Dad asked abruptly.

"He went to see about his boat. He said he'd be here."

Carolyn looked at the clock. She felt uneasy about inviting Kent. Everyone would be scrutinizing him, as if he were some new character on a soap opera. Kent, who drove a truck for the Kentucky Loose-Leaf Floor, was a part-time student at Murray State. He was majoring in accounting. When Carolyn started going with him early in the summer, they went sailing on his boat, which had "Joyce" painted on it. Later he painted over the name, insisting he didn't love Joyce anymore—she was a dietician who was always criticizing what he ate—but he had never said he loved Carolyn. She did not know if she loved him. Each seemed to be waiting for the other to say it first.

While Carolyn helped her mother in the kitchen, Dad went to get her grandfather, her mother's father. Pappy, who had been disabled by a stroke, was cared for by a live-in housekeeper who had gone home to her own family for the day. Carolyn diced apples and pears for fruit salad while her mother shaped sweet potato balls with marshmallow centers and rolled them in crushed cornflakes. On TV in the living room, *Days of Our Lives* was beginning, but the Christmas tree blocked their view of the television set.

"Whose name did you draw, Mom?" Carolyn asked, as she began seeding the grapes.

"Jim's."

"You put Jim's name in the hat?"

Mom nodded. Jim Walsh was the man Carolyn's youngest sister, Laura Jean, was living with in St. Louis. Laura Jean was going to an interior decorating school, and Jim was a textiles salesman she had met in a class. "I made him a shirt," Mom said.

"I'm surprised at you."

"Well, what was I to do?"

"I'm just surprised." Carolyn ate a grape and spit out the seeds. "Emily Post says the couple should be offered the same room when they visit."

"You know we'd never stand for that. I don't think your dad's ever got over her stacking up with that guy."

"You mean shacking up."

"Same thing." Mom dropped the potato masher, and the metal rattled on the floor. "Oh, I'm in such a tizzy," she said.

As the family began to arrive, the noise of the TV played against the greetings, the slam of the storm door, the outside wind rushing in. Carolyn's older sisters, Peggy and Iris, with their husbands and children, were arriving all at once, and suddenly the house seemed small. Peggy's children, Stevie and Cheryl, without even removing their jackets became involved in a basketball game on TV. In his lap, Stevie had a Merlin electronic toy, which beeped randomly. Iris and Ray's children, Deedee and Jonathan, went outside to look for cats.

In the living room, Peggy jiggled her baby, Lisa, on her hip and said, "You need you one of these, Carolyn."

"Where can I get one?" said Carolyn, rather sharply.

Peggy grinned. "At the gittin' place, I reckon."

Peggy's critical tone was familiar. She was the only sister who had had a real wedding. Her husband, Cecil, had a Gulf franchise, and they owned a motor cruiser, a pickup truck, a camper, a station wagon, and a new brick colonial home. Whenever Carolyn went to visit Peggy, she felt apologetic for not having a man who would buy her all these things, but she never seemed to be attracted to anyone steady or ambitious. She had been wondering how Kent would get along with the men of the family. Cecil and Ray were standing in a corner talking about gas mileage. Cecil, who was shorter than Peggy and was going bald, always worked on Dad's truck for free, and Ray usually agreed with Dad on politics to avoid an argument. Ray had an impressive government job in Frankfort. He had coordinated a ribbon-cutting ceremony when the toll road opened. What would Kent have to say to them? She could imagine him insisting that everyone go outside later to watch the sunset. Her father would think that was ridiculous. No one ever did that on a farm, but it was the sort of thing Kent would think of. Yet she knew that spontaneity was what she liked in him.

Deedee and Jonathan, who were ten and six, came inside then and immediately began shaking the presents under the tree. All the children were wearing new jeans and cowboy shirts, Carolyn noticed.

"Why are y'all so quiet?" she asked. "I thought kids whooped and hollered on Christmas."

"They've been up since *four,*" said Iris. She took a cigarette from her purse and accepted a light from Cecil. Exhaling smoke, she said to Carolyn, "We heard Kent was coming." Before Carolyn could reply, Iris scolded the children for shaking the packages. She seemed nervous.

"He's supposed to be here by noon," said Carolyn.

"There's somebody now. I hear a car."

"It might be Dad, with Pappy."

It was Laura Jean, showing off Jim Walsh as though he were a splendid Christmas gift she had just received.

"Let me kiss everybody!" she cried, as the women rushed toward her. Laura Jean had not been home in four months.

"Merry Christmas!" Jim said in a booming, official-sounding voice, something like a TV announcer, Carolyn thought. He embraced all the women and then, with a theatrical gesture, he handed Mom a bottle of Rebel Yell bourbon and a carton of boiled custard which he took from a shopping bag. The bourbon was in a decorative Christmas box.

Mom threw up her hands. "Oh, no, I'm afraid I'll be a alky-holic."

"Oh, that's ridiculous, Mom," said Laura Jean, taking Jim's coat. "A couple of drinks a day are good for your heart."

Jim insisted on getting coffee cups from a kitchen cabinet and mixing some boiled custard and bourbon. When he handed a cup to Mom she puckered up her face.

"Law, don't let the preacher in," she said, taking a sip. "Boy, that sends my blood pressure up."

Carolyn waved away the drink Jim offered her. "I don't start this early in the day," she said, feeling confused.

Jim was a large, dark-haired man with a neat little beard, like a bird's nest cupped on his chin. He had a Northern accent. When he hugged her, Carolyn caught a whiff of cologne, something sweet, like chocolate syrup. Last summer, when Laura Jean brought him home for the first time, she had made a point of kissing and hugging him in front of everyone. Dad had virtually ignored him. Now Carolyn saw that Jim was telling Cecil that he always bought Gulf gas. Red-faced, Ray accepted a cup of boiled custard. Carolyn fled to the kitchen and began grating cheese for potatoes au gratin. She dreaded Kent's arrival.

When Dad arrived with Pappy, Cecil and Jim helped set up the wheelchair in a corner. Afterward, Dad and Jim shook hands, and Dad refused Jim's offer of bourbon. From the kitchen, Carolyn could see Dad hugging Laura Jean, not letting go. She went into the living room to greet her grandfather.

"They roll me in this buggy too fast," he said when she kissed his forehead.

Carolyn hoped he wouldn't notice the bottle of bourbon, but she knew he never missed anything. He was so deaf people had given up talking to him. Now the children tiptoed around him, looking at him with awe. Somehow, Carolyn expected the children to notice that she was alone, like Pappy.

At ten minutes of one, the telephone rang. Peggy answered and handed the receiver to Carolyn. "It's Kent," she said.

Kent had not left the lake yet. "I just got here an hour ago," he told Carolyn. "I had to take my sister over to my mother's."

"Is the boat O.K.?"

"Yeah. Just a little scraped paint. I'll be ready to go in a little while." He hesitated, as though waiting for assurance that the invitation was real.

"This whole gang's ready to eat," Carolyn said. "Can't you hurry?" She should have remembered the way he tended to get sidetracked. Once it took them three hours to get to Paducah, because he kept stopping at antique shops.

After she hung up the telephone, her mother asked, "Should I put the rolls in to brown yet?"

"Wait just a little. He's just now leaving the lake."

"When's this Kent feller coming?" asked Dad impatiently, as he peered into the kitchen. "It's time to eat."

"He's on his way," said Carolyn.

"Did you tell him we don't wait for stragglers?"

"No."

"When the plate rattles, we eat."

"I know."

"Did you tell him that?"

"No, I didn't!" cried Carolyn, irritated.

When they were alone in the kitchen, Carolyn's mother said to her, "You dad's not his self today. He's fit to be tied about Laura Jean bringing that guy down here again. And him bringing that whiskey."

"That was uncalled for," Carolyn agreed. She had noticed that Mom had set her cup of boiled custard in the refrigerator.

"Besides, he's not too happy about that Kent Ballard you're running around with."

"What's it to him?"

"You know how he always was. He don't think anybody's good enough for one of his little girls, and he's afraid you'll get mistreated again. He don't think Kent's very dependable."

"I guess Kent's proving Dad's point."

Carolyn's sister Iris had dark brown eyes, unique in the family. When Carolyn was small, she tried to say "Iris's eyes" once and called them "Irish eyes," confusing them with a song their mother sometimes sang, "When Irish Eyes Are Smiling." Thereafter, they always teased Iris about her smiling Irish eyes. Today Iris was not smiling. Carolyn found her in a bedroom smoking, holding an ashtray in her hand.

"I drew your name," Carolyn told her. "I got you something I wanted myself."

"Well, if I don't want it, I guess I'll have to give it to you."

"What's wrong with you today?"

"Ray and me's getting a separation," said Iris.

"Really?" Carolyn was startled by the note of glee in her response. Actually, she told herself later, it was because she was glad her sister, whom she saw infrequently, had confided in her.

"The thing of it is, I had to beg him to come today, for Mom and Dad's sake. It'll kill them. Don't let on, will you?"

"I won't. What are you going to do?"

"I don't know. He's already moved out."

"Are you going to stay in Frankfort?"

"I don't know. I have to work things out."

Mom stuck her head in the door. "Well, is Kent coming or not?"

"He *said* he'd be here," said Carolyn.

"Your dad's about to have a duck with a rubber tail. He can't stand to wait on a meal."

"Well, let's go ahead, then. Kent can eat when he gets here."

When Mom left, Iris said, "Aren't you and Kent getting along?"

"I don't know. He said he'd come today, but I have a feeling he doesn't really want to."

"To hell with men." Iris laughed and stubbed out her cigarette. "Just look at us—didn't we turn out awful? First your divorce. Now me. And Laura Jean bringing that guy down. Daddy can't stand him. Did you see the look he gave him?"

"Laura Jean's got a lot a more nerve than I've got," said Carolyn, nodding. "I could wring Kent's neck for being late. Well, none of us can do anything right—except Peggy."

"Daddy's precious little angel," said Iris mockingly. "Come on, we'd better get in there and help."

While Mom went to change her blouse and put on lipstick, the sisters brought the food into the dining room. Two tables had been put together. Peggy cut the ham with an electric knife, and Carolyn filled the iced tea glasses.

"Pappy gets buttermilk and Stevie gets Coke," Peggy directed her.

"I know," said Carolyn, almost snapping.

As the family sat down, Carolyn realized that no one ever asked Pappy to "turn thanks" anymore at holiday dinners. He was sitting there expectantly, as if waiting to be asked. Mom cut up his ham into small bits. Carolyn waited for a car to drive up, the phone to ring. The TV was still on.

"Y'all dig in," said Mom. "Jim? Make sure you try some of these dressed eggs like I fix."

"I thought your new boyfriend was coming," said Cecil to Carolyn.

"So did I!" said Laura Jean. "That's what you wrote me."

Everyone looked at Carolyn as she explained. She looked away.

"You're looking at that pitiful tree," Mom said to her. "I just know it don't show up good from the road."

"No, it looks fine." No one had really noticed the tree. Carolyn seemed to be seeing it for the first time in years—broken red plastic reindeer, Styrofoam snowmen with crumbling top hats, silver walnuts which she remembered painting when she was about twelve.

Dad began telling a joke about some monks who had taken a vow of silence. At each Christmas dinner, he said, one monk was allowed to speak.

"Looks like your vocal cords would rust out," said Cheryl.

"Shut up, Cheryl. Granddaddy's trying to tell something," said Cecil.

"So the first year it was the first monk's turn to talk, and you know what he said? He said, 'These taters is lumpy.' "

When several people laughed, Stevie asked, "Is that the joke?"

Carolyn was baffled. Her father had never told a joke at the table in his life. He sat at the head of the table, looking out past the family at the cornfield through the picture window.

"Pay attention now," he said. "The second year Christmas rolled around again and it was the second monk's turn to say something. He said, 'You know, I think you're right. The taters *is* lumpy.' "

Laura Jean and Jim laughed loudly.

"Reach me some light-bread," said Pappy. Mom passed the dish around the table to him.

"And so the third year," Dad continued, "the third monk got to say something. What he said"—Dad was suddenly overcome with mirth—"what he said was, 'If y'all don't shut up arguing about them taters, I'm going to leave this place!' "

After the laughter died, Mom said, "Can you imagine anybody not a-talking all year long?"

"That's the way monks are, Mom," said Laura Jean. "Monks are economical with everything. They're not wasteful, not even with words."

"The Trappist Monks are really an outstanding group," said Jim. "And they make excellent bread. No preservatives."

Cecil and Peggy stared at Jim.

"You're not eating, Dad," said Carolyn. She was sitting between him and the place set for Kent. The effort at telling the joke seemed to have taken her father's appetite.

"He ruined his dinner on nigger toes," said Mom.

"Dottie Barlow got a Barbie doll for Christmas and it's black," Cheryl said.

"Dottie Barlow ain't black, is she?" asked Cecil.

"No."

"That's funny," said Peggy. "Why would they give her a black Barbie doll?"

"She just wanted it."

Abruptly, Dad left the table, pushing back his plate. He sat down in the recliner chair in front of the TV. The Blue-Gray game was beginning, and Cecil and Ray were hurriedly finishing in order to join him. Carolyn took out second helpings of ham and jello salad, feeling as though she were eating for Kent in his absence. Jim was taking seconds of everything, complimenting Mom. Mom apologized for not having fancy napkins. Then Laura Jean described a photography course she had taken. She had been photographing close-ups of car parts—fenders, headlights, mud flaps.

"That sounds goofy," said one of the children, Deedee.

Suddenly Pappy spoke. "Use to, the menfolks would eat first, and the children separate. The womenfolks would eat last, in the kitchen."

"You know what I could do with you all, don't you?" said Mom, shaking her fist at him. "I could set up a plank out in the field for y'all to eat on." She laughed.

"Times are different now, Pappy," said Iris loudly. "we're just as good as the men."

"She gets that from television," said Ray, with an apologetic laugh.

Carolyn noticed Ray's glance at Iris. Just then Iris matter-of-factly plucked an eyelash from Ray's cheek. It was as though she had momentarily forgotten about the separation.

Later, after the gifts were opened, Jim helped clear the tables. Kent still had not come. The baby slept, and Laura Jean, Jim, Peggy, and Mom played a Star Trek board game at the dining room table, while Carolyn and Iris played Battlestar Galactica with Cheryl and Deedee. The other men were quietly engrossed in the football game, a blur of sounds. No one had mentioned Kent's absence, but after the children had distributed the gifts, Carolyn refused to tell them what was in the lone package left under the tree. It was the most extravagantly wrapped of all the presents, with an immense ribbon, not a stick-on bow. An icicle had dropped on it, and it reminded Carolyn of an abandoned float, like something from a parade.

At a quarter to three, Kent telephoned. He was still at the lake. "The gas stations are all closed," he said. "I couldn't get any gas."

"We already ate and opened the presents," said Carolyn.

"Here I am, stranded. Not a thing I can do about it."

Kent's voice was shaky and muffled, and Carolyn suspected he had been drinking. She did not know what to say, in front of the family. She chattered idly, while she played with a ribbon from a package. The baby was awake, turning dials and knobs on a Busy Box. On TV, the Blues picked up six yards on an end sweep. Carolyn fixed her eyes on the tilted star at the top of the tree. Kent was saying something about Santa Claus.

"They wanted me to play Santy at Mama's house for the littluns.

I said—you know what I said? 'Bah, humbug!' Did I ever tell you what I've got against Christmas?"

"Maybe not." Carolyn's back stiffened against the wall.

"When I was little bitty, Santa Claus came to town. I was about five. I was all fired up to go see Santy, and Mama took me, but we were late, and he was about to leave. I had to run across the courthouse square to get to him. He was giving away suckers, so I ran as hard as I could. He was climbing up on the fire engine—are you listening?"

"Unh-huh." Carolyn was watching her mother, who was folding Christmas paper to save for next year.

Kent said, "I reached up and pulled at his old red pants leg, and he looked down at me, and you know what he said?"

"No—what?"

"He said, 'Piss off, kid.' "

"Really?"

"Would I lie to you?"

"I don't know."

"Do you want to hear the rest of my hard-luck story?"

"Not now."

"Oh, I forgot this was long distance. I'll call you tomorrow. Maybe I'll go paint the boat. That's what I'll do! I'll go paint it right this minute."

After Carolyn hung up the telephone, her mother said, "I think my Oriental casserole was a failure. I used the wrong kind of mushroom soup. It called for cream of mushroom and I used golden mushroom."

"Won't you *ever* learn, Mom?" cried Carolyn. "You always cook too much. You make *such* a big deal—"

Mom said, "What happened with Kent this time?"

"He couldn't get gas. He forgot the gas stations were closed."

"Jim and Laura Jean didn't have any trouble getting gas," said Peggy, looking up from the game.

"We tanked up yesterday," said Laura Jean.

"Of course you did," said Carolyn distractedly. "You always think ahead."

"It's your time," Cheryl said, handing Carolyn the Battlestar Galactic toy. "I did lousy."

"Not as lousy as I did," said Iris.

Carolyn tried to concentrate on shooting enemy missiles, raining through space. Her sisters seemed far away, like the spaceships. She was aware of the men watching football, their hands in action as they followed an exciting play. Even though Pappy had fallen asleep, with his blanket in his lap he looked like a king on a throne. Carolyn thought of the quiet accommodation her father had made to his father-in-law, just as Cecil and Ray had done with Dad, and her ex-husband had tried to do once. But Cecil had bought his way in, and now Ray was getting out. Kent had stayed away. Jim, the newcomer, was with the women, playing Star Trek as if his life depended upon it. Carolyn was glad now that Kent had not come. The story he told made her angry, and his pity for his childhood made her think of something Pappy had often said: "Christmas is for children." Earlier, she had listened in amazement while Cheryl listed on her fingers the gifts she had received that morning: a watch, a stereo, a nightgown, hot curls, perfume, candles, a sweater, a calculator, a jewelry box, a ring. Now Carolyn saw Kent's boat as his toy, more important than the family obligations of the holiday.

Mom was saying, "I wanted to make a Christmas tablecloth out of red checks with green fringe. You wouldn't think knit would do for a tablecloth, but Hattie Smoot has the prettiest one."

"You can do incredible things with knit," said Jim with sudden enthusiasm. The shirt Mom had made him was bonded knit.

"Who's Hattie Smoot?" asked Laura Jean. She was caressing the back of Jim's neck, as though soothing his nerves.

Carolyn laughed when her mother began telling Jim and Laura Jean about Hattie Smoot's operation. Jim listened attentively, leaning forward with his elbows on the table, and asked eager questions, his eyes as alert as Pappy's.

"Is she telling a joke?" Cheryl asked Carolyn.

"No. I'm not laughing at you, Mom," Carolyn said, touching her mother's hand. She felt relieved that the anticipation of Christmas had ended. Still laughing, she said, "Pour me some of that Rebel Yell, Jim. It's about time."

"I'm with you," Jim said, jumping up.

In the kitchen, Carolyn located a clean spoon while Jim washed some cups. Carolyn couldn't find the cup Mom had left in the refrigerator. As she took out the carton of boiled custard, Jim said, "It must be a very difficult day for you."

Carolyn was startled. His tone was unexpectedly kind, genuine. She was struck suddenly by what he must know about her, because of his intimacy with her sister. She knew nothing about him. When he smiled, she saw a gold cap on a molar, shining like a Christmas ornament. She managed to say, "It can't be any picnic for you either. Kent didn't want to put up with us."

"Too bad he couldn't get gas."

"I don't think he wanted to get gas."

"Then you're better off without him." When Jim looked at her, Carolyn felt that he must be examining her resemblances to Laura Jean. He said, "I think your family's great."

Carolyn laughed nervously. "We're hard on you. God, you're brave to come down here like this."

"Well, Laura Jean's worth it."

They took the boiled custard and cups into the dining room. As Carolyn sat down, her nephew Jonathan begged her to tell what was in the gift left under the tree.

"I can't tell," she said.

"Why not?"

"I'm saving it till next year, in case I draw some man's name."

"I hope it's mine," said Jonathan.

Jim stirred bourbon into three cups of boiled custard, then gave one to Carolyn and one to Laura Jean. The others had declined. Then he leaned back in his chair—more relaxed now—and squeezed Laura Jean's hand. Carolyn wondered what they said to each other when they were alone in St. Louis. She knew with certainty that they would not be economical with words, like the monks in the story. She longed to be with them, to hear what they would say. She noticed her mother picking at a hangnail, quietly ignoring the bourbon. Looking at the bottle's gift box, which showed an old-fashioned scene, children on sleds in the snow, Carolyn thought of Kent's boat again. She felt she was in that snowy scene now with Laura Jean and Jim, sailing in Kent's boat into the winter breeze, into falling snow. She thought of how silent it was out on the lake, as though the whiteness of the snow were the absence of sound.

"Cheers!" she said to Jim, lifting her cup.